To
Find Her
Place

Books by Susan Anne Mason

COURAGE TO DREAM

Irish Meadows
A Worthy Heart
Love's Faithful Promise

A Most Noble Heir

CANADIAN CROSSINGS

The Best of Intentions
The Highest of Hopes
The Brightest of Dreams

REDEMPTION'S LIGHT

A Haven for Her Heart
To Find Her Place

✦ Redemption's Light · 2 ✦

To Find Her Place

Susan Anne Mason

BETHANYHOUSE
a division of Baker Publishing Group
Minneapolis, Minnesota

© 2021 by Susan A. Mason

Published by Bethany House Publishers
11400 Hampshire Avenue South
Bloomington, Minnesota 55438
www.bethanyhouse.com

Bethany House Publishers is a division of
Baker Publishing Group, Grand Rapids, Michigan

Printed in the United States of America

Library of Congress Cataloging-in-Publication Data
Names: Mason, Susan Anne, author.
Title: To find her place / Susan Anne Mason.
Description: Minneapolis, Minnesota : Bethany House, [2021] | Series: Redemption's light ; 2
Identifiers: LCCN 2020056512 | ISBN 9780764235207 (trade paperback) | ISBN 9780764239243 (casebound) | ISBN 9781493431496 (ebook)
Subjects: GSAFD: Christian fiction. | Love stories.
Classification: LCC PR9199.4.M3725 T6 2021 | DDC 813/.6—dc23
LC record available at https://lccn.loc.gov/2020056512

Unless otherwise indicated, Scripture quotations are from the New Revised Standard Version of the Bible, copyright © 1989 National Council of the Churches of Christ in the United States of America. Used by permission. All rights reserved.

This is a work of historical reconstruction; the appearances of certain historical figures are therefore inevitable. All other characters, however, are products of the author's imagination, and any resemblance to actual persons, living or dead, is coincidental.

Cover design by Koechel Peterson & Associates, Inc., Minneapolis, Minnesota/Jon Godfredson
Cover photography by Ron Ravensborg

Author is represented by Natasha Kern Literary Agency.

21 22 23 24 25 26 27   7 6 5 4 3 2 1

—— ❧ ——

To all the dedicated social workers
who strive tirelessly to help
children in need in their communities.
May God bless you and them!

—— ❧ ——

Be strong and courageous; do not be frightened or dismayed, for the LORD your God is with you wherever you go.

JOSHUA 1:9

1

September 1943

“I’m leaving now, Mama. Are you sure you’ve got everything you need?”

Jane Linder glanced from her mother, seated in her favorite plaid armchair, to the wooden mantel clock and tried to ignore her rising anxiety. Today she needed to catch an early bus in order to attend an unexpected board meeting.

One that could affect the future of her job.

And today, of all days, Mama was having a bad morning.

“I’ll be fine, Janey.” Mama plucked at the fraying hem of her bathrobe sleeve. “Don’t worry about me.”

Jane pulled a napkin from the breakfast tray on the side table and set it on her mother’s lap. “You have your toast and tea right here. And there’s leftover soup for lunch. I’ll come home at noon and check on you if I can.”

Mama gave a wan smile that accentuated the bluish tinge to her mouth and pushed a lock of gray hair off her forehead. “I know it’s an important day for you. I don’t want you worrying about me. I’m sure I’ll feel better soon.”

“All right. I hope so.” Jane made a quick scan of the narrow living room, ensuring the drapes covering the front window were open no more than a few inches—enough to let in some light, but not enough that the neighbors could see inside. She also made sure Mama's favorite floor lamp was on and that her crossword puzzles and *Good Housekeeping* magazines all sat within easy reach.

"If it's too hectic and I can't come home, I'll call Mrs. Peters and have her come check on you." Jane slid the telephone across the coffee table, closer to Mama's chair. "In the meantime, if you start to feel worse, please call me at work." She knelt and grabbed her mother's thin hand. "Promise me you will. I don't want you to worry about bothering me. Nothing's more important than you."

Mama's thin lips trembled. "You're such a good daughter. I couldn't ask for anyone better." Tears formed in her eyes, creating red rims around the edges.

Jane held back a sigh. Whenever Mama had a bad spell, she became overly emotional. And sometimes rather clingy, often begging Jane not to go into the office. At times, Jane gave in and stayed home, but then felt guilty about not living up to her commitment at work. There were even days Jane considered resigning her position at the Children's Aid Society, but with her brother away fighting in the war, Jane's income was the only real thing keeping them afloat.

Besides, the children were too important for her to quit her job. They were the reason Jane had become a social worker in the first place—so she could help disadvantaged children find a family to love them. It was a mission entrusted to her by God, she was certain. One she couldn't in good conscience abandon. If it meant eventually hiring a nurse to stay with Mama during the day, Jane would find a way to do so.

But for now, she needed to be on time for this meeting.

"I have to go, Mama. I'll see you later." She kissed her mother's papery cheek, whispered a quick prayer for the Lord's protection over her, then grabbed her satchel and rushed out the door.

———❖———

Jane's heels clattered on the tile floors as she hurried toward the conference room situated on the second floor of the municipal building. The interior of the stone structure remained cool, a fact that Jane welcomed. Dressed in her best green suit and ivory blouse, she wanted to make a good impression and not appear like a wilted flower.

The double doors of the meeting room stood slightly ajar, and a murmur of voices drifted outward. Nerves dampened Jane's palms as she paused to gain her bearings and take a breath.

She had a fair idea why the board wished to see her today. Her boss, Mr. Mills, had done her the courtesy of calling yesterday to let her know before it was announced that he had decided to retire and that the position of Managing Director of the Toronto Children's Aid Society would now be open.

For the past six months, Jane had been filling in for her ailing boss as acting directress, a position that carried a lot of responsibility. Yet she'd welcomed the chance to prove herself in the role, hoping to garner the board's favor. And today's meeting might be the culmination of that goal, since she fully intended to submit her application as a contender for the position. If Vera Moberly could successfully run the Toronto Infants' Home, there was no reason Jane couldn't do the same with the Children's Aid Society. As a caseworker, she'd longed to make policy changes but lacked the power to do so. Now, excitement bubbled through her at the potential good she could bring about for the children.

Focus, Jane. Don't get ahead of yourself.

She smoothed down her skirt, adjusted the sleeves of her jacket, and stepped through the door, making certain her best smile was in place.

A large oval table dominated the room. Several men and women were seated around it, while others stood by the coffee cart in the corner. She made a quick scan of the faces, trying to match the names with the various board members.

"Mrs. Linder. Thank you for coming in on such short notice."

Mr. Fenmore, the chairman of the board, approached her with a tight smile. For a man in his mid-to-late fifties, he was tall and fit. He wore a dark suit and thin silver eyeglasses that matched the color of his hair.

"My pleasure, Mr. Fenmore." She shook his hand. "I hope I haven't kept you waiting."

"Not at all. You're right on time. If you'll take your seat, we can get this meeting started."

Jane pasted on a pleasant expression, one she hoped hid her nerves, and took the chair Mr. Fenmore indicated, while the other board members returned to their seats.

Mr. Fenmore took his place at the head of the table and nodded to a woman at the far end. "Marcie, are you ready?"

The woman, obviously here to take the minutes, raised her head, pen poised over a notepad. "Yes, sir."

He inclined his head. "Then I officially call this emergency board meeting to order."

Jane swallowed. She'd been invited to a few board meetings in her six months as directress, but they hadn't seemed quite this formal. The word *emergency* sent a chill of foreboding down her spine, but she told herself the term simply meant that the gathering was out of the ordinary from the group's usual monthly meeting.

"Thank you again for coming, Mrs. Linder," Mr. Fenmore said. "Although I could have come to your workplace, we felt that discretion would be better served if we met here."

"I understand." The foreboding chill spread down her legs to her toes. Why would they need such secrecy over Mr. Mills's retirement? Everyone at the Children's Aid would know soon enough.

The man shifted on his chair. "Mrs. Linder, I assume you are aware of the difficulties facing the agency right now—the additional workload, the lack of available foster families, and the decrease in funding, just to name a few."

"I'm very aware of it, sir," she said with quiet dignity. "I deal with these problems and more on a daily basis."

Mr. Fenmore's gray eyebrows rose slightly. "Of course you do. And you're doing an admirable job in Mr. Mills's absence. I only hope you don't take offense to what I'm about to tell you."

Jane's stomach clenched. This did not sound good. And so far, it didn't appear to have anything to do with Mr. Mills's announcement.

"After going over the financial statements from the last several months, it has become evident that the agency is in worse straits than we imagined."

"Considerably worse," one of the other members added.

The man who'd just spoken up was Mr. Warren. He was the accountant, a rather surly man who always went over their financial records each month with a magnifying glass.

Jane's shoulders stiffened as she looked around the table. Far from seeming sympathetic, some of the members were giving her hard stares that made her throat constrict. Surely they didn't blame her for the conditions at the agency. Mr. Fenmore knew the problems stemmed from the effects of the war. What control could she have over that?

"It's true," she said carefully, "that the last few months have been particularly difficult. However, I'm confident this is a temporary problem that will rectify itself in short order."

"We hope that is the case as well." Mr. Warren spoke up again. "But to make certain, we would like to have access to the Children's Aid's financial statements for the last two years as well as any other pertinent records."

"I see." Her brain whirled with the logistics of gathering that much paperwork together.

Mr. Fenmore leaned forward in his chair. "These records will be made available to an independent advisor whom we have hired to make a thorough study of the organization. His name is Garrett Wilder, and he will examine not only the finances, but the agency as a whole. We felt it would be beneficial to get an objective outside opinion about what we are doing right and what we could improve upon."

Jane's chest suddenly felt hollow, as though all the air had seeped out. An auditor? This could not have come at a worse time. She didn't need an outsider casting judgment on her methods right when she planned to make a bid for the director's job.

"Mr. Wilder will be arriving tomorrow morning." Mr. Fenmore's chair squeaked as he leaned back. "We would like you to provide him with an area to work and give him your full cooperation."

An area to work? Where was she to find space when they were so overcrowded already?

"May I ask how long he'll be spending with us?" Jane asked. Hopefully only a day or two. It would be tight, but they could manage.

"Likely several weeks."

Jane leaned forward, her cheeks heating. Something wasn't adding up here. Why were they doing this now? From that stony look Mr. Fenmore gave her, it made her suspect there was another reason for this audit. One he wasn't willing to share with her.

"May I inquire about Mr. Mills?" she asked when she found her voice again. "I understand he has officially decided to retire."

Mr. Fenmore nodded. "Yes. We learned that late yesterday. I assume he informed you as well."

"He did. He felt it was only fitting that I know of his decision since—" she inhaled and did her best to slow her heartbeat— "since I intend to put my name forth as a candidate for the permanent position."

A few murmurs went around the table.

Jane eyed some of the female board members, hoping for their support at least. But their stoic features gave nothing away.

"I see." Mr. Fenmore stroked his mustache. "Well, we won't be making any decisions until Mr. Wilder presents us with his recommendations. At that point, we will be pleased to accept your candidacy, along with all the rest."

A wave of relief washed over her. They weren't opposed to her application. All she had to do was make sure Mr. Wilder found everything in tip-top shape and gave her a glowing report.

"I suppose it's only fair to tell you," Mr. Fenmore went on, "that Mr. Wilder plans to put his name forth for the position as well. In addition, with jobs being so scarce now, we're likely to get dozens of other applications. I just want you to be aware of the level of competition there will be for the job."

"I understand." Jane did her best to keep her composure.

"However, for now, let's take it one step at a time, shall we?" He looked around the table. "If we are all in agreement, I believe we can declare this meeting adjourned."

As the board members began to file out, Jane's stomach sank to her shoes, her anticipation turning to ashes.

If she were to get this job, she'd have some major hurdles to navigate first.

She only prayed she would be up to the challenge.

2

The next morning, while walking from the bus stop to the Children's Aid office, Jane allowed herself a few moments to fume over the events of the previous day—in particular, the board's high-handed tactics. She'd been given barely any time to prepare her staff for today's invasion of Mr. Wilder. Once she returned from the meeting yesterday and had made the announcement of both Mr. Mills's retirement and the arrival of *the interloper*, as she'd come to label the man, the rest of the day had been consumed with preparing for his arrival.

Resentment bubbled under her skin. What was the real reason the board was bringing in this businessman to scrutinize the organization? She sensed there were things Mr. Fenmore hadn't told her, and being kept ignorant didn't sit well with her. If they felt she wasn't doing her job or that she was lacking in some way, they should have just come out and told her.

Jane waited for a break in traffic to cross the street. Initially, some of the board members had not been pleased when Bob Mills insisted on Jane taking over for him while he recuperated from his heart surgery, but she'd hoped her hard work and dedication would have won them over by now. Obviously, she'd been mistaken.

Now, as much as she hated the prospect, she would have to

set aside all animosity toward Mr. Wilder and treat him with as much grace as she could muster.

For everyone's sake.

Her team was under enough pressure as it was. It would be up to her as directress to set the tone and guide everyone through the uncertain weeks ahead. If she had to put in more hours over the next few weeks until matters settled down, then she would do it.

Thankfully, Mama was feeling somewhat better than yesterday, which had given Jane one less problem to deal with this morning. She would need all her wits about her to handle everything on her plate today.

Unusual quiet surrounded the main hallway as she entered the Children's Aid building. Jane took a moment to allow her system to settle before stepping into the clerical office.

"Good morning, Melanie," she said to the girl seated at the reception desk. "No sign of Mr. Wilder yet, I hope."

"Not yet." The cheerful blonde looked up from the papers on her desk. "Any idea what this audit is really about?"

Jane hesitated. Knowing Melanie's propensity for gossip, Jane decided to keep what little knowledge she had to herself. "I'm not really sure. Mr. Fenmore was very vague about the whole situation."

"Well, I, for one, find the timing suspicious." Melanie leaned closer. "Do you think it's a coincidence that they're bringing someone in to do an audit the day after Mr. Mills announced his retirement?"

Jane removed her hat and patted her hair back into place, attempting to ignore the jump in her stomach. Melanie was voicing the very thoughts that had plagued her all night. "I don't know. I hope it's merely a matter of wanting a clearer picture of where things stand before the new director is hired."

"Or directress." Melanie winked at Jane. "Did you tell them you want to apply yourself?"

"I mentioned it." Jane shifted, uncomfortably aware of the

other staff in the room straining to listen. "The board won't be interviewing anyone until the audit is complete. Now, were you able to reschedule my meeting with the mayor?"

She hated to put off Mayor Conboy, since he held the majority of the Children's Aid's purse strings, but it couldn't be helped. Not knowing what to expect from Mr. Wilder, Jane wanted to be available as much as possible during his first day on the job. She imagined the interloper to be a middle-aged businessman who knew nothing about running a social agency. Their organization was very different from big corporations, and she intended to make sure he understood how they worked. That making a profit wasn't their main goal. And that the welfare of the children was their ultimate concern.

"Yes. Mayor Conboy was actually relieved, since he'd had a conflict arise as well. It's now moved to next Thursday at one o'clock."

"Good. And what about the budget meeting with Mr. Warren and the other board members?"

"It's now on Friday at four o'clock." Melanie glanced over at Jane, as though anticipating her next question. "Don't worry. I rearranged your schedule to make room for it. I figured one of the upstairs rooms should be free at that time."

"Thank you." Jane's shoulders sagged a little. She hated having meetings that late in the day, but the lack of space in this building made it necessary to either rent outside facilities for meetings or wait until later in the day, when most of the caseworkers had vacated the rooms upstairs.

"When Mr. Wilder does arrive," Jane said, "please show him to my office right away and then hold my calls."

"Sure thing, Jane. I mean, Mrs. Linder." Melanie turned back to her typewriter.

Jane shook her head as she turned down the hall. It had been a tough adjustment for everyone having to address her as Mrs. Linder. For Melanie, in particular. Her friendship with the younger girl hadn't seemed quite so problematic when Jane was simply another caseworker. However, it had proven challenging over the last six months to keep her professional life separate from her personal one.

She unlocked the door and slipped into her office—or more accurately Bob Mills's office—which she currently occupied while he was away. With a sigh, she sat down in the captain's chair, realizing that he would never be back to run the organization. Making a mental note to speak to the board about a retirement party for him, she pulled a file open on her desk. When Mr. Wilder arrived, she wanted to appear hard at work, in control, and not as flustered as she felt.

A few minutes later, a soft knock on her door made her jump. "Come in."

"Good morning, Mrs. Linder." Bonnie Dupuis, one of the newer caseworkers, entered the office.

Relief loosened Jane's shoulder muscles. "Bonnie. You're in early. What can I do for you?"

"I thought you'd want to know that Mrs. Bennington called first thing this morning. They have another woman at the maternity home wanting to place an infant for adoption and asked if someone could come over. I know you prefer to handle Bennington Place personally, but Melanie said you'd be tied up with the auditor who's coming in." Her voice held a question, her gaze curious.

"Unfortunately, yes. I'll have to see to Mr. Wilder." Jane suppressed a flare of disappointment. She had a great rapport with the two women who ran the Bennington Place Maternity Home and looked forward to helping the expectant mothers who took refuge there. Now that she was acting directress, however, she often couldn't afford the time to go out into the field. "I'd appreciate it if you could go over in my stead. Please give Ruth and Olivia my regards."

"I will. Thank you, ma'am."

When the door closed again, Jane released another soft sigh. Being called *ma'am* made her feel fifty instead of just shy of thirty. She flipped through the remaining pages on her small desk calendar. Well, she'd be twenty-nine for another three months anyway. Why was the thought of turning thirty so depressing?

As an eager girl of eighteen, she'd never imagined herself being divorced and living with her widowed mother at this age. She'd pictured herself happily married with at least four children by now. Her chest constricted on a familiar spasm of pain—the same pain she did her best to hide whenever she held a new baby or witnessed the joy of adoptive parents receiving their first child. For most people, the term *miscarriage* was barely a blip on their consciousness. But for Jane, the word meant more than just the loss of a child. To her, it meant the disintegration of her marriage and the death of her dreams for the future.

She could still hear her doctor's words. *"I'm terribly sorry, Mrs. Linder, but it's my professional opinion that you are incapable of carrying a baby to term. I would strongly advise against getting pregnant again."*

Jane released the calendar page, allowing it to float back to September. Over the past four years, she'd had time to mourn her losses and had come to accept her fate, pouring all her energy into her career. Apparently, God had other plans for her life. A different way for her to minister to children.

Which was another reason why this job was so important to her.

And why she would do everything in her power to keep it.

———— ❧ ————

Garrett Wilder stepped off the streetcar and fixed his fedora more securely on his head in order to counteract the gust of air that blew up around him. The streetcar chugged ahead with a clang, causing a small cyclone of dirt and leaves to swirl about the road. He'd decided to leave his car at home since he was unsure

of the parking situation at the Children's Aid office. Surprisingly, he found that he rather welcomed taking public transportation.

As he began the walk toward Isabella Street, his morning coffee from the boardinghouse churned in his unsettled stomach. Perhaps he should have skipped his usual beverage, knowing that the uncertainty of the day ahead would likely be hard on his digestive system.

Pushing all doubts aside, he forged ahead with a determined stride. This was only a matter of first-day jitters, nothing more. He had no cause to feel guilty about being brought in to the Children's Aid Society to analyze its current operations, even if his arrival might create resentment on the part of Mrs. Linder, the woman who'd been filling in as acting directress for several months now.

Garrett conjured up the image of a plain, rail-thin woman, possibly in her mid-fifties, who wore no-nonsense clothing to match a military-like demeanor. It was rather unusual for a woman to receive such a promotion, even on a temporary basis. For Mrs. Linder to be put in charge of the whole office, she must have been working at the agency for some time.

The fact that the board of management deemed it necessary to bring in Garrett to investigate was even more unusual. The board hadn't come out and said she was responsible for the financial difficulties facing the agency or the mysterious discrepancies with the books, but the hints had been pretty strong.

"Pay close attention to the directress," Mr. Fenmore had urged him. *"If there's anything to be found that might point to her as contributing to the downturn in the department's efficiency, we need to hear it."*

Garrett shifted on the sidewalk as he came closer to the address he sought. Finding evidence to destroy a woman's career wasn't exactly a prospect he looked forward to. However, if her mismanagement was putting an important public service at risk, and if proving himself here meant he'd be favored for the newly vacant director's position, then Garrett would find a way to navigate a few difficult weeks. It would be a small price to pay to secure his future.

Even if that future looked nothing like what he'd pictured before the loathsome war had started.

Absentmindedly, he rubbed his hand over his chest, where one of the deadly pieces of shrapnel remained lodged. Strange how the trajectory of one's life could be changed by an ill-timed grenade and two precariously imbedded fragments of metal.

When he reached 32 Isabella Street, Garrett stopped at an opening in the brick-and-iron wall. A brass plaque on the post read *The Children's Aid Society*. Pressing his lips together, he turned down the stone pathway that led to a majestic-looking brick building, one that, if all went well, might become his permanent workplace. He couldn't afford to let sentiment or regret derail his plans. His career—and more importantly his family's well-being—depended on it.

On a deep inhale, he opened the front door and stepped inside, finding himself in a narrow hallway with open arched doorways on either side. From the left, the clicking of typewriter keys could be heard, and the scent of brewed coffee and lemon furniture polish hung in the air. Garrett set his hat on the hall coatrack, straightened his jacket, and walked across the polished wooden floors. He poked his head into the room on the left, where a woman, presumably the secretary, stopped typing.

"Good morning. Can I help you?" She gave him a bright smile, revealing a small gap between her front teeth. Her blond hair hung in soft waves to her shoulders.

Garrett came forward and glanced down at the nameplate on the desk. "I believe you can, Miss Benton. I'm Garrett Wilder. I'm here to . . ."

The welcoming expression fell away from her face.

Garrett stiffened but through sheer force of will kept his expression the same. "I see you're aware of who I am."

Miss Benton squared her shoulders, rose, and stuck out her hand. "Nice to meet you, Mr. Wilder."

He shook her hand. "And you, Miss Benton."

"I'll take you back to Mrs. Linder's office." Miss Benton came around the desk. "She said to notify her as soon as you arrived."

"I'm sure she did," he muttered.

"I beg your pardon?"

He gave her one of his winning smiles. "I'm eager to meet her as well." Garrett followed the woman down the hall to where the corridor branched into a *T* shape. At the first office to the left, Miss Benton stopped to give the door two sharp raps.

"Come in." The voice was melodic yet authoritative.

Miss Benton opened the door. "Mr. Wilder is here, Mrs. Linder."

"Thank you, Melanie. Please send him in."

Garrett bristled. She sounded like a queen inviting a peasant into the throne room. Mrs. Linder might be older and more ex-perienced, but at almost thirty-one, Garrett wasn't a child, and he would not be intimidated.

Miss Benton waved him in. "Go on in, Mr. Wilder."

Garrett pulled himself up to his full height and stepped inside. "Good morning, Mrs. Lind—" He stopped short, his mouth fall-ing open.

The woman seated behind the desk couldn't possibly be the acting directress. This woman was young—possibly younger than he was. She wore her chestnut hair in a tidy roll off her forehead that showcased porcelain skin and stunning green eyes. But it was her boldly painted red lips that claimed his attention. Realizing he was staring, he blinked and attempted to regain his equilibrium.

Mrs. Linder regarded him steadily, her slim brows lifting in a silent query.

"Forgive me," he said. "Because of the job title, I had expected someone of a more . . . mature age." He summoned his profes-sional charm and extended his hand. "Garrett Wilder. Good to meet you."

"Likewise." She rose in one fluid motion and shook his hand, never breaking eye contact. "However, I must admit that I too was expecting someone older."

He gave a sheepish grin. "Thank you for saying that. I feel a little better now."

He waited for her to resume her seat, then loosened the buttons on his suit jacket and sat down, setting his briefcase on the floor beside him.

Mrs. Linder folded her hands on the desktop. "I admit that learning about your impending arrival yesterday came as quite a surprise, Mr. Wilder. All Mr. Fenmore told me is that you are here to study our operations and advise us how we can improve our situation." She glanced down at a piece of paper. "From your file, I see you have excellent credentials, including a business degree. I presume you'll wish to study our financial records first."

Garrett held back his surprise. She knew a lot more about him than he'd expected. "The finances are part of it, certainly, but my job here encompasses a great deal more than that."

"I see." She twisted a plain gold wedding band on her left hand.

A fleeting thought crossed his mind about what type of man her husband must be. How did he feel about his wife working in such a demanding position, one that would likely require long hours and come with a great deal of responsibility? Would Garrett ever be as open-minded when he married? Granted, his mother helped his father with the family farm, but that wasn't quite the same as this type of career.

"I plan to study all areas of the agency's operations," he continued. "I'll observe how things are done, then make recommendations for overall improvement." He didn't add that a big part of his job would be studying her.

A slight frown creased her brow. "Given the current economic situation, my employees are understandably nervous. Will these recommendations lead to any potential layoffs?"

Garrett knew he had to tread with care or he would alarm the staff unnecessarily, which in turn might hinder their performance. "Only if it makes sense and only as a very last resort. I simply wish to see how we can streamline procedures in order to maximize everyone's time and eliminate unwarranted expenses."

Brushing some lint from his pant leg, he rose. "Now, if you'd be kind enough to show me to my office, I'll get settled in and prepare to meet the other staff members."

She stood and tugged her suit jacket into place. "Of course. Follow me."

As she came around the desk, he stepped back. She was tall for a woman. In fact, with the heels on her shoes, she stood almost at his eye level. At six foot two, however, he still had several inches over her.

"There's a room at the end of the hall we've fixed up for you." She moved by him, leaving a lingering floral scent. "You'll find we are rather cramped for space in this building. However, we make do the best we can."

He followed her to a room not much larger than a broom closet, which looked as though it were normally used as a storage area, but now contained a rather beat-up desk, a captain's chair, and a metal file cabinet. A wooden letter tray and an office lamp were the only items on the desktop. Not exactly the executive suite he'd hoped for. He set his briefcase on the desk's scarred surface and frowned. "I will need a telephone."

"I figured as much. The phone company should be here sometime today or tomorrow to install one." She shrugged. "I know it's a little rough in here, but feel free to add your own touches. Whatever will make your job easier." She smiled, and though she was saying and doing all the right things, he sensed her aversion to having him here.

"Most of the supplies are kept in that cupboard." She waved a hand toward the corner. "But if there's anything else you need, Melanie can help you."

"Melanie?"

"Miss Benton, our secretary and receptionist. She handles all the office supplies, orders, typing, et cetera. In truth, this place couldn't run without her." She gave a light laugh as she backed toward the door. "Well, I'll let you get settled. . . ."

Garrett bit back an oath. This awkwardness was no way to begin a working relationship. He needed to establish some sort of rapport with this woman in order to gain her cooperation. "Before you go, Mrs. Linder, I'd appreciate it if we could clear the air."

Jane froze, caught in the man's hypnotic blue gaze, and found herself wishing for the paunchy middle-aged man she'd envisioned. An older man's experience might have intimidated her but not as much as this man's incredible good looks did. "I'm not sure what you mean."

She tilted her chin, doing her best not to allow her facial expression to give away her unease. At all costs, she had to come across as cool and professional. Totally in control of all aspects of the agency, but, most importantly, in control of her emotions.

Mr. Wilder leaned a hip against the desk and crossed his arms, still managing to look elegant in his three-piece suit with not a wrinkle in sight. "I realize this is a less-than-desirable situation, but my time here will be much less stressful if we can establish some sort of understanding. After all, we're both working toward the same ultimate goal—to improve the agency's functionality so we can help the most children."

The tension in her shoulders eased slightly. He was right. Every aspect of the Children's Aid Society centered around the welfare of the children. "Do you really believe that, Mr. Wilder?" she asked coolly. "Or do you care only about the pluses and the minuses in the ledger book?"

A nerve jumped in his jaw. "I care a great deal about the children who come through these doors, but if we don't address the agency's financial problems and the office is forced to close, what will happen to the children then?"

Alarm ricocheted through her system. "Surely there's no threat of the agency closing. The government wouldn't allow it."

"Then why did the board of management feel the urgent need to hire me?"

Jane bit her lip. This was the question that had plagued her since she first learned of Mr. Wilder's impending arrival. "Mr. Fenmore said they were bringing in an objective third party to study the agency. I assumed this would mainly consist of a financial audit and recommendations for how to optimize our funding."

Mr. Wilder gazed directly at her. "Believe me, Mrs. Linder, this is much more serious than a simple audit. But I'm confident that if we work together, we can find viable solutions to get this agency running in peak condition." He pushed away from the desk and held out his hand. "Can I count on your cooperation?"

Jane hesitated for a fraction of a second. It would serve no purpose to be at odds with this man. If she worked closely with him, she'd be in a better position to figure out exactly what was going on here. And also to see just how serious he was about applying for the director's job. She forced her lips into a smile and shook his hand. "As long as I can expect the same courtesy from you."

He gave her an appraising look and nodded. "Fair enough, Mrs. Linder. Fair enough."

3

After an hour at his desk in the windowless cubbyhole that now served as his office, Garrett rose and stretched. Time to see the rest of the building. He plucked his suit jacket off the back of his uncomfortable chair and put it on. First impressions in meeting the staff were of utmost importance. They needed to know that although he wasn't officially in charge, he did hold a position of some authority.

He headed down the narrow hall toward Mrs. Linder's office. Paying better attention this time, he noted the nameplate beside the door read, *Robert Mills, Managing Director*. So, this wasn't Mrs. Linder's actual office. Where did she normally sit? And what had her position been before she became acting directress?

He knocked on her door.

"Come in."

She was on the telephone and gestured for him to sit down.

"I'm glad Miss Dupuis was able to help." A pause. "That's sweet of you to say, Olivia. I miss working with you too, but right now I'm too—" Mrs. Linder's gaze swung to him. "In my new role, I'm afraid I have to leave the maternity homes to my caseworkers. But as soon as I have a day off, I'll come for a visit and we can catch up. In the meantime, my staff are always happy to help." Another pause. "You too, Olivia." Mrs. Linder replaced the receiver and looked up with a smile. "That was one of the matrons from Bennington Place, a local maternity home we serve."

He frowned. The conversation—or what he'd heard of it—sounded like two friends rather than a professional exchange. "Rather chummy with them, aren't you?"

She bristled like an annoyed peahen. "When I was a caseworker, I visited the maternity home often. We developed a friendly working relationship. What's wrong with that?"

"Nothing, I suppose, as long as you're able to remain objective."

Red patches bloomed in her cheeks, and she pressed her lips into a hard line. "Was there something you needed, Mr. Wilder?" she asked between clenched teeth.

Garrett inhaled and let out a breath. He would have to remember not to be so blunt. He wasn't among the soldiers in the trenches anymore, and Mrs. Linder deserved to be treated with more sensitivity. "I'm ready to see the rest of the building and meet the other staff members, if you don't mind."

Her nostrils flared as she got to her feet. "Certainly. I would have taken you around earlier, but I thought you'd appreciate a bit of time to settle in first."

"Well, consider me fully settled."

She stared at him as if uncertain whether he was serious or not. Then she moved by him into the hall, where she stopped by the narrow front room. A variety of people from all walks of life filled the seats—adults as well as children, some nicely dressed, others more bedraggled-looking.

"This is our waiting area where clients wait to meet with the caseworkers. Across the hall is our stenographer pool. Any of our volunteers who come in to help with clerical duties also work in there."

"Do any of these volunteers have access to the agency's financial records?" He hoped the question sounded casual enough so as not to arouse suspicion.

However, Mrs. Linder's brows rose slightly. "Yes. Mr. Bolton is a bookkeeper who volunteers his time to help balance our ledgers."

"I assume someone oversees his work?"

"If you mean once he's finished, then yes. That job belonged to Mr. Mills, who was quite fastidious about the finances." She shrugged. "That responsibility now falls on me."

Garrett bit his tongue to keep from blurting out more questions. There would be plenty of time to delve into the minutiae of the operations later. But this nugget of information could prove vital to some of his investigations.

"Upstairs you'll find the rooms where the caseworkers meet with the parents." She headed to the staircase and started up. As they reached the top, she glanced over her shoulder with an almost embarrassed air. "I should warn you that the space limitations are even worse up here. Once you see this, you'll probably appreciate having your own area to work in, even if it is cramped."

He snorted. "And here I thought you were trying to punish me."

A strangled sound met his ears, and for a second, he could have sworn she was smothering a laugh.

She stopped at the first open door and made room for him to peer inside. He stared open-mouthed for the second time that day. Nothing could have prepared him for the overcrowded quarters and the cacophony of conversations within. He'd heard the comings and goings of people in the building, but he'd never expected this crowd.

In the middle of the room, three tables were pushed together to form one large working area, surrounded by at least ten chairs. More tables and chairs lined the walls around the perimeter, along with a row of filing cabinets and some sort of storage cupboard. Every available space was taken up with people—parents with young children on their laps and staff members writing on notepads. Some were on telephones, speaking loudly to try and be heard over the din.

How did they accomplish anything in such chaos?

He turned to Mrs. Linder. "Is this how your day-to-day operations are normally handled?"

"I'm afraid so. This is a rather tame day. It sometimes gets far more crowded, depending on the number of children involved."

One tot let out a piercing yell.

Garrett cringed, repressing the urge to cover his ears. "This doesn't seem like a good time to introduce myself."

"You're right. The best time might be after closing, when only the staff remain to finish their paperwork."

He stepped back into the corridor and moved several paces away.

"There's another room similar to this on the opposite side of the stairs. That room holds about seventeen workers, while this one generally holds ten to twelve." Mrs. Linder walked ahead and pointed out the washrooms as well as a small closet where one worker sat on a stool, balancing a notepad on her knee.

Mrs. Linder shot him a wry look. "People use whatever space is available to them. Even a closet."

"What plans are being made to solve this crisis?" Garrett couldn't believe the agency could function at all in such disorder.

"The board is saving toward an eventual new office complex, but plans were put on hold for reasons I'm not privy to. You'd have to ask Mr. Fenmore about that." She shrugged. "In the meantime, we make do."

They made their way slowly down the stairs.

"Some of our problems are likely temporary," Mrs. Linder said. "The war is to blame for a great deal of our overcrowding and increased workload."

Garrett frowned. "How so?"

"For one thing, the number of neglected and abused children has risen greatly. With the men away, the mothers are finding it difficult to cope. Most are taking some sort of work to bring in money while still fulfilling all the usual duties at home. We also have fewer volunteers to help with the workload as well as fewer foster families willing to take in extra mouths to feed. Everyone is focused on their own problems, striving to keep their families afloat. Understandable, but unfortunate." She paused at the foot of the staircase. "I imagine the economic upheaval from the war is also part of the reason why the expansion plans have been put on hold. In such uncertain times, it seems unwise to invest in real estate."

Garrett nodded, impressed by her perceptive views. "You're probably right. No one thought this war would last so long, and now it seems never-ending."

"I know." Sadness washed over her features. "It seems like forever since I've seen my brother."

Garrett discreetly rubbed a hand over his chest, attempting to quell his guilt over the fact that he wasn't still overseas with his fellow comrades. If fate hadn't intervened, he might be fighting alongside Mrs. Linder's brother at this very moment.

Jane attempted to shake off the feeling of melancholy that talk of the war always evoked. From Mr. Wilder's grim expression, she imagined he felt the same. However, now was not the time to focus on anything other than work.

They stopped outside Jane's office.

"Could you clarify something for me, Mrs. Linder?" Mr. Wilder flipped the page on his notepad. "I understand Mr. Mills reorganized the agency into three separate areas: the shelter, the child placement department, and the family protection department."

"That's right."

"What exactly does the family protection unit do?"

Jane leaned against the doorframe, affection for her mentor softening her mood for the moment. "Mr. Mills was passionate about preventing cruelty to and neglect of children. We receive countless calls about parents abusing their children or simply neglecting them, leaving them without proper food and clothing. We investigate every claim and determine whether it's safe to leave the child in the home or better to remove them to foster care. We also do regular inspections of our foster homes to ensure the parents are living up to their promise to care for the children entrusted to them."

Mr. Wilder scratched his chin. "This is a more complex organization than I realized. My estimated time for a complete study may have been somewhat optimistic."

Just then, the front door of the agency burst open, claiming Jane's immediate attention. A stout woman entered, dragging a scowling boy with her.

Jane recognized the child and immediately rushed toward them. "Martin. Mrs. McElroy. What can I do for you?"

The woman propelled the boy forward. "I'm sorry, Mrs. Linder, but I'm afraid I have to return Martin to the shelter. Mr. McElroy and I can no longer tolerate his shenanigans."

Jane's stomach sank, along with her hopes for the boy. She'd prayed the McElroys would turn out to be Martin's permanent home. What had gone wrong this time?

The boy crossed his arms in front of him, his mouth curved down in a permanent scowl.

Conscious of the people in the waiting room nearby and of Mr. Wilder hovering behind her, Jane made a quick decision. "Martin, I'd like you to go with Mr. Wilder here. He'll take you to the staff room while I talk to your . . . to Mrs. McElroy." She lowered her voice and leaned toward Mr. Wilder. "The staff room's down the back hall. There's a cookie jar on the counter and drinks in the refrigerator."

If he was surprised, he hid it well. He simply nodded and waited for Martin.

As the boy stalked by her, Jane resisted the urge to lay a comforting hand on his shoulder. "Mrs. McElroy, won't you come into my office and we can discuss the situation?"

"There's no point." Mrs. McElroy's shrill voice echoed through the hall. "I'm leaving the boy here and no discussion is going to change my mind."

Jane stiffened and summoned her sternest demeanor. "Ma'am, you have a responsibility to this child. You signed papers that say so."

"You can just tear up those papers." She glanced at the wall clock. "I have to go. I need to get back before school lets out and the rest of the young'uns arrive home."

Jane followed her to the door. Short of tackling the large woman, she had no way to make her stay. "Are you sure you won't change your mind? Maybe once you—"

"I won't."

From the grim set to the woman's jaw, Jane realized that arguing would be a waste of time. "Then I'll have someone come by tomorrow with release forms. When would be a good time?"

"Anytime when school's on." The woman waved a hand as she sailed out the door, slamming it behind her.

The air whooshed from Jane's lungs, and she fought the urge to sink against the wall.

Mr. Wilder appeared from the back hall. "Martin is eating cookies in the staff room."

"Alone?" Her voice came out as a screech.

Mr. Wilder frowned. "He's perfectly safe in there. . . ."

"You don't understand." Alarm spurted through her as she raced by him. "You can't leave Martin alone." Why hadn't she stressed that point? Told him that Martin had a tendency to run off?

Her fears were confirmed when she reached the staff room. The cookies and juice sat untouched on the table, the room empty.

"Oh no." Jane flew down the back corridor to the rear entrance and out the door. "Martin! Martin, come back!"

Finding nothing but a few dead leaves lying on the patio stones, she continued down the side alley between the buildings where the trash cans were stored. "It's all right, Martin. Mrs. McElroy is gone."

She stood still, her ears strained for any sign he was near. He couldn't have gotten far, could he?

Out on Isabella Street, she scanned the sidewalk in both directions. No sign of the boy anywhere. Taking a breath to calm her racing heart, she retraced her steps into the alley. A slight movement by the trash cans caught her eye, and she quickly moved to peer behind them. The collar of Martin's blue shirt was visible between the cracks.

Relief spilled through her tense muscles. She inhaled slowly as she took a minute to consider the best course of action. The boy used to trust her, but after several unsuccessful foster placements, she understood why that might no longer be the case.

"I'm sorry things didn't work out with the McElroys," she said quietly. "Would you like to come in and tell me about it?"

Silence reigned for a moment, then a sniff followed. "No."

She bent closer to the trash cans. "How can I help you, then? You can't stay out here all night." Even though it was the beginning of September, the temperature had already turned cooler, especially at night.

"You'll make me go back to the shelter. I don't like it there. Mrs. Shaughnessy hates me."

Jane held back a sigh. "She doesn't hate you, Martin. If you obey the rules, you won't have any trouble with her."

"The other kids don't like me either. They make fun of me." Another sniff followed.

"It's getting chilly out here." She rubbed her arms. "Come inside and we can talk there."

"Is Mr. Mills here?"

Jane paused. The last time Martin had been sent back, Mr. Mills had lost patience with him and had raised his voice at the boy in a moment of exasperation. Even though he apologized later, the damage had been done. "No. Mr. Mills is . . . away right now. I'm in charge for the time being."

"You are?" A note of hope rang in Martin's voice.

"Yes, I am." Jane held her breath, praying her past connection with the boy would win out.

Finally, the metal cans rattled, and Martin stood up, his brown eyes staring at her in silent accusation.

Jane's heart pinched with regret. *Oh, Martin. I'd do anything to give you the family you deserve.* How she wished someone could see past the anger and the surly attitude to the hurting child beneath. With a little love and understanding, she was sure Martin would blossom. She held out a hand. "I could use something warm to drink. How about some cocoa?"

He nodded and reluctantly took her hand.

Jane longed to pick him up and hug him. But at eight years old, Martin considered himself too old for such gestures. She contented herself with clasping his small hand in hers and giving it an encouraging squeeze.

When she looked up, her steps slowed. Mr. Wilder stood at the end of the alley, his arms crossed in front of him, a mixture of puzzlement and disapproval on his face. How long had he been watching them?

Garrett scratched his head as Mrs. Linder led the unruly boy back into the building. Why wasn't she scolding the child for his outrageous behavior? A good spanking would be in order if one of his nephews had pulled such a stunt. Instead, Mrs. Linder intended to make him cocoa?

He followed them into the staff room, an area only slightly larger than Garrett's so-called office, where a round table and six odd chairs occupied most of the space. Beside the narrow stove and tiny refrigerator, a tiled countertop held a kettle and some ceramic jars.

After seating Martin at the table where his juice and cookies remained, Mrs. Linder looked up. "This is Martin Smith, one of our favorite residents." She winked at the boy. "Martin, this is Mr. Wilder. He's working here for the next few weeks."

"Nice to meet you, Martin."

The boy only shrugged a shoulder in response.

Jane pulled a pot from a lower cupboard and got out a jar of milk from the small fridge. She shivered as she turned on the burner and stirred several tablespoons of cocoa powder into the milk.

"You keep the kitchen well stocked, I see," he said.

She glanced over her shoulder. "We like to have refreshments on hand. You never know when a hot drink or a cookie will come in handy."

"I wouldn't mind a cup, if you have enough," he said.

Martin glared at him. "Why are you here?"

Mrs. Linder whirled around. "Martin, mind your manners."

"Sorry." The boy dropped his head toward his narrow chest.

Garrett glanced over at Mrs. Linder, who shook her head, an expression of pleading in her eyes. He gave a slight nod of understanding. Martin looked to be around the age of his oldest nephew. How would his sister handle this situation with her son? Cassie was always more tactful than Garrett or his parents, doling out spankings only when absolutely necessary.

Garrett pulled out a chair and sat down. "Sounds like you're having a rough day," he said.

Martin speared him with a glare.

The sound of a metal utensil whisking against the pot seemed to increase. Time for a different tactic.

"Do you play baseball, Martin?"

The boy shook his head.

"How about soccer or football?"

"No. I like hockey."

"Ice hockey?"

Martin shot him another flinty stare. "I don't have any skates. I play on the road."

"Ah, I see. That sounds fun."

Mrs. Linder brought two cups over to the table. "Here you go, fellows."

Garrett picked up one of them. "Thank you. This looks delicious." He took a quick sip that practically scalded his tongue and sucked in a breath. "They don't call it hot cocoa for nothing."

Martin snorted and leaned over to blow on the surface of his cup.

Mrs. Linder turned off the stove, poured the remaining liquid from the pot into a chipped teacup, then took a seat beside Martin.

"Mr. Wilder," she said. "Would you excuse us, please? I'd like to talk to Martin in private."

"Certainly. Nice to meet you, Martin. Maybe we'll throw a ball around one day."

Why had he said that when he doubted the opportunity would ever arise?

Back in his tiny office, Garrett found it difficult to concentrate on the numbers in front of him, since his mind kept wandering to Mrs. Linder and Martin. The two seemed quite familiar with each other. What sort of history did they share?

Something about Martin tugged at Garrett, and as he mulled over the possible reason, he realized the boy reminded him of Nelson, his childhood friend. Martin bore the same haunted look Nelson had worn when he first came to live with Garrett's neighbors on the next farm over. Gradually, thanks to Mr. and Mrs. O'Neill's patience with the boy, Nelson had learned to relax and understand that he was truly safe. The last Garrett had heard, Nelson had come back to help his adoptive father run the farm after the death of Mrs. O'Neill. Garrett hoped that Martin would be as lucky as Nelson and someday find a permanent home.

About twenty minutes passed before Garrett heard Mrs. Linder's voice.

"Do you have a jacket, Martin?"

"No, ma'am."

"That's all right. We'll find one for you. Let me see if Mr. Wilder would like to accompany us."

Footsteps sounded outside his door and Mrs. Linder peered inside. "I'm taking Martin over to the shelter now. I thought it might be a good opportunity to give you a tour."

Garrett closed the ledger and rose. "I'd like that. Thank you."

Mrs. Linder stepped inside and lowered her voice. "Martin isn't happy about going back. I'll need a quick word with the matron when we get there to make sure she treats him with sensitivity."

Garrett barely kept the surprise from his face. Surely tighter discipline was warranted, not sensitivity. But now was not the time to begin voicing his opinion. Not when he didn't fully understand the dynamics involved. "Whatever I can do to help, let me know."

A relieved look came over her face, and she flashed him a warm smile. "Thank you. That poor child has been through so much. I want to make this transition as smooth as possible."

"Then smooth is what we'll aim for." Garrett grabbed his overcoat from the hook. "Lead on."

4

n the hallway, Jane stopped to put on her coat, since the overcast skies indicated it might rain. She had hoped to give Mrs. Shaughnessy more than five minutes' notice before she brought Mr. Wilder over for the first time, so the matron could have the house and the children in tip-top form. But it made sense for him to come with them now.

Jane reached for her satchel and allowed the tension to ease out of her shoulders. Despite all the commotion over Martin, she'd managed to telephone Mama while Melanie was seeing to the boy and was relieved to find her mother in better spirits. Even so, Jane was thankful that she'd asked their neighbor to check on Mama, as she had the previous day. Mrs. Peters was quite familiar with her mother's condition, and Jane trusted her to know if the situation called for Jane to come home.

"The children's shelter is just a short walk around the block," she said as they waited for Martin and Melanie.

"It's certainly handy having the shelter so close by." Mr. Wilder had donned his fedora and trench coat, then waited for Jane by the door.

"It is indeed. I usually go over at least once a week to speak with the matron, check on things, and visit the children."

His dark brows rose. "Really? Is that part of your job as directress?"

Heat rose in Jane's cheeks. "That's a matter of interpretation. Mr. Mills's view was that the shelter was best run by Mrs. Shaughnessy. He preferred to concentrate on the child protective services. But since I'd already established a good rapport with the children and staff at the shelter, I decided to remain as involved as possible, without sacrificing any other aspect of my job. So even if it's on my lunch, I make time to visit them."

Just then, Melanie emerged from the reception area, one hand on Martin's shoulder. He was wearing a brown knitted sweater, one of several they kept on hand for just such an emergency. It would be fine for the short walk to the shelter, where they would have to find more clothes for him until they could retrieve his few belongings from the McElroys.

"Thank you, Melanie," Jane said. "We should be back in half an hour or so." Jane took Martin's hand. "All right. Let's go get you settled, young man."

She led the way outside and along the sidewalk. The cool autumn air was a nice change from the stuffiness inside, chasing away the beginnings of a headache. Jane inhaled deeply. Somewhere a fireplace was going, the lingering smell of smoke scenting the air.

They walked in silence for several minutes until Jane felt the need to break the ice between the two males. Clearly Martin did not trust Mr. Wilder, and the man wasn't doing much to change Martin's view.

"I was a caseworker with the agency for several years," she said to Mr. Wilder, "which is where I met Martin. Isn't that right, Martin?"

The boy nodded, but his eyes remained glued to the ground.

"You must be very familiar with the children, then," Mr. Wilder said.

"I am. I try to learn something about each one and spend time talking to them individually."

Mr. Wilder slowed his long strides to match hers and Martin's. "I'm glad you'll be able to introduce me. A stranger appearing out of nowhere might make them uncomfortable."

"That's very perceptive of you. Have you had much experience with children, Mr. Wilder?"

He glanced over at her. "If that's your subtle way of asking if I have any children of my own, the answer is no. But I do have a niece and two nephews, so I know a bit about kids."

"That's not what I meant," Jane hastened to clarify. "But your familiarity with children could prove helpful in this job."

"I also know a little about the foster care system. When I was growing up, our neighbors were foster parents for several children, one of whom became my best friend." He lowered his voice. "Nelson told me a few sad stories of some of the places he'd lived before he came to our neighbor's farm."

She nodded. "There are many unfortunate cases, which is why we do frequent inspections and why we try to make the shelter a welcoming place."

Martin gave a slight snort, which Jane pointedly ignored.

They rounded the corner, and the ivy-covered building came into view.

"This home used to belong to a former president of the Children's Aid, Mr. John MacDonald," Jane said. "The agency bought it after his death in 1928."

"It's beautiful." Mr. Wilder stopped to gaze up at the high rooftop and the rows of shuttered windows. "Looks spacious."

"It is. Even though the children share the bedrooms, they each have their own space. There's a dining room, a living room, and a common area that's used as a classroom and activity room. But most of the children attend a neighborhood school."

"Is there a yard in back?"

"A small one, yes. There's also a park several blocks away. The staff makes sure the children get lots of fresh air and exercise."

She walked up the few stairs to the front door, tugging Martin along with her. "Come in and I'll introduce you to the matron."

Mrs. Shaughnessy was waiting in the front hallway for them. She was a short, plump woman with a homey sense about her that the children responded to quite well. Yet, at the same time, she managed to uphold strict discipline in the shelter, so that everything ran smoothly.

"Good afternoon, Mrs. Shaughnessy."

"Good afternoon, Jane." The woman smiled, then turned to Martin. "Hello, Martin. I trust your stay with us will be more successful this time around."

The boy didn't respond.

Jane tapped his shoulder. "Martin, it's polite to answer when Mrs. Shaughnessy speaks to you."

Martin quickly straightened his posture. "Yes, ma'am. Thank you, ma'am."

Jane turned to the man behind her. "Mrs. Shaughnessy, this is Mr. Wilder."

The woman bobbed her head. "How do you do, sir? I wish we'd had more notice of your arrival. We would have had the children all assembled and waiting. Most of them are out at school right now, but the younger ones are upstairs in the play-room."

Mr. Wilder removed his hat. "No need to worry, Mrs. Shaughnessy. I'd prefer to see them in their natural state anyway." He walked down the hall, scanning the area as he went.

A trickle of annoyance crept through Jane's system. Politeness dictated that he should wait for the matron to invite him in for a tour.

Jane hurried after him. "Before we show you around, Mr. Wilder, I have something to discuss with Mrs. Shaughnessy. Martin, will you take Mr. Wilder and wait in the parlor, please?"

"Yes, Mrs. Linder." He pointed to a doorway across the hall. "It's in here."

With little recourse, Mr. Wilder nodded. "Thank you, Martin."

They went into the main living area, which housed several couches, a fireplace, a wooden table and chairs, and a piano. Mrs. Shaughnessy liked to play music in the evenings and even attempted to teach the children to play a few simple songs.

"We won't be long," Jane said. "Make yourself comfortable." Then she took Mrs. Shaughnessy by the arm and guided her down the hall. They entered Mrs. Shaughnessy's cozy office, formerly Mr. MacDonald's study, and took a seat by the hearth.

"I presume this is about Martin," Mrs. Shaughnessy said once she'd situated herself. "Or is it Mr. Wilder who's got you in a flap?"

Jane huffed out a breath. "Both. A child being dumped off like unwanted goods is not the best impression to make on Mr. Wilder. Especially on his first day here."

"It's unfortunate but not your fault, dear." Mrs. Shaughnessy gave her a sympathetic look.

Jane unfastened her coat. "I only hope we can find a better fit for Martin this time around."

"That doesn't seem likely with the shortage of families available." Mrs. Shaughnessy's ample chest rose with her sigh. "What are we to do with Martin until then? He clearly doesn't want to be back here."

"You're right. He doesn't do well in group settings. He acts up to get the attention he doesn't even realize he's seeking. I'll have to double my efforts to see if we have any families who might take him." Jane shifted on her seat. "In the meantime, we need to make sure the other children treat Martin better than they have in the past. No more bullying or mean-spirited teasing. It will only set off his temper." She paused. "Could one of the older girls take him under their wing? Perhaps Rachel or Bettina? That way he'd have someone looking out for him while giving him the attention he needs."

"That might work. I'll speak to the girls when they get back from school." The matron shook her head. "It's a shame that an older couple couldn't adopt Martin. I think he'd thrive with one-on-one attention."

"So do I. Unfortunately, the agency has fairly rigid criteria on adopting." Jane rose from the armchair. "If only this dreadful war would end. Maybe then we'd have more families willing to give these children the homes they deserve."

"From your lips to God's ears, my dear."

———◆———

Jane hurried back to the living room, praying Mr. Wilder and Martin were both in one piece. The harsh plunking of piano keys met her ears as she entered.

Mr. Wilder sat on one of the sofas, a pained expression on his face.

"I see you're in dire need of some piano lessons, Martin," Jane said with a light laugh. "Should I let Mrs. Shaughnessy know?"

The boy glared at her, likely miffed that his attempt to annoy Mr. Wilder hadn't worked.

Jane turned to the man, who had risen from his seat. "Would you care to see the dining room and the kitchen before we go upstairs?"

"I'd prefer to start where the children are, if you don't mind."

"Very well."

They walked out into the hallway, where Mrs. Shaughnessy hovered by the telephone stand.

Before Jane could explain their intentions, Mr. Wilder started up the wide central staircase.

Jane laid a comforting hand on the matron's shoulder and spoke as quietly as she could. "Try not to worry, Mrs. Shaughnessy. Remember, he's here to help the agency, not make matters worse. I'd better go up before he startles the children. Come along, Martin."

She hurried up the stairs as fast as her high heels and slim-fitting skirt would allow, with Martin right behind. Jane caught up to Garrett at the far end of the corridor, where he stood peering into the playroom. As she approached, he moved aside to let her by.

She clasped Martin's hand in hers and entered the room. Most of the children were seated on the floor with various toys scattered around them. The small tables contained tidy piles of paper and a basket of pencils. Jane nodded to Miss Channing, one of the shelter's aides, who sat at a desk in the corner.

"Children," Jane said in a loud voice. "May I have your attention for a moment, please?"

The laughter and murmurs stopped as the children all looked up.

"Good afternoon, everyone."

"Good afternoon, Mrs. Linder," a chorus of voices sounded.

"I'm here to introduce you to two people. Some of you may remember Martin Smith." She put her hands on the boy's shoulders and gently guided him forward. "He's going to be staying here with you again for a while. I hope you'll make him feel welcome."

One of the girls, Denise Turner, stood up. "Hi, Martin. You can sit with me if you'd like."

Jane felt the muscles in Martin's shoulders relax a bit. Thank goodness for little Denise, who despite getting into her own share of trouble, had a generous heart and a lovable spirit.

"And this gentleman beside me is Mr. Wilder. He'll be working with us for a few weeks to study how we run things at the Children's Aid. I trust you will be cooperative and polite if he asks you any questions."

"Hello, children." Garrett stepped forward, a wide smile on his face as he pulled a small bag from his pocket. "If you'll come forward, I have a treat for each of you."

Squeals of delight rang out as the children scrambled into line.

Frowning, Jane leaned forward to see what exactly he intended to give out. Her stomach dropped. Peppermint candies? Mrs. Shaughnessy would have a fit. Candy was forbidden contraband, except on the rarest of occasions, because visits to the dentist were less than desirable. But Jane couldn't say anything now or she would undermine Garrett's position.

"Can I have two candies, Mr. Wilder?" Bobby asked. "One for my sister when she gets back from school?" Bobby hopped up and down beside the toy box. A red-and-blue-striped ball slipped from his fingers and rolled across the floor, unheeded.

"Me too, Mr. Wilder," Denise said. "I have a . . . brother."

Jane was about to step in and chastise the girl for fibbing, but Garrett held up a hand.

"Sorry, one candy each," he said firmly. "I'll leave the bag with Mrs. Shaughnessy. She can give them out to the other children when they return from school."

One of the girls, Elsie, tugged on his jacket. "Will you come to the park with us tomorrow, Mr. Wilder? They have a slide."

"Do they?" Both brows rose. "That sounds like fun, but I'll be busy in the office tomorrow. Perhaps another time."

Jane stepped forward. "Say good-bye to Mr. Wilder, children." She forced a note of authority into her voice and glanced at Miss Channing, who had remained seated the whole time. Jane made a note to discuss her performance with Mrs. Shaughnessy the next time they met. The young woman seemed a trifle too reserved to be in charge of the children who required a firm hand. However, they couldn't really afford to lose even one worker.

"Thank you, Miss Channing. Forgive us for interrupting your playtime." Jane gave Mr. Wilder a pointed look and headed out into the hall.

"Am I correct in thinking you're annoyed with me, Mrs. Linder?" A hint of amusement laced the man's voice as he followed her.

She huffed out a breath. "You really should have asked about the candies before handing them out. Certain rules must be respected. Not to mention that disrupting their routine is not conducive to—"

He laid a hand on her arm. "I only wanted to put the children at ease. Surely one little peppermint won't hurt."

She clamped her mouth shut, while attempting to ignore the heat from his hand filtering through her sleeve. With effort, she forced her muscles to relax. "If you're ready, I'll show you the rest of the shelter."

"I'd appreciate that." He gave her a quick smile.

She forced her attention away from his appealing dimples and focused on giving him a tour of the upper floors. She'd been around good-looking men before. Why did this one fluster her so much?

Before they returned to the main level, she checked on Martin in the playroom. Little Denise sat beside him at one of the desks, a game board in front of them.

"Looks like Martin's made a friend." Mr. Wilder's low voice sounded by her ear.

A tingle traveled down her spine, and she moved a step away. "If anyone can befriend Martin, it's Denise."

"She does seem to be a charmer. Reminds me a little of my niece, Amanda."

As much as Jane hated to leave Martin, she couldn't stay all day and watch over him. "Shall we go downstairs?"

"Yes, please."

They were just finishing the tour of the kitchen and dining area when Mrs. Shaughnessy appeared in the hall. "I hope everything met your approval, Mr. Wilder."

He reached for his hat on the coatrack. "From what I've seen so far, you seem to have the home well in hand."

"That's a relief to hear, sir. We certainly try our best."

"Thank you for your time, Mrs. Shaughnessy." He smiled as

he settled his hat on his head. "I'm sure we'll see each other again soon."

"I certainly hope so, sir." The older woman actually blushed.

Jane shook her head in mild amusement. It seemed she wasn't the only one affected by those dimples.

5

"Melanie said you wished to see me?" Mrs. Linder stood in the doorway of Garrett's office the next day, looking crisp and neat in another trim suit. Navy blue this time.

"Good morning." Garrett laid his pencil down. "I hoped you might have some time to answer a few more questions."

He'd spent the morning going over his preliminary notes about the Children's Aid office as well as the shelter. It was important to record his initial impressions, even if those impressions changed after he learned more about the operations.

Mrs. Linder folded her arms in front of her and moved farther into the room. "What sort of questions?" Her gaze darted to the ledger, then skimmed over the other items on his desk.

Why did she always seem on the defensive with him? Did she have something she didn't want him to discover?

"In going over some of the files," he said, "I've seen numerous mentions of the Infants' Home. It appears the Children's Aid and the Infants' Home are intertwined somehow, but I can't quite figure out exactly how they work."

Her shoulders eased away from somewhere around her ears. "Don't feel bad," she said. "At times even we aren't sure how it works." She gave a light laugh as she moved closer to the desk and glanced down at the framed photo he'd set out. His favorite snapshot of his sister's kids.

She picked up the frame. "Are these your niece and nephews?"

Ah, so she'd remembered what he'd told her yesterday. He smiled. "Yes. Kevin, Dale, and Mandy. They're the loves of my life." Warmth spread through his chest just thinking of them and the fact that he'd get to see them at the end of the week.

"They're beautiful." A strange hitch invaded her voice as she ran a finger across the glass.

For an instant, as her eyes met his, a flash of longing appeared. Then she blinked and set the photo down, her features settling into what he'd come to think of as her business face.

"Thank you," he said. "I think they're pretty great, but then again, I'm biased."

She looked at her watch. "It's almost noon, and I have a meeting at one o'clock. If you don't mind giving up part of your lunch hour, I could fill you in on our role with the Infants' Home."

"I don't mind at all. I often work through lunch anyway." He rose from his seat. "Why don't we take a walk? I could use some fresh air and a bit of exercise."

She nodded. "That sounds good. Let me make one more phone call and we can go."

Ten minutes later, Garrett walked down Isabella Street beside Mrs. Linder, enjoying the cool air and open space, a treat after spending all morning in his windowless office. Even though it was only the beginning of September, fall was on its way, a season he enjoyed more than the others. It was always a busy time at his parents' farm, but one he relished nonetheless.

"This was a good idea," Mrs. Linder said suddenly. "I don't get out of my office enough these days."

"I always find a change of scenery helps recharge my energy, even if it's only for a few minutes." He looked over at her. "How do you like overseeing the agency?"

She walked in silence for a few seconds. "It's challenging, I'll admit. There's a lot more to it than I originally realized. But when Mr. Mills took ill, he said he didn't trust anyone else to handle things in his absence." She lifted one shoulder. "And as much as I loved my job as a caseworker, I couldn't let him down."

"It sounds like you have a close relationship with Mr. Mills."

"I do. He's a wonderful boss and mentor."

"You must have mixed feelings about him retiring, then." It was a statement more than a question. One she confirmed with a nod.

"Of course, I'm happy for him," she added quickly. "But I'm going to miss him terribly. He leaves big shoes to fill. I only hope I can live up to his legacy."

Garrett almost stumbled over a crack in the sidewalk. She made it sound as though she intended to stay on in her current role. The board had certainly never mentioned any such thing. But if they were both competing for the same job, it would make his position here even more stressful, for both of them.

She glanced over at him. "I understand you might be applying for the position yourself." Her words were more than blunt, almost accusatory.

"That's right. I intend to use my time here to see if I would be a good fit for the organization. And it for me."

"Don't you already have a job?" The sharp question sliced through the air between them.

"Not really. For the past year or so, I've been doing freelance audits for various companies. But I'm ready to put down roots and settle into a permanent job, and I'd like it to be a meaningful position. Somewhere I can make a difference in the world. Working with needy children seems to be a perfect way to do that." Heat built under his collar. He hadn't meant to reveal so much of himself. Or how important getting this position was to him.

"Exactly why I want the job." Her gaze was steady on his, not angry or challenging, simply calm and direct.

His stomach clenched. He'd never imagined this scenario, assuming that because she was a married woman, the high-level job must be a temporary position for her. He winced inwardly, imagining what his mother and sister would think of that idea. Cassie already called him a chauvinist. Perhaps she had a point.

"I hope this isn't going to affect our working together," he said quietly. "I have to believe that in the end the best person for the job will be the one who gets it."

Her features relaxed a little. "I agree. Mr. Fenmore told me that given the current high level of unemployment, he expects dozens of applications for the job once they post it. I have to believe that God will allow the right person to take over the helm." She shrugged. "I see no reason for it to affect our interactions while you work here. You will have my full cooperation."

He nodded, a growing admiration for her fairness and sensibility loosening the tightness in his chest. "I appreciate that, Mrs. Linder. You shall have the same from me."

"Thank you." She tilted her head. "Perhaps you should call me Jane. It will be easier that way."

He smiled. "Very well. And I'm Garrett."

She looked at her watch again. "Let's head back and I'll answer your questions about the Infants' Home on the way."

"Thanks. It's my fault we got off track."

"That's all right. I think it was a productive conversation, don't you?"

"I do indeed."

By the time they neared the office, Jane had filled Garrett in on the intricate way the Infants' Home worked. He walked beside her in silence as though trying to digest what she'd told him.

"It makes sense that the infants are housed in a different building from the older children," he said. "But why create a separate organization? And why does the Children's Aid handle the adoptions?"

"I can't really explain the reasoning behind it all. It's just the way things evolved. However, I can tell you that Miss Moberly has done wonders with the Infants' Home. She and Mr. Mills have worked closely together over the years to establish foster care for children of all ages. I'm not sure why our department handles the infant adoptions, but it seems to work out well."

"I suppose to insiders it makes sense. But for someone new, the whole process seems convoluted." His brows pulled down in a frown.

"If you really want to know more, I'd suggest speaking with Miss Moberly. You could give her a call and set up an appointment if you'd like."

He nodded. "That might be a good idea. The better the understanding I have of all the pieces in this puzzle, the easier it will be to make the best recommendations possible."

Jane repressed the spurt of alarm that continued to wind through her. She'd hoped that once they'd cleared the air and established their respective positions about the director's job, she'd feel better about the man's presence in her office. Yet an invasive feeling of unease persisted. The feeling that she was simply playacting the part of directress and didn't really deserve the role. The feeling that Garrett Wilder was infinitely more qualified for the job than she.

In reality, he probably was. But she couldn't allow her own insecurities to destroy her chance to make effective changes to the agency, especially with regard to the way adoptions were handled. Children like Martin deserved the opportunity to find a permanent home. And if she didn't use her position to effect the types of changes she envisioned, who would?

Even though Mr. Mills often agreed with her in principle, he'd never been open to expanding the criteria for adopting older children to possibly include single people or even older couples. She had no guarantee that Garrett would either.

When they reached the office, Jane led the way inside. They'd taken a lot longer than the fifteen minutes she'd intended. If she hurried, she could eat half of the sandwich she'd brought from home and gulp down a cup of tea before her next meeting.

"Jane. Thank goodness you're back." Melanie rushed into the hallway, her expression anxious.

Jane stopped cold. "What's wrong?"

The young woman's gaze swung to Mr. Wilder and back to Jane again. "There was an urgent phone call from your neighbor. Your mother needs you to come home right away."

6

arrett watched the color drain from Jane's face as her hand went to her throat.

"How bad is it? Did she say?" Her voice came out in a rasp.

Melanie shook her head. "Only that she's not well."

Jane turned to Garrett. "Excuse me, but I have to leave. Melanie, please cancel my one o'clock meeting and send my sincerest regrets."

"I will."

Garrett laid a gentle hand on her arm. "Is there anything I can do to help?" He didn't know Jane well, but as usual, his impulse to rescue people came charging to the forefront.

"No, thank you." When she looked at him, raw anguish twisted her features. "I hope to be back, but if I don't return today, please see Melanie or one of the caseworkers if you need help with anything."

She headed down the hall to her office, then came back carrying her handbag.

He stood by, feeling utterly useless. "I hope everything's all right with your mother. And please don't rush back on my account."

She looked up from her change purse as she counted out coins. "Thank you. In that case, I will see you tomorrow."

When she left, the very energy in the building seemed to shift, leaving the atmosphere considerably more somber.

Garrett returned to his office, took out a notepad and pen, and attempted to focus on writing down what he'd learned about the Infants' Home. But his mind kept wandering back to Jane and her mother. He could only imagine how distraught he'd be if he got a call about an emergency with his own mother. He'd be on the road to the farm so fast his tires would burn rubber. Another thought crossed his mind. Jane had been counting her coins as though preparing to take a bus. If the situation was so urgent, why wouldn't she call her husband and have him pick her up?

He ran a hand over the back of his neck. Perhaps her husband worked out of town or had a job where he couldn't be disturbed. Perhaps they didn't own a vehicle. Garrett suddenly wished he knew more about the woman and her background. After auditing various companies over the past year, he usually tried to find out as much as possible about the people he was investigating. Tomorrow he'd make some subtle inquiries about the directress, an idea that didn't seem out of place since the board had specifically asked Garrett for feedback on her. Anything that might affect her performance was, in his mind, fair game.

A few hours later, he set down his pen and stood up. There wasn't much more he could do here today. He might as well take some of the files home to read this evening after dinner at the boardinghouse. Tomorrow he'd tackle the problems with a fresh outlook.

His thoughts turned to Jane once again, and he resolved to make a phone call to his parents tonight. This war had taught him the hard way that life was too precious and far too fleeting to take for granted.

It was only by the grace of God that he'd recovered from his injuries and made it home in one piece. Since then, he'd vowed never to let a single day go by without a healthy dose of gratitude.

———— ❧ ————

The next morning, Jane sat at her desk and did her best to quiet her conscience, telling herself that she had no real reason to fret. Mama's episode had turned out to be a mild heart fluctuation, one that Dr. Henshaw had handled easily. As a precaution given her mother's medical history, he'd decided to keep her overnight for observation, and if events followed their usual pattern, she'd be released later that afternoon.

Jane twirled a pen between her fingers, her nerves refusing to settle. What a disaster the past two days had been. She couldn't have orchestrated a worse introduction for Mr. Wilder to their organization. First there was Martin's unceremonious return and the unplanned tour of the shelter, followed by the emergency with her mother requiring Jane to cancel a meeting and leave work hours earlier than normal. He must think her totally incompetent as directress, and she couldn't blame him. She'd have thought the same thing.

"Good morning, Jane." Garrett Wilder stood in her doorway. "How is your mother faring today?"

Jane straightened her shoulders, realizing she'd been staring blankly at the papers on her desk. "A little better, thank you. The doctor kept her in the hospital overnight, so I'll pick her up later this afternoon." Another day that she'd have to leave work early.

"The hospital?" Frowning, he came into the room. "Was it something serious, then?"

Concern shone in his eyes, yet Jane couldn't help but wonder if the emotion was sincere or if he was searching for any weakness he could find. She hated that he'd already seen her at her worst, but there was no point in trying to hide Mama's condition now.

"I'm afraid so. My mother suffered rheumatic fever several years ago, and it left her heart in a weakened state."

"I'm sorry to hear that." His gaze fell to Jane's left hand and the plain band she still wore. "Does she live with you and your husband?"

Tension snapped up Jane's spine, and she drew in a sharp breath. These were natural questions that someone who didn't know her would ask. Thankfully, she'd perfected a generic answer that kept her curious co-workers at bay. "My husband is away fighting in the war, as is my brother. I moved back to live with my mother since she couldn't stay on her own."

Garrett frowned. "I didn't realize your husband was overseas. That must be such a worry for you."

Jane murmured something nondescript.

"But it appears that living with your mother has turned out to be a mutually beneficial arrangement."

Jane gripped her hands together. "For the most part, it has." The toll of caring for her mother often seemed overwhelming, yet Jane couldn't bear the alternative. Dr. Henshaw, Mama's physician, had gently suggested that the day might come where she would be better off in a nursing facility; however, Jane would not allow herself to think of that time yet.

Garrett took a seat and crossed one leg over his knee. "I'm grateful that my own parents so far enjoy good health. They own a farm about an hour from here."

She forced herself to relax. The man was simply making pleasant conversation, as one would with a co-worker. "I take it you don't live with them. That would make for a long drive to work each day."

"That it would. No, I live in a boardinghouse in the city, but I go home almost every weekend to help with the chores and enjoy my mother's cooking." He smiled as he continued to study her. "I hope you manage to get some time to relax on your days off. Or does this place keep you too busy for that?"

Tension screamed back into Jane's muscles. It seemed like he was probing for more information. Now that he knew she wanted the director's job, was he trying to find ammunition to use against her? "I spend most Saturdays working here, along with the rest of my employees," she said briskly. "As you will learn, we are severely understaffed." She shoved on her reading glasses, ones she only needed for small print, but that gave her a more authoritative air. "Now, how can I help you this morning?"

Garrett stared at the woman before him, realizing the door had slammed shut on the brief glimpse he'd gained into her personal life. Once again, she'd donned her professional armor, complete with dark-rimmed glasses. Yet, far from rendering her unapproachable, the spectacles only added to her charm.

Not that he should be noticing anything of the sort. He glanced down at her slim gold wedding band to hammer home that idea, then cleared his throat. "I'd like to discuss the financial records with you today, if you can spare some time. When I was going over them last night, I made note of a few items I'd like to clarify."

"Very well. I have some time now before my next appointment."

"Perfect. Shall we work in here, then?"

"I think that would be best."

"I'll get my notes and be right back."

An hour later, they had gone over several months' worth of expenses with amazing efficiency. Jane was indeed a thorough recordkeeper, although she admitted that finances weren't her strong suit and that Mr. Bolton, the volunteer she'd previously mentioned, did most of the detailed figure work. So far, Garrett had found no hint of mismanagement of funds, which, he could admit, was a relief. The more time he spent with Jane, the more he admired her skills. Her integrity had shone through in all their dealings so far. He couldn't imagine her being responsible for perpetrating any type of fraud.

"Tell me," he said as they wrapped up, "how did you come to

have a career at the Children's Aid?" He leaned back in his chair, aiming to adopt a casual air. He truly was interested in her history, since strong, independent women in high positions were a rarity.

Her brows rose above her glasses. "I started working here as a clerk out of high school. Over the years, I got my college diploma in social work and became a caseworker, which is the position I enjoyed the most—where I felt I made a real difference in the children's lives."

"I can imagine how fulfilling that must be." He tilted his head, one glaring question consuming his thoughts. "I'm curious, though. This job obviously requires long hours and a great deal of dedication. Does your husband not object to your spending so much time here?"

Her smile instantly vanished. "This is the forties, Mr. Wilder. Modern women do work outside the home now." Her nostrils flared. "Besides, with my husband gone, it's up to me to support my family."

"I see." He hesitated, then purposely gentled his voice. "Does your family include children?" There were no photos of her husband or children around the room, but then again, the office still technically belonged to Mr. Mills.

Her head flew up, and her green eyes flashed. Then just as quickly, a mask seemed to come over her features. "Unfortunately, my husband and I weren't blessed with children, which makes me all the more grateful to have my career to fall back on."

Despite her crisp tone, Garrett sensed the underlying pain beneath her words. How difficult must it be to yearn for a child, yet bravely soldier on to place other people's children in good homes?

"Well, I admire your fortitude. And as far as I can tell, you're doing an admirable job filling in for Mr. Mills."

She looked up at him, the first hint of vulnerability on her face. "Do you really think so?"

"I haven't delved into all areas yet, but from what I can see at the outset, you have stepped in and kept things running smoothly.

I can find nothing out of the ordinary in the expenses, except for one or two minor additions and—"

"What additions?" she snapped.

"Well, for one, this entry here." He reached across the ledger to point out a figure. "It's marked as *birthday gifts*. I presume that means gifts for the children?"

"Correct." She pulled off her glasses and frowned. "What's wrong with that?"

"It's a sizeable expense for something unnecessary."

"I disagree. I think every child deserves a birthday present. It increases their morale and gives them something to look forward to."

"From a business standpoint, however, it's an unnecessary expense. One I will recommend be stopped."

Her eyes widened. "Next, you'll want to cancel Christmas."

He held back a laugh at her exasperated tone. "Just call me Mr. Scrooge."

"You can't be serious? Children must have Christmas. That is non-negotiable."

He narrowed his eyes. "Did Mr. Mills support this practice?"

She hesitated for a second. "Not exactly. I implemented it after he took sick."

"What did you do in previous years?"

"People in the community donated toys and candies for them."

"Did this cost the agency anything?"

"No."

"Then I suggest we continue with that practice. There are many ways to provide children with a nice Christmas and birthday gifts without spending agency funds. It just takes a little creativity." He waited, hoping she wouldn't continue to argue with him.

When her shoulders slumped, he took it as a sign of victory.

"You have a point," she said. "I guess the newfound authority went to my head a little." She gave a sheepish shrug, and a faint blush stained her cheeks.

He hoped it was the only way it had gone to her head and that she had nothing to do with any missing funds. The more he got to know her, the higher his opinion of her grew, and he hated to think she could be involved in anything like that. If indeed there were some sort of mismanaged funds, he prayed it was just an honest mistake, one easily rectified.

He rose from his seat. "Thank you for your time. I'll continue my investigation and make note of any further ways to cut costs."

With a nod in her direction, he tucked the ledger under his arm and made his way back to his cubbyhole, where he tossed the book onto the desk with a sigh and rubbed the place on his chest where the shrapnel resided. Even if Jane was completely innocent, which he prayed she was, he needed to remember that they were vying for the same position.

He could not allow his growing respect for the woman to interfere with his plans to secure his future.

7

he taxi company says they won't be able to send a car out for another half an hour. Something about a traffic accident and several cabs being stuck." Melanie shrugged one shoulder in apology as she hung up the phone.

Jane set her handbag on Melanie's desk with a thud. "Well, that's inconvenient timing." She blew a piece of hair off her forehead. She was already leaving work later than she'd hoped. Now, Mama would have to wait a bit longer while Jane caught the bus.

"What's inconvenient?" Garrett appeared in the open doorway.

Jane's spine stiffened. She'd hoped to leave without him noticing. "Just a delay in getting a cab. I'll take the bus instead."

"Do you need a ride home?" He came more fully into the room. He'd shed his suit jacket at some point and rolled his shirtsleeves up to the elbow, revealing finely muscled forearms sprinkled with dark hair.

"Thank you, but no. I'm going to pick up my mother at the hospital."

"Even more reason to accept a ride." His brow rose as he looked at her. "My car is right outside. Please allow me to do this for you."

She bit her lip. If she accepted his offer, she'd have to make small talk in the car. But it was only a fifteen-minute drive, and there were usually several taxis waiting at the hospital. Once Mama was released, they could take a cab home. She let out a weary breath. "Very well. I would appreciate a lift if it's not too much trouble."

A grin brightened his features. "Wonderful. Let me grab my jacket."

Jane stared at the empty doorway, frowning. Something about this man unsettled her in ways she couldn't explain.

"What's the scowl for?" Melanie asked, amusement lacing her voice. "It's only a car ride."

"I don't know. I just sense there's an ulterior motive in everything Mr. Wilder says or does." She shook her head. "Maybe I'm being paranoid."

"Or perhaps it's something else." Melanie leaned back in her chair, the wood creaking in protest. "I know this audit has us all on edge, but you have to admit, the man is gorgeous."

Jane aimed a fierce glare at her friend. "I'm married. Remember?" Melanie was the only one in the office who knew Jane was divorced, and therefore, single.

She laughed. "Fair warning, Boss. I intend to do my best to catch Mr. Wilder's attention while he's here. After all, with this blasted war dragging on, there aren't many eligible men around."

"I thought you were interested in Harold Bolton." Jane hadn't approved of Melanie dating one of the agency's volunteers, but since Mr. Bolton wasn't an official employee, there was little Jane could do, except warn Melanie to be discreet.

"A girl has to keep her options open. Besides, I'm pretty sure he's seeing other people, so why shouldn't I?"

Jane shook her head. "For all you know, Mr. Wilder could be married."

"He's not. I asked him."

Why did that thought bother her? "Be careful, Melanie. You know that dating co-workers is frowned upon."

Melanie doubled over in a sudden fit of coughing.

"Are you all right, Miss Benton?" Garrett's concerned voice came from behind Jane. "Can I get you some water?"

"I'm fine. Thank you." Melanie's scarlet face belied her words, yet Jane believed the blush was more from embarrassment than from her cough.

Jane picked up her bag. "Good night, Melanie. Would you cancel the taxi for me, please?"

"Right away."

As she walked past a bewildered Garrett, Jane resisted the urge to roll her eyes. In so many ways, the man's presence in the building was creating chaos. Who knew how many of the other employees had their eyes on him?

Jane only hoped his investigation would wrap up as soon as possible. Maybe then some semblance of normalcy would return to the Children's Aid offices.

⁓ ❧ ⁓

As Garrett drove toward the hospital, he risked a sidelong glance at Jane in the passenger seat of his car. Earlier, he'd gotten the impression that he'd walked in on a private conversation between the two women, and she now seemed rather sullen.

"Dare I ask what that was all about back there?" he asked. "Was I the butt of some joke?"

"Not really." Her lips twitched at the corners. "But I do believe Miss Benton has set her cap for you, Mr. Wilder."

He shook his head. "I'm flattered but not interested. I'm here to do a job and only that."

"Right. No fraternizing with the enemy." The hint of sarcasm in her voice had him looking over at her again.

"Is that how you view me? Or how you think I view you? As the enemy?"

"No. I mean . . ." A rosy hue invaded her cheeks. "I'm not sure exactly how to view you."

"Well, as I've already explained, we're on the same team, working toward the betterment of the agency."

"I hope you mean that," she said quietly. "I'd hate to think I had to guard every word and action around you, for fear you might use some piece of information against me."

An itch crept up his neck as her words cut a bit too close for comfort. But his interest in Jane wasn't malicious. He was only doing his job. "Believe me, I don't deal in gossip or innuendo. I will only report what I deem necessary to effect a positive change in the department's operations. You have my word on that."

They drove on in silence for a few minutes. Garrett drummed his fingers against the steering wheel.

"Tell me more about young Martin," he said at last. "How did he end up in the system?"

Her rigid posture relaxed slightly. "He was abandoned by his mother when he was nine months old. Dropped off at a church with a note saying she couldn't keep him."

"That young." Garrett whistled. "Although I imagine a healthy infant would've been in great demand for adoption."

"You're right. He was placed with a young couple who were initially thrilled to get him. Unfortunately, when Martin was just under two, they brought him back. He stayed at the Infants' Home for a while until another family was found. But just after his fourth birthday, the same thing happened, and this time he was brought to our shelter."

"Right. Because the Infants' Home only keeps children until the age of four." Garrett remembered that from their talk the other day.

"Yes." Jane sighed. "Martin's been in and out of foster homes ever since."

Garrett's chest tightened. What could a child have done to deserve such callous treatment? "Did these people give a reason why they returned him?"

Jane shot him an uneasy look while twisting her fingers into a tight pretzel. "If I tell you, it must remain confidential."

"That goes without saying."

She hesitated for a moment, then seemed to come to a decision. "Martin suffers from epileptic seizures. We think it's probably what led his mother to give him up in the first place. It was certainly the reason why the adoptive parents brought him back. They had no interest in a child with special needs. His medical problems, coupled with constant rejection, caused increasingly bad behavior as he got older, all contributing factors that have made him difficult to place." She lifted her chin. "But I'm determined to find him a permanent home if it's the last thing I do."

Garrett sifted through the information. "I presume that once Martin's condition became known, any potential parents were made aware of the situation."

"Of course."

"Wouldn't they have been prepared for his seizures, then? Received medical training on what to do?"

"Yes, but sadly the reality proves harder to deal with than reading about the condition on paper."

"I see. So, what do you intend to do now?"

She released a long breath. "What I always do. Keep him in the shelter until another family can be found." She shook her head. "I keep praying that God will find him the right home. I don't know why my prayers seem to go unanswered."

Garrett drove in silence, shifting gears as he accelerated. "Have you ever considered a different type of adoption for Martin? A widow, perhaps? Maybe a grandmotherly type? It sounds like Martin could benefit from some one-on-one attention."

Jane nodded. "I've often thought an unconventional family would be more suited to Martin." She paused, as though reluctant to continue. "I've mentioned the idea in the past to Mr. Mills, but he didn't agree with changing the usual criteria to suit one child and didn't feel it merited bringing such a change before the board."

Garrett turned a corner, then gave her a cautious glance.

"Forgive me if I'm overstepping, but what about you and your husband? You're obviously fond of Martin." Given her attachment to the boy, Garrett couldn't imagine that she hadn't at least considered the idea of adopting him herself.

Jane's knuckles went white around her purse handle. Her throat worked up and down until Garrett thought she might have choked on something. "Donald didn't wish to adopt," she finally said.

Those five clipped words didn't mask the river of pain beneath them. Garrett could only imagine the tense conversations they must have had on the subject. Some men believed strongly in propagating their own offspring to carry on the family name. Perhaps Jane's husband was one of them.

A short time later, he pulled up to the front of the hospital entrance and slowed to a stop.

"Thank you for the ride," she said. "It was very kind of you."

Once again, her guard was up, her professional façade in place. Before he could untangle himself from behind the wheel, she had pushed out of the passenger door.

"I'll wait here for you," he called after her.

She turned to look over her shoulder. "Please don't. I have no idea how long it will take to get my mother discharged. I'll see you tomorrow in the office."

She lifted her hand in a quick wave, then hurried toward the entrance, leaving Garrett feeling that he'd pulled the scab off an old wound without knowing exactly how to make it better.

8

Jane strode down the hospital corridor, attempting to shake off any residual tension from her car ride with Garrett. Those fifteen minutes had been even worse than she'd expected.

"What about you and your husband? You're obviously fond of Martin."

It almost seemed like he was trying to provoke her with his personal questions.

Probing for her secrets.

Secrets she had no intention of divulging.

If she were to survive this trying period with him watching her every move, it was imperative to keep a professional distance. Her personal life needed to remain strictly off-limits.

Setting her resolve, Jane made her way to her mother's room on the sixth floor. Thankfully, Mama was dressed and sitting on the side of the bed, her bag clutched on her lap. Ugly green curtains were pulled around the other three beds in the ward.

"There you are, dear." Mama stood as soon as she spied Jane in the doorway. "I am more than ready to go home." She rolled her eyes toward the bed nearest her.

As if to punctuate Mama's veiled insinuation, a loud, hacking cough sounded from behind the curtain.

"Wait until I get a wheelchair, Mama, and we'll head out."

"No need," a cheerful voice called out.

Jane turned to see a nurse in a white short-sleeved uniform rolling a chair through the door.

"I have one right here for you, Mrs. Mitchell." The young woman parked the wheelchair, then moved to the foot of the bed, where she lifted the chart from a hook. "Looks like your paperwork has been signed and you're ready to go."

The lines in Mama's face relaxed. "Thank you for your kindness, Betty."

"All part of the job." The nurse smiled, transforming her plain features. "I hope we don't see you back here again anytime soon."

"I'll do my best." Mama allowed Betty to help her into the wheelchair without a peep.

"Any instructions?" Jane asked as she gripped the chair's handles.

"Her heart has resumed a normal rhythm. Just make sure she gets plenty of rest, interspersed with a little mild activity to keep the joints moving." She winked at Mama. "We don't want you getting spoiled."

"Thank you, Betty." Jane smiled at the woman. "We appreciate your care."

As Jane wheeled her mother out into the corridor, she spotted Dr. Henshaw coming toward them.

"Ah, is my patient leaving me already?" he teased.

Mama chuckled. "As much as I love your company, I'm glad to be going home."

Jane's tense muscles eased a fraction, more relieved than she realized to see the doctor before they left. He was a kind man with a wonderful bedside manner, one Mama thrived under. And even though he wasn't much older than Jane, she trusted him implicitly to never sugarcoat the truth. "You're certain my mother's all right to go home?"

The doctor turned frank hazel eyes on her. "Yes. Luckily this was a mild arrhythmia. Nothing some rest won't cure." He handed Jane a piece of paper. "I was coming to give your mother this note for the pharmacist. I've made a slight alteration to the dosage of her medication. The next time you get it filled, give them this."

Jane took the slip and stared at the writing, the familiar anxiety crawling across her chest. "So, it's not urgent to fill right away?"

"No. Next time will be fine." He tilted his head, studying her. "Why don't I stop by the house in the next day or two, just to be safe?"

Relief rushed through her system so quickly that she almost felt dizzy. "I'd appreciate that. Thank you, Doctor."

"Not at all." He turned back to Mama. "Remember to take it easy for the next few days, Mrs. Mitchell, and avoid all stress."

"I will." Mama smiled weakly. "Thank you again."

When Dr. Henshaw left, Jane resumed her position at the wheelchair. "Let's get you home, Mama."

Several hallways and an elevator ride later, Jane wheeled her mother through the lobby to the front door, where she paused to take a breath and allow the stress to drain out of her. Mama's health was stable for the moment, which was all that really mattered. She gave a silent prayer of thanks as she moved the wheelchair to a safe spot and patted her mother's shoulder.

"Wait here, Mama. I'll see if there's a taxi handy." Jane exited through the revolving door, scanning the area in front of the building. But the place where the taxis usually parked was empty. She blew out a breath. Hopefully, it wouldn't be long until another one showed up.

Just then, a familiar-looking car approached the front of the building.

Her shoulders stiffened. What was Garrett still doing here? She'd made it clear that she didn't want him to wait. Why hadn't he listened to her?

Before her temper could come to a full boil, the man unfolded himself from the driver's seat and jogged over.

"Jane." He waved as he approached her. "Is your mother with you?"

Irritation climbed farther up her spine. "I told you not to wait."

"I tried to go, honestly. But it bothered me leaving you and your mother without a dependable way to get home. So, I kept circling around until I saw you come out." He gestured to the area where the cabs usually congregated. "Good thing, since the last taxi took off a few minutes ago." He shrugged, appearing totally unrepentant for disregarding her wishes.

"I'm sure another one will be along any moment." She craned her neck to see around him, but no other vehicles came into view. More than anything, she didn't want this man mixed up with her personal life and meeting her frail mother would let him see far too much.

He frowned. "Are you actually going to refuse a ride home? With your ill mother waiting inside?" He stared at her as if she'd lost her mind.

She pulled the strap of her purse tighter. The rational part of her brain told her she was being unreasonable, but she couldn't help it.

He came closer. "If I've offended you in any way, I apologize. I simply want to help."

A wave of shame overrode her irritation. She exhaled loudly. "It's not your fault." She stared at a button on his jacket, not quite able to meet his gaze. "I guess I'm a little on edge, but I shouldn't take it out on you."

"Fair enough. My offer still stands if you care to take me up on it." His quiet statement caused another round of shame to heat her cheeks.

"Janey? Is everything all right?"

She whirled around to see her mother hobbling along the walkway.

Jane rushed to her side. "Mama, you shouldn't be out of the chair."

"I didn't know what was keeping you."

"There aren't any taxis available right now." She shot a glance at Garrett, who stood watching them, and her resistance drained away. Her mother needed to get home to rest. Dr. Henshaw had specifically advised her to avoid stress. "But my colleague, Mr. Wilder, has offered to give us a lift."

A tremulous smile lit her mother's face. "How nice of him."

Jane turned to Garrett. "This is my mother, Hildie Mitchell."

He came forward, hand outstretched. "Glad I can help, Mrs. Mitchell. After all, what's the point of having a vehicle if I can't give people a ride?"

A hint of color returned to Mama's cheeks. "Thank you, Mr. Wilder."

"Please, call me Garrett."

As he helped Mama into the car, she seemed to perk up right before Jane's eyes.

Jane bit her lip. She should be relieved, happy even.

But as she climbed into the back seat, she still couldn't seem to let her guard down.

Garrett pulled away from the curb and glanced over at the older woman beside him. "How are you feeling, Mrs. Mitchell?"

Her shoulders and back were slightly stooped, giving her the appearance of a much older person, though she couldn't be more than sixty.

"A little weak, though I'm sure I'll feel better once I'm home." She gave him a thin smile and leaned her head against the seat. "So, you work at the Children's Aid with Jane?"

"Yes, ma'am. I just started there, and so far, I must say I'm impressed with your daughter's work ethic." He resisted looking in the mirror to see Jane's reaction.

"My Janey does work hard. Too hard, in my opinion."

He nodded. "It appears all the staff is overworked."

"Tell me about yourself, Garrett." Mrs. Mitchell shifted to look at him, her eyes bright with sudden interest.

The tension in Garrett's shoulders eased at this much safer topic of conversation.

"Well, I grew up not far from here. My parents own an apple orchard and farm over in Huttonville, about an hour's drive away."

"Goodness. Do you drive into the city from there every day?"

"No, ma'am. I rent a room in town, but I usually go home on the weekends to help out."

"I'm sure your parents appreciate that." Mrs. Mitchell gave a loud sniff. "Makes me miss my Brandon just hearing about it."

Garrett felt the weight of Jane's sigh from the back seat. "Is Brandon your son, the one who's away fighting in the war?"

"Yes. I pray every day that God sees fit to send him home safe and sound."

Garrett swallowed hard. From his own mother's reaction to him going off to fight, and then coming back injured, he knew how hard the war was on the soldiers' families. He looked over at her. "I was overseas for a time as well. Until I got injured and sent home. My parents are very happy to have me back."

"I can understand that. Not that I want Brandon to be injured. Just that he comes home safe."

Garrett reached over and patted the woman's arm. "I'll pray that he does, Mrs. Mitchell."

"This is our street up here on the right," Jane said.

Garrett welcomed the interruption, glad that no one asked about his injuries or why he hadn't been sent back to the fighting. He pulled up in front of the house Jane indicated and turned off the engine. Then he ran around to open the passenger door for Mrs. Mitchell.

Jane was quick to help her mother onto the sidewalk, while Garrett grabbed her small case.

"Where shall I put your bag, Mrs. Mitchell?"

"Just leave it on the porch," Jane said over her shoulder. "I'll get it later."

Garrett frowned. Why did she seem so determined not to accept any help? Perhaps she simply liked to keep her professional life separate from her personal one. He carried the bag to her front porch and set it down.

"Thank you." Jane shot him an indecipherable look as she opened the screen door.

"Won't you come in, Garrett?" Mrs. Mitchell peered around her daughter. "The least we can do is offer you something to drink after going out of your way for us."

"Really, Mama," Jane huffed as she twisted the key in the lock. "We've taken up enough of Garrett's time as it is. I'm sure he has to get home for dinner at the boardinghouse." She gave him a pointed stare, almost daring him to contradict her.

"Jane's right, ma'am. I should get—"

Suddenly, Mrs. Mitchell's eyes rolled back, and she pitched to one side. Garrett dashed over to catch her before she hit the porch floor.

"Mama!" Jane whirled around, letting the screen door bang shut. "What happened?"

Mrs. Mitchell's thin eyelids fluttered.

"She was about to topple over," Garrett said. "Here, let me take her inside." He scooped the woman into his arms and carried her into the house. She weighed barely more than a child.

"Bring her into the parlor." Jane rushed into the room ahead of him and gestured to a worn armchair beside the couch.

Gently, he set Mrs. Mitchell down, making sure her head rested against the cushioned back.

Jane grabbed a blanket and tucked it around her mother's legs. Her features were pinched, her brow furrowed. "Mama. Can you hear me?"

"Yes, dear," Mrs. Mitchell said, not opening her eyes. "I'm not deaf."

Garrett bit his lip to keep from chuckling.

"I just had a moment of weakness. I'll be fine in a few minutes." She opened one eye. "A cup of tea would certainly help."

"Of course. I'll put the kettle on." Jane turned to look at him, a question in her eyes.

"Don't worry. I'll sit with her while you're gone."

Jane swallowed. "Thank you."

"You're welcome." He laid a hand on her arm. "Take a minute to breathe, Jane. Everything's fine."

Surprisingly, moisture appeared in her eyes. She nodded and then headed down the hall.

Garrett stared after her for a moment. Between working so many hours at the office and constantly worrying about her mother, she had to be exhausted. What toll did that level of stress take on a person?

He turned his attention back to the parlor. The room was long and narrow, with a window that overlooked the street. Garrett let his gaze wander around the room, noting that a sofa, several wooden side tables, and an upright piano rounded out the furnishings.

Although the room was cozy, it had definitely seen better days. The furniture appeared to be from another era, and the curtains were faded, as were the wallpaper and the rug. Near the ceiling, the paint had started to peel and bubble.

"Like me, this house is a bit tired-looking," Mrs. Mitchell said as though reading his thoughts. "Ever since my husband died twelve years ago, I'm afraid I've let things slide. My son never was very handy, and he's been away almost four years now." She let out a sigh.

"And Jane's husband is overseas as well," Garrett added. Then again, maybe he wasn't the handy type either.

For a moment, Mrs. Mitchell appeared startled, her fingers flying to the neck of her blouse. Then, she nodded. "You're right. Donald has been gone just as long as Brandon."

Garrett rose and walked over to the piano, the one piece of furniture that looked in better shape. Several family photos sat on top. The largest portrayed a younger Mrs. Mitchell with the man who must have been her husband and their two children. Garrett peered closer at a young Jane, with her hair in a bow and long ringlets over each shoulder. The fair-haired boy beside her favored their father. Another picture showed the same boy, now a young man in uniform, fresh-faced and smiling. A third depicted Jane in a black graduation cap and gown. The innocent beauty in her features made his breath catch. He scanned the top of the piano again and then the rest of the room. Why weren't there any pictures of Jane and her husband? Surely they must have taken a wedding photo.

Footsteps entered the room. Garrett turned to see Jane setting a laden tray on the coffee table.

He took a seat on the sofa while she poured the tea. A shroud of silence seemed to descend on the room, where only the sounds of a clock ticking and the tea dribbling into the cups could be heard.

"So, who is the piano player in the family?" he asked to break the quiet.

"Mama is." Jane's features softened. "She used to teach students here." She handed her mother a china cup and saucer.

Mrs. Mitchell smiled. "Oh, but Jane is a wonderful pianist too. I know because I taught her myself."

"Don't exaggerate, Mama." Color bled into Jane's cheeks, highlighting the hue of her lips. "How do you take your tea, Mr. Wi—I mean Garrett?"

"Just a bit of milk, please."

She handed him a dainty cup with a slight tremor in her hand. He took it from her, astonished by his longing to steady her hand with his.

Mrs. Mitchell took a rather noisy sip of her tea, then looked over at him. "If you live in a boardinghouse, I take it you aren't married."

Jane started to cough and set her cup down with a loud clink. "Mama, that's rather personal, don't you think?"

Garrett stifled a smile. "It's a fair question." He looked at Mrs. Mitchell. "No, ma'am. I'm not married."

"Why hasn't a handsome young man like you found a good woman?"

From the side, he caught Jane's annoyed expression.

"I had a girlfriend years ago," he said. "But after high school, our paths went in different directions, and she broke off our relationship." He leaned back in his seat, the memory of Adeline bringing up bittersweet feelings.

"That's too bad." Sympathy washed over Mrs. Mitchell's features. "First loves can leave a scar that's hard to heal."

Garrett nodded. "It was a difficult time. I wanted to go to college, but the Depression was at its height, and my parents needed me on the farm. Adeline was upset that I wouldn't marry her right away. She didn't understand why I couldn't leave my parents and she had no interest in life on the farm." Normally, he avoided talking about Adeline at all costs, but for some reason, reliving his past now didn't seem as terrible as it once did. After the war, that seemed like a lifetime ago.

Mrs. Mitchell shook her head. "A woman should stand by her man if she truly loves him."

"Unfortunately, Adeline thought differently." He shrugged one shoulder. "She married someone else six months later."

"How sad." Mrs. Mitchell leaned over to pat his arm.

"But you did eventually get your degree," Jane observed. "That's something no one can take away from you."

"True. Although with all the unemployment right now, it's still hard to find work." He pressed his lips together. He understood Jane's reason for wanting the director's job, but he didn't want her to know how much he was depending on getting it. It would add even more pressure to their tenuous working relationship.

Mrs. Mitchell nodded. "I can't imagine how hard it will be

when Brandon and all the other men come back from the war. Thank goodness for Janey's salary. Without it, I don't know where we'd be." She set her cup down on the table with a sigh. "Well, as much as I've enjoyed our conversation, I think I need to lie down for a while."

Right away, Jane sprang into action, rushing to assist her mother.

Garrett got to his feet as well. "Can I help?"

"No, thank you. Mama's room is just down the hall." She wrapped an arm around her mother's waist.

"Then I'll take my leave. Thank you for the tea."

"And thank you for the ride. I appreciate it." Jane gave him a somewhat distracted smile.

"Anytime." He paused. "Jane, if your workload permits, why don't you take tomorrow off? Make sure your mother is settled and feeling well."

Her mouth tightened. "I'll see how the morning goes and decide then."

He nodded. "Nice to meet you, Mrs. Mitchell. I hope you're feeling better soon." He retrieved his hat. "I can see myself out."

On his way back to the boardinghouse, Garrett's mind spun with all he'd learned about Jane's family. The war had certainly produced more casualties than just the soldiers who served overseas. He'd just left two brave women, struggling to survive on their own without the men in their lives to look after them.

And both wore the scars to prove it.

9

Late Saturday morning, Garrett stepped out of his car and inhaled deeply, filling his lungs with the scent of sunshine and ripe apples. The city was great, but nothing could beat coming home to his parents' quaint two-story farmhouse on the edge of the rolling orchard. In the summer, the fields to the west grew raspberries and strawberries, and even now in September, Garrett could still smell their lingering sweetness that perfumed the air.

Noise erupted from the open barn door. One of the goats raced out, followed by both of his nephews. Dale tripped, sprawling in the dirt, then quickly sprang back up and scrambled after his older brother, Kevin, who leaped onto the goat's back. The animal gave a loud bleat, bucked and twisted, but Kevin stayed stuck like a burr. Dale joined the fray and grabbed the rope around the goat's neck.

"Got him!" Dale raised a fist in victory.

"No, *I* got him. I'm the one who jumped on him." Hopping off, Kevin scowled.

Garrett suppressed a smile as he went to join them. "I'd say it was a team effort. Good job, you two." Ramsey, the unruliest of the goats, was always trying to escape either the pen or the barn. Of course, sometimes he had a little help.

"Uncle Garrett!" Kevin raced over to hug him. "Grandpa says we can have a bonfire tonight when it gets dark."

"That sounds like fun." Garrett moved to help Dale wrangle the stubborn goat back to the barn. "Where is Grandpa now? In the orchard?"

Kevin scampered after them. "Yup. Mom says we can help him after lunch."

Garrett tied the goat to one of the posts near a feed bucket. "Let's go up to the house. I have a hankering for one of your grandma's oatmeal cookies."

"Me too." Dale took off before Garrett could even blink.

Kevin kept pace beside Garrett as they made their way across the grass to the farmhouse. Dale had already rushed inside and left the screen door flapping open. Garrett let Kevin enter first, then walked into the kitchen, where his mother and sister stood elbow-deep in flour.

The boys headed right for the sink to wash their hands, likely knowing their grandmother would have their heads if they didn't. Not to mention, they wouldn't be allowed a cookie with dirty hands.

"Garrett. I was beginning to wonder where you were." Mom lifted her cheek for a kiss. "It's almost lunchtime."

"Sorry, got a late start this morning. Hi, Cass."

His sister swooped some blond hair off her cheek with her forearm, leaving a dusting of flour behind. "I hope you're ready to do some picking. I promised the kids we'd help Dad this afternoon."

"Sure thing." Garrett studied his sister, noting the worry lines between her brows. "Anything I should know about?"

Cassie shot his mom a look.

Mom punched the dough a little harder. "We can't get enough pickers again this year. I fear we'll lose a lot of the crop."

With so many of the men off at war, there was a shortage of people willing to do manual labor. A fine line existed between picking the ripened fruit and waiting a day too long, which ran the risk of the fruit falling to the ground, becoming nothing more than feed for the animals.

Garrett picked a cookie from a tin on the counter. "What if I post some ads at the office? Some of the people coming in might be in the market for some seasonal work. Couldn't hurt."

"That's for sure. Any way we can bring more help to the farm is a good thing." Mom applied the rolling pin to the dough, thinning it out with a precision born from experience. Just the sight of her in her checkered apron, a kerchief tying back her brown hair, warmed Garrett's heart.

"Apple pie, Mom?"

"What else at this time of year?" She winked at him.

Garrett finished off the cookie and wiped his hands. "Where's the princess?"

Cassie laughed out loud at his nickname for her daughter. "Your *princess* was misbehaving and was sent to her room."

"Aw, what did she do now?" In truth, Mandy was more tomboy than princess, having to work hard to keep up with her brothers.

"She punched Dale."

Garrett bit his lip to contain his laugh.

Cassie wagged a floury finger at him. "We do not condone violence in this family, Garrett Wilder. So don't you be encouraging her—or any of them for that matter." She walked over to the sink and washed the remains of the dough from her hands, drying them on a towel.

He held up his hand. "I won't. I swear."

"Good." Cassie's features softened as she picked out a cookie and handed it to him. "You can take one up to her, but don't let on I know."

Garrett laughed. "Must be tough having to be the only disciplinarian."

"Are you kidding? If Jack were here, Mandy would have him tied up in knots." Cassie's bottom lip trembled as she turned away.

Garrett's hand stilled. Poor Jack had missed most of Mandy's life. She'd been only six months old when he'd enlisted four years ago. Garrett remembered being furious with his brother-in-law for leaving Cass and the kids. Most married men with children were exempt from enlisting, but since Jack had already been a member of the Toronto militia, his patriotic duty had outweighed his personal one. And if Cassie could forgive him for going, how could Garrett do any less?

He dropped a kiss to his sister's cheek. "I'll take this up and make sure her royal highness isn't getting into any more trouble."

———◆———

That night, as Garrett and his family sat around the firepit with the flames crackling in front of them, a wave of pure contentment settled over him. Overhead, a blanket of stars winked out a greeting to all below.

In Garrett's opinion, this was the best place on earth, where every problem seemed to fade into the background amid the wonder of nature. Where his connection to God seemed the strongest. Here, he always made it a point to appreciate the opportunities he'd been given, most especially his second chance at life. Even if it meant he couldn't do as much of the physical farm work as he'd like.

Mandy sat on Dad's lap, her fair head leaning against his chest. The two boys held sticks over the fire, competing for the best-cooked marshmallow. Mom and Cassie each sat on an old wooden chair, while the rest of the gang toughed it out on two fallen logs.

"I had a letter from Jack yesterday," Cassie said suddenly.

"How's he doing?" Other than their disagreement over Jack enlisting, Garrett and his brother-in-law had always gotten along well.

Cassie shook her head. "The way he's living sounds horrible. And I'm sure he's not telling me the half of it." She sniffed. "But at least he's alive, which is all that matters. I only pray he comes back to us soon." She glanced over at Garrett. "This might sound selfish, but I almost wish he'd be wounded, like you were, so they'd send him home."

Mom put an arm around Cassie's shoulders. "No one wants to see Jack get hurt. Why don't we pray instead for the end to this horrible war so that all the soldiers can come home?"

Cassie nodded but remained silent.

"Hey!" Kevin shouted. "You knocked my marshmallow off."

"Did not." Dale jumped up from the log. "Your stick hit mine."

"Boys!" Cassie moved quickly between them. "I think it's time to go in."

The kids started to grumble, but Dad placed a hand on Kevin's shoulder. "Do as your mother says now."

"Yes, sir." Kevin's subdued tone seemed to calm his brother, and they each laid down their sticks.

Mom reached over to scoop Mandy from Dad's lap. "If there's no more fighting, maybe Uncle Garrett will read you a story after your bath."

Garrett nodded. "I'll be up in a while. Make sure you scrub those elbows and knees."

Dale snickered.

"Me too?" Mandy piped up, peering over Mom's shoulder.

"You too, princess."

Dad chuckled as he watched the group trek across the lawn toward the house. "Those kids sure keep us on our toes."

"No doubt. I'm glad Cassie has you and Mom to help her. I can't imagine her trying to do it all on her own." He stirred the embers with a stick, bringing the flames back to life. Then he snagged the two chairs and brought them over. Dad got up from the log and they settled back onto the seats.

"As much as I hate this war," Dad said, "I'm cherishing this time with Cass and the kids. It's something we'll always remember, long after Jack gets back."

"I love seeing them every weekend too." Garrett lifted his mug of almost-cold coffee. "How are things really going with the orchard, Dad?"

Now that Mom and Cassie were out of earshot, he hoped his father would be more forthcoming.

Dad stroked his chin, staring into the fire. "Because of the unseasonably warm weather this summer, the fruit is ripening faster than normal. And we don't have enough pickers." He shook his head. "All we can do is trust the Lord to work it out for us."

"Is that all? There's nothing more I need to know?"

His father's mouth tightened. "Just the same old issues. Too many expenses and not enough income."

Garrett heaved out a breath. Things must be bad for Dad to even mention money. "I'll try to figure out where we can recruit some more workers. Have you tried the church?"

"I have. Pastor Craig is spreading the word among the parishioners. He said he'd make an announcement at the end of service tomorrow, so we'll see if we get any new takers."

"I'll see what I can do in the city. Maybe post a notice in the employment office."

"That would be a help. Thanks, son." Dad glanced over. "So, how's the new job going? Do you still intend to apply for the director's position?"

"I think so. I'm already starting to see how I could make a difference. There will likely be a lot of interest in the position. But if I do a good job with the audit, I'm hoping to have an advantage over the other candidates."

His heart gave a tug thinking of Jane and how, with her years of experience at the Children's Aid Society, she really deserved it more than he. But he couldn't afford to think that way. He needed to stay objective and let the board members make their choice.

"As long as you're happy, that's what's important." Dad rose and poured a pail of sand over the last of the embers. "Guess we should head up."

"You go on. I'll be right there."

"You sure?"

"Yeah. I think I need a few minutes alone with the stars. And with the Lord."

Dad gave a knowing nod. "Give Him my regards."

10

Jane arrived late to the office on Monday morning, frazzled to find Garrett already seated in one of her guest chairs, his shirtsleeves rolled up as though he'd been working for hours.

"Good morning," he said, lifting his gaze from the notebook on his lap. "I hope you don't mind my waiting in your office. I had an idea I wanted to run by you as soon as possible."

Even though she'd come in to work for a few hours on Friday after she'd made sure Mama was feeling better, she hadn't seen much of Garrett. He'd spent most of the day shadowing one of the caseworkers to observe a typical workday. Which had suited Jane just fine. She was having a hard time reconciling the fact that Garrett had seen her at a weak moment. Just the idea that he'd been inside her house made her uncomfortable. She'd always done her best to keep her personal life private, and she had no intention of changing that.

"Good morning." She skirted by his chair, mentally counting to ten to get her emotions under control. Keeping her back to him, she undid her jacket and hung it up. Before she turned around, she patted her hair to make certain it was still intact, then forced a neutral expression as she took her seat.

"How's your mother?" he asked. "No additional fainting spells, I hope."

"She's doing much better, thank you." Jane pulled out a pad of paper as she spoke. "We had an uneventful weekend, and she seems steadier today."

"I'm glad to hear it." He narrowed his eyes. "And how are you holding up?"

"I'm fine, thank you." She folded her hands on top of the papers. "Now, what is this idea you had?"

A slight frown creased his brow, as though he didn't quite believe she was fine. But thankfully he let it go.

"Do you ever take the children at the shelter out on any special trips?"

She paused to consider the unexpected question. "They walk to the park quite often in the good weather, and I do believe there might have been a trip to the Riverdale Zoo a few years ago."

"How did that happen? Did someone rent a bus? Did you require chaperones?"

Jane blinked, surprised at the barely suppressed energy he exuded. "I'm not sure. We must have had some help with supervision, but they likely took the city transit. Why?"

His blue eyes brightened even more. "I had an idea when I was home this weekend. My niece and nephews had a great time helping my dad pick apples all afternoon. I couldn't help but think how much fun an outing to our orchard would be for the kids at the shelter. Fresh air, sunshine, a hayride. They would love it." He paused, his face animated. "What do you think?"

"I don't know," she said slowly, then frowned. "Wouldn't that fall under your category of a 'frivolous expense'?"

His lips quirked up. "Touché. But I'm trying to find a way to do this with as little cost as possible. I think it would be a great experience for them."

Jane forced herself to look away from the hopeful excitement on his face and remain objective. "I'm sure the children would love it, but there are practicalities to consider. How would we get sixteen children all the way out to your farm, which you said was about an hour away?"

"I thought I'd see how much it would cost to rent a school bus for the day."

"And we've circled back to the second problem. We have a very limited budget for the children's entertainment. A trip like that could use up the entire amount for the year." She gave him a pointed look. "Much more than birthday gifts."

"We'll come back to that. What else is there to consider?"

"You mentioned it already. Supervision. We'd need several adults willing to come on this trip."

"How many?"

"I think I'd feel comfortable with two or three. We can't use Mrs. Shaughnessy, since she'd have to stay behind to manage the shelter in case any new children are dropped off as well as look after any of the current children who may not be able to go on the outing for one reason or another."

"Got it. So, some of the usual helpers—"

"Would have to agree to come."

"Right. One or two of them, plus you and I, and we'd be set."

"Me? You expect me to come?"

"I hope you'd want to." His eyes brightened. "And your mother would be welcome to join us, if she were feeling up to it."

Jane resisted the urge to argue and forced her shoulder muscles to relax. She needed a minute to process his request. To take her emotions out of the equation and view the situation objectively. Sure, it would be fun for the kids. But would the logistical nightmare to arrange it be worth the trouble?

And then there was her mother. Would she be well enough for such an outing? Or would it cause a setback in her fragile health? Yet if Jane left her alone, she'd only worry about her all day. True, she often worked at the office on a Saturday, but she was only a streetcar ride away, should her mother need her. Not a sixty-minute drive away. She ran a hand over her brow. This was not the way she'd envisioned starting her week.

Garrett rose from his seat. "If you need some time to think about it, I understand. In the meantime, I'll see what I can find out about the cost of transportation."

"Very well."

He stopped at the door. "If we can make this happen, I do hope you'll consider coming. It'll be a day you won't soon forget." He gave her a wide grin, then ducked out the door.

Jane blew out a breath. Why did this man send her senses reeling every time she saw him? She needed to remember she was a professional. In control. Logical and calm.

If only her unsettled nerves would listen.

———❖———

Later that afternoon, Garrett knocked once on Jane's open door, then stepped inside her office. "I've got great news." At least, he hoped she'd think it was. "I've found a way we could transport the children to the orchard for free."

She looked up, her glasses perched on the end of her nose. "That was fast."

"What can I say? I'm inspired." He dropped onto the guest chair. "A friend of the family is a bus driver who owns his own vehicle. When he heard about my idea, he offered us the use of the bus for free. Which will save us a bundle. And"—he grinned—"it will hopefully remove any objections to the trip."

"That is good news. It will definitely make my decision easier."

"Does this mean you've given the idea some more thought?"

"I have. And I've spoken to the staff at the shelter. Two of the assistants are willing to come along to help with the children."

"That's great." He paused. "And what about you?" He leaned forward, a little unnerved at how much he wanted her to come. Deep down, he felt the trip to the country would be just as beneficial for Jane as for the children.

"It will depend on my mother, but if I can, I'll join you."

He couldn't stop the spread of his smile. "Fantastic. You'll love it, I promise. And the expressions on those kids' faces will be worth any effort it takes to get them there."

"When will this take place?"

"The apples are ripe for the picking now, so I thought this Saturday, if possible. If not, the Saturday after will work too."

She pursed her lips for a moment, then nodded. "I think we can make that work. Saturday it is." For a moment, her features softened, and when she looked up, a sheen of moisture appeared in her eyes. "Martin is going to love this. That alone will make it worthwhile for me."

He regarded her thoughtfully, and she continued, "He's had so much misery in his eight years. He deserves some happy memories."

"Well, he's going to love our farm. I guarantee it."

11

The next morning, Garrett whistled as he entered the office, still basking in his victory over the upcoming orchard trip. He looked forward to sharing the beauty of the farm with the children, an experience he knew they'd remember for a long time to come.

As he shed his overcoat, he became aware of a strange buzz of conversation that whispered through the main floor. Something was going on. Something out of the ordinary.

Not another crisis with a child, he hoped.

He peeked into the stenographer's office, where a strange hush permeated the room. Several of the volunteers sat at their desks, staring off into the distance. Melanie stood by the window, a hand over her mouth.

He walked over to her. "What's wrong?" he asked quietly.

Melanie looked up and shook her head. "Jane just received a telegram. From the war office."

A cold chill slid down Garrett's spine. "Do you know what it said?"

"No." Melanie twisted a handkerchief in her hand. "She's holed herself away in her office. I don't know if I should go in or let her be."

Garrett paused. Melanie had a point. From what he'd seen of

Jane, she preferred to handle personal problems on her own. Yet it didn't seem right not to at least check on her. "I'll look in on her." He could take Jane's wrath better than Melanie, who was already upset.

Relief flashed across the woman's face. "Tell her I'm here if she needs me."

"I will."

A feeling of dread rolled in his stomach as he approached Jane's office, one that intensified when he heard weeping coming through the door. He hesitated. Should he intrude or let her grieve in peace?

But he'd feel terrible if he didn't at least try to help. He knocked once, then stepped inside and quickly closed the door again.

Jane was hunched over her desk, shoulders shaking with the force of her sobs.

He couldn't be certain she'd even noticed him entering. He paused for a second, unsure what to do, until the need to offer comfort compelled him to go over and put a tentative arm around her.

He wasn't sure what to expect. For her to push him away? Yell at him? Order him to get out?

Certainly not for her to turn and bury her face in his shoulder.

Crouched in an awkward position by her chair, he ignored the cramping in his calves and held her while she wept. Whatever the news, it had clearly caused her grief. Was it her husband or her brother?

When she finally pulled away, he handed her his handkerchief. "What's happened?" he asked softly.

Holding the handkerchief to her mouth, she pointed to her desk. He lifted the crumpled telegram and rose to read it.

We regret to inform you that your son, Corporal Brandon Mitchell, has been listed as Missing in Action and presumed dead. Any new information we receive will be furnished immediately.

Garrett closed his eyes briefly. "I'm so sorry, Jane." His thoughts

94

flew to Mrs. Mitchell and how this news would affect her. "You probably need to go home."

She glanced up. "How am I going to tell my mother?"

"Wouldn't a similar telegram have gone to the house?"

She shook her head. "I made sure they knew to send it here. I didn't want my mother to ever receive this kind of news alone." A shudder rippled through her frame. "Poor Brandon. I pray he's not suffering. Or being tortured in some prisoner-of-war camp."

"There's still a chance he could be found unharmed," he said. "You have to hold on to hope." But the odds of that outcome were highly unlikely. Everyone knew an MIA designation didn't usually end well.

She looked at him with red-rimmed eyes. "I'm trying. But I know Mama will jump to the worst possible conclusion." She brushed the tears from her cheeks. "Maybe it would be kinder not to tell her anything. Not until something more definite has been determined."

As much as he'd like to agree with her, he couldn't. He remembered hearing about how his own parents had reacted to learning he'd been wounded. Sure, he wanted to spare them from knowing how serious his injuries were, but it wouldn't have been fair in the long run. They had a right to know the truth. As did Mrs. Mitchell.

"Do you really think it would help? This way, at least she'll have the chance to pray for him and to be more prepared for any bad news that might arrive."

Jane let out a long sigh. "I suppose you're right. I wouldn't want anyone to keep the news from me. As much as I'd like to, I guess I can't spare my mother."

"No, you can't. But you'll be there to help her cope."

She sighed again and blew her nose.

"I can give you a drive home if you'd like," he offered.

"Thank you." Her eyes appeared to mist over again.

He nodded. "I'll give you some time. When you're ready, just come and find me." He started toward the door.

"Garrett?"

"Yes?"

"Would you mind telling Melanie and the others for me? I know they'll be worried, and I don't think I can face them right now."

"Of course." Wishing he could do more for her, he left the room to give her time to compose herself.

He found Melanie in the hall, waiting for him. "How is she? Was it very bad news?"

He drew in a deep breath and nodded. "Fairly bad. Her brother has been declared missing in action."

"Oh no." Melanie's brow crumpled. "I only met Brandon a few times, but he seemed like a good person. Always looking out for their mother."

Garrett started down the hall toward his office. "At least it wasn't bad news about Jane's husband. I suppose that's some consolation."

Melanie made a face. "Jane would far rather that jerk was missing than Brandon." Her eyes went wide, and she clapped a hand over her mouth.

Garrett stiffened. "Why would you say that?"

Melanie bit her bottom lip and wrapped her arms around her middle. "Forget it. I shouldn't have said anything."

He leaned closer, pinning her with a direct stare. "Why would you call Jane's husband a jerk? Did he mistreat her? Or cheat on her?"

Melanie's words had just confirmed the unease he'd felt standing in Mrs. Mitchell's living room the other day. Something about Jane's marriage seemed off. Why were there no pictures of her husband at the house or in her office? And why had Mrs. Mitchell seemed surprised when he mentioned the man?

"I'm sorry." The color rose in Melanie's face. "It's not my place to say. You'll have to ask Jane."

Then before he could say another word, she fled down the hall.

---- ❖ ----

Pushing through the fog of her sorrow, Jane climbed the stairs to her house, vaguely conscious of Garrett's car driving away. His calming presence during the drive home had steadied her and allowed her to get her emotions under better control so she could break the unfortunate news to her mother.

Why couldn't it have been Donald?

That one thought, as gruesome as it was, kept circling her brain. She almost wanted to rail at God for depriving her of her brother, the one decent man in her life and the light of Mama's existence. Now, the real possibility existed that Brandon would never return, and Jane and Mama would be on their own for the rest of their lives.

Her legs felt like lead as she let herself in the door.

"Jane, is that you?" Mama's concerned voice came from the living room.

"Yes, Mama." She removed her overcoat and hung it on the rack.

Taking a deep breath, she entered the room, where her mother was seated in her favorite chair.

Mama looked up, deep lines grooving her forehead. "Why are you home at this hour? Are you ill?"

The room spun around Jane in a sickening circle, forcing her to grasp the back of a chair. *Be strong, Jane. Your mother needs you.*

She squared her shoulders and moved to sit beside her. "I received some bad news this morning, Mama."

Her mother dropped the knitting onto her lap. "Did you lose your job?"

"No, Mama. That's not it."

"Is it . . . is it Brandon?" The words were a mere whisper, holding a thread of hope that the answer would be no.

Jane pressed her fingers to her trembling lips and nodded. "He's been declared missing in action." She would not add the "presumed dead" part. Mama didn't need to hear that proclamation. Not until it had been proven beyond a shadow of a doubt.

For a moment, her mother sat there in stunned silence, staring at Jane as though she spoke a foreign language. Then her mouth fell open and a keening wail escaped as she crumpled over her knees.

Jane knelt in front of her and rubbed her back. "You mustn't give up hope, Mama. There's still a chance he'll come back to us."

Lost in her sorrow, Mama appeared not to hear her. "Oh, my beautiful boy. Why, Lord? Why would you take my only son?"

Jane shivered as Donald's similar rant came back to haunt her. He'd said almost those exact words when she'd miscarried the second time. *My son. Why would God take my son?*

Donald had been inconsolable—so much so that he could offer Jane no comfort in the midst of her own devastating grief. She'd been forced to wallow in her guilt and pain alone, never imagining her life would get worse a few weeks later when Donald walked out on their marriage.

Yet losing Brandon would be worse for her mother because he had been her rock all these years since Papa died.

She wept with her mother, then at last when Mama raised her head, Jane handed her a handkerchief.

"Did they say anything else?" Mama asked.

"Just that they'd let us know if any new information came to light."

"You mean when they find his body." More tears trickled down Mama's wrinkled cheeks. She looked as though she'd aged ten years in ten minutes. "We all know missing in action really means dead."

There was no point in arguing with her, especially when Jane couldn't dispute the truth of her statement.

"This has been a terrible shock, Mama. Maybe you should lie down for a while."

She shook her head. "I want to go to church to pray for Brandon."

The idea took hold of Jane, certainty growing that church was exactly where they should go. As she helped her mother get ready, Jane remembered Garrett's parting words.

"Your mother will need you today, Jane. Don't worry about anything at the office. We can handle it. Take all the time you need." Garrett's gaze had held hers, silently communicating his sympathy.

His expression had said more, had meant more to her, than all the verbal platitudes in the world. For the first time, she didn't worry that he had a hidden agenda or would use her weakness against her.

Perhaps she didn't need to view Garrett Wilder as her enemy after all.

12

Garrett sat under the dim light of his desk lamp and rubbed his eyes. A glance at the clock on the wall indicated that it was after ten in the evening. No wonder his vison was blurry. He'd been staring at columns of numbers for hours.

Once he'd finished dinner at the boardinghouse, he'd come back to the office, needing the quiet of the empty building to aid in the detailed work he wanted to accomplish.

After the shocking news Jane had received earlier in the week, she'd been leaving the office right at five o'clock each day to go home to her mother. He hated seeing the change in Jane, her shoulders weighted with sorrow, her eyes dimmed. Gradually, though, the shock seemed to be wearing off, which was a blessing, since it could be years before the women ever learned of Brandon's fate. In the meantime, it would be better to carry on with their lives as best they could.

Another issue had been bothering Garrett since that day. He couldn't get Melanie's inadvertent remark about Jane's husband out of his mind. Though he wanted to trust Jane with every fiber of his being, he couldn't ignore the fact that he felt like she was hiding something. And that fact alone made it difficult to rule her out as a potential suspect in the missing money.

Especially now that he'd found evidence that seemed to corroborate the board members' suspicions.

Someone had indeed been changing figures in the ledger and skimming money from the accounts. Granted, he needed a magnifying glass to really see how the numbers had been altered, but Garrett had found several such cases over the last six months of entries where a decimal place had been changed, or a zero had been changed to an eight, or a one had been added in front of a number. Not huge amounts of money, but in the end they all added up.

And Jane's initials were on every page.

He pinched the bridge of his nose. There was no way to prove if the changes had been made by someone after the fact, or if Jane herself had made them. Was it merely a coincidence that these alterations had begun only after Jane had taken over for Mr. Mills?

Garrett's stomach ached just thinking about it. But after witnessing the run-down condition of the Mitchell residence and remembering Mrs. Mitchell's remark about relying on Jane's salary, it wasn't outside the realm of possibility that Jane could be in some sort of financial trouble and had given in to temptation.

Could this tie in somehow with Melanie's bad opinion of Jane's husband? Had he possibly racked up huge debts before he went off to war, leaving Jane to deal with the consequences?

Garrett rubbed the back of his neck. The more he considered his options, the more he concluded that he would have to address this with Jane herself. He could see no other way around it.

Yet the thought of facing her with any type of accusation made the acid rise in his throat.

The only thing that might help him now was prayer.

Lord, help me to discern the true culprit behind these thefts. And give me the words to approach Jane without accusation. Let her see that I'm only seeking the truth. And I ask that if Jane is guilty that I might treat her with the same compassion as you would. Amen.

With his heart not much lighter, Garrett put the ledger away in his top drawer, turned off the lights, and headed home for the night.

———— ❧ ————

This has to be the longest week in history.

Late on Thursday afternoon, Jane opened her office, weariness weighing her down. The arrival of the telegram on Tuesday had only been the start of the bad news.

Mrs. Shaughnessy's reports on Martin were less than encouraging as he continued to cause problems with the other children at the shelter. Jane had asked Bonnie Dupuis to do the preliminary work in searching for potential foster families for the boy, but so far, she hadn't come up with anything. It looked like Jane would have to take over his case. After all, she knew Martin's history better than anyone, and she would be the best judge of a family that might suit him.

She let out a sigh as she set her satchel on the floor. If only there were more hours in the day. This week she'd been working fewer hours than normal, wanting to spend more time with Mama and make certain that stress over Brandon didn't result in another visit to the hospital.

Once again, Jane struggled with her duty to her mother versus her commitment to her career, and unfortunately, it was becoming evident that her job was suffering. Ever since Garrett Wilder's arrival, Jane couldn't seem to get her feet under her. And instead of feeling more confident in the position, she felt as though she were floundering, barely keeping her head above water.

Her meeting this afternoon with the mayor was one more example. It had not gone at all the way she'd hoped. He'd flatly refused to increase the city's funding for the Children's Aid, claiming that the downturn in the economy made it necessary to pour more money into helping the unemployment situation as well as other social services. Long lines at the Scott Mission and various other soup kitchens around the city proved the truth of his words, but it didn't lessen the sting of rejection. Mayor Conboy had gently advised her to focus her efforts on seeking additional funding from private sources. He reminded her of the presentations Mr. Mills liked to make to various philanthropic committees to plead their cause.

Jane was well aware of her boss's efforts in this regard. He'd achieved great success in the past, convincing the wealthy to part with their coins. If only Jane could follow in his footsteps. But the idea of standing up before rooms full of people begging for money, even for a good cause, made spots dance before her eyes. Not only that, but many of the groups Mr. Mills solicited were men's groups, and she'd had no luck in getting them to agree to meet with her. The best she'd been able to do was send out a barrage of letters attempting to solicit donations, but her efforts thus far had met with virtually no response.

She pressed her fingers to her temples, wishing she could erase the doubts that kept surfacing. Doubts that she truly had the skills and the stamina to do this job. Was she letting Mr. Mills down with her reticence? Letting the children down by not doing everything in her power to acquire more funding?

A knock interrupted her tortured thoughts.

"Come in."

Garrett stepped inside. "Do you have a few minutes? There's something I need to discuss with you."

At the bleak expression on his face, Jane's spirits sank even lower. Whatever he had to say, it couldn't be good. But there was no point in putting it off.

"I can spare some time."

"Thanks." He made a point of closing the door firmly behind him before taking a seat. He set a book and a notepad on the chair beside him, then let out a long breath before focusing his attention on her. "I'm afraid this is going to be an unpleasant conversation, and I ask for your patience at the outset."

Tingles of alarm crept up her spine. Surely he didn't have the power to fire her. No, that would have to be Mr. Fenmore and the board's decision. But the grimness of Garrett's features told her it was something equally as serious. She reached for her eyeglasses and slipped them on. "What's on your mind?"

"I'm about to bend the rules a bit." He ran a hand over his jaw. "But I don't see a way around it."

Jane straightened her back against the spokes of her chair. She'd never seen Garrett so serious. "Go on."

"Despite the short amount of time I've been here, I feel you and I have developed a certain level of trust between us. Would you agree?"

"I would," she said carefully. Her mind flew in all directions, but she couldn't come up with any reason for this talk.

"What I'm about to say must remain absolutely confidential. The board would not be pleased with what I'm about to tell you."

Jane's hands began to shake. She clasped them together on the desktop to disguise their trembling. "I understand."

"One of the main reasons I was brought in to the Children's Aid Society," he said, staring directly into her eyes, "was to find out if someone is skimming money from the accounts."

Jane blinked, then shook her head. "No, that's not possible. I go over the books every month and—" She stopped, a cold pit opening up in her stomach. "Are you saying the board suspects me?"

Garrett's blue gaze remained steady. "Unfortunately, no one is above suspicion. No matter how much I wish it wasn't the case."

She fought to stay calm. "Could you elaborate a bit more about these missing funds? I've never noticed anything out of the ordinary with the books." But then again, finances were not her strong suit. If someone wanted to, it would be fairly easy to get something by her. But not by Mr. Warren.

Oh. Her stomach dropped as sudden understanding dawned. No wonder the man wasn't exactly oozing friendliness at their last meeting. Did he suspect her of theft?

Garrett picked up the book and opened it to a page that had

been marked with a ribbon. "If you look closely, you'll see where several figures have been changed on this page alone."

He pointed to the three different numbers in question.

Jane peered at them, then pulled a magnifying glass out of her drawer to look even closer. Sure enough, the figures had been altered. In one case, a one had been added in front of an amount of 130 dollars, making the entry 1,130 dollars.

"There are other such alterations done over the past six months. Not all of them as big as this one. Still, they add up." He had resumed his seat, watching her with an unreadable expression.

Was he waiting for her to explain the situation away? How could she when she had no idea what was going on?

"I don't know what to say. I feel terrible that I didn't notice this." She gave a shrug. "Perhaps I didn't go over every entry as thoroughly as I should have. But then again, that's why Mr. Warren goes over them as well."

Garrett nodded. "It was Mr. Warren who made the discovery of the discrepancies."

"And sent in a third-party auditor to find the culprit."

"Among other things, yes."

"So, what do we do now? Do you want to speak to Mr. Bolton?" Her hands continued to tremble, the tremors spreading all the way down her legs.

"Eventually. But first I need you to be honest with me." Garrett leaned toward her. "Are you telling me that you have no knowledge of this whatsoever?"

She looked him straight in the eye. "Until you brought this to my attention, I had no idea of any discrepancy with the books."

He closed his eyes for a moment, then with a sigh, he opened them. "I have to ask you another uncomfortable question. And I need full transparency from you, Jane. No secrets."

She dropped her gaze to the desktop, her mind searching for what he could be insinuating.

"During a recent conversation, Melanie hinted that your

husband might not be the most . . . upstanding of men. But she refused to say anything further. Which only reinforced my own suspicion that something was amiss."

Panic sputtered to life in her chest. What had Melanie said?

"Normally, I wouldn't bring this up; however, in this situation where any hint of impropriety must be explored . . ." He trailed off, looking miserable. "I'm sorry, but I must insist on the truth. When your husband joined the war, did he leave you in financial difficulties?"

Her heart seemed to stop, then stutter back to life. She longed to be able to get up and walk out. Simply leave all her problems behind and disappear. But even if she dared, the weakness in her legs wouldn't allow her to move.

Garrett seemed to be insinuating that Donald had left her in financial trouble and that she might be skimming money from the books to counteract the debt. She should be outraged at such an asinine assumption, but all she could muster up was sheer terror. Terror that she wouldn't be able to prove her innocence, that the board would agree with Garrett's conclusions and fire her. Or, worse yet, have her arrested.

She ran her tongue over her dry lips. "You asked for my discretion at the outset of this conversation," she said. "Now I am going to ask for the same courtesy from you."

Garrett stared at Jane from across the desk. Her face had lost all color, except for the stark red lipstick that stood out against her pale skin. A slight film of perspiration shone on her forehead, and her hands trembled visibly, despite the way she gripped them together in front of her. What was she about to tell him?

"As long as it isn't something criminal, then you have my word." He held his breath, praying he wasn't making a terrible mistake in uttering that promise.

"It's true that my mother and I aren't in the best financial shape. I have assumed the expense of running her house, plus I have a bank loan that I'm slowly paying off." She lifted her chin. "But I'm not in dire straits. And I would certainly never steal from anyone. Especially the children."

Garrett narrowed his eyes. "I'm hearing a lot of *I* statements. Where does your husband fit into all of this?"

Jane's gaze darted to the wall behind him. "He doesn't." Lines pinched around her mouth as she let out a sigh. "I . . . no longer have a husband."

"What?" His mouth fell open. "Did he . . . was he killed in the war?" Could she have been keeping his death quiet all this time? More importantly, why would she want to?

"No. As far as I know, Donald is alive and well." Several seconds went by before she finally met his eyes. "But he no longer plays a role in my life . . ." She swallowed, and her voice became a whisper. "Because we're divorced."

His stomach clenched as though someone had sucker punched him. *Divorced?* The word ping-ponged around his brain. That had never crossed his mind. "When did this happen?"

"Two years ago."

Garrett pushed up from his seat and paced the room, palming the back of his neck. "Wait. Hasn't he been away at war for years?" Or maybe that was just a convenient excuse to explain his absence.

"Yes. He's been gone since the start."

Garrett scratched his head. "You're telling me that in the middle of combat, Donald took time out to divorce you?"

She stared down at her hands. "Our marriage was pretty much over before he enlisted. Apparently, he met someone in England. Someone he was in a big hurry to marry."

The air seemed to seep from Garrett's lungs. Suddenly everything he knew about Jane shifted. The pain in her eyes. The outer armor she wore most of the time. It all made sense now.

Her husband had divorced her to marry someone else. What must that do to a woman's self-esteem? To her soul?

A thousand other questions raced through his mind. Questions he had no real right to ask. He fought to stay focused on the issue at hand. "I'm sorry you had to go through that, but I don't understand the need for such secrecy. Divorce isn't as uncommon as it used to be."

"That may be true. However, it's still a stigma. One I didn't want to negatively affect my career." She folded her arms in front of her like a shield. "I did tell Mr. Mills about it. I had to explain why I needed time off to see lawyers and go to court. But he respected my right to keep it private. Melanie is the only other person in the office who knows, and only because she overheard me on the phone with my lawyer."

"And now I know."

"Yes." She stared at him as though trying to read his thoughts. "I hope I can count on your discretion as well."

He hesitated, the vulnerability in her eyes tearing at his conscience. What did he do in this situation?

"You mentioned that we have a degree of trust between us," she continued, a thread of despair in her tone. "I hope my impression of you as a man of honor isn't wrong. For all I know, you could use this information against me to help you get the director's position."

He ran a hand over his jaw. "How would your divorce help me?"

"I already have one big strike against me by being a woman, but a divorcée?" She shook her head. "I doubt the board would consider me at all if they knew that."

Garrett studied her face and saw only honesty. He had to admit, she had a point. Most of the board members—Mr. Fenmore in particular—didn't strike Garrett as being very open-minded. When they'd asked Garrett to investigate her, were they simply looking for any excuse to dismiss her? He repressed a sigh. This was one of those pivotal moments in life where what he did next could decide not only his fate, but hers as well.

He returned to his seat and met her nervous gaze. "First of all, I believe that you didn't know anything about the missing money. Second, your personal life and your marital status should have no bearing on your ability to do your job. If I'm ultimately awarded the position, I want to get it because they feel I'm the best candidate. Not because I did something underhanded to discount my competition." He nodded. "You have my word the board will not hear about your divorce from me."

Jane's bottom lip trembled, and a sheen of moisture appeared in her eyes, magnifying their greenness. "Thank you. I appreciate that more than you know." She swallowed hard and lifted her chin. "Now, how are we going to figure out who's been stealing our money?"

Garrett shook his head, a reluctant smile forming. She was gutsy, he'd give her that. "Why don't you start by telling me everything you know about Harold Bolton?"

13

"hanks for meeting me, Olivia. I hope I didn't pull you away at a bad time." Jane smiled at her friend as she slipped into the booth at Marty's Diner.

"Not at all. Ruth doesn't mind covering for me. And my mother-in-law has the baby, so the timing couldn't be better." Olivia set her purse on the seat beside her. "Besides, I could tell by your voice on the phone that something's bothering you." Olivia's brown eyes darkened with concern. She looked as fresh and pretty as always, in a yellow dress and light blue cardigan. These days, an aura of peace surrounded her. Marriage and motherhood certainly agreed with her.

Jane suppressed a slight pang of envy at the way everything had turned out for her friend, despite the hardships she'd endured. Hardships that Jane had unwittingly played a part in.

The waitress arrived to take their order. Since it was close to lunchtime, they each ordered a ham sandwich and a cup of tea.

"You're right," Jane said once the waitress had left. "I have a lot weighing on me right now. I need advice from someone who will be honest with me." She gave Olivia a wry smile. "I can always count on you for that."

"True." Olivia laughed, then quickly sobered. "Does this have anything to do with the auditor you said the board hired?"

The waitress arrived with their drinks, promising their food would be ready soon.

"Yes. Things are far worse than I thought." Jane poured milk into her tea and quickly explained the difficulties facing the agency and the discrepancies with the finances.

"They don't suspect you, do they?" Olivia's eyes widened.

"Garrett didn't come right out and say that, but I can read between the lines. The discrepancies started after I took over as directress. Of course it looks suspicious."

Olivia set her cup down a little too forcefully. "That's crazy. You've been working there for more than a decade with an exemplary record."

Jane sipped her tea. She'd made her share of mistakes over her career, but none of them had anything to do with money.

"Why would they think that you would suddenly start stealing from them?" Olivia shook her head, the overhead light shining off her dark hair. "It doesn't make sense."

"It doesn't have to. The fact remains that under my direction, the agency's situation has gotten worse, not better. Now that Mr. Mills has officially retired, of course the board members are going to examine my performance."

Their sandwiches arrived, and Olivia dug right in. However, with the knots in Jane's stomach, she doubted she could swallow a bite.

"Did you manage to convince the auditor that you're not responsible?"

"I think so," Jane said slowly, "but I had to end up telling him"— she lowered her voice—"about the divorce."

Olivia gasped. "Why would you do that?"

Her friend knew how diligent Jane had been in guarding her secret, and given Olivia's own unsavory past, she understood Jane's desire to keep her private life quiet.

"He thought Donald might have left me wallowing in debt and that I might be desperate to repay his bills." She shrugged.

"I had to make him understand that Donald no longer had any impact on my life."

"Will he tell the board members?"

"He says he won't." Jane fiddled with her spoon, suddenly uncertain if dumping all this on her friend had been wise.

"Then what's the problem?"

Jane stared out the window at the parade of pedestrians. What *was* the real issue bothering her?

"I'm not sure," she said at last. "I guess with Garrett knowing I'm not married, I feel exposed. Vulnerable. He knows too many details about me. He's been to the house, knows about Mama's illness, and has seen me at my worst. Now this." She let out a long breath. How had Garrett become so entwined in her life in such a short amount of time?

Olivia set her sandwich on the plate and studied Jane, her thin brows rising. "Are you attracted to him?"

Jane almost choked on her tea. "What? No. Absolutely not." Yet the rush of heat to her cheeks branded her a liar. "It's just unnerving to be under such scrutiny. He's questioning how we do everything, trying to change the way things are run. He even wants to take the kids from the shelter on a trip to his parents' orchard."

Olivia's lips twitched. "How Machiavellian. What other evil plans does he have up his sleeve?"

"Very funny." Jane shook her head. "Seriously, though, he's making me question myself. What if I'm not cut out to do this job?" She swallowed hard. That was what it all boiled down to, the overwhelming question that continued to plague her.

Olivia reached across the table to squeeze Jane's hand. "Of course you are. You're an intelligent and competent woman." She tilted her head to one side. "Unless it's more than the audit that's bothering you. Is the strain of the job proving too much?"

To Jane's horror, the burn of tears threatened. She blinked rapidly. "Maybe. I think Martin being returned to the shelter yet again is bringing back all my guilt over the mistakes I've made with him."

"Oh, Jane. I'm sorry. I know how much you'd hoped this family would be the right fit for him. But you can't keep going over the past. It won't do you or Martin any good."

Olivia was the only person who knew the whole story about the mistake Jane had made in Martin's case, the first case she'd been given as a newly graduated social worker. How she'd broken the rules by contacting Martin's birth mother after the first adoption fell through to see if she would take him back. Not only had Jane reopened the woman's wounds, but she'd made her feel even worse, knowing her baby had been rejected by his adoptive parents. And in a misguided effort to make amends, Jane had promised Martin's mother that she would find the perfect home for her son.

A promise she had yet to fulfill.

"Listen to me." Olivia's quiet voice brought Jane out of her self-recriminations. "If I can recover from my horrible past and end up with the wonderful life I have now, you can too." She grabbed Jane's fingers and squeezed again. "I have faith in you. More importantly, I trust that God has a plan for your life. You just need to be patient."

"I-I'm scared, Olivia." She'd never uttered those words aloud before. "What if the board declares me responsible for the thefts? What if they fire me or try to have me arrested? What will happen to Martin and to Mama then?"

Jane wished she shared her friend's steadfast faith. The unwavering belief that everything would work out fine. Jane couldn't quite believe that, not after all the tragedies she'd experienced: the miscarriages, her inability to have more children, her husband's abandonment and remarriage, and now her brother's disappearance. How many more disasters did God have in store for her?

"The board has no proof of any wrongdoing because you're innocent," Olivia said fiercely. "Even if the worst happens and they let you go, you'll find another job. It won't be the end of the world."

"That could take months, though, and Mama and I are barely scraping by as it is." Jane pushed back a wave of terror. "We could lose the house."

"There is another option. One that selfishly I hope might happen." Olivia gave a sheepish smile.

"And that is?"

"You could give up the directress position and go back to your old job. You're a wonderful caseworker, Jane. We miss you at Bennington Place."

Jane's chest warmed at Olivia's praise. "I do miss that part of the job."

Olivia patted a napkin to her lips, then sat back with a sigh. "The new girl, Miss Dupuis, is doing fine. She just doesn't have the same way you have with the women. The exact balance of gentle yet firm, direct yet compassionate."

"That balance took years to perfect. You of all people know I wasn't exactly a shining star at first." Jane would always regret the high-handed way in which she'd taken Olivia's firstborn child into the custody of the Children's Aid. Over the years, Olivia had admitted that giving up her son had been the best thing for him at the time, and Jane was always humbled by her friend's gift of forgiveness.

"Won't you at least consider my idea? We could be a good team again." Olivia's pleading look cinched another string around Jane's heart.

"You know I love working with the mothers and their babies, but my heart bleeds for the forgotten children, the ones no one wants." Jane swallowed hard to force her emotions back. "As directress, I could authorize adoptions for those children to people who might otherwise be overlooked. An older couple. A spinster with loads of love to give. People who Mr. Mills and the board automatically discounted."

"I understand that, and I admire you for it." Olivia removed a small mirror from her purse and reapplied her lipstick. "I promise

I'll pray about your job, that you'll be able to discern God's will for your life. Other than that, I'm afraid I haven't been much help."

"You're wrong there." Jane opened her wallet and fished out some bills. "Just talking to someone about everything is a relief."

"I'm glad. In the meantime, try to relax. Go and enjoy that trip to the orchard with the children. I think it will be a wonderful outing for them and for you." She winked. "Especially with a handsome tour guide."

Jane swatted her arm. "Who said anything about handsome?"

"You didn't have to. I could tell by the way you talked about him."

"Handsome is a distraction I do not need." Jane gave her friend a stern look as she rose from her seat.

"If you say so." Olivia laughed. "Just remember to leave the details up to God. He's the one who will figure it all out."

14

On Saturday morning, Garrett awoke at six o'clock, more excited than a kid on Christmas morning. He was meeting Ken, the bus driver, at the shelter for the trip to the orchard. Once the children were loaded, Garrett would follow the bus in his own car. Though he would have loved to ride with the others, he needed his car for the rest of the weekend. Besides, if Jane and her mother ended up coming with them, he could at least offer them a more comfortable drive.

As Garrett navigated the quiet streets, he found his thoughts consumed with Jane. He still had a hard time coming to grips with the idea that her husband had divorced her and married someone else. His fingers tightened on the wheel just thinking about what he'd like to do to the man. What possible reason could Donald have had to abandon his wife like that? And why hadn't Jane fought the divorce? For her to simply accept Donald's actions and release him from their marriage seemed contrary to everything he knew of her feisty personality. His gut tightened. There was much more to that story, he was certain of it, but he had no right to ask.

The fact that Jane was single had added a new edge to their interactions, making his attraction to her harder to ignore. But ignore it he must. For several reasons. For one thing, he was supposed to be working with her as an objective auditor. For another, he might eventually be competing with her for the same job. Third, and most importantly, Jane's colleagues believed her to be married, and he would never tarnish her reputation by acting inappropriately.

The best thing he could do was treat Jane the way he treated his sister—with respect and brotherly affection. Maybe then he could get through this assignment with his integrity intact.

The bus was waiting in front of the shelter when Garrett arrived. By the time he got out, Ken appeared on the sidewalk.

"Hey there, Garrett," the big man said. "I got Bertha all cleaned and polished for you. Inside and out."

Garrett shook Ken's hand. "You do realize you're driving sixteen children, don't you?"

A loud laugh vibrated around him. "Yes, sir. But they deserve clean seats too."

"Don't say I didn't warn you."

A taxi pulled up behind his car and Garrett turned. Jane got out, then went to help her mother alight from the other side.

Warmth curled through Garrett's chest, much like the grin that spread across his face. "Jane, Mrs. Mitchell. I'm so glad you both could come."

Jane assisted her mother onto the sidewalk, then lifted her head to grace him with a wide smile. "We're looking forward to this. It will be like a mini vacation."

Garrett's attention shifted to her outfit, and he couldn't help but stare. Today, she wore denim pants rolled up to the ankle over a pair of work boots. A blue blouse and matching cardigan completed her outfit, along with a floral kerchief that held her chestnut hair away from her face.

She looked . . . completely adorable.

Garrett forced his gaze away and went to greet Mrs. Mitchell. "I thought you ladies might like to ride in my car. It will be a lot more comfortable than the bus."

"That does sound better." Mrs. Mitchell smoothed her hands over her belted dress, her smile creating a network of lines around her eyes. "Thank you for inviting me, Garrett. I've never picked apples before."

Jane's brow puckered. "Now, Mama, you know you won't be climbing up any ladders."

Garrett laughed. "I'm sure there will be some low branches where you can snag a few apples for yourself," he said with a wink. "And don't forget the hayride. Everyone loves that part."

Mrs. Mitchell looked much better than the last time he'd seen her. Today she seemed stronger, and her pale eyes were bright. If this outing could take her mind off her worries about her son for a little while, then it would be well worth it.

A rumble of feet and voices, much like a thunderstorm about to erupt, came from the direction of the shelter.

Garrett turned his head. "Ah, sounds like the kids are ready."

Seconds later, the children poured out onto the lawn in one loud, manic mess. The two volunteers appeared frazzled already as they attempted to corral them into some semblance of order. At last, the children stood in a row by the bus, awaiting instructions from Ken, who then ushered them all onto his vehicle, like a captain directing new recruits onto his ship.

Garrett motioned to his car. "Ladies, shall we?"

Jane stood staring at the bus, frowning. "I hope we're doing the right thing. What if something goes wrong?"

He could almost feel the anxiety rolling off her. "Everything will be fine, Jane. Trust me."

Her eyes met his and she nodded.

As they got into the car, Garrett prayed his confidence would not be misplaced.

Jane watched the scenery roll by from the back-seat window. She'd insisted that Mama sit up front to enjoy the view. Secretly,

Jane wanted a little distance from the man who lately seemed to scramble her thoughts as well as her pulse.

Back here, she could breathe easier and observe his interaction with her mother without feeling forced to make conversation that often resembled a ping-pong match of wits.

Now that Garrett knew she wasn't married, she'd become aware of a subtle shift in the current between them. Without the safeguard that had kept any romance off-limits, Jane now found herself adrift in unfamiliar territory. Suddenly, it was a lot harder to deny her attraction to the man, an attraction that could not be acted on. She twisted the ring still on her finger, reminding herself that everyone else believed she was married, and she needed to act accordingly.

With the car windows cracked open, a lovely breeze blew around her, and despite her harried thoughts, Jane began to relax. Within minutes, the scenery changed from bricks and cement to gently sloping greenery, interspersed with lines of trees that stretched for miles. In some fields, herds of either cattle or sheep roamed, while in others, rolls of baled hay dotted the vista.

Garrett kept up a running commentary on what Mama was seeing, and Jane could tell by her delighted response that she was enjoying every moment. How long had it been since she'd taken Mama anywhere other than a doctor's appointment? Jane swallowed back a rush of guilt. She was always so busy working that she didn't have time for the simple pleasures in life. But that shouldn't mean Mama had no fun. She made a mental note to try to plan some outings for the two of them, ones that wouldn't be too taxing on her mother's health. The winter would be upon them soon enough, and Mama would be housebound once again.

Finally, Garrett turned onto a gravel lane where a sign indicated they were entering Wilder's Orchard and Farms. They drove past a crudely built fruit stand toward a brick farmhouse and a large barn that stood off to the right. In the distance, Jane could make out a tractor attached to a flatbed wagon filled with hay, which she assumed would be used to take them out to the orchard.

Garrett pulled up in front of the house and shut off the engine. "Welcome to our farm." He grinned as he got out of the car and came around to open Mama's door for her.

Jane stepped outside and breathed in the country air, scented with newly mown grass. There was no bus in sight yet, which gave her a few moments to relax and examine their surroundings. Shoving her hands on her hips, she surveyed the land that stretched from the house to the barn and beyond. "This is amazing."

"It sure is," Mama agreed. "Thank you again for inviting me."

"It's my pleasure." Garrett closed the door and leaned one hip against the car. "I love sharing the beauty of our farm with others."

Renewed optimism flowed through Jane's veins. There was something freeing about being surrounded by nature. For today, she would set aside her problems and try to enjoy herself.

A sudden frenzied barking sounded, accompanied by the swoosh of a black-and-white ball of fur racing across the grass.

Garrett moved away from the car to intercept the creature hurtling toward them. The dog ran in circles around his legs before Garrett bent to pat the animal, who wriggled with kinetic joy.

"Hey, Jett, buddy. I missed you too." He scrubbed the dog's head.

The absolute love on Garrett's face brought a flood of warmth through Jane.

He straightened with a smile. "This is my dog, Jett."

Jane stepped closer and held out her hand for Jett to smell. "What breed is he?"

"He's a border collie. Smart, loyal, and great at rounding up errant goats."

"Isn't that supposed to be sheep?"

Garrett let out a long laugh, his blue eyes twinkling. "Sheep, goats. He's not fussy."

Jane couldn't help but laugh too as she patted Jett. Garrett's joy was infectious. He obviously loved it here, so why did he choose to live in the city?

The farmhouse screen door squeaked open. "I hope my son isn't keeping his guests standing in the yard." A tall woman with light brown hair came down the stairs, sporting a wide smile. She wore a flowered housedress and a bulky beige sweater.

"Sorry, Mom. Jett sidetracked me." He held out his arms and wrapped his mother in a huge hug. "Mom, this is Jane Linder and her mother, Mrs. Mitchell."

"Hello and welcome. I'm Sarah. My husband, Ben, is out in the orchard already."

"It's nice to meet you, Mrs. Wilder." Jane immediately liked this friendly woman.

"Please, call me Sarah. Everyone does."

"Then I'm Jane, and my mother is Hildie."

Sarah came forward to drape an arm around Mama. "Hildie. What a lovely name."

"Why, thank you. It sounds better than Hilda. My daddy gave me the nickname and it stuck."

The screen door opened again, and two boys ran out, followed by a slim blond woman balancing a young girl on her hip. The boys ran over to Jett and threw themselves on the dog, who didn't seem the least bit perturbed by the friendly assault.

"Where are all the other kids?" the older boy asked. He appeared to be about seven or eight.

"They'll be here any minute." Garrett tousled the boy's hair. "These are my nephews," he said to Jane. "This is Kevin, and the younger one is Dale." He turned slightly as the other woman approached. "This is my sister, Cassie, and this pretty one here"—he plucked the girl from her arms—"is my niece, Amanda, or Mandy, as we call her." He kissed her cheek and she giggled.

Jane smiled at Cassie. "Hello, I'm Jane, and this is my mother, Hildie." Up close, Jane marveled at the woman's fragile loveliness.

With her fair hair, clear skin, and wide gray eyes, she resembled the angel Mama put on top of their Christmas tree each year.

"Nice to meet you," Cassie said. "We're so glad you could come. We welcome any help we can get in the orchard this time of year."

Jane laughed. "I only hope the children don't eat more apples than they pick."

The sound of an engine rumbled up the lane.

"Speaking of children," Jane said, "that must be them now."

The bus appeared over a slight hill, and as soon as it stopped, the doors opened and a harried-looking Miss Channing got off with the other aide, Miss Tate, right behind her.

Miss Tate immediately took charge. "Children, you may get off and line up beside the bus."

Amid whoops of laughter, the youngsters all poured out, spilling out like apples from an overturned barrel.

Jane immediately picked out Martin, who stared wide-eyed at his surroundings, a look of awe on his face. The moment he spied Jett, he shot forward, stopping in front of Garrett.

"Is this your dog, Mr. Wilder?"

Garrett placed a hand on the dog's head, keeping him from jumping toward Martin. "Yes. This is Jett."

"Can I pet him?" The pleading expression on the boy's face tore at Jane's careful composure. Martin should be living in a home with a family and his own dog to love.

"Sure. A quick pat and then you have to join the others."

"Yes, sir." Martin knelt down and stroked the dog's head.

Jett's tongue lolled out in apparent bliss.

"Martin," Miss Tate called. "Get in line, please."

The boy rubbed Jett's ears one more time, then hurried back.

Once the children had come to order, Jane addressed them. "Good morning, everyone. This is Mr. Wilder's family farm. While you're here, I expect you to obey his instructions and stay where you're told to go. We want this to be a fun day for everyone. Now, I'll let Mr. Wilder explain what will happen next."

Garrett came over to stand beside her. She couldn't help but notice how relaxed he seemed, clearly in his element. He'd taken off his jacket, and underneath he wore a blue plaid shirt that complemented dark pants and work boots. Standing with his hands on his hips, he exuded confidence and masculinity.

"I hope you're looking forward to picking some apples," he said to the kids. "I'll give you a quick lesson once we get there. There are a couple of rules you'll need to follow. Stay with your group, no climbing the trees, and only use a ladder if an adult says you may." He clapped his hands together. "Who's ready for a hayride?"

Jane raised her hand along with all the kids.

Garrett turned to her with a wink. "All right, then. I'll find my dad and we can get going."

With his father at the wheel of the tractor, Garrett inspected the group of kids on the wagon and made sure they were all safely seated.

"All set, Dad," he called.

"Aren't you coming?" Jane frowned at him.

It appeared she'd saved him a spot beside her. A very cozy spot indeed.

"I prefer to walk. But I'll catch up with you in the orchard."

He tried not to let the confusion on Jane's face worry him as he walked beside the wagon. In all likelihood, she would press him with questions once they got there, but he had his answer prepared. One that didn't go into details as to why the jarring of the tractor ride was not an option for him. No one except Cassie and his parents knew the severity of his war injury. At first, he hadn't wanted to upset his parents with the truth of his situation, knowing they'd only coddle him. But in the end, he'd had to explain why he couldn't shoulder the bulk of the farmwork anymore.

Garrett shook off the negative thoughts and focused on the children. As he'd hoped, they appeared to be having a ball. Some of the younger ones were huddled on the hay in the middle of the wagon, while the older boys swung their legs off the edge, hooting every time Dad turned a corner. Jane and her mother sat together, smiling widely as they scanned the scenery.

It was the perfect day for apple picking. The sun provided enough warmth to make a jacket unnecessary, and every now and then, a light breeze picked up, bringing with it the scent of ripe apples and fresh hay.

The tractor passed several rows of trees until they came to the area where they would be picking. His father cut the engine and jumped to the ground.

"Okay, folks, hop down and gather over by that first tree. Garrett will fill you in on what's next."

"Thank you for the ride, Mr. Wilder," one of the kids said.

"You're welcome. My family is happy to have you here. We don't even mind if you snack on the apples while you pick." Dad winked at the kids, who laughed.

Garrett waited until the group was assembled by the tree. "All right, everyone. Today we'll be picking McIntosh apples, my personal favorite. I'm going to let Miss Tate divide you into four groups, and we'll get started. Cassie, you and the kids can join whichever group you wish."

Once they were organized, Garrett gave them a quick lesson in how to tell a ripe apple from ones that weren't ready to be harvested. He provided them with bushel baskets and taught them how to place the apples gently inside so as not to bruise them.

"Pick as much ripe fruit off each tree as you can before moving to the next," he instructed. "If you see apples that are too high, ask an adult to get them for you. Never reach too far. An apple isn't worth the risk of falling and hurting yourself." He paused. "Any questions?"

Murmurs of "no, sir" met his ears.

"Let's get started. Remember, at the end we'll see which team has picked the most baskets. There could be a prize involved."

More whoops of glee followed.

Garrett assigned each group to its own row of trees. Then, once he was sure each of the adult supervisors had everything in hand, he found himself gravitating toward Jane and her young charges. He wasn't surprised to find Martin with her, along with Denise. Another boy and girl, who looked to be about ten and twelve, rounded out the group. They had placed their basket at the base of the tree trunk and were chatting and laughing, comparing the size of their apples before depositing them in the container. Garrett chuckled to himself. At this rate, they'd be lucky to get two bushels by lunchtime. But as long as they had a good time, that was the only thing that mattered.

Jane was standing on her tippy-toes, reaching for some of the higher clusters, her expression intent. Once she tugged the large bunch off the branch, her whole face brightened. "Gotcha." She pulled off the extraneous leaves and placed the fruit in the basket.

When she straightened and saw him watching her, a flush infused her cheeks.

"I think you missed your calling in life," he teased.

She laughed. "I never knew picking apples could be this much fun." She rubbed a piece of fruit on her pants until the skin shone and then bit into it. Her eyes closed as she chewed. "That's the best apple I've ever tasted." When she opened her eyes again, tiny specks of gold sparkled in their depths.

He'd never seen this side of her. She seemed so at ease . . . so full of life . . . so beautiful.

Garrett's chest muscles seized, and he gulped in a lungful of air. He had to stop thinking of her that way and maintain a professional distance. "I'm glad you're enjoying it," he said. "If you need me, I'll be cruising the rows, checking on everyone."

Jane smiled. "Thanks. I'm sure we'll be fine."

Garrett took one last look at the group, reveling in the un-guarded joy on Martin's face, before he headed for the row farthest away from temptation. His boots thudded heavily against the hard-packed earth as he walked.

Peering up through the branches at the sunlight filtering through the leaves, he had the distinct feeling he knew exactly how Adam must have felt in the Garden of Eden.

Even though Garrett's temptation had little to do with fruit.

15

"Can I climb the ladder to get those apples, Mrs. Linder?" Martin pointed to a spot high in the tree they were presently picking.

Matt and Trudy had dragged the almost-full basket away from the tree trunk, while Denise sat on the grass, contentedly enjoying a polished apple. With almost four bushels full, the kids deserved a break.

Jane shaded her eyes and looked up. "I don't think we need to go quite that high."

"But Mr. Wilder said we had to finish each tree before we move to the next one."

Jane recognized the boy's obstinate tone. Still, she didn't feel comfortable letting any of the children go up the ladder. Perhaps she should do it, even if the idea of heights threatened to make her break out in a rash. "I'll go," she said. "I'm a lot taller, and I'll be able to reach them."

"But I'm good at climbing ladders." Martin jumped onto the bottom rung as though to prove his point. "Mr. McElroy made me use a big one to clean the gutters on his roof."

Jane pushed that disturbing piece of news to the background for the time being to focus on the matter at hand. "That may be so, but I'm not comfortable with you going up. So I'll go. Each of you hold the legs while I climb."

She scanned the height of the wooden structure, which had to be twenty feet tall, trying not to let her fear show. At least she'd worn her sturdy boots, which steadied her as she started to climb. If she kept her attention focused upward, she should be fine.

As she neared the top, she stopped to collect herself and assess the situation. Glancing over to the left, she simply stared. At this height, she could see above the trees to the amazing vista before her. She made out a neighboring farm in the distance, its red silo a beacon against the blue sky.

"Oh my," she breathed. "The view is magnificent."

"The apples are the other way, Mrs. Linder." Denise's voice floated up to her.

Jane turned her attention to the tree. "I see them." The apples were ripe, and if they weren't picked soon, they'd likely fall to the ground as fodder for the squirrels.

She stretched out her hand, her fingers just able to reach them. With one sharp tug, the clump broke free. Jane wobbled for a second, her heart slamming into her throat as the ladder quivered, but she managed to regain her balance. "Got them!" she shouted.

The children's triumphant cries surrounded her as she started back down. Descending, she discovered, was a far more difficult process than going up. It didn't help that while clutching the apples in one hand, she couldn't get a good grip. Still, she persevered, slowly making her way downward.

As she was getting nearer to the ground, about to congratulate herself for her prowess, one of the kids yelled, "Mr. Wilder! Mr. Wilder! Did you see? Mrs. Linder got the apples way at the top."

Her foot slipped on the rung, but she quickly righted herself. Had Garrett been watching her all along? She took a deep breath and continued down.

With two or three rungs left to go, strong hands grasped her by the waist and lifted her the rest of the way down, setting her feet lightly on the grass.

"That was quite the effort." With one finger, Garrett nudged her kerchief back in place. An amused expression lit his features.

She took an awkward step back and gave a breathless laugh. "It was worth it. The view from up there is fabulous. Plus, I got what I went for." She held out the cluster of apples. "Here, Trudy. Put these in the basket for me, please."

The girl ran over to retrieve the fruit.

"Can I go up next time?" Martin tugged on her sleeve.

"Definitely not," she said. "Now that I've been up there, I know it's much too dangerous."

Garrett laid a hand on Martin's shoulder. "Mrs. Linder is right. Too many accidents happen on ladders."

"Yes, sir."

"Okay. I came to tell you we're going to break for lunch now." Garrett pulled his cap back on. "Let's go find out what my mother has made for us to eat."

Jane made sure all the kids were accounted for on blankets under a pair of oak trees and checked that they were following the instructions of the adults, then went over to the wagon to help Sarah unpack the baskets of food. Mama was sitting under a tree where she'd been observing the pickers all morning, now talking with Ben Wilder.

"I hope this wasn't too much trouble for you," Jane said as she removed the wrapped sandwiches.

"Not at all. I'm used to feeding the workers, though they're not usually this animated and lively." Sarah gave her a wide smile. "As soon as everyone's settled, I'll take Hildie back to the house. I've offered her one of our rooms if she'd like to rest for a while after lunch."

Jane straightened. "That's kind of you, but I don't want to put you out."

Sarah laid a hand on Jane's arm. "It's no trouble. I'll enjoy having some company up at the house. Please try not to worry."

Jane could only nod. It was obvious Garrett must have filled Sarah in on her mother's condition.

"Why don't you start handing out these sandwiches?" Sarah said. "I'll bet the country air has made those little ones ravenous."

Ten minutes later, the children were seated on the ground, happily munching their food amid giggles and bursts of laughter. From her spot on the blanket, Jane forced herself to set her worries aside and relax, taking a moment to enjoy the carefree pleasure on the children's faces. By habit, her gaze found Martin, and warmth spread through her chest. In this setting, Martin seemed like a different boy. Relaxed and loose-limbed, laughing with the other children, as though for the first time he hadn't a care in the world.

Jane smiled as she unwrapped her sandwich. Giving the kids this taste of life outside of the city was better than a tonic for their health—both physical and mental. Perhaps these types of excursions were something they should incorporate more often into the children's schedule. They deserved to be exposed to more of what life had to offer than simply going to school and coming back to the shelter at night.

"May I join you?"

Jane blinked up at Garrett standing in front of her. She hadn't seen him for a while and assumed he'd gone back to the house.

"Of course." She scooted over to the far side of the plaid blanket to give him space.

He plopped down beside her, a roast beef sandwich in hand. "The kids seem to be having a great time." He took a huge bite from his bun.

"I was just thinking the same thing. It's been a real treat for them. And so far, no disasters." She gave a nervous laugh.

"That's always good." He smiled, his dimples flashing.

Away from the office, he seemed different, so relaxed, clearly in his element. Out here, he exuded a type of confidence that Jane found immensely appealing. Surrounded by his family and the children, she could picture what a good husband and father he would make one day.

The hair on her arms prickled, and she suddenly realized just how close he was to her. Close enough to see the silver flecks in his blue eyes. Close enough to notice a tiny white scar by one of his eyebrows and to smell the clean scent of his soap.

Trying to ignore the flutter of her pulse, Jane took a small bite from her sandwich and chewed slowly, then washed it down with a swallow of lemonade.

"What about you?" he asked. "Are you enjoying yourself?"

"How could I not? It's beautiful here."

"Then why don't you seem as relaxed as you were earlier? Your shoulders are bunched up tighter than a corkscrew."

She shifted her position, purposely trying to loosen her muscles. "I guess I'm not very good at relaxing. It seems there's always something to worry about."

Ever since her father died when she was sixteen, the world had become an unsafe place. She'd worried how her family would survive without her dad. Worried about her brother's wild streak that took over without their stern father to keep him in check. And later, once she'd married Donald, she worried about being able to give him the family that was so important to him. Now, she worried about excelling in her career while trying to keep her mother in good health. Not to mention her concern over all the lost and abused children who came through the agency's doors each week.

Sometimes it all seemed too much to bear.

He regarded her steadily for several moments. She could feel the weight of his gaze as she focused on the orchard in front of them.

"I think it's time we remedy that fact. This afternoon, I want you to think only about the fresh air, the sunshine, and the trees.

It really is God's country out here, and He'd want you to appreciate its beauty."

Jane held back a sigh. He made it sound so easy. But she'd been bearing the burden of responsibility for so long, she couldn't just let it go at the snap of her fingers. "I'll try," she said, knowing he wouldn't be satisfied until she gave an answer.

"Good. I intend to make sure you do."

Needing a distraction from his disarming gaze, Jane reached in the picnic basket and took out a small jar. "Is this homemade applesauce?"

"Sure is. It's Mom's famous recipe, with a secret ingredient she won't divulge to anyone. Not even me. Go ahead and try it."

"I will." Jane found a spoon, took off the lid, and lifted a spoonful to her mouth. A burst of amazing flavors hit her tongue. Tart apples, brown sugar, cinnamon, and some other spice she couldn't quite place. Likely the secret ingredient. "It's wonderful. The best I've ever tasted."

He laughed. "I'll make sure to tell her."

"I suppose you can't go wrong when you're using apples right off the tree." She smiled and tilted her head to peer over the orchard. "I can see why you love this place. What I don't understand is why you aren't working here with your family. Why are you living in a rooming house in the city and working in an office?"

When the muscles in his jaw hardened, she wished she could take back her questions. "I'm sorry. Forget I asked."

He scrubbed a hand over his jaw. "I do love this place, and I always intended to take over the farm one day. I even got my degree in order to help Dad run the business side of things." Shadows lurked in the depths of his eyes.

"What happened?" she asked softly.

"The war happened." Bitterness twisted his handsome features.

She drew in a slow breath. "Your injuries . . . ?"

"Yes."

A calming breeze flowed over them as she waited for him to

elaborate. Yet Garrett's thunderous expression was anything but calm.

"A grenade went off when I was helping a fellow soldier. I woke up in a hospital with no idea where I was or how I'd gotten there." He rolled his napkin into a tight ball. "I was one of the lucky ones, though. I managed to keep all my limbs. But my injuries still prevent me from being able to fully embrace life on a farm."

"Was that the reason you wouldn't ride on the wagon with us?"

He looked away and nodded. "The jostling of the tractor over uneven ground isn't good for"—he hesitated—"my back." A nerve pulsed in his neck.

There was much more Garrett wasn't saying, Jane was sure of it. She'd never seen any evidence of him favoring his back. In fact, he seemed nimble enough, quick to jump up to help anyone who needed it. She imagined someone with a back injury would move carefully, maybe even limp a little. But Garrett appeared perfectly healthy.

"I'm sorry," she said. "That must have been hard to accept."

"It was. When I realized I couldn't do the physical labor any-more, I took some more business courses geared toward finance and auditing to give me a better chance at a job behind a desk."

"But that's not what you really wanted to do with your life, is it?"

"No," he admitted. "It's not."

How sad that he'd had to forfeit the desire of his heart and settle for second best. Much like her situation in a way. Her dream of having a family had died with her miscarriages, and now she too was making the most of her second chance.

It seemed they had more in common than she thought.

***

Garrett glanced at Jane's face, trying to interpret her reac-tion to his admission of weakness. Why had he told her about his injury? Now she'd view him with pity, maybe even with less respect than she did before. But at least he'd held back the worst of his condition and the uncertainty that would forever hold his future hostage.

"I imagine it's hard to come home every weekend," Jane said. She peered at him under her lashes, as though afraid of saying the wrong thing.

"Not really." He plucked a blade of grass and ran it through his fingers. "I've learned to accept my limitations and help with whatever chores I'm able. Plus, seeing my niece and nephews is more than enough incentive to come home. They ground me. Make me remember what's truly important in life."

"I'm sure they do." A flash of emotion passed over her features. "There's nothing like children to put everything into perspective." She gave a soft smile and gestured to Martin, playing ball with Garrett's two nephews. "If only Martin could be this happy and carefree every day."

The ball dropped to the ground and rolled onto their blanket.

Martin raced over to retrieve it. "Sorry, Mr. Wilder. I missed."

"It's all right. You just need more practice." Garrett snatched up the ball and got to his feet, happy to have a distraction from the charms of the woman beside him. "It'd be easier if we had a catcher's mitt, but for now, let's practice without one." He lobbed the ball in a high arc.

Martin ran, reaching upward, but it fell through his fingers.

"Nice try." Garrett jogged across the space to join the group of boys.

"Uncle Garrett! Throw it to me." Kevin jumped up and down behind Martin.

Garrett complied, and after a few more throws with his nephew, he paused. "I think Martin needs some practice. How about we teach him to catch the way I taught you?"

"I can catch too." Dale's lower lip protruded, the boy always wanting to be as good as his big brother.

Garrett laughed. "Of course you can. Now, what's the number one rule I taught you?"

"Keep your eye on the ball," his nephews yelled in unison.

"That's right. Got that, Martin? Don't look away as it comes toward you." He threw the boy another easy ball.

This time, Martin managed to catch it.

"That's it. Now, you throw one to me."

Martin screwed up his face as he leaned his arm back and let the ball fly.

Garrett could have jumped for it but coming down on the uneven grass might jar his back, so he gave the appearance of a good effort, letting the ball roll out of reach.

Martin stared, waiting Garrett's reaction.

"Good throw, Martin. I wasn't fast enough to catch it."

Garrett retrieved the ball and handed it to Kevin. "Why don't you give Martin a few pointers? I'm sure you could help him a lot."

Kevin grinned. "I can do that."

They'd only thrown a couple of balls when Dad's voice boomed over the field. "All right, everyone. Who's ready for more picking?"

The kids all leapt up from wherever they were and took off at a run. Garrett picked up the forgotten ball and walked back to the blanket.

Jane had already packed up the remains of their lunch. "Thank you for doing that," she said as he approached.

"Doing what?"

"Giving Martin some attention. I could tell it meant a lot to him."

He shrugged. "I only treated him the same way I would my nephews."

She folded the blanket over one arm with a smile. "Exactly. It's good for Martin to see that not all men are stern taskmasters. That some treat kids with kindness."

He shook his head. "It's a shame what he's been through. I

can't imagine anyone not loving kids the way I do." He had to look away from the admiration shining on her face, afraid it might go to his head. Afraid he might think her comment meant more than it did. "Well, have a good afternoon, and watch out for those ladders."

As he walked away, her laugh followed him, seeping under his skin and warming his soul. "Get a grip," he muttered under his breath, sternly reminding himself that Jane was a co-worker and nothing more.

It didn't matter that she wasn't married. It didn't even matter if she found him attractive or admirable. The nature of his war wounds made it impossible to share anything other than friendship with a woman.

Because how could he promise a future to someone when he didn't know if he'd even have one himself?

16

In direct contrast to the idyllic time spent at the Wilders' farm, the next week created a host of new problems at the office for Jane.

Garrett had been looking into Mr. Bolton's background in order to learn as much as possible about the man before he interviewed him about the missing money. He'd found out that Mr. Bolton had been let go from his full-time job several months ago and hadn't told anyone about it. Garrett's theory was that the man had been stealing from the Children's Aid out of desperation, not greed, which made Garrett want to be extra careful in throwing out accusations. Jane had enough on her plate and was happy to let Garrett handle that particular problem.

Because, at the moment, her biggest concern was Martin.

Despite the fact that the boy had enjoyed his outing to the orchard and seemed to get along with the other children, his behavior when he returned to the shelter hadn't improved. Mrs. Shaughnessy was losing patience with him, since he continued to get into trouble—not only at the shelter but at school as well. After several attempts to discipline Martin for disrupting the classroom, the principal had requested he be tutored at home, so as not to interrupt the lessons of the rest of the hardworking students.

Which left Jane in a predicament.

She had no funds to hire a tutor and the other staff members, both at the shelter and in the office, were already overworked. In the end, it fell to Jane to become his temporary teacher. Each morning, Martin would walk over from the shelter and report to Jane. She would then set him up in the staff lunchroom with some books, notepaper, and pencils. She'd spend half an hour going over the lesson for the day and leave him with work to do on his own. During her lunch hour, she would look over his work and give him an assignment for the afternoon.

To her relief, Martin seemed to love his time away from the shelter and hadn't tried to run off. Part of the reason, Jane surmised, was Martin's new hero worship of Garrett. Ever since the trip to the orchard, Martin talked nonstop about Mr. Wilder, his dog, and the farm. The fact that Garrett made a special point of checking in with Martin several times each day only added to the boy's idolization.

As if her thoughts had conjured the man, Garrett knocked once and entered her office.

"Any thoughts on what we're going to do about Martin?" He pulled over a chair. "He can't stay in the lunchroom indefinitely."

Jane looked up from the papers on her desk and attempted to ignore the flutter in her belly. "I'm working on a new placement. I still believe that if we find him a permanent home, he'll feel secure enough to stop misbehaving."

She lowered her gaze. Lately, she'd been having a difficult time keeping herself from staring at Garrett. His compassion toward her since she'd received the awful news about Brandon and the time she'd shared with him on his family's farm had only enhanced her opinion of him, leading her to entertain all kinds of silly fantasies.

She pulled out a folder. "I've narrowed it down to three possible families."

"Mind if I take a look?" He held out his hand.

"Not at all." She passed him the file. "Though I'm surprised you'd want to dive into the minutiae of the organization this soon."

He glanced up. "I'm here to analyze everything, Jane, minutiae and all. Might as well take it as it comes." He studied her. "Come to think of it, I'm surprised you're involved in this. Shouldn't this be the job of Martin's caseworker?"

She removed her glasses and folded them. "Technically, I still am Martin's caseworker. I suppose I should reassign him, but since he trusts me—and believe me, he doesn't trust easily—I felt I should handle this one personally."

"That makes sense." He removed the papers and scanned the details about the three potential families.

Jane fiddled with a pen while she waited. She'd gone over them again and again but couldn't decide which one would be the most suitable. After her misjudgment of the McElroys, her confidence had slipped a little. Frankly, she welcomed Garrett's opinion.

He closed the folder with a frown. "None of these are ideal, are they?"

"Not really. But as I've said, with the war on, we've lost a great number of foster families and have to choose from the ones we have left—ones who haven't already rejected Martin, or who don't want an older child, or who only want girls. That leaves very few candidates."

"Which family are you leaning toward?"

Jane hesitated, strangely reluctant to share her opinion. "I think I'd probably eliminate the Harrisons. They're an older couple, and my instincts tell me they only want someone to do work on their property. I don't believe they're really interested in creating a family for a child."

One dark brow rose. "How do you know?"

"I've been to their place. It's a rather large farm. When the Harrisons' last foster child reached the age of eighteen, he left to pursue a job out West. I feel they're merely looking for a re-placement."

"That might not be a bad thing."

"Perhaps not. But I can't help but wish for a real family for Martin. With parents who would treat him as their own child. Nurture him, help him grow into the wonderful young man I know he could be." Her throat cinched shut. She was breaking one of the cardinal rules by becoming emotionally involved with a child she was trying to place. But how could she not after the promise she'd made to Martin's mother? And the guilt that, six years later, she was still trying to fulfill that vow?

"Ever the optimist, I see," Garrett said.

"I can't help it. I want every child to feel loved and safe."

"An admirable goal."

His approving gaze did funny things to her stomach.

"So, which family do you think might give Martin this idyllic life?" His words had a teasing quality that Jane chose to ignore.

"I would pick the Jeffersons. They're in their early forties and have had success with foster children in the past. I think they could provide Martin with the stability he needs." She pulled over one of the sheets of paper. "On the other hand, the Blackwood family might work out too, except they've never had a foster child before, and it would be risky to place a potentially difficult case with an untried couple."

"Or it could be a perfect fit. They indicate that they're hoping to eventually adopt. This could be the permanent family you want for Martin."

"Possibly." She bit her lip. "But something tells me that being so new to the foster care system, they wouldn't be prepared for a child with special needs."

A sudden shriek sounded from the front of the building, followed by the slam of a door.

"Martin, come back here!" a woman shouted.

"That sounded like Melanie." Jane jumped up from her chair. "What's Martin done now?"

Garrett beat her out of the office. They both ran out the front door and found Melanie on the lawn, staring out toward the road.

"Martin! Get back here now!" The girl's mouth was pinched, her arms crossed.

Jane rushed past her down the walkway, the brisk fall air biting through the thin fabric of her blouse.

Martin knelt in the middle of the road beside a black furry heap.

Jane's heart stuttered. What was he doing? She looked both ways up the street as she ran toward him. "Martin, you need to get out of the road."

"Mrs. Linder!" He raised his head, his face awash with tears. "This dog is hurt. He needs help."

She peered down at the lifeless-looking animal and her heart squeezed. From the blood matting its hindquarters, it was likely he'd been hit by a car. "I'll call for help, but first, you need to come inside."

"I'm not leaving him." Martin jutted his chin out. "A car might run over him."

"A car might run over *you*!" Anxiety raced through Jane's system as she tugged on his shirtsleeve.

Martin wrenched away and threw his arms over the dog. "No. I'm staying here."

Garrett strode into the street and bent over the injured animal, quickly running his hands over its body, murmuring soothing words while feeling its limbs. The dog appeared to be unconscious, since it didn't move when Garrett touched its broken right hind leg. Likely the animal had internal injuries as well, but only a vet would be able to determine the severity.

"Is he dead, Mr. Wilder?" Martin's voice quavered.

"No, but he's in rough shape. We'll need to take him to a veterinarian to be checked out." Garrett laid a hand on Martin's shoulder. "You go in with Mrs. Linder. I've got my car here so I can take him. We just need to find the nearest clinic."

A defiant light shone in the boy's eyes. "I want to go with you."

"Martin," Garrett said in a firm voice. "Mrs. Linder is in charge. You need to listen to her." He glanced at Jane, wishing he knew what she was thinking. "Maybe Martin could help you look up the nearest veterinarian office?"

She nodded. "I have a telephone directory in my office." She held out her hand, which wasn't quite steady, and waited, an expectant look on her face.

Reluctantly, Martin took her hand and stepped onto the curb, his focus never leaving the animal.

As gently as possible, Garrett scooped the dog into his arms. "My car's just down the street. I'll put him inside and come back for the address."

Jane nodded again and led the boy back inside the building.

Garrett let out a long breath. Poor Martin. He couldn't seem to help but find himself in the midst of trouble. Yet Garrett had seen by the boy's reaction to Jett how much Martin loved animals. Could anyone really blame him for trying to rescue this one?

He opened the back door of his Ford and laid the dog on the back seat. "Hang in there, buddy. I'll be back soon. We're going to get you some help." He felt around for a collar but found none. But the dog looked too well fed to be a stray.

No matter. First, they needed to make sure he would live. The rest of the details could be sorted out later.

17

The next morning, as Jane made her way to the office, she couldn't shake the cloud of worry that had kept her awake a good portion of the night. Had she made the right decision in allowing Martin to go with Garrett and the dog to the veterinarian?

Part of her could admit she was often too lenient with the boy, yet forcing her authority only seemed to make him dig in his heels even more. Over the years, she'd learned to pick her battles with Martin, and other than missing an hour of school time, no real harm had been done.

Except she was letting Martin get attached to a stray dog—a severely injured dog, at that. Jane knew the boy was setting himself up for a huge disappointment, but aside from cruelly banning him from seeing the dog ever again, there wasn't much she could do.

The offices sat hushed in an unnatural stillness as Jane let herself into her office and flicked on the light switch. She closed the door behind her, needing a brief time of solitude before the workday began, with its host of phone calls and meetings, paperwork to go over and problems to solve. She took her seat and rubbed the bridge of her nose, the start of a headache already brewing. For some reason, she couldn't seem to muster any enthusiasm for the issues requiring her attention. Had she lost her passion for the directress position? Or did she simply miss the more hands-on job of being a caseworker?

Maybe Olivia was right. Maybe the directress position wasn't for her. Jane really didn't care about paying the plumber for unclogging pipes or dealing with her employees' constant complaints. Nor could she summon the motivation to solicit private donations to keep the agency afloat. But if she wanted to effect any real change in the way the Children's Aid was run, this was the price she would have to pay. As a caseworker, she had no power over policy.

A knock sounded on her door. So much for her moment of peace and quiet.

"Come in."

Garrett sailed through the door. "Good morning, Jane."

"Good morning." Her lackluster greeting had the smile fading from his face.

"What's wrong? You look like your dog just died."

She speared him with a flinty glare.

"Okay, bad joke, given yesterday's events." He dropped into her guest chair. "That's why I'm here, actually. With an update on Blackie."

"You named him Blackie?"

Garrett leaned back in the chair, waving aside her question. "I called the vet this morning, and it looks like Blackie's going to make a full recovery. He's malnourished as well as dehydrated, so they want to keep him until he's stronger."

At Jane's sigh, Garrett frowned. "What? I thought you would be happy for Martin. He'll be glad to hear the good news when he gets here."

"I'm glad the dog is going to be all right," she said, "but it does bring up a concern I have."

"What's that?"

"I don't want to encourage Martin's interest in the animal."

Garrett's frown deepened. "Why not? After all, he did help rescue him."

She twisted a pen between her fingers. "Well, first off, Martin's focus today is going to be all about the dog and not on his schooling. But mostly I'm afraid he'll get too attached. It will only hurt him in the long run."

"Well, I was thinking, if they can't find the owner . . ." Garrett gave a sheepish shrug, his expression reminiscent of Martin's. "I might take Blackie. We can always use another dog on the farm."

She set her jaw and removed some papers from her briefcase. Why did that idea annoy her even more? "That's your prerogative. But my request stands. Please don't encourage Martin to bond with this dog."

"Jane." The gentle insistence of his voice stilled her fingers on the files.

She tried to keep her features intentionally blank as she looked up.

"Everything is going to be fine."

She shook her head, a ridiculous lump of emotion tightening her throat. "You don't realize how easily Martin gets his hopes up, only to have them dashed time and time again." She swallowed. "Please don't make him any promises you can't keep."

"I understand." He leaned across the desk and laid a hand on her arm, his warmth seeping through her sleeve. The look of sympathy on his face made her want to crumple like a used tissue.

"If you'll excuse me," she said in a strangled voice, "I need to get to work."

He removed his hand and nodded. "Me too."

With that, he walked out of the office, leaving Jane's stomach churning with a confusing mix of emotions—worry over Martin, doubts about her passion for her job, and an unwanted attraction to her co-worker.

She pressed her fingers to her temples. She was tired of being strong all the time. Tired of the constant weight of responsibility with no one to share it. Garrett made her want to lean on him in ways that just weren't possible. Or practical. She gave herself a mental shake, slid on her glasses, and opened the folder on the top of the pile.

Half an hour later, Jane checked the clock on the wall, sudden alarm rippling through her. Martin should have been here ages ago. Perhaps she should—

The telephone on her desk rang. She snatched up the receiver. "Yes, Melanie."

"I have Mrs. Shaughnessy on the line for you," Melanie announced.

"Put her through."

A few seconds went by, then Mrs. Shaughnessy came on.

"Mrs. Linder." The woman sounded out of breath. "You need to come over right away. Martin is in a state, and I'm at my wits' end. I need your help."

Jane's lungs seemed to stop working. *Oh, Martin. What have you done now?* She drew in a breath and let it out. "I'll be right over, Mrs. Shaughnessy. Try to stay as calm as you can."

She hung up without waiting for a reply and shot out of her chair. Grabbing her jacket, she rushed into the hallway, where she slammed into something solid. A grunt escaped as strong hands gripped her arms to keep her upright.

"Whoa." Garrett's amused voice sounded by her ear. "Where's the fire?"

"Sorry." She stepped back, not looking at him. "I have to get to the shelter. There's a problem with Martin."

She scooted around him toward the front door, stopping to tell Melanie where she was headed. Only after she was partway down the sidewalk did she realize that Garrett was right behind her.

A ridiculous sense of relief rippled through her at the thought of having his steadying presence there, should she need it. As soon as they reached the shelter, she entered the front door. Right away, she could hear loud voices coming from the second story and headed directly up the stairs.

Utter chaos met her eyes as she entered the playroom. Toys were scattered across the rug, many of them broken. Dolls with missing limbs, cars without wheels, stuffed bears with their eyes or ears torn off. Several younger children sat in the corner, crying, with Miss Tate doing her best to console them.

Mrs. Shaughnessy stood with her arms folded near Martin, who was on top of a desk, wielding a small baseball bat like a sword.

"Mrs. Linder. Mr. Wilder. Thank goodness." The matron turned, relief edging her features. "Maybe you can get this hellion to come down."

Jane took one look at the wildness in Martin's glassy eyes and fresh anxiety cinched her throat. She'd seen him in this state before, and it hadn't ended well. Stress, she'd learned that day, was one of the triggers for his seizures. She sent up a silent prayer for guidance as she approached the boy.

"Martin," she said in her calmest tone, "please give me the bat and come down from there." She held out a hand toward him.

He shook his head, frozen in his battle stance.

"Are the other children all right?" Jane asked the matron, her eyes never leaving Martin.

"Other than terrorized, they're fine."

Jane took a breath and forced her taut muscles to relax slightly. No one had been physically hurt. The destruction of property could be dealt with later. "Miss Tate, please take the other children from the room."

The woman nodded and, with remarkable speed, whisked the younger, inconsolable children into the hallway and down the stairs.

"If you come with me now, Martin, we can talk about whatever is bothering you." Jane only prayed he'd take the lifeline she was offering.

But he didn't move. Didn't even acknowledge her words.

"Remember what I told you before. We don't solve problems with violence. We talk about what's bothering us and come up with reasonable solutions."

"Talking is stupid." Martin's legs began to shake, and a muscle under his eye twitched.

Jane feared he'd topple off the desk. If only she had an idea of what had set him off, she might be better equipped to say something that would calm him down. "Well, destroying toys is no way to solve anything. Whatever the problem is, we can find a way to fix it."

"No!" His face turned red, right up to the tips of his ears. "You always say that, and nothing ever changes." He swung the bat in a wide arc in front of him. "I hate it here. I hate them." He pointed to the door that Miss Tate and the children had disappeared through. "And I hate you too."

Jane pushed back the zing of hurt coiling through her system. She knew he didn't mean it. He was simply taking out his anger and frustration on her, and he'd apologize once this episode was over. Even so, the words sank deep into her bones. She set her jaw, searching for words that would soothe him.

But before anything came to mind, the boy's eyes glazed over, and his muscles began to shudder. The bat fell from his stiffened fingers, bouncing off the desk to the ground.

Jane's heart pounded, her lungs stretching in her chest like an overfilled balloon as she rushed forward. *A seizure.* Just what she'd feared might happen.

She grabbed Martin off the desk, quickly lowering his jerking body to the rug in the middle of the room. "Call Dr. Henshaw," she barked over her shoulder.

Mrs. Shaughnessy was already out the door. Fortunately, the other children weren't here to witness the episode, which could be quite frightening.

Jane turned Martin on his side and loosened the top button

of his shirt. "It's all right, honey," she murmured. "I'm right here with you. It's going to be fine."

Garrett kneeled on the other side of the boy. "What can we do?" Furrows stretched across his brow like small trenches.

Martin's body continued to convulse.

"We have to let the seizure run its course," she said. "All we can do is make sure he doesn't hurt himself and let him know he's not alone."

She laid a soft hand on Martin's shoulder, hoping that his brain would register the comfort. "We're right here, Martin. You're going to be okay." Tears clogged her throat, but she swallowed hard. She'd been through this before, and even though she believed he'd be fine, it still ripped her heart out to see him like this.

Garrett reached over and laid a hand on her shoulder. She glanced up at him, his concerned blue eyes giving her strength.

"You might want to move back a little," she advised. "He might vomit."

She expected Garrett to shoot up from his position, but his gaze remained steady.

"I'm not worried." He glanced down at Martin's shuddering body. "Poor kid. I can't imagine having to go through this."

Her chest warmed. Most people didn't have such a stoic reaction to witnessing their first seizure. But it didn't seem to faze Garrett at all.

Under Jane's hand, Martin's body gradually grew lax, and then finally he stilled. His face was whiter than the walls, his eyes closed. His breathing had evened out, which was a good sign.

She rubbed his arm. "Martin. Wake up, honey."

Garrett frowned. "Shouldn't we let him rest?"

"We have to make sure he's conscious first. Once he comes around, he'll be quite sleepy, and he can rest then. Dr. Henshaw will tell us if there's anything else we can do when he gets here."

Martin's eyelashes fluttered, then he blinked and slowly opened his eyes.

Jane laid a hand on his cheek. "You had a seizure, honey, but you're all right. Just lie still until the doctor gets here."

He stared off somewhere beyond her shoulder. Tears welled in his eyes and slowly rolled down his face.

Oh, Martin. Jane's heart squeezed hard. With quiet resolve, she gathered him in her arms and brought his head against her chest. She didn't care how bad his behavior had been or how many toys he'd destroyed. This child needed love and compassion, and she would give him as much as she could. "Shh. It's all right. You're safe here." A tear escaped and slid down her cheek, but she didn't care. This boy deserved so much more than her tears.

So much more than empty words promising a better future.

If only she knew how to get it for him.

18

Garrett paced the lunchroom, feeling more and more like a caged lion as he waited for Jane to return from the shelter. Once the doctor had arrived and moved Martin to his bed in the dormitory, Jane had suggested that Garrett go back to the office since she would have to meet with Mrs. Shaughnessy to get to the bottom of the incident, and there was no point in both of them wasting the morning.

Unfortunately, he'd found it impossible to concentrate on the columns of figures in front of him, unable to erase Martin's seizure from his mind. When they'd first entered that playroom amid the destruction Martin had wrought, Jane's actions in the face of such a volatile situation had astounded him. The calm and assertive manner in which she'd handled Martin's seizure was nothing less than brilliant. Only her tears at the end had revealed just how deeply she'd been affected. He'd had to hold himself back from taking her in his arms and comforting her the same way she comforted the boy.

He shook his head. That type of thinking needed to stop. He had to remember he was here to do a job, not get entwined in the drama of everyone's lives.

Footsteps sounded in the hall seconds before Jane walked in.

"Oh, Garrett. I didn't expect anyone to be in here." She headed straight for the coffeepot on the stove and poured the strong brew into a mug.

"How did it go after I left?" he asked.

She took a long sip. "Not well."

He stiffened. "Is Martin going to be okay?"

"He'll be fine. Dr. Henshaw gave him a mild sedative to help him sleep better."

"What didn't go well, then? The talk with Mrs. Shaughnessy?"

Jane nodded and pulled out a chair, seeming to deflate onto it.

"Did she say what happened to make Martin behave that way?"

"She wasn't totally sure. Miss Tate told us that one of the boys said something that set Martin off. And the other kids started laughing, which made everything that much worse." She glanced over at him. "Martin hates being laughed at. Apparently, he started grabbing the toys away from the other kids and destroying them. He was trying to hurt them the way they'd hurt him." She shook her head. "Which is not an excuse for his behavior."

He sat down across from her. "No, it's not. But at least you understand why he did it."

"I do. However, it doesn't solve the problem." She ran a hand over her eyes. "Mrs. Shaughnessy has reached her limit with Martin. She wants him out of the shelter as soon as possible." Two vertical grooves formed above her nose. "She said if we don't remove him by the end of the week, she'll quit." A loud sigh escaped. "I can't afford to lose her, Garrett. Without Mrs. Shaughnessy, the shelter would have to close, and where would the other children go?" Her shoulders slumped, and an air of defeat surrounded her.

"What other options do you have?" Garrett leaned over the table, his mind spinning to come up with possible solutions. He wished his parents' neighbors still took in foster kids. However, Mrs. O'Neill had passed away a few years back, and Mr. O'Neill had his hands full keeping up with the farm.

"I'm going to appeal to some of the clergy in the area and see if they might have a parishioner who'd be willing to take Martin temporarily. At least until I have time to do more extensive interviews with the potential foster families I've picked out."

"That sounds like a good plan." He narrowed his eyes. "Then why do you seem so discouraged?"

She shrugged. "I've been down this road several times before, with no success. And I hate having to tell Martin he's not welcome at the shelter." Moisture welled in her eyes, magnifying their gold flecks.

His chest tightened. How he wished he could solve all her problems, ease her load so she could simply rest. "Hey, let's think positive. I'm sure one of those families you've chosen will be a good fit for him. We just need an interim solution until then."

She looked so defeated that he longed to make her feel better. But there was nothing he could do except pray for her and for Martin.

He rose and gave a brief nod. "I'd better let you get started making those calls. Let me know if I can do anything."

"Thank you, Garrett. It helped having you there today." Her lips lifted into a semblance of a smile.

"I'm glad." He paused in the doorway. "You were amazing, by the way. Martin's lucky to have you on his side." Then, before he revealed any more of his feelings, he forced himself to leave.

—— ❖ ——

Jane's hands shook as she hung up the receiver. Only one pastor out of the five she'd called had offered to try and find a family to take Martin. The others had turned her down flat. She wasn't proud of the fact that she'd lost her temper with two of the clergymen who, in her opinion, had displayed an extremely uncharitable response to her request.

Not her finest moment.

Not when she prided herself on the good connections she'd

developed with the various resources in the city. In truth, she shouldn't have made those calls when she was already in a heightened state of anxiety. She'd allowed her irritated mood to affect her professionalism, and that was something she usually never did.

She lowered her head to her hands. Everything in her life seemed to be spinning out of her control. Her head throbbed with all the unanswered questions, and she ached with the uncertainty of Martin's future.

The thought of him staying in a place where he clearly wasn't wanted tore at her conscience. She'd love nothing more than to go in there, scoop him up, and take him somewhere safe. However, in his weakened condition right now, he needed to stay put and rest. But tomorrow, if he was feeling better, and if she still had nowhere to take him, what would she do then?

Opening her bottom drawer, she rummaged at the very back for a dog-eared folder. With care, she brought it out and removed the top sheet of paper.

Application to Become Foster Parents
Name: Mr. and Mrs. Donald Linder
Status: Approved

Jane stared at the rest of the information penned on the sheet, remembering the feeling of anticipation she'd had when she'd filled out the forms four years earlier. Before Donald had destroyed Jane's last hope for ever having a family. Perhaps it had been unwise to start the application without telling him, but she'd reasoned that if they passed the first stage, he would surely change his mind about adopting, and by the time the home inspection started, he would be as eager as she was. How could she have misread her husband so completely?

Jane stared at the document. Did she dare use this now to become Martin's temporary guardian?

Would it constitute a conflict of interest? A violation of ethics? An outright lie?

She drew in a breath and exhaled slowly. At this particular moment, she didn't care, not when Martin's well-being hung in the balance. Tomorrow, she would take him home with her and she'd deal with the consequences later.

19

The next day, Garrett parked his car outside Jane's house and turned off the engine. He sat for several seconds, rubbing his palms on his pant legs in a futile attempt to reduce his apprehension. Was he doing the right thing coming here, or should he let the situation wait until tomorrow before talking to Jane about it?

Confronting her might only make matters worse, but he couldn't go back to his room in the boardinghouse knowing she might be making a mistake that could ruin her bid for the director's job.

This morning, a very subdued Martin had felt well enough to return to Jane's tutelage in the staff room. Other than a brief interaction with Martin concerning his schoolwork, Jane had remained behind closed doors, more than likely making more phone calls to find a temporary home for the boy. Garrett did ask Jane if they should talk to the boy about his behavior the day before, but she'd advised against it.

"I don't want to upset him and possibly trigger another seizure," she'd said. "When the time is right, I'll speak to him about it. For now, I'll concentrate on finding a temporary placement."

Later in the day, the vet had called to say Blackie might be ready to go home sooner than expected, and Garrett thought the good news might cheer Martin up. When he went looking for the boy, he'd found the staff room empty and Jane's office closed for the day as well. A niggling sense of unease had wound through his system. Had she found a placement for the boy and taken him there? If so, why wouldn't she have told Garrett about it?

When he asked Melanie where Martin was, she reluctantly told him that Jane had left early and taken the boy home with her. Only for the night, she'd explained, until further arrangements could be made.

But Garrett didn't quite believe that. He had an uneasy suspicion that she planned to keep him indefinitely, which in his mind constituted a conflict of interest.

He'd hate to have to report it to the board at their scheduled meeting on Monday, along with the fact that he'd found more evidence of missing money. He'd come to care about Jane and didn't wish to add to her troubles. Yet if she did plan to keep Martin long term and he didn't report it, he might lose the board's trust, as well as his own chance of applying for the director's job.

Garrett hesitated, his hand hovering above the doorbell. If ever he needed divine guidance it was now. He bowed his head. *Heavenly Father, you know the depths of my heart, my motives, and my intentions. Please help me to keep a clear head and act in the best interest of everyone involved.*

The steadiness he'd gained with prayer evaporated the moment Jane answered the door.

"Garrett? What are you doing here?" Her nervous tone matched the way she didn't quite meet his eyes. She kept her hand on the door, open only wide enough to see her face.

"Hello, Jane. May I come in?"

"That depends on your answer to my question." A defiant light glowed in her eyes.

He hesitated, the need to tread carefully very apparent. The wind picked up, ruffling his jacket collar. "Do you mind if we talk inside? I didn't bring my overcoat."

For a second, he thought she'd refuse, but then she reluctantly opened the door and allowed him entry.

"Come back to the kitchen where we can have some privacy." She headed down the narrow hallway toward the rear of the house.

As he passed the opening to the living room, he glanced inside. Martin and Mrs. Mitchell were engrossed in what appeared to be a serious game of checkers.

"Hello, Mrs. Mitchell," he said. "Looks like Martin is keeping you busy."

The woman lifted her head with a smile. "Hello, Garrett. He is indeed."

Her eyes seemed brighter than usual, perhaps due to having a child around. Garrett knew from his own family how youngsters could raise a person's spirits.

Martin looked up. "I'm winning, Mr. Wilder. Do you want to watch?"

Garrett smiled, relieved to see a return to the boy's good humor. "Maybe later. I have some business to discuss with Mrs. Linder first."

He followed the hallway to the kitchen, where he found Jane at the sink, filling a kettle with water. He could almost see the waves of tension vibrating off her stiff frame.

She turned off the faucet and set the kettle on the stove, all without looking at him.

He came farther into the kitchen, admiring the hominess of the space—the round table with its checkered cloth, the pots of ivy hanging by the window, the display of blue plates in the corner cabinet. An enticing smell of what might be meatloaf lingered in the air, making Garrett's stomach grumble, reminding him that he was missing dinner at the boardinghouse.

"We need to talk," he said quietly. "Could we sit down, please?"

She nodded and gestured to the table.

He pulled out a chair for her, and once she was seated, he took a spot across from her, giving her as much space as he could. The last thing he wanted was for her to feel attacked.

"I have some serious concerns about Martin staying here," he said in a low voice. "It feels like a conflict of interest."

Jane squared her shoulders and met his gaze. "It's a last resort until we can find another foster home. If I'd had any other option, I would have taken it."

"What if I told you I have a possible solution?" The idea had come to him on the way over, and he hadn't had time to fully flesh it out yet. Still, it merited a conversation.

"What kind of solution?" The guarded look she gave him reminded him of a cornered animal.

He took a deep breath. "What would you think about Martin staying on the farm with my parents until you find him a foster home?"

"The farm?" Jane struggled with her first thought—that the farm might be the perfect place for Martin.

"Yes. I'd have to talk it over with my parents, but I'm fairly confident they'd agree. As a temporary measure, of course."

Jane stared, her heart thumping loudly. Martin had just gotten here. Already the house seemed brighter, and Mama seemed happier having the boy around. They couldn't lose him so soon. "That's an interesting idea, but I . . . I don't think it would work."

"Why not?" He tilted his head, unblinking in his regard.

She clamped her mouth shut to keep from gaping at him. She thought Garrett of all people would understand why she was doing this. He knew her complicated history with the boy and how she wanted—no, *needed*—to protect him. Her mind whirled with possible arguments. "Your parents haven't been approved. They'd have to fill out the necessary paperwork and pass the requirements for temporary guardianship."

"Did you do that?" He speared her with a hard stare.

"Of course I did." Guilt trickled through her. She'd completed the paperwork all right. It just happened to be four years old.

He narrowed his eyes. "A single working woman who looks after her ailing mother? That doesn't sound like it would fit the requirements."

Heat crept into her cheeks, but she jutted out her chin, refusing to admit anything.

"Ah. I see." He leaned closer. "You filled out those forms and approved them yourself. If that's not a breach of the rules, I don't know what is."

"That's not true. I—no, *we*—were approved. Donald and I, while we were still married."

The kettle whistled. She pushed up from the table, clamping her teeth together to keep from growling at him as he shook his head. "And besides, Martin is perfectly safe here. You know that. No one cares about him more than I do."

He threw out his hands. "Don't you see? That's the problem. As acting directress, it's critical you remain objective. But you can't be objective where Martin is concerned."

She took the kettle off the stove and poured the water into the teapot. Her hands shook, sloshing water over the side of the pot.

"Jane." His quiet voice cut through her. "I have a meeting with the board of management on Monday. They want an update on my findings so far." He came to stand beside her, his brow puckered. "I . . . what am I going to tell them about this?"

Her head whipped up, fear coiling in her belly. "Why do you have to tell them anything?" She hated the note of pleading in her voice. "This is just a temporary measure. No harm is being done."

"Are you sure about that?" He stepped closer. "You didn't want Martin getting attached to the dog. How is it fair to let Martin get attached to you?"

She gasped, his words slamming through her, the truth convicting her. She *did* want Martin to get attached to her, to love her as much as she loved him. But how was that fair to him when she couldn't give him the home he deserved? Even if she applied to adopt Martin, the board would never allow it. In all her time at the Children's Aid, she couldn't recall a single instance when Mr. Mills had ever granted custody to an unmarried person. And with her as directress, it put her in an even more tenuous position. No, they would laugh her right out of the boardroom.

Still, there was nothing she could do about it tonight, and it was pointless to keep hashing it over with Garrett. She steeled herself against his knowing gaze. "I have nothing more to say. I think it's time for you to leave."

A muscle ticked in his jaw. "Fine. But I'm going to talk to my parents, and if they agree, I'll have them fill out the paperwork for temporary guardianship." He stopped by the kitchen door. "And for the record, I intend to sit in on the interviews with the foster parents when you meet with them. I believe an objective second opinion is in order." He gave her a long look, then walked out the door.

All the air seemed to seep from her lungs, then almost immediately a hot burst of anger rushed in to fill the space. Couldn't he see what an impossible situation she was in?

And why did his disapproval sting so much?

She gritted her teeth as she stirred sugar into Mama's tea. Tonight, she would have to spend a lot of time on her knees praying for clarity for herself and for Martin, because it appeared that only divine intervention could help her out of this mess.

20

On Monday, Jane read over Mr. and Mrs. Wilder's application for the third time, unable to find anything out of the ordinary, no matter how much she wished she could. Garrett had beaten her to the office this morning and left the forms on her desk before he'd headed out to the board meeting. She picked up the rubber stamp and rolled it between her fingers. As soon as she stamped the application approved, she'd lose Martin.

She let out a sigh. Having the boy under her roof for the weekend had been such a gift. He'd slept in Brandon's room, across the hall from her, and for the first time in ages, the tight grip of loneliness in her chest had eased. Ever since her mother's health had deteriorated, Mama slept downstairs in the dining room, which they'd converted into a bedroom for her, so she didn't have to climb the stairs. Jane never admitted it, but she'd always felt rather isolated on the second story. Knowing Martin was across the hall had been a comfort she hadn't realized she'd been missing. And the boy had been a definite blessing for Mama, keeping her company and giving her an infusion of new energy.

Still, Jane understood that living on the Wilders' farm would be a better fit for the boy. He would have Garrett's nephews to play with, the fresh country air, and the animals that he adored. An experience he would remember for the rest of his life.

For Martin's sake, she had to do the unselfish thing. She pressed the rubber into the ink and stamped her approval on the application as well as the carbon copies.

When Garrett returned from his meeting, she could tell him the good news.

She put the stamp away in her drawer with a sigh. If the news was so good, why did she feel so terrible? She swiped away a tear with a determined slash, questioning once again the prudence of remaining in her job here. How much sadness could her soul take, seeing so many children in need of loving homes and never being allowed to adopt a child of her own?

Was it some sick form of self-torture to stay here?

Perhaps she should follow Donald's example and make a complete change in her life. Start over, do something completely new, though nothing as drastic as joining the army or marrying someone else. If only she had any inkling of what that could be. The Children's Aid was all she'd ever known.

A quick knock preceded Garrett into her office. "Hello, Jane. Have you had a chance to go over my parents' application?"

He was wearing a full three-piece suit with a brass-buttoned vest and a crisp white handkerchief in his front pocket that matched his shirt. His hair, which often seemed a bit disheveled after he'd run his fingers through it, now sat perfectly groomed off his forehead, highlighting those amazing eyes.

Her pulse began an unsteady gallop. "I have." She handed him the papers. "If your parents are ready, you can take Martin to the farm tonight."

He fingered the sheets, his gaze trained on her with microscopic intensity.

She swiveled in her chair to open one of the credenza drawers and pretended to search for a file. Anything to keep him from seeing how much this was hurting her.

"Why don't you come with us?" he asked, his voice gentle. "My mother said to invite you for dinner. Perhaps it will make the transition a little easier for everyone."

For her, he meant. Tears burned the backs of her eyes. Blindly, she pulled a folder out of the drawer and turned back to her desk. "Thank you, but I don't think so."

"Jane."

She squared her shoulders. "It's better to make a clean break."

"What about Martin? Do you want him to sense you're not in favor of this move?"

She whipped her head up. "I didn't say I'm not in favor of it. I know living on the farm will be wonderful for him. It's just . . . hard." She ducked her head and picked up a pen.

"My mother's chicken and dumplings might make it a bit more bearable." He wiggled his brows at her, one dimple winking out.

She stared at him. Why was he being so nice? Was he feeling guilty about something else? "You didn't tell the board about Martin or about my divorce, did you?" Her voice wasn't much louder than a whisper.

His smile disappeared. "No. When I got here this morning, I didn't feel ready for the meeting. I decided I wanted more time to determine Bolton's part in the financial discrepancies. So I called and postponed our meeting for a couple of weeks." He gave her a pointed look. "By then I assume Martin's situation will be settled."

Relief flooded through her. She got the distinct feeling that he'd postponed the meeting more for her sake than for the Mr. Bolton situation. She nodded, pressing her lips together to contain her emotions that were too near the surface. "Can I think about dinner?"

"Sure. Mom always cooks enough for ten people, so it won't

be a problem." He folded his parents' copy of the approved application and shoved it inside his jacket. "I'll be by for Martin around five o'clock. You can let me know then."

With the barest of smiles, he left the room.

Jane sagged back against her chair, the energy draining from her. She almost wished Garrett wouldn't be so noble, that he'd stayed *the interloper* in her mind. Because lately he was becoming far too appealing to resist. Even if they weren't co-workers who would eventually be vying for the same job, a future with Garrett wasn't possible. He deserved someone unblemished by life. Someone fresh and pure. Not a divorcée who couldn't give him the children he deserved. She slid her glasses back in place and focused back on her work.

Nothing could be gained by indulging in some romantic fantasy.

Her heart wouldn't survive if she did.

"Really?" Martin's brown eyes sparkled. "I can go and stay at Mr. Wilder's farm?"

Jane had expected excitement, yet it still stung that Martin was so eager to leave. She held her tight smile in place. "For now, yes. Just for a few weeks until we make other arrangements." She didn't want him to think he could stay there permanently.

"When do we leave?"

"Soon. But first we need to have a talk." Jane motioned for him to sit beside her on the sofa. Mama was taking a nap, so this was the perfect time to address the incident at the shelter.

He must have sensed what was to come because he sat perfectly still, his head bent.

"I need you to understand that your behavior at the shelter was totally unacceptable and that Mrs. Shaughnessy had every right to ask you to leave."

His gaze remained glued to his knees.

"Even if the older boys taunt you and try to provoke you, you have to learn to ignore them."

"I don't like it when they laugh at me," Martin said so quietly Jane could barely make it out.

"I understand that laughing at someone is hurtful. Mrs. Shaughnessy has spoken to the other children very sternly about it. But that doesn't make it okay for you to destroy the toys and threaten them with a bat."

Martin lowered his chin to his chest.

"You only ended up . . . hurting yourself." She almost said *causing a seizure*, but she didn't want him to be worried that any time he got upset it could happen again.

"I'm sorry, Mrs. Linder."

"I accept your apology. And I trust you will remember this conversation when you're at the farm. Mr. and Mrs. Wilder are very nice people, but they won't put up with bad behavior either. You will have to get along with the other children in the house and be as helpful as you can."

"I will, Mrs. Linder. I promise." His fearful gaze flicked up to hers.

Jane had to hold herself in check at his remorseful expression and not give in to the urge to hug him. She couldn't reward bad behavior, no matter how much she wanted to. Even allowing him to go to the farm almost seemed like a gift.

"Mr. Wilder will be here soon," she said. "Do you need help getting your things ready?"

"No, thanks. It won't take long." With that he scampered out of the room and up the stairs, his feet thumping loudly on the carpeted runner.

Jane shook her head with a bemused chuckle. Despite her sadness at their impending separation, she couldn't help but be happy for him. Martin would thrive on the farm, she was certain. Maybe it would give him a better idea of what a true family looked like.

As Jane got up from the sofa, her mother came into the living room.

"Mama, did you have a good rest?"

"Yes, I did." She took a seat in her chair and picked up her knitting.

"What would you like for dinner? There's some leftover stew from yesterday."

Her mother looked over. "It's the church potluck tonight, remember? Mrs. Peters is picking me up at six. That's why I made sure to have a rest."

"Oh. It slipped my mind completely." Jane bit her lip. In all the uproar with her job lately, had she been neglecting her mother? She should have made something for her mother to take with her to the church.

"Why don't you come with us, dear? There might be some nice young men bringing their mothers." Mama winked.

"Really, Mama. Will you ever stop trying to marry me off again?" Jane gathered the few dirty dishes from her mother's lunch and swept a glance over the rest of the room, its faded charm a testament to her childhood. She should think about doing some redecorating. Something simple that wouldn't cost too much.

"Not until I see you happy and settled with a family of your own."

"You are all the family I need." She dropped a kiss on top of her mother's head.

"And Brandon, when he returns." Her mother gave her a sharp look. "Don't count him out yet, Janey. He's strong and tough. He'll come back to us."

"I pray you're right, Mama. I really do." At least her mother's attitude had become more positive.

She carried the dishes to the kitchen and set them in the sink. Then she opened the refrigerator and peered inside. Judging by the sparse interior, she would need to make a trip to the market soon.

The doorbell rang. Jane ran a hand over the printed dress she'd changed into after work. Perhaps she should accept Mrs. Wilder's dinner invitation. It would be better than moping around the empty house, missing Martin's chatter.

As she headed down the hall, footsteps pounded from upstairs, and the eager boy beat her to the door.

"Hello, Martin." Garrett stepped into the hallway.

"Mr. Wilder! I can't believe I get to come and stay on the farm."

Garrett ruffled the boy's hair. "My family is looking forward to having you. Especially my nephews." He lifted his head, and his gaze met Jane's. "Are you going to join us for dinner?"

Jane did her best to ignore the leap of her pulse. "Since Mama's busy at the church tonight, I'd be pleased to accept your mother's invitation."

His smile widened. "That's great." He looked over at Martin. "Do you have a bag I can carry out for you?"

"It's by the stairs. I'll get it." He raced off before anyone could move.

Jane reached for her jacket on the coatrack, and immediately Garrett moved to help her. "I must warn you about something." His breath tickled the hair by her ear.

"Oh?" she said, trying to keep the heat from rising in her cheeks.

"I have a surprise for Martin." He gave a sheepish shrug.

"A surprise for me?" Martin appeared, lugging his small suitcase.

"That's right." Garrett grinned, looking like a mischievous boy himself. "It's in the car."

Jane didn't know who was more excited, Garrett or Martin. "Let's say good-bye to my mother first."

Martin rushed into the living room. "Good-bye, Mrs. Mitchell. It was great playing checkers with you. And learning that song on the piano."

Mama smiled at him. "You have fun on the farm and be careful. Mind Mr. and Mrs. Wilder."

"I will."

"Have a good time at the potluck, Mama." Jane bent to kiss her cheek. "I shouldn't be too late."

"Enjoy yourself, dear. And please give my best to Sarah and Ben."

By the time Jane got her purse and made her way outside, Martin was huddled in the back seat of Garrett's car. A large black dog lay on the seat beside him, a bandage wrapped around one back leg.

Jane folded her arms and shot an annoyed look at Garrett on the sidewalk.

Garrett came over and laid a hand on her shoulder, his eyes earnest. "They couldn't find the owner, so I'm taking the dog. At least Martin will know Blackie has a good home."

Jane watched the dog lick Martin's hand and pushed back a wisp of envy. Garrett was giving Martin everything she'd always hoped to—a home, a family, and a pet, even if only on a temporary basis. Was it terrible to wish that she could be the one to provide him with such happiness?

With a sigh, she rounded the car. The only thing that mattered was Martin's well-being. He would enjoy living on the farm, and it would give Jane time to find him the permanent home he deserved.

She needed to focus on that and be grateful for God's small mercies.

———— ❖ ————

Later that night, Garrett stood in the shadows of his parents' porch, observing the kids as they introduced Jett and Blackie. He'd decided to delay the meeting until after dinner, keeping Jett outside while Blackie got accustomed to the house and the new people. Blackie had lain on a blanket in the corner of the kitchen while they ate, and when he seemed perfectly at ease, they decided to see how the two dogs would get on.

In typical Jett fashion, the border collie raced in circles around the injured lab. Blackie laid on the grass, his tongue lolling, watching Kevin and Dale run after Jett. Martin stayed by Blackie's side, his arm draped across the animal's back.

Garrett worried that all the chaos might be too much for the older dog, but Blackie seemed to be taking it all in stride.

Jane came out the screen door and joined him by the railing. "They certainly are having fun."

Her wistful tone made Garrett take a closer look. A definite aura of sadness surrounded her, evident in the downturn of those full lips and the bow of her shoulders.

"He's going to be fine. You're doing the right thing."

She shook her head, her attention still trained on Martin. "Then why does it feel so terrible?"

The urge to comfort her proved too strong, and since they weren't at work, he indulged his impulse to put an arm around her and pull her close. "You're welcome to come and visit him anytime. Mom and Dad would love to have you. They think you're pretty special, in case you haven't noticed."

She gave a quiet sniff. "I like them too."

"For the record," he said, "I think you're pretty special as well."

She looked up at him, her eyes wide and damp.

His gaze fell to her lips, his heart thudding loudly in his chest. Temptation knotted his insides and dampened his palms, but before he could do anything, she suddenly moved away from him.

"I've already said good-bye to your family. I think I'd like to go home now, if you don't mind."

"Of course." Her subtle rejection stung, though it was probably for the best. "Let me get my jacket and keys."

"Okay. I'll go give Martin a hug good-bye."

By the time Garrett came back outside, Jane was already seated in his car, her features stoic.

He walked over to the kids on the lawn. "Hey, boys," he said to his nephews. "I'm going back to the city now. I know you'll do your best to make Martin feel at home."

"Don't worry, Uncle Garrett." Kevin tugged on Jett's collar. "We'll show Martin around the barn and the orchard and tell him where the cookies are kept."

Garrett laughed. "All the important things, I see."

"And we'll make sure Mandy doesn't bug him too much." Dale jumped into Garrett's arms. "She can be a real pest."

Garrett had grown up thinking the same things about his own little sister, but he gave Dale his sternest look. "Mandy just wants to do all the things you do. Remember it's your job to watch out for her." He hugged the boy and set him on the grass. Then he patted Kevin's shoulder and turned to an unusually subdued Martin, who still sat with his arm around Blackie. "Martin, I have to go now, but I'll see you again on Saturday. I'll telephone tomorrow to make sure you're settling in all right."

The boy looked up. "Bye, Mr. Wilder. Thank you for bringing me here. And thank you for bringing Blackie too."

"You're welcome." He patted the boy's head. "Be good. I'll see you soon."

Garrett was still smiling as he drove down the country roads. The sun had long since set over the trees in the distance, and the moon was beginning to rise.

"I think my nephews are going to be good for Martin," he said to a quiet Jane. "Maybe, if we're lucky, he can spend several weeks with them before his new placement begins."

Jane shook her head. "He'll just start feeling comfortable and then he'll have to leave for somewhere new."

What could he say? She was right, but there wasn't anything else they could do at the moment.

They traveled the rest of the way back in silence, broken only by Garrett's attempts to make her laugh with stories about his family. When he finally turned onto her street, he searched for some way to ease her mind or perhaps lift her spirits.

"Was my mother's chicken and dumplings as good as I claimed?" The question sounded silly as soon as it left his lips.

"Of course. It was fabulous." Her mouth twitched in the barest of smiles. "I even asked her for the recipe."

"Now, that might be tricky. Mom doesn't share her family recipes with just anyone."

Her brows rose. "She said she'd give it to me. I didn't even have to twist her arm."

"That's because Mom is a great judge of character. And I must say I have to agree with her."

Scowling, she shook her head. "Well, you're both wrong. In fact, lately I can't seem to do anything right." She bit her bottom lip, her eyes cast down.

Suddenly, the confident woman from the agency, the advocate for abandoned children, had vanished. Instead, all he saw was her vulnerability, her self-doubt. The emotions he'd been holding back all day built up inside and threatened to spill over. How could she not know how amazing she was?

He pulled up to the curb in front of her house. The shadows from the trees overhead gave them privacy, making him bolder. He slid closer toward her. Close enough to inhale her intoxicating scent of lavender soap. "You couldn't be more wrong, Jane. You're smart, beautiful, and compassionate. And brave. So very brave. You're like no other woman I've ever met." He ran a finger down her satiny cheek, feeling the tug of attraction all the way to his toes. "I want to kiss you," he murmured. "I've wanted to for a long time now. But only if you want it too."

Her gaze fell to his mouth, and her lips parted. But she didn't pull away. Not even as he leaned closer.

When she gave a tiny nod, he let out a soft groan and brushed his lips slowly across hers. She tasted darkly mysterious, exotic almost. His heart thumped a wild rhythm as she slid her arms around his neck and kissed him back. He ran his fingers through her hair, knocking loose the pins, letting the chestnut waves fall to her shoulders.

She was so lovely, her skin a porcelain sheet, her eyes so filled with emotion that they glowed. He kissed her again, filled with the sensation that until this moment he'd been sleepwalking through life, and now, with the taste of her lips on his, every sense had awakened with roaring intensity.

At last, he pulled his mouth away and rested his forehead against hers. The windows had fogged up, the air inside the car overly warm. He cranked the window down an inch and allowed the cool night air to enter.

With it, cold reality rushed in as well. What was he thinking? This kiss would change everything and likely not in a good way.

Jane kept her eyes closed, her heart almost beating out of her chest. In the space of a few minutes, Garrett's kiss had transported her from the depths of despair to the heights of pleasure, his lips coaxing a reaction from her that she'd never experienced, not even with her former husband.

The intensity of it shocked her. Frightened her. How could she feel something so strong for someone she'd only known for a matter of weeks?

"Garrett." She let out a breath. "I . . . I'm not sure this is a good idea."

He gave a barely perceptible nod. "I know." He sighed. "I should have resisted, but tonight I just couldn't."

She looked into his eyes, gratitude and regret warring within her. "You'll never know how much your words meant to me. I've been struggling to do everything on my own for so long. . . ." She swallowed hard. "It's nice to know someone else is on my side for once."

"I'll always be on your side." He cupped his palm against her cheek. "But you're right. This probably wasn't wise. Not now, anyway, while we have to work together."

She gave a soft sigh. "I agree."

A slow grin crept across his face. "I did succeed in doing one thing, though. I made you forget about your problems for a bit."

She chuckled. "I suppose you did."

"Do you want me to come in with you? Make sure your mother's all right?"

"That's sweet of you. But I'll be fine." She ran a hand over her head, gasping. Where had all her hairpins gone?

"Sorry." He tugged gently on a loose strand. "That was my fault."

"Mama can't see me in this state, or she'll know I've been up to something." She grabbed a few pins from her lap and shoved them back in place.

"Like kissing a man in his car?"

She stopped and stared at him. "Are you teasing me?"

"Yes, but only because you're such fun to tease." He gave her a flirtatious wink.

A legion of butterflies unfurled in her belly. What was happening to her? She was always so sensible. So practical. She never crossed boundaries with co-workers. She certainly didn't swoon over handsome men or lose herself in passionate kisses.

Garrett reached over to tip up her chin. "Relax, Jane. Everything's fine. And please don't worry about Martin. It will all work out. You'll see."

"Are you always such an optimist?"

"Most of the time." He grew serious. "Are you sure you're all right?"

She nodded. "I'll see you tomorrow."

Gathering her wits about her as much as possible, she opened the car door and got out. Her legs wobbled slightly as she climbed the stairs, but she held her spine erect. She couldn't let him see how he'd turned her senses upside down.

Once she unlocked the door, she turned and gave a casual wave, then stepped in and shut the door with a sharp click.

How in the world was she supposed to forget about that kiss and carry on the next day as though nothing had happened between them?

21

The next morning, Jane sat in the passenger side of Garrett's car on the way to interview the Jefferson family, glad that despite their moment of intimacy the previous evening, they had managed to resume their working relationship.

Her relief, however, was soon replaced with the discomfort she'd hoped to avoid.

"How was the rest of your evening yesterday after I left?" A slight twinkle gleamed in his eye.

"Fine, thank you." She trained her gaze ahead so he wouldn't see that it hadn't been fine at all. That she couldn't sleep for reliving their kisses and for missing Martin terribly. The boy had only been with her for a few days, yet his presence in her home had felt so right.

He peered over at her. "I hoped you wouldn't feel awkward, but so far today you haven't even looked me in the eye."

She shrugged. "As we agreed, I think it's best we forget all about last night." Her cheeks grew warm just thinking about it.

Silence filled the car for a moment until he let out a breath. "Very well. We won't discuss it again."

Thankfully, they were approaching the Jeffersons' residence. "The house should be up ahead on the right," Jane said.

Today they would meet with the Jeffersons and the Black-woods, and she prayed one of them would be a suitable foster family for Martin.

Or more than suitable. Perfect, even.

He deserved a perfect match.

Garrett pulled into a driveway that wound around to a large brick house, and he shot her a sideways look. "Try not to worry. If these people don't work out, another family will."

Jane frowned. Easy for him to say. He hadn't been Martin's caseworker for the past six years.

"And maybe try smiling." Garrett's lips twitched as he parked the car. "We don't want to scare the nice people off."

She held back a sarcastic retort and plastered an exaggerated smile on her face. "Better?"

He grimaced. "A little scary, actually. Maybe tone it down a bit."

She tried to scowl at him but couldn't help chuckling. "Point taken. Let's go."

The Jeffersons were as nice a couple as she remembered from their initial interview several years ago. Mr. Jefferson had been teaching for over twenty years and Mrs. Jefferson was a housewife who loved caring for foster children. Their home was stylish but cozy, having been handed down from Mr. Jefferson's parents. With five bedrooms and a large backyard, there was plenty of space for several children.

"Why have you never adopted any of the foster children you've had?" Jane asked after Mrs. Jefferson served them tea.

Mrs. Jefferson set the pot on a tray. "We did consider adoption earlier on. In fact, one time we came very close, but the mother changed her mind after we'd had the little girl for ten months. I never got over that loss. It took me a few years before I could consider being a foster parent again." She smiled. "Then my husband and I realized we could help a lot more children if we didn't adopt."

"I see." Jane put her cup down. "And you've never been tempted to adopt an older child? One who was in no danger of being taken away?"

A slight frown appeared. "Not really, no."

Jane bit her lip and made a notation on her pad.

"I take it you're looking for a permanent home for this child," Mr. Jefferson said.

"Yes. Martin is a special case. In addition to having a medical condition, he suffers from abandonment and rejection issues, which I feel would be helped by a family who could give Martin undivided attention and love."

"What is the medical condition?" Mr. Jefferson gave her a curious look.

"Epileptic seizures. Which can be very frightening for someone witnessing it for the first time."

"I've had several students with epilepsy. I'm familiar with how to handle a seizure. And I could train my wife what to do."

"That's encouraging to hear." Garrett, who had been unusually silent for most of the interview, now spoke up. "Who knows? Perhaps Martin will win you over, and you'll change your mind."

"I wouldn't count on it," Mr. Jefferson said.

Mrs. Jefferson put a hand on her husband's arm. "That's not to say we wouldn't be willing to have him here for a long time."

"Just no adoption."

"That's right," the man replied. "We prefer no permanent legal entanglements. It's better to see the child through school and send them off on their way to adulthood. Then we're free to start over with another child in need."

Jane laid her pen down. "Martin has been shuffled around many times in his eight years. He tends to act out either for attention or as a test to see if the parents will send him back. We would need assurance that you wouldn't give up on Martin at the first sign of trouble."

"I'm used to dealing with all types of children, Mrs. Linder," Mr. Jefferson said calmly. "I'm certain Martin wouldn't be a problem."

Jane did her best to hide her disappointment. Other than their unwillingness to adopt, the Jeffersons seemed a perfect fit. "Well, then. Thank you both for your time." Jane rose and extended her hand. "We'll be in touch as soon as we make our decision."

———❖———

"What did you think?" Jane asked Garrett as they made their way to the Blackwoods' residence.

"Overall, they're a lovely couple. I admire their dedication to helping as many children as they can." He did his best to go over in his head what he'd learned about the Jeffersons so he'd remember it for his more detailed notes later.

"Yes, but would they be a good fit for Martin? That's what we need to determine."

"I reserve the right to withhold judgment until I've met the next couple."

"Fair enough." Her lips pulled up in a slight smile. "That's the house. Number fifty-three." She pointed at a semidetached house with a pristine front lawn and a tidy flower bed under the front window.

"The Blackwoods are going to be very different from the Jeffersons," she cautioned as he parked the car out in front. "They're younger, which means they could possibly be more naïve and idealistic."

"Understood. Lead the way."

During the interview that followed, Garrett observed the skilled manner Jane used to draw information out of the younger couple with her intelligent questions. In their early thirties, Debra and Larry Blackwood had not been blessed with children and had decided that while waiting for that possibility, they would apply to be foster parents to children who needed them. They were open to the idea of adoption; however, they made no secret of the fact that they wanted an infant.

They were saying all the right things, their eagerness and enthusiasm shining throughout the interview. Other than their desire to adopt a newborn, Garrett felt they might indeed be the best option. This couple at least entertained the idea of adoption, whereas the Jeffersons did not.

"Clearly the Blackwoods are too big a risk for Martin," Jane said the moment they were in the car.

"How so? They seem the better match to me."

"Did you see their reaction when I mentioned Martin's medical condition? They looked very nervous."

He frowned. "I didn't see that. I saw two committed people who were willing to take a chance on a difficult child."

"Which is admirable. But they just don't have the experience necessary to handle Martin. You've seen how demanding he can be."

"I have. And I still think the Blackwoods are the better option."

Jane shook her head. "I guess we'll have to agree to disagree on this."

He glanced over at her frowning profile. "Look, there's no need to be hasty. Let's write down our impressions when we get back to the office, along with a list of pros and cons, then give ourselves a little time to digest all we've seen and heard."

"All right." Her shoulders slumped forward.

He hated the defeat in her demeanor, how lately the odds seemed to be stacked against her—her mother's fragile health, the bad news about Brandon, Martin's rejection from his foster family and expulsion from the shelter. All that in addition to the other problems at the agency had notably increased the stress she was under.

Garrett wished he could agree with her choice of the Jeffersons, but it would be unprofessional to concede simply to cheer her up.

"I could use a bite to eat," he said moments later. "Why don't we stop at a diner before we head back? Think of it as a working lunch."

"I don't know." She looked at her watch. "I have a lot of work to get through this afternoon. I should get back."

"You have to eat. We'll be quick, I promise."

"All right," she said reluctantly. "I am a little hungry, and I forgot to pack a sandwich today."

Twenty minutes later, they were seated in a small diner with their food in front of them. The restaurant was almost empty since it was past the usual lunch hour.

"Martin is certainly enjoying his time with my parents," Garrett said as he bit into his sandwich. "He loves the farm and the animals."

"His first night went well, I hope?"

"He did have an argument with Dale and Kevin, but Mom made them sit at the kitchen table until they achieved a truce." He chuckled. "But Mom has lost the battle on not allowing dogs in the bedrooms. Blackie will be bunking in with Martin."

Jane sipped her water. "I'm glad, in a way. I think the unconditional love of an animal is good for him. Yet I worry how leaving the dog will affect him." She blinked rapidly several times. The soup she'd ordered remained untouched. "Do you think . . ." She hesitated, then lifted hopeful eyes to his. "Do you think your parents would ever consider adopting him?"

His hand stilled on his glass of iced tea. In no way had he expected that question.

"I doubt it," he said gently. "It's a big commitment for people my parents' age. Especially now that they've taken in my sister and her kids."

"I know." Jane's features crumpled.

"Hey, don't give up yet." He clasped her hand in his. "We'll find the right home for him. I've made it my mission to see that it happens."

"I made it my mission years ago, and I'm still searching." Her lids fluttered closed, and she dabbed a napkin to her lashes.

At that moment, he wished he could adopt the boy himself, if only to ease her burden and see the relieved gratitude in her eyes. He squeezed her fingers. "Really, Jane, we'll do everything we can."

"You feel as strongly about this as I do, don't you?" she asked softly.

He felt strongly all right—and not just about Martin. But he couldn't admit that, not with the director's job standing between them, among other things.

"I do. Martin has captured my heart as completely as he's captured yours."

"That's the best news I could hear." Her lips trembled as she leaned across the small table. "Now I can trust you'll do what's best for him."

It took every bit of self-control not to kiss her. But he couldn't repeat the same mistake twice. So, he released her hand and sank farther back on his seat.

"Speaking of Martin," Garrett said, "he's very excited about Thanksgiving next weekend. I guess he's never had a true family celebration before." He smiled and shook his head. "He's been hounding my mother about helping her bake the pumpkin pies."

"I'm glad he'll get to experience Thanksgiving on the farm. I'm sure it will be special." Jane lifted a spoon of soup to her lips.

"What are your plans for the holiday?"

A hint of dejection returned to her features. "Nothing too grand. I'll roast a small chicken and make a pie. Apple is Mama's favorite."

"Just the two of you?"

She nodded. "It's been just us since Brandon enlisted."

"You and your mother should join us at the farm," he blurted out before his brain had fully processed the idea. "We'll have more than enough food, and my parents would love to have you both."

She frowned. "You don't know that."

"Yes, I do. Mom is always inviting extra people. She hates to think of anyone spending the holiday alone. And she adores you and Hildie."

Her gaze flicked to his and then away. "I-I'll talk to Mama about it and get back to you."

"Fair enough. But I really hope you'll come."

And he did. No matter how hard it would be to keep his feelings in check.

22

*W*hy did I ever agree to this?

Jane gripped the car's armrest as her mother's laughter drifted to the back seat of Garrett's Ford. She must have been overcome with temporary insanity. A full day with Garrett and his family could prove more than her resistance was capable of withstanding.

"Are you flirting with me, young man?" Mama's cheery tone was almost unrecognizable.

"I can't help myself when I'm around a beautiful woman."

At his teasing tone, Mama's laugh became a girlish giggle.

The knots of tension in Jane's neck loosened at the sound. If Garrett's silliness distracted Mama from missing Brandon and kept her from thinking they might never share a Thanksgiving with him again, then it would be worth the trip. Besides, Jane would get to share the holiday with Martin.

The only real drawback would be spending so much time around Garrett in a such a personal setting. Her unrelenting attraction to him was proving most annoying. Hopefully with so many people around, she would find it easy to keep her distance.

Sarah welcomed them into her kitchen, wearing an enthusiastic smile and a blue apron with huge sunflowers. "Hildie, Jane. So wonderful to see you again." She came forward and gave them both hugs.

The kitchen smelled of turkey, onion, and celery, with a hint of pumpkin.

Jane handed her a covered pan. "I brought some candied yams. I would have brought pie, but Garrett assured me you would have more than enough of those."

Sarah laughed out loud. "Yes, indeed. But I will gratefully add this to our table."

"Where's Dad?" Garrett set his offering of bakery rolls on the kitchen counter.

Cassie walked in, carrying Mandy on her hip. "He's with the boys outside. Kevin is teaching Martin how to play football."

Jane smiled. October was such a nice time of year for Thanksgiving, since the weather was often nice enough to spend time outdoors, and the leaves were usually at their peak of color.

"They won't let me play, Unca Garrett." Mandy's lower lip jutted out.

"That's my cue." Garrett laughed as he swept the girl from her mother's grip. "Let's go, sweetie. If they won't let you play, we'll start our own game."

A smile broke free, and the little girl's brow cleared. "Or we could have a tea party."

Garrett stared at her in mock horror. "And ruin our appetite for turkey? Never."

Mandy chortled, her pigtails bobbing.

"I'll leave you ladies to your work." Garrett gave his mother a kiss and disappeared out the back door.

Jane dragged her attention from Garrett back to the kitchen. "She certainly is a charmer, isn't she?"

Cassie snorted. "That's one way to put it." She opened the icebox and took out a covered bowl. "It's good to see you two again. I'm glad you could join us."

Sarah steered Mama over to the table. "Have a seat, Hildie. The craziness is about to begin."

"What can I do to help?" Jane stood somewhat awkwardly in

the middle of the room. It seemed every space on the counter and kitchen table was filled with bowls and chopping boards.

"How are you at mashing potatoes?"

"I'm a pro."

"Terrific." Sarah handed her a masher. "Cassie will drain them, and then you can take over. Excuse me while I stir the gravy."

They worked in unison with Sarah providing cheerful banter. In no time at all, she called in the men and children to wash up, and everyone gathered around the long dining room table.

Jane found herself seated between Garrett and Martin. Across from her, Cassie settled Mandy into her chair, giving Dale a glare as he stole a slurp of milk. Mama sat near Sarah's end of the table, across from Kevin, who was making faces at Martin.

Ben took his place at the head and proceeded to carve the impressive bird. A host of delicious smells wafted around as they passed the steaming bowls and platters. Once their plates had been filled, Ben held out both hands. "Shall we say grace?"

Garrett instantly took his father's hand, then extended his other to Jane.

With a tentative smile, she placed her hand in his, attempting to ignore the way nerves fluttered in her stomach. She reached for Martin's hand on her other side and motioned for him to bow his head.

Ben closed his eyes and began. "Heavenly Father, we thank you for this day, for the family and friends we have gathered here with us. We thank you for the bounty of food you have provided and the rich harvest of crops we've had this year. We ask that you watch over the soldiers fighting in this war. In particular, we ask your protection for Jack and for Brandon. Keep them safe and bring them back to us, Lord."

The slight pressure from Garrett's fingers filled Jane with emotion. Tears pushed at her lids, but she squeezed her eyes tight, refusing to let them fall.

"Thank you," Ben continued, "for Garrett's healing from his

injuries and for allowing him to return to us. Bless the leaders across the globe. Guide their decisions toward bringing an end to this war and bringing peace to our world. We give you praise and thanks for our many blessings. Amen."

Slowly Jane opened her eyes as Garrett released her hand. She glanced at her mother, who was dabbing a napkin to her eyes.

"That was beautiful, Ben," Mama said. "Thank you for including my boy. He's been on my mind all day."

Ben nodded. "Sarah told me about Brandon's situation. He's been in our daily prayers ever since. I remember when we were notified that Garrett had been injured. We had no idea how serious his condition was, or if we'd ever see him again." His throat muscles worked up and down. "Our prayers were answered, and our son came back to us. I pray yours will too."

Sarah gave a loud sniff. "Enough of such maudlin talk. Let's start eating before the food gets cold."

From then on, the meal passed in wonderful camaraderie. Jane found Ben and Sarah's relationship so heartwarming. Their obvious affection for each other, as well as for their children and grandchildren, filled the room with an aura of love.

After Jane finished a slice of the best pumpkin pie she'd ever tasted, she pushed back her chair with a sigh. "That was delicious, although I think my stomach is protesting the amount of food I ate." She picked up her plate as well as Martin's. "Sarah, please let me do the dishes. I need to burn off this meal somehow."

"Great idea." Garrett jumped into action beside her, gathering the other dessert plates. "Mom, you and Cassie go and relax with Dad, Hildie, and the kids. Jane and I will handle the cleanup."

Sarah just blinked. "Well, if you insist."

"We do," Jane said firmly. "Keeping Mama company would be a big favor." She winked at her mother.

"That will be no hardship at all." Sarah laughed as she passed Jane her plate.

"I wish I had the strength of my youth," Mama said. "Sometimes I feel downright useless."

"Nonsense." Sarah helped Mama from her chair. "At our age, we deserve to let the younger ones do their share."

Jane carried the dishes through the swinging door into the kitchen and began to fill the sink with hot water and soap. She looked around, noting that Sarah and Cassie had already tidied up a good part of the kitchen as they'd cooked. Some of the bigger pots sat drying upside down on the dish rack.

Garrett entered and placed his stack of dishes on the counter.

Jane's pulse began to dance through her system. Being alone in the kitchen with Garrett was probably not the best idea. Standing here, close enough to feel the warmth of his arm as they worked side by side, did nothing to lessen the attraction she felt for him. Best to focus on the job at hand as much as possible. She lowered as many dishes into the water as she could and searched for a dishrag.

"We use a sponge. It's right here." Garrett reached over her shoulder, his arm brushing hers. He grabbed the yellow sponge and tossed it in the water, causing a few suds to splash out.

His warm chuckle vibrated down her neck.

She pinned him with a mock glare. "If you're going to help, you'd better behave yourself."

"You're no fun." He grinned at her.

"How old are you? Twelve?" She huffed, but she had to force her lips not to twitch as she scrubbed the plates and set them in the tub of rinse water.

Garrett reached in and extracted a dish to dry. "Everything is more enjoyable when you add a little fun. You should try it sometime."

She shot him a look. "Maybe I will when I'm not in someone else's kitchen."

They worked in harmonious silence for several minutes. Jane added a second load to the water and glanced over at Garrett. He'd rolled his shirtsleeves up past his elbows, and his well-sculpted arms strained against the material as he reached into the cupboard above to put away the dried dishes.

"You're lucky, you know," she said quietly, "to have such an amazing family." She scoured one of the casserole dishes, exceedingly aware of his attention on her. "This was the type of Thanksgiving I've always dreamed of—a big noisy family, laughing and teasing each other." She paused to steady her voice. "Thank you for sharing them with us today." She dared to glance over at him.

His intense blue eyes were trained on her, filled with some emotion she couldn't quite define. "You're welcome." He reached over to push a lock of hair behind her ear, his fingers lingering on her jaw with a mere whisper of a touch.

A parade of goosebumps traveled down her arms. As he moved a step closer, the breath tangled in her lungs. Would he kiss her again? Her lips parted almost of their own volition as she stared into his eyes. Memories of their last embrace burned brightly in her mind, scrambling her pulse.

"Need any help in here?" The door swung open and Cassie stopped short. "Oh, sorry." She grinned mischievously. "I'll come back later."

Warmth blasted up Jane's neck to her ears. Good grief. Where was her self-control when she needed it?

Garrett resisted the urge to groan out loud. He'd almost broken his vow not to act on his feelings for Jane. That he would keep their relationship strictly friendly . . . and nothing more.

Something about the lure of this woman wore down his defenses faster than hot butter on mashed potatoes. He seemed to lose all sense of reason around her, yet he couldn't make himself stay away.

Jane moved to the kitchen table, where she began to scour the surface with frantic strokes of the sponge. "I can't imagine what Cassie must think of me. Does your family even know I'm divorced?"

"They do. I hope you don't mind that I told them."

She kept scrubbing the already-clean table.

"I'm sorry," he said quietly. "I promised myself I wouldn't kiss you again, but I got carried away. Something that happens far too often around you."

Her head flew up, her mouth falling open.

"You're just too appealing to resist." He waggled his brows at her, hoping for a laugh or at least a smile.

Instead, her nostrils flared, annoyance blooming in her eyes. "If I was so appealing, my husband wouldn't have traded me in for another wife." She lowered her head and continued her attack on the table.

Garrett studied her. Was she mad at him or embarrassed at being caught in a compromising position by his sister?

He laid a hand over hers to still her fingers, then gently removed the sponge from her grip. "Donald was a fool."

She stood still, her hands trembling.

Garrett took a step back. Perhaps they could both use a change of scenery. "Why don't we get some air? You can help me feed the animals." When she hesitated, he added, "We could take the kids along as chaperones."

A huge breath rushed out of her. "That's a good idea."

"Great. Meet me at the front door in five minutes."

While Jane finished wiping down the other surfaces in the kitchen, Garrett rounded up the kids, avoiding Cassie's smug gaze. "Put on your jackets," he told them. "It's cool outside now."

"Can I feed the goats, Mr. Wilder?" Martin's voice rose over the crackle of the parlor radio. "Mr. Ben lets me do it sometimes."

Garrett shared an amused glance with his father, then laid a hand on Martin's shoulder. "Sure. As long as you take turns with the others. Mandy loves feeding the baby goats too, don't you, princess?"

The girl bobbed her head up and down. "Petunia is my favorite. But you can feed Ramsey. He bites."

Martin only scoffed. "I already figured out how to get my fingers out of the way in time."

Kevin, Dale, and Martin raced out the front door. Cassie finished buttoning Mandy's coat just as Jane appeared. An immediate flush colored Jane's cheeks. She ducked her head, pulled her coat from the hook, and they all stepped out onto the front porch. Mandy immediately sped across the lawn after the boys.

Cassie put a hand on Jane's arm. "You're smart to bring the kids along. Hopefully it will force my brother to behave himself." With a light laugh, she gave Jane a one-armed hug.

The tension in Jane's expression eased. "I'm not sure that's possible."

Cassie laughed again. "And don't worry about your mother. She's having a wonderful time. She even seems enthralled by Dad's farm stories."

Garrett snorted. "Hildie's being polite. No one could be enthralled by those." Dad was notorious for his long-winded tales about the crops and the animals, not realizing that some people weren't as interested in such topics.

"Oh, no. Mama loves hearing about farms. It reminds her of her childhood." Jane smiled at Cassie. "It means so much that Mama is having a nice Thanksgiving."

"We're happy to have her."

Garrett's gaze swung between the two women. If he didn't do something, Cassie would stay here talking all night.

"See you later, sis." Garrett took Jane's hand and led her down the steps, relishing the feel of her hand in his, not even caring what his sister might think.

They strolled across the lawn to the barn. The kids were already in the far pen with the goats.

Garrett led Jane to the stalls where the two horses were housed. "You remember Elias and Elliott from the hayride?"

"Not really."

"These two are the workhorses. They do everything from plough-ing the fields to pulling the wagons. They're very gentle." He grabbed the pitchfork to loosen some hay from the bale and topped up the horses' troughs, then made sure they had enough clean water.

Jane leaned against one of the posts, watching him work. She seemed a little nervous about getting too close to them. Or maybe she was afraid of getting too close to him.

"Does your back give you much pain?" A hint of concern laced her words.

Garrett set the empty pail on the ground. Dad's mention of his healing had probably reminded her of his injury. "It's intermit-tent. Most times it's bearable." A measure of guilt wound through him. Given how close they'd become, it felt dishonest to withhold the truth about his condition.

He wiped the dust from his hands and looked her in the eye. "The worst part about my injury isn't the residual pain." He in-haled slowly. His next words could change everything between them. "It's the shrapnel that's lodged near my spine."

She frowned, tiny ridges forming above her brows. "That doesn't sound good."

He brushed a few pieces of hay from his sleeve. "It's not. Un-fortunately, it's also . . . dangerous." A film of perspiration formed on his forehead. He'd only ever told Cassie and his parents the full extent of his injuries.

"Dangerous?" The glow from the nearby lantern reflected twin golden spheres in her wide eyes. "How so?"

Children's giggles drifted over to them, accompanied by the bleats of the goats. It seemed wrong to be discussing something so serious on what was supposed to be a day of thanksgiving. But now that he'd started, he might as well continue.

"It's possible that the shrapnel could shift and . . . damage my spine." He moved over to pat Elliott's long snout so Jane wouldn't read the true gravity of the situation on his face.

"That's why you have to be so careful," she said. "To keep from jarring it."

He nodded.

"What would happen if it did move?" Her voice wasn't much above a whisper, yet he sensed the fear in her words.

Trust Jane to ask the one question he'd hoped to avoid.

"Garrett?" She reached over to still his hand on the horse's nose.

With a sigh, he turned around. "It could cause paralysis."

Her mouth fell open. "Isn't there anything they can do? An operation or something?"

"Afraid not. Not one worth the risk in my doctor's mind." An opinion Garrett happened to agree with. "No more bronco riding for me, I guess." He forced out a laugh, hoping she'd take his cue and lighten the mood.

Instead, she wrapped her arms around his waist and laid her head against his chest. "Oh, Garrett. I'm so sorry."

He closed his eyes, his arms automatically encircling her, drinking in her comfort. She had to be able to hear the erratic beat of his heart beneath her ear, feel the catch of his breath in his lungs. When would the reality hit her that he was damaged goods? He should never have kissed her, never dragged her into his orbit when he knew it was futile.

Before he got too comfortable in her embrace, he gently set her away from him, distressed to see moisture glittering in her eyes. "Hey, it's not that bad. I'm alive and able to lead a relatively normal life. It could have been a lot worse." He thumbed a tear from her lashes. "Let's go see what the kids are doing to those poor animals."

Anything to bring a smile back to her face. And if baby goats couldn't do that, nothing could.

23

J ane did her best to enjoy the antics of the children as they fed the goats, yet her mind whirled with all that Garrett had told her. How did he live with such uncertainty, knowing that one slip of the metal inside him could relegate him to a wheelchair for the rest of his life?

"Time to head back," Garrett finally announced.

A flurry of activity ensued as the children bid the animals good-night. The boys raced each other back to the house while Garrett carried Mandy.

If they'd been alone, Jane might have been tempted to take his hand. Show him that he could lean on her for support. She suspected he'd trusted her with information that not many people were privy to.

Cassie met them on the porch. "Jane, I don't want to worry you, but your mother took a bit of a bad turn, and now she seems to have fallen asleep."

Alarm burst through Jane's system. Why had she left her mother for so long? She sprinted inside the house and straight into the living room. Her mother was lying on the couch, her eyes closed, a blanket over her. "Mama?" *Oh please, Lord, no. Not when we're so far away from a hospital.*

Seated on a chair near her, Sarah got to her feet. "She's all right,

194

Jane. She had a bit of a dizzy spell and became a little fatigued, so I suggested she lie down."

"Thank you. That was smart." Jane took her mother's hand and felt for the pulse at her wrist. It was weak but not as bad as it could be. Yet Mama's breathing was shallow, a sign that she wasn't getting enough oxygen. Jane pulled the blanket up a little higher, worry spiking through her. With her mother in this state, the long car ride home would be too much for her. Why hadn't Jane thought of that and insisted on leaving earlier?

Because I was too preoccupied with Garrett, that's why.

Sarah laid a hand on her shoulder. "Why don't you both stay the night? We have plenty of room. That way Hildie can get a good sleep, and you can leave in the morning."

"Mom's right." Garrett came into the room.

"I don't know. . . ." Jane hated to put the Wilders to any trouble. Hated to be an imposition. But what option did she really have?

"Cassie's already offered to bunk in with the kids. You and your mother can take her room." Garrett's whole demeanor exuded steady calmness.

Jane's gaze darted to the hallway. "Mama can't climb the stairs."

"It's no problem. I'll carry her up." Garrett kept his attention on Jane, poised to act.

As soon as she gave a reluctant nod, Garrett moved across the room to gently lift Mama into his arms as though she weighed nothing. She barely stirred, which was both a good sign and a bad one.

Jane trailed behind as he carried Mama up the main staircase to one of the bedrooms. He waited inside the door while Jane pulled back the quilt on one of the twin beds, then he set Mama down with great care.

Jane swiftly removed her mother's shoes and settled the blankets over her. Only the faint rise and fall of Mama's chest gave Jane any comfort. She straightened and looked over at Garrett.

"Thank you. I know it's still early, but I'll just sit with her for a while to make sure she's all right."

"Sure." He pulled a ladder-back chair from the corner and placed it by the bed. "Let me know if you need anything else. I'll be out helping my dad with a few evening chores, but it won't take long." He stopped by the door. "My room's right across the hall. If you think Hildie needs a doctor, I want you to wake me up, no matter what time it is."

Her throat tightened. "That's very generous of you. I'm sorry to be such a bother."

"You're no bother, Jane. You don't have to handle this alone."

She pressed her lips together, desperate to shove all her unwanted emotions down deep where they belonged. With a quick nod, she took a seat on the chair to keep watch.

Half an hour later, when Jane was assured her mother was sleeping peacefully and that her breathing had returned to normal, she made her way to the kitchen. She would take up a glass of water for Mama, who often woke in the night with a dry mouth.

A small lamp glowed on the counter, but the room appeared deserted. Grateful that she knew where the glasses were kept after watching Garrett put them away, she opened the appropriate cupboard and took out the smallest glass.

"How's Hildie doing?" Sarah's soft voice came from the kitchen table.

Jane looked over in surprise. "Sarah, I didn't see you there. Mama's sleeping comfortably. Thank you again for suggesting we stay. I think it's best for her."

"No trouble at all. Will you join me for a cup of chamomile tea? The kettle should still be hot."

"Thanks, but no." She pulled out a chair. "I'll sit with you for a few minutes, though, if that's all right."

"Sure. I'd love the company."

Jane sat down with a sigh. It had been a long day, but she had something she wanted to discuss with Sarah. "I hoped to have a chance to talk to you about Martin." She scanned the kitchen and the area in the hall to make sure he wasn't around.

"Don't worry. The kids are upstairs with Cassie. What do you want to know?"

"How is he fitting in? Is he behaving?"

"Ever since we established a few ground rules, he's been fine." Tiny lines crinkled around Sarah's eyes. "It certainly helps that being outdoors so much uses up a lot of energy."

"What about schooling?"

"He goes with the kids. Since he's in the same grade as Kevin, he seems keen to go. And so far we haven't had any negative feedback from the teacher."

Jane let out a breath. "That's good news. He certainly seems happier than I've seen him in a long time."

Sarah set her cup down. "He's important to you, isn't he?"

"He is. I've been his caseworker since he was two years old. I can't help feeling I've failed him." She swallowed hard.

Sarah's hand covered hers. "From what Garrett's told me, you've been trying your best."

"Somehow it doesn't seem enough."

They sat in silence for a few seconds until Jane got the nerve to broach the question that had been on her mind for a while. "Sarah, is there any chance you and Ben might consider adopting him permanently?" Even though she'd already asked Garrett, Jane needed to hear the answer from his mother herself.

Sarah gave her a sympathetic look and sighed. "If circumstances were different, I'd say yes without hesitation. But right now, with Cassie and the kids here and with the farm in such a precarious financial state, I know Ben will say it's not feasible to take on the responsibility of raising another child." She shook her head. "Not that I wouldn't love to give him the home he deserves."

The air in Jane's lungs seemed to leak away, leaving her hollow inside. She blinked to clear her vision. "I understand."

"Maybe if Garrett gets the director's job, things might change."

Jane frowned. "What does that have to do with the farm?"

"I thought he'd have told you." Sarah's fair brows rose. "Garrett sends whatever money he can home to us, keeping only enough for his room and board in Toronto. If he gets this job, it will mean a raise and a secure income, as opposed to the sporadic jobs he's had since he got home from the war."

Jane sank back on her chair. She'd never realized one of the main reasons Garrett wanted the director's position was to be able to give his family more financial help—help they clearly needed.

"This job opportunity seems heaven-sent for several reasons," Sarah continued. "Garrett has a true spirit for helping children, and this job would allow him to do that. But mainly it's a good fit because he can't do the heavy farmwork anymore, which is a struggle for him. All he ever wanted to do was work in partnership with Ben."

"Garrett told me about the shrapnel," Jane said quietly. "I can't imagine how hard it is to live with that."

Sarah nodded. "I want him to see a specialist to determine if anything can be done, but there's a long waiting list." She looked up. "The piece by his spine is bad enough, but it's the one near his heart that worries me the most."

"Near his heart?" A cold pit opened in Jane's stomach.

"Mother." The harsh voice came from the doorway. Garrett stood glaring at Sarah, sweat glistening on his forehead.

"I'm sorry, Garrett. I thought . . . Jane said you told her about the shrapnel." The anguish on Sarah's face squeezed a fresh wave of anxiety through Jane.

She rose and went to face Garrett. "Why didn't you tell me the whole story?"

He stalked over to the icebox, grabbed out a pitcher of lemonade, and poured himself a glass. Then, without answering, he drained it.

Sarah gave Garrett an apologetic glance and stood up. "I'll leave you two to talk. Sleep well, Jane. I'll see you in the morning."

With Sarah's departure, a strained silence fell over the room. Jane leaned against the wall, waiting to see how Garrett would respond. She tried to see it from his perspective. Maybe he'd planned to reveal the news a bit at a time, to soften the blow, so to speak.

He stood at the counter, his hands clenched into fists. At last, he expelled a loud breath and turned to face her. "I know I should have told you about both pieces of shrapnel. But it's hard enough to admit I could be dealing with paralysis. Facing death is a whole new level of gravity." He shook his head. "And I hate being the object of people's pity."

A band of sorrow tightened around her chest. "I don't pity you, Garrett. I have sympathy for you. That's very different."

"It doesn't feel different." He raked a hand through his hair. "This . . . condition has made me feel useless, feeble, not in control of my life. I thought I'd made peace with it all, knowing how lucky I was to still be alive. I'd resigned myself to living a life alone, hopefully in the service of others, so that, in some small way, my life would have meaning." He raised haggard eyes to hers. "And then I met you."

Her lungs ceased working as he took a step toward her. She should leave, flee from the explosion of feelings rioting through her. But her feet remained rooted to the wooden floorboards.

"My heart," he continued, still staring at her, "the one I'd safely cordoned off for my own good, began to beat a new, exciting tempo, one I couldn't ignore. For the first time since I returned from the war, I railed against God for leaving me in this condition, because you make me want to live fully again."

He moved closer. Close enough that she could feel the heat radiating from his body. He raised a hand to her cheek. Searching her face, he seemed to wait for her to move away. But she remained transfixed by the longing in his eyes, torn by her own yearning for him. Yet, there were things she needed to say as well.

"I know all about feeling useless," she whispered. "After two miscarriages and being told I couldn't carry a baby to term, followed by my husband leaving me, I felt broken inside. Painfully aware that no man would want a divorced woman, especially one incapable of having children. I thought I'd lost my one chance at happiness and resigned myself to being alone for the rest of my life."

He studied her in silence for several seconds, his expression dark. "Is that why Donald left you?"

She nodded. "The second miscarriage happened when my pregnancy was further along. Losing our son was devastating for both of us. Donald couldn't accept the doctor's prognosis that I wouldn't be able to give him a child, and he refused to consider adoption." A hard breath shuddered out of her. "When he left me, I felt unwanted. Worthless. Nothing more than damaged goods."

A growl rumbled up from his chest. "You're not damaged, Jane. You're beautiful, inside and out. Any man would be lucky to have you."

With that, he leaned forward and slowly brought his mouth to hers. His insistent lips coaxed a response from her until she could no longer resist him. With a small cry, she wrapped her arms around him and kissed him back. He pulled her closer, and the combined sound of their heartbeats echoed in her head. Tremors of electricity traveled the length of her body, igniting every nerve ending within her. She buried her face in his neck, relishing the scent of soap and hay, as the truth became evident. Her feelings for this man were too strong to ignore. Too thrilling to turn away from. If he felt the same, despite all he knew about her, who was she to reject him?

———— ❧ ————

Garrett pressed his face into the softness of Jane's thick hair. His heart swelled with a rush of such fierce love that he wasn't sure how to contain it. Yet all the while his head screamed at him. *You're being selfish. What type of life can you offer her?*

On a loud exhale, he moved away from her. "You deserve so much more than a man who could end up paralyzed, or worse yet, die without warning."

A shudder went through her. "And you deserve a woman who can give you the children I know you'd love."

He leaned his forehead against hers. "So, what do we do now?"

"I-I'm not sure."

"It won't be easy, but I'll back away from you, if that's what you want, Jane. I mean it this time."

"To be honest, I don't know what I want. My head and my heart are saying two different things." She sighed. "And there's still the issue of the director's job standing between us."

His immediate thought was to take himself out of the running. However, even if he did, there was no guarantee the board would give Jane the position.

"Why don't we take some time to think about it?" He managed to force his lips into a smile. "Pray about it. Discern what God has in store for us."

A flood of relief washed over her features. "That sounds sensible. In the meantime, we'll remain strictly professional at work. Agreed?"

His chest tightened. Why did this sound as if she was already regretting his declaration? But she made a valid point. The last thing either of them needed, especially Jane, was any whisper of impropriety in the workplace. Neither of them would get the job then. "Agreed."

"Well, I should get back to Mama and make sure she's still sleeping."

"Of course." He tried to ignore the pang of disappointment that twisted inside him at the thought of not being around her, even for just a short time.

"Before I go, would you do something for me?" She looked up at him, raw uncertainty on her face.

"Sure. Name it. Whatever you need."

Her brows rose slightly. "Would you mind . . . kissing me again?"

Warmth spread through his chest, and he grinned. "I wouldn't mind in the least."

Maybe she wasn't quite so ready to distance herself from him after all.

24

Back at work on Tuesday morning, Jane gave thanks to God for the many blessings she and her mother had received over the weekend. Getting to experience a true family Thanksgiving with wonderful people like the Wilders had been an unexpected gift.

Garrett's kisses had also been unexpected in the most wonderful way. Her stomach fluttered just thinking about his lips on hers. The strength of his arms around her. The heat in his eyes.

She shook her head to rid herself of memories that were much too distracting when she needed to focus on her work. Thankfully, Mama was feeling better today after resting most of holiday Monday once they'd returned from the farm, which meant Jane could come into the office with a clear conscience.

A knock sounded on her door.

Right away her heart thumped to life in her chest. After silently admonishing herself to behave in a professional manner if it was Garrett, she said, "Come in."

"Good morning, Mrs. Linder." Bonnie Dupuis entered the room, looking somewhat frazzled for so early in the day.

Jane pushed away a slight twinge of disappointment. "Good morning. How was your Thanksgiving?"

"Lovely, as usual. All my siblings managed to make it home this year, which was nice."

Jane made a note to take time to converse more with the caseworkers about their personal lives and not only about work issues. "I'm glad. What can I do for you?"

"I had a call from Mrs. Bennington first thing this morning. She wants someone to go over and speak with one of the residents as soon as possible." Bonnie shifted from one foot to the other. "I have back-to-back appointments today. Clarine called in sick with the flu, and all the other workers are overextended as well." She held up some file folders. "I wanted to get your opinion on which client could be delayed."

Jane mulled it over for a second. "No need for that. As it turns out, my calendar is light this morning. I'll go over to Bennington Place myself." Besides, she could use the distraction.

All the color drained from the girl's face. "Oh no. That's not necessary. I can push one of these cases off until tomorrow."

"It's fine. I've been wanting a chance to go over and see Ruth and Olivia anyway."

"Are you sure you have the time?" Bonnie's eyes widened, and she gestured to the piles of paper on Jane's desktop. "I mean, I know how busy you are . . ."

"Normally, yes. But my morning meeting was just canceled." Jane rose and came around the desk. "Will you please tell Melanie where I'm going and have her let Mr. Wilder know when he arrives?"

"Certainly. Th-thank you." Bonnie ducked her head and left the room.

After a quick bus trip, Jane arrived at the maternity home. It had been more than six months since she'd been here, and though she'd kept in touch with Olivia, she looked forward to seeing the other matron of the home. Ruth was a lovely older widow who, with Olivia's help, had turned her home into a shelter for unwed mothers.

With a smile on her face, Jane climbed the stairs and knocked on the front door.

A young pregnant woman answered.

"Good morning. I'm Mrs. Linder from the Children's Aid Society. May I speak with Mrs. Bennington or Mrs. Reed?"

"Yes, ma'am. Please come in." The girl ushered her into the parlor.

Two minutes later, Olivia appeared, a chubby baby on her hip. The dark-haired boy kicked his legs and bounced, as though eager to be let down.

"Jane! I didn't expect you to come." Olivia rushed over to give her a hug. "It's good to see you again."

"You too. And this can't be little Costas? He's gotten so big."

"He certainly has. He's almost seven months old now. And too mobile for his own good." She tweaked the boy's nose. "You never let Mama get any work done, do you?"

He laughed and a string of drool dripped from his chin.

"Do you bring him with you every day?"

"No, most days my mother-in-law watches him, but today she had an appointment."

"Well, lucky for me or I wouldn't have gotten to see him." Jane brushed a lock of hair from the boy's forehead. "My, he favors his father. He's the spitting image of Darius with those big blue eyes."

Olivia beamed. "Yes, indeed. I'm a lucky woman to have two such handsome men in my life as well as two beautiful daughters."

"You deserve it after everything you've been through."

"What about you, Jane? How are things going with Mr. Wilder?" Olivia asked.

Heat rose from Jane's neck to scorch her cheeks. "Fine. He's doing a very thorough job."

Olivia's eyes narrowed. "Judging from that blush, I'd like to know just how thorough."

Jane bit back a groan. How was she going to keep their relationship a secret if she couldn't stop blushing at the mere mention of Garrett? "We may have developed a friendship over the course of his time at the office."

"Only a friendship?" Olivia's arched brows rose almost to her hairline.

Jane shifted her weight and rearranged her satchel. "For now. After all, we have to keep things professional."

"Ah. But what happens when he's finished his work there?" Olivia grinned, bouncing the baby to keep him amused.

"I honestly don't know. But for now, it's . . ."

"Terrifying?"

The air rushed from Jane's lungs. "How did you know?"

"I felt the same way about Darius at first." Olivia laughed. "I'll take that as a good sign."

Jane leaned closer. "I'd appreciate your prayers. The whole situation is rather complicated. He's likely going to be in the running for the director's position."

"Oh dear. Well, I'll definitely step up my prayers for you and for the whole agency."

"Thank you. Speaking of which, I came to see the new mother."

"Right. Her name is Polly Breen." Olivia leaned closer. "She's been a bit hard to get to know. At first, she was adamant about giving up her baby, and now it looks like she's changed her mind. Perhaps you can give her some advice."

"I'll certainly do my best."

"She's in the second bedroom at the top of the stairs."

Jane smiled. "Tell Ruth I'd love to catch up with her when we're finished."

Jane climbed the stairs to the second story and found the bedroom easily enough. The door was open, so she gave a light knock on the doorframe and went in.

A young woman was seated in a rocking chair near one of the twin beds, holding a swaddled baby in her arms. She looked to be in her early twenties and was quite pretty, with fair hair and serious brown eyes.

"Hello," Jane said, walking forward with a smile. "Are you Polly?"

"Yes." A frown creased the woman's brow. "Who are you?"

Jane came to a halt. Wasn't the girl expecting her? Or had Ruth called without telling her? "I'm Mrs. Linder from the Children's Aid Society. I understand you wished to speak to someone about your newborn."

Polly clutched her baby tighter against her body. "I-I was expecting Miss Dupuis."

Jane sat on the edge of the bed so as not to intimidate Polly by towering over her. "I'm afraid Miss Dupuis's schedule didn't afford her the time to come today, so I'm here instead." She gave her a kind smile. "How can I help you, Polly?"

The woman's lips began to tremble. "I've changed my mind about putting my baby up for adoption. I want to keep her." She lifted her chin, a defiant gleam in her eyes.

"First of all, congratulations on your little girl." Jane leaned forward to peer at the tuft of hair peeking out from the blanket. It was always good to let the mothers know that the Children's Aid wasn't ready to snatch the baby from their arms. Something Jane had learned the hard way with Olivia. "And secondly, it's your prerogative to keep your child if you're able to provide for her."

"Thank you." Polly let out a breath. "I thought the agency would be mad that I'd changed my mind." Her features softened as she looked down at the baby. "But I just can't give Pearl away."

"What a lovely name." Jane set her satchel on the floor. "Have you determined how you're going to provide for your daughter?" she asked in a soft voice.

"Not yet." Polly's features hardened. "But I had a job before as a seamstress. I'm sure I can find another one once I'm ready."

"I imagine that Mrs. Bennington and Mrs. Reed have spoken to you about the difficulties a single mother faces in this regard. Do you have anyone—a family member, perhaps—who might be willing to help you until you get back on your feet?" Above all, Jane had to ascertain that the child would be in no danger of neglect.

She sensed the girl's hesitation. Polly was probably worried that if she gave the wrong answer, she might not get to keep her baby.

Jane continued, "If you truly wish to raise your little girl alone, it will be difficult, but know that we all want to help you. Many times, the ladies here will allow a new mother to stay on until she has a job and has found adequate care for her child. In fact, the other residents often watch each other's babies while the mother goes for an interview or works a short shift."

Polly gave a slight smile. "Yes, Ruth and Olivia have been more than kind about that. And one of the girls here has already offered to watch Pearl when I'm ready to look for work."

"That's good. I'm glad you have the beginning of a plan in place." Jane studied the girl, noting the nervous way she wouldn't meet Jane's eyes. "However, I'm wondering why you needed to see a social worker. You could have simply told us over the phone that you'd changed your mind."

Polly ran her tongue over her lips. "I'm sorry, but since I'm keeping Pearl, I'll need my money back."

"Money?" Jane's heart began a hard thump in her chest. "What money?"

"The money I paid Miss Dupuis to find my baby a good home." Polly stared at Jane in confusion. "She said that the mothers who could afford to pay got special treatment and their babies would have a better chance to be adopted by wealthier parents."

A hot burst of anger ran up Jane's spine. "Miss Dupuis told you that?"

"Y-yes." Doubt crept into Polly's eyes. "Isn't that how it works?"

"No. It's not." Jane drew in a breath. "How much did you pay for this special treatment?"

"Two hundred dollars." Polly's eyes filled with tears. "It was all I had to give. I'd have paid more if it meant Pearl would have the best home possible."

Jane shook her head. "Polly, we don't accept payment for our services. Did none of the other women here tell you that?"

Polly's mouth opened and closed again. "Miss Dupuis said not to discuss it with anyone because of privacy issues. And she didn't want the women who couldn't afford to pay anything to feel bad about it."

Jane pressed her lips together, the enormity of the situation pressing down on her.

"Did I do something wrong?" Fear laced Polly's voice.

Jane forced a sympathetic expression on her face. "No. None of this is your fault." She opened her satchel and took out a notebook and pen. "But I need your help. What Miss Dupuis has done is illegal. I'd like you to write down everything you can remember about what she said and did, and the approximate dates." Jane looked at her. "Do you think you can do that for me, Polly?"

The girl nodded. "I'll put Pearl in her cradle and do it right now."

"Thank you. That would be most helpful, especially if you can recall how the subject of money even came about."

Polly rose with the baby and laid her in the bassinet by her bed. "I'm sorry. I didn't know it was wrong to pay her."

Jane laid a hand on her arm. "This is not your fault. You had no reason to question her word." She picked up her bag. "I'm going down to speak with Ruth and Olivia and give you some time to write down what you remember. If you need anything, please come and find us."

"I will."

As Jane headed downstairs, a grim determination took hold. She had a strong feeling that this could somehow be tied to the discrepancies with the books and couldn't wait to get Garrett's thoughts on the matter when she returned.

———❖———

Garrett's anticipation to see Jane again on Tuesday morning faded into mild disappointment when he learned she'd gone out to visit one of the maternity homes. Perhaps it was just as well. It would give him a chance to get some work done without picturing her in the office down the hall.

Without obsessing over how he'd missed her after she left the farm.

Without wanting to kiss her again.

Enough of that, Wilder. You're in the workplace. You need to keep your priorities straight and resist temptation.

Easier said than done.

Still, he managed to transcribe his notes from the interviews with the Jefferson and Blackwood families last week, along with his observations and recommendations about both couples. He was dropping them off on Melanie's desk for typing when he heard the front door open.

"I'm back, Melanie," Jane called as she bustled into the room. "Do you know where Bonnie is? She said she had a full schedule today."

"I believe she's upstairs with a client." Melanie frowned. "Do you need to speak to her?"

"Not now. It can wait until later. I actually need you to hold my calls until further notice. Something pressing has come up—" She stopped short as soon as she spied Garrett. "Oh, good. I need to speak to you right away."

He tamed his lips into a neutral expression. "Good morning, Jane. I trust you had a pleasant long weekend." He didn't know if she'd told anyone that she was spending Thanksgiving with his family.

Her cheeks began to turn crimson, almost matching the shade

of her lipstick. "Very pleasant, thank you." She turned back to Melanie. "As I was saying, I have a pressing matter to attend to. Please hold my calls until further notice."

"Yes, ma'am."

Jane turned to Garrett. "Can you come to my office as soon as you have a chance?"

The urge to tease her faded. Something wasn't right. Jane seemed nervous and edgy. Rattled, even.

"I can spare some time now," he said. "I wanted to discuss the foster family interviews with you."

She gave him a long look, then nodded. "Good. Come on back."

"What's wrong?" he said without preamble after he'd closed her door. "Is it your mother? I hope she hasn't suffered a setback from her visit with us?"

She blinked. "No. Mama is fine. This concerns the agency." She lowered her voice. "At the maternity home this morning, I discovered a serious problem. And I need your advice on how to handle it." Her face had lost most of its color and tight lines bracketed her mouth.

"I'll do my best."

"I don't know if this ties in with the financial discrepancies, but I suspect it does."

Garrett leaned forward, his senses on high alert. "Go on."

"I learned today that Bonnie Dupuis made one of the mothers pay her two hundred dollars to find a good home for her baby."

"What? That's illegal!"

"It most certainly is. The mother in question changed her mind about placing her child for adoption and wanted her money back." Jane bent to take a notebook from her bag. "I had her write down all she could remember of her interactions with Miss Dupuis."

Garrett flipped through the pages of notes and gave a low whistle. "How many other mothers has she done this to, I wonder?"

"I don't know." Jane passed a hand over her eyes and let out a breath. "I can't understand how this happened. I thought I was doing a good job as directress, but clearly I was mistaken if these sorts of things are going on under my very nose."

He reached out to squeeze her arm. "Jane, you can't blame yourself. There's no way you could have known this was happening."

"Do you think it's tied in with Mr. Bolton somehow? It seems too much of a coincidence that he's skimming funds and at the same time Miss Dupuis is extorting money from unwed mothers."

"You're right. I have a feeling they could be connected. Maybe the two of them are working together."

Jane's eyes went wide. "What do I do now? Call the police?"

Garrett got up to pace the room, trying to determine the most logical course of action. "I think it would be best to allow the authorities to handle this. For now, I'd let Miss Dupuis carry on so as not to raise suspicion. But it might be advisable to pull her records and see how many infants she's placed lately to get a better idea of the scope of her crime."

Jane nodded. "She just started going to the maternity homes. Up until now, she'd been handling the older children. So hopefully there won't be many."

"That's good news. Still, we'll have to play this carefully so as not to tip her off before the police can act."

Jane sagged back against her chair on a loud exhale. "I can't believe one of our employees is doing something so . . . vile."

He wished he could comfort her, but he'd promised to stay professional in the workplace, and he would honor that vow. "I'm going to take the falsified ledgers down to the police station. I imagine an officer will at least question Mr. Bolton. Perhaps then he might confess Miss Dupuis's role in this whole affair. Either way, I wouldn't let him back in the building. And I'd have Miss Dupuis's termination papers ready."

She squared her shoulders and flashed him a grateful smile. "Thank you for your input. It's a relief to share the burden with someone."

Warmth spread through his chest. "I'm glad I could help."

"Tomorrow, if you have time, we should get back to the matter of Martin's placement."

"Sounds good." He hesitated, oddly reluctant to leave her. "I guess I'll be on my way, then."

She slipped on her glasses with a nod. "Good luck with the authorities. I'll be anxious to hear what they say."

"Try not to worry," he said. "It will all work out. I promise."

25

Two days later, Garrett walked up Queen Street toward one of the city's municipal buildings, reflecting on the surprising ease with which the fraud case had concluded. Mr. Bolton had ended up confessing everything to the police, and they had subsequently arrested both him and Miss Dupuis. Apparently, the two were romantically involved and had cooked up the schemes together. At least the culprits had been caught, and one of Garrett's main purposes in being hired at the Children's Aid Society had been fulfilled.

Now, with the issue resolved and Jane's innocence proven, Garrett no longer felt the need to avoid meeting with the board. By all rights, he should be bursting with pride that he and Jane had helped solve this crime, yet he couldn't ignore a certain gravity that weighed heavily on his soul.

On one hand, he was immensely proud of the report he'd put together, confident that his recommendations could make a real and lasting difference to the Children's Aid Society going forward.

On the other hand, he still struggled with one particular issue, one he'd wrestled with for some time.

Inside the main doors, he draped his overcoat over his arm and made his way up the wide stone staircase to the second floor. When he reached the conference room, he glanced at his watch.

With twenty minutes before the meeting started, he welcomed the quiet of the hushed hallway to hopefully come to terms with the difficult decision he'd made.

He crossed to one of the large windows overlooking the street below and stared at his hazy reflection in the glass. *Am I doing the right thing, Lord? Am I being truly unbiased, or is my judgment clouded?*

After accusing Jane of not being objective enough in her job, Garrett hated to admit that he'd lost the neutrality required in undertaking this study. Somehow along the way he'd become entwined in Jane's life and in Martin's. Over the past two days as he'd prepared his report, Garrett realized that in order to fulfill his mandate, he would have to set aside his personal feelings and be totally honest in his final recommendations.

Even if his honesty could be hurtful or possibly considered a betrayal.

Garrett peered closer at his reflection, straightening his tie and smoothing back a stray lock of hair. It all boiled down to one thing. What kind of man did he wish to be, both in the business arena and in his personal life?

The war may have cost him a lot of things, but Garrett still prided himself on his integrity. The belief that a man's word was worth only as much as his actions behind it. That doing the right thing no matter what was paramount. He let out a weary breath, then stiffened his spine. As much as it might pain him to do so, his path remained clear. The path he'd known he must follow all along.

With a prayer on his lips, he continued down the hall toward the meeting room. Outside the double doors, nerves swirled in his stomach as he waited for the members to invite him inside.

Minutes later, the door opened, and Mr. Fenmore motioned him over. "Hello, Garrett. We're ready for you to join us."

Garrett forced a confident expression to his face as he followed the man inside.

Twelve men and four women of varying ages sat around the long conference table. A haze of smoke rose above their heads from the numerous ashtrays on the table, filled with freshly lit cigarettes and pipes.

Garrett did his best not to waver under their scrutiny. "Good morning, everyone."

"Mr. Wilder." The white-haired man at the end of the table gestured to an empty chair. "Please have a seat."

Garrett placed his briefcase on the table and sat down. He removed a folder and laid it before him. "As you requested, I am prepared to report on my findings."

Mr. Fenmore resumed his seat. "Excellent. The board and I are eager to hear them."

Garrett loosened the knot of his tie and cleared his throat. "I'd like to start by saying that except for my conclusions on the child protection department, this report is complete. Once I finish my last interview with the supervisor, I will combine my results and submit the total package."

"Very well. Please continue."

"I'd like to start with my biggest area of concern, the severe physical limitations of the building." Garrett took out another sheet. "In particular, the meeting rooms on the second floor are severely overcrowded, which makes it impossible to conduct an interview with any semblance of privacy." He looked up. "Mrs. Linder indicated that plans for expansion, or a possible relocation to larger quarters, have been put on hold, likely due to the war."

"That's correct," Mr. Fenmore said. "It didn't seem prudent in these unsettled times to make such a drastic and costly change. We remain hopeful that once the war ends, we can continue with these plans."

"It makes sense given the uncertainty of the economy. However, with the increase in the caseloads, finding more space has become a requirement that cannot be ignored. Do you realize the social workers see over two hundred clients a day in that building? How they manage is nothing short of a miracle. As an interim solution, I propose that we look into leasing temporary space. Given the economy, I believe we should be able to find a rental at a reasonable rate, one that could tide the agency over until expansion is prudent."

Garrett paused for a moment. "I would also advise keeping the office staff separate from the caseworkers. Right now, the waiting area for clients is situated directly opposite the clerical space, which leads to much disruption. The constant comings and goings are most distracting and not conducive to an efficient workplace. If a separate location isn't possible, I would suggest designating a separate floor for the clerical staff. In addition, the caseworkers themselves require more privacy in which to conduct their client interviews. I propose that any future space procured for them be sectioned off into smaller, more private work areas. This might even be doable on a temporary basis with the present facilities for a minimal cost."

Several heads nodded around the table, and pens scratched over their notepads.

"Another concern I have is the heavy reliance on volunteers in the office, something I would like to see changed in the future."

"I disagree, Mr. Wilder." One woman spoke up. "Volunteers have been the backbone of the Children's Aid for many years. I doubt we'd be able to function without them."

From her passionate response, Garrett presumed she had likely started out as a volunteer herself. "I'm not disputing that, ma'am. Certainly, I have seen how beneficial the volunteers can be for services such as visiting the children at the shelter, sewing and knitting clothes, and donating gifts and food. All are greatly appreciated. What I take issue with is them being privy to certain confidential records, particularly the finances."

Garrett's gaze moved to Mr. Warren, who leaned forward in his seat. "I would have to agree with Mr. Wilder on this account."

"I've had the opportunity to study the agency's financial records in some detail, both during Mr. Mills's time and during his absence." Garrett glanced at his notes and straightened his back. "Overall, the records appeared to be in order. However, in more recent entries, I did find evidence of the tampering Mr. Warren mentioned. I brought the issue to Mrs. Linder's attention, and she was greatly distressed by it." He made a point of looking directly at several of the board members. Eye contact was a crucial way to inspire trust.

"Did you learn who is behind this?" Mr. Warren said.

"One obvious suspect was Mr. Bolton, the bookkeeper. But before we accused him, I wanted to dig deeper to see if anyone else might be involved. Mrs. Linder discovered that Miss Dupuis, one of the caseworkers, was using her position to exact unwarranted payments from unwed mothers to find their babies the best possible homes. Apparently, the two were dating and had concocted the schemes together."

Audible gasps sounded from several of the members.

Mr. Fenmore's already ruddy complexion grew crimson. "Has this situation been handled?"

"Rest assured, sir, it has. As of two days ago, the police have taken over, and both Mr. Bolton and Miss Dupuis have been arrested."

"Can we hope the authorities will keep our name out of the matter? We certainly don't need this type of publicity."

"The police have assured us they will be as discreet as possible."

Mr. Fenmore expelled a loud breath. "That's good news. We owe you a debt of gratitude, sir. I had no idea anything so nefarious was going on within our walls."

Mr. Warren scowled. "Which doesn't say much for the current directress. She not only initialed the fraudulent ledger entries, but she was unaware of worse crimes going on in her midst."

Garrett clenched his fingers around a pen. "That's hardly fair, sir," he said in an even tone. "Unless one of the women involved had come forward, no one could have known. We have Mrs. Linder's quick actions to thank for resolving this situation so expediently. Otherwise, Miss Dupuis might have continued her crimes unchecked."

An uneasy silence descended over the room. Garrett paused to focus back on his notes before forging ahead.

"Now that Mr. Bolton is gone," he continued, "I propose that the agency hire a part-time accountant to keep the books. Records of such a confidential nature should be safeguarded."

Mr. Warren slapped the table. "Which is what I've been saying for years now."

"Duly noted," Mr. Fenmore replied with a wry lift of his brow.

"Before we move on from this topic, I would also recommend that all records be kept in fireproof storage. I've noted too many cardboard boxes and wooden file cabinets for my liking. These records need to be safeguarded against any potential damage and archived in the same manner."

"That sounds wise," another woman said. "I could look into the cost of obtaining fireproof cabinets."

"Thank you, Mrs. Browning. That would be appreciated." Mr. Fenmore turned back to Garrett. "I'd like to know your findings on the children's shelter and the matron."

"Certainly. From what I've observed, Mrs. Shaughnessy runs a tight ship. The children are healthy, well cared for, and well-disciplined." He pushed the thought of Martin out of his mind. His case was out of the ordinary, to be sure. "One recommendation I have is that a building maintenance fund be established for future repairs. The residence is starting to age and will soon need updating as well as additional ongoing maintenance."

Several members made notations on their pads in front of them.

"A sensible plan." Mr. Fenmore nodded, then tapped his fingers on a folder in front of him. "And now we come down to the heart of the matter. What have you found out about Mrs. Linder? Does she have any bearing on the downturn in the agency?"

A bead of sweat trickled down Garrett's back. This was the part he'd been dreading. "I've not ascertained any direct connection between Mrs. Linder and the agency's troubles. Nor did I find anything amiss in her conduct as directress. She has a wonderful rapport with both the staff and the children."

One man snorted. "That isn't exactly an asset. The director's position requires respect and absolute authority. Not camaraderie."

"I disagree, sir. I believe it requires a healthy balance between the two. And speaking of balance, it's my opinion that Mr. Mills might have had too close an involvement in all areas of the agency, perhaps to the detriment of his health." Garrett's thoughts turned to Jane and how she tried so valiantly to fill her mentor's shoes. "It seems to me that the director should delegate more responsibility to the department supervisors instead of immersing himself in the minutiae of the day-to-day operations. Biweekly or monthly staff meetings with the department heads would allow him to keep up with the details, leaving him more time to devote to the overall concerns of the agency."

"You have a point." Mr. Fenmore leaned forward. "Tell me, how is Mrs. Linder coping with the stress of the position?"

Garrett ran a finger under his collar. Despite the open windows, the room had started to feel overly warm. He drew in a breath, dreading to give the statement that would seal Jane's fate. "I would have to say that Mrs. Linder appears . . . overwhelmed by the duties involved with the position. She admits she doesn't have a head for finance, and her efforts to obtain additional funding, which is so sorely needed, have been minimal at best." He hesitated. *Forgive me, Jane.* "While Mrs. Linder has done no direct harm to the agency, neither has she provided much benefit. Although she has managed to keep the agency afloat in this time of transition"—he paused as his chest constricted—"I cannot see her being a good fit to take the Children's Aid Society into the future."

A murmur went around the table. Several heads bent together, whispering.

Garrett's chest ached. How could Jane take this as anything other than a betrayal? But he had to be honest, and the truth was that he didn't feel she was the best person for the job.

"Her talents," he continued, "are much better utilized in the area of social work, where she indeed excels. I have witnessed firsthand her passion for the children and her unwavering commitment to ensure every child has a loving home."

Mr. Fenmore nodded thoughtfully. "Thank you for your honesty, Mr. Wilder. I believe your findings concur with our assessment of Mrs. Linder's performance as well."

Mrs. Browning lowered her glasses to glance around the table. "I've always held Mrs. Linder in high regard, and I propose we do all we can to keep her as a caseworker."

"Thank you, Mrs. Browning. I agree." Garrett smiled at the woman. "Continuing on that subject, I intend to officially present some of Mrs. Linder's ideas for reforming the adoption criteria. As you know, the war has made it harder to find people willing to adopt, and those who do often wish to adopt newborns. Mrs. Linder feels, and I concur, that if we were more flexible regarding the adoption of older children, more of them could be placed in loving, albeit slightly unconventional, homes."

An uncomfortable silence descended on the room until one woman spoke up. "I think this is a commendable idea. One we should study in greater detail. I look forward to reading your full report, Mr. Wilder."

"Thank you, ma'am."

"Is there anything else you wish to say before we conclude the meeting?" Mr. Fenmore asked.

"I believe those are the highlights, sir. A more detailed account will follow in my written report."

"Very well." Mr. Fenmore rose, a sign that the meeting was

over. "Thank you for your efforts, Mr. Wilder. We will take all your recommendations under consideration."

Garrett rose as well and handed Mr. Fenmore a piece of paper. "At this time, I'd like to offer my official application for the director's position. Now, more than ever, I feel I could be an asset to the Children's Aid Society as we move forward."

Mr. Fenmore accepted the paper with a nod. "Very good. I will be in touch."

Garrett closed his briefcase and stood. "Thank you for your time, ladies and gentlemen." He gave a slight bow. "Until our next meeting."

———— ❖ ————

Regret set in as soon as Garrett returned to the office, guilt slicing through him the moment he passed Jane's door. Though everything he'd told the board members was the truth, he couldn't help feeling that he'd betrayed Jane's trust. Yet he couldn't in all good conscience allow his personal feelings to interfere with his professional duty. He only prayed that she would see it that way as well.

He shoved his briefcase onto his desk, then palmed the back of his neck as he paced his work area. What would Mr. Fenmore do now that he'd heard Garrett's opinion on Jane's performance? Would he call Jane in for a meeting, or would he simply inform her over the phone that she would not be considered for the position?

Garrett owed it to Jane to inform her what he'd reported so she wouldn't be caught off guard by such a call. Even if it meant she would hate him.

With a heavy heart, he walked down the hall to her office and knocked.

When there was no answer, he checked the time and realized it was past noon. He went into the lunchroom but found only Melanie seated there.

"Jane's gone over to the shelter, in case you're looking for her," she said.

"I hope there's no problem."

"No, she just went to visit the children." Melanie set her sandwich on a plate. "She likes to do that whenever she can."

"Right." He remembered her saying that the first time they'd gone to the shelter. "Well, I'll catch up with her later, then."

"Is anything wrong? You don't seem yourself today."

Garrett forced a smile. "Everything's fine." *Except I've just crushed Jane's dreams.*

"I guess you'll be leaving us soon, once your final report is complete."

He nodded, attempting to ignore the twist in his stomach. "I'll likely be done by the end of the week or maybe early next week."

"It's been fun having you here." She winked at him. "You certainly added some interest to the place."

He chuckled. Now that he had gotten to know Melanie, he could tell she just enjoyed flirting with him and wasn't serious about pursuing him. "Thank you . . . I think."

Instead of returning to his work area, Garrett grabbed his overcoat and left the building, heading toward the shelter. Perhaps he would run into Jane on her way back.

When he'd first arrived over six weeks ago, he'd been filled with blind optimism, thinking he could sweep in, make his study, and in his infinite wisdom, lay out all the solutions to the agency's problems. How naïve could he have been? He kicked a pebble off the cement, watching it bounce over the street. Not even the beauty of the fall day or the swirl of colorful leaves on the sidewalk could lift his somber mood.

He was almost at the shelter when Jane emerged. She lifted her collar against the brisk breeze and started toward him, stopping in sudden surprise when she noticed him on the sidewalk.

"Garrett. Were you looking for me?"

"Yes. I hoped we could talk for a minute before going back to the office."

Two grooves formed between her brows. "Is something wrong?"

"Not exactly. But I'd like to let you know what I reported to the board this morning."

"I see." She fell into step beside him.

For a while they walked in silence, with only the sound of traffic breaking the stillness. Garrett knew he was stalling. Trying to stretch out this time when they were still on good terms.

Finally, he couldn't put it off any longer. "Jane, it's no secret how much I admire you, not only for the work you do but for the person you are. Your intelligence, your compassion, and your heart for children are all qualities that make you such an excellent social worker."

Her steps slowed until she came to a stop. She looked up at him with a question in her eyes, eyes that seemed the color of jade today. "I appreciate the compliments," she said slowly, "but I sense you're trying to tell me something."

His chest constricted as though already feeling the pain he would inflict. "As part of my overall analysis, the board asked for my opinion on your efficacy in the position of directress. It was hard, but I had to remove all personal feelings from the equation and be honest in my assessment." He bunched his hands into fists. "I told them that though you were an excellent social worker, I didn't feel you were the right person to run the agency."

A well of hurt bloomed in her eyes. She swallowed, then squared her shoulders. "What made you say that? Was it the way I handled Martin's situation?"

"That played a small part. But I could see the stress eating away at you as the weeks went on. And to be honest, the performance of the agency has declined somewhat in the last six months. Funds are not coming in the way they did when Mr. Mills was in charge. The caseworkers aren't working as efficiently as they once did—partly due to the space restrictions, but part of it, I believe, is because they see you as a co-worker and not as their manager. You're too familiar to them since you used to be one of them."

She stared at him, not saying anything. He'd expected anger, arguments, insults even.

Her silence was far more unnerving.

"I'm recommending in my report that someone from outside the organization be made director. Someone who would come in with a fresh perspective and be able to bring order to the present chaos."

"Someone like you, perhaps?" Her sarcasm bit as sharply as a whip.

"I don't know. It depends on who the other candidates are. I may not be the right person for the job either." He stuffed his hands into his coat pockets. "On a positive note, I wanted to let you know that I've incorporated your ideas for untraditional adoptions into my recommendations, so that whoever takes over the position will have your ideas in writing."

"That's something, I suppose." She let out a shaky breath, staring at a point past his shoulder. "If you'll excuse me, I have to get back for a meeting." She started down the sidewalk at a brisk pace.

Garrett's feet remained rooted to the cement, his heart just as heavy. "I'm sorry, Jane," he called after her.

But she kept on walking, never once looking back.

26

"I understand. Thank you for letting me know." Jane hung up the phone, leaned back in her chair, and closed her eyes.

The phone call she'd been expecting since Garrett's unsettling revelation yesterday had finally come. Mr. Fenmore had just called to inform her that the board had narrowed down the candidates for the director's position to the top three, and unfortunately, she was not one of them. But he hoped she would continue to be a valued part of the team in her former role of caseworker. And would she mind staying in the directress position until he'd chosen the new man for the job?

How ironic that she'd been so worried about the board members finding out about her divorce, when in the end it didn't matter anyway.

Now, as Jane sat facing the mountain of paperwork on her desk, all her enthusiasm seemed to have deserted her. It wasn't just the utter humiliation of having failed. It was the deep sense of betrayal she felt from Garrett. How could he not say something to her before reporting her shortcomings to the board? If he had, if she'd been more prepared for what he was thinking, maybe it wouldn't have torn such a hole in her soul.

She gave a short laugh. Who was she kidding? This cut so

deeply because of their personal relationship. If Garrett had remained *the interloper*, his report wouldn't have stung nearly as much.

But instead, they'd grown close. Too close, apparently.

If he cared about her the way he claimed, how could he have done this? He could have simply given a generic report of her performance and let the board decide for themselves, without his opinion to sway them.

Instead, he killed any chance she might have had.

She swallowed hard to push back the lump constricting her throat. Somehow, she'd have to survive the next week or two as directress until a replacement had been hired. Then return to her former position, at a much lower salary.

A terrible thought arose. What if Garrett was made the director? Could she hand over the reins and continue with him as her boss? Even if she managed to get past the hurt, it would mean the death of any romantic relationship between them. They could never be involved if he became her superior.

She dropped her head into her hands. How had this become such a tangled web?

The phone rang. For a minute, Jane was tempted to ignore it. But on the third strident ring, she picked up the receiver.

"Jane." Melanie's voice sounded strangled.

"What is it?"

"You'd better come out here right away."

Goose bumps pebbled along her skin as she hung up the phone. What else could go wrong today?

On slightly unsteady legs, Jane exited her office and headed down the main corridor, unsure of what calamity she was about to face. A man in a gray trench coat stood just inside the front door.

Jane blinked, then froze, all the blood seeming to drain from her body.

Staring directly at her, the man removed his hat, and a tentative smile inched over his face. "Hello, Jane. I see you haven't changed a bit. You're as beautiful as I remember."

She stumbled forward a step. *It can't be . . .*

"D-Donald," she whispered. "How . . . what are you doing here?"

"I came to see you, of course." He rolled the brim of his hat between his fingers, his nervous glance bouncing to the other workers who now peered out from the front office. "I telephoned the house, and your mother told me you were here." His eyes held a haunted quality, reinforced by deep grooves that bracketed his mouth.

"But . . . but why aren't you overseas? I don't understand . . ." Her legs wobbled.

Garrett appeared from somewhere behind her to grasp her elbow and steady her.

Donald's expression took on a pleading quality. "Look, could we maybe get a cup of coffee somewhere? There's a lot I need to tell you. A lot I want to explain."

Jane's lungs didn't seem to want to expand, rejecting the need for oxygen. Her husband—correction, *former* husband—whom she hadn't laid eyes on in four years, was standing in front of her, asking her out for coffee.

As if that were perfectly normal.

As if she should be grateful he'd taken the time to look her up.

As if he hadn't discarded her and married someone else.

Scathing words hovered on her tongue, and though she wanted nothing more than to throw him out on his ear, the curious stares of her co-workers held her rooted to the spot. Almost everyone here believed that she and Donald were still married. How would it look if she reacted with rage and not the tearful welcome home that would be expected?

Yet there was no way she could throw herself into his arms and pretend to be the doting wife, patiently awaiting her husband's return. Not even Vivien Leigh was that good of an actress. Getting Donald out of the building seemed the best option for the moment. She forced a tight smile to her lips. "Let me get my coat and purse."

Ignoring the stunned expression on Garrett's face, she whirled around and went back into her office, where she leaned against the door and gulped in several large breaths. Her hands shook as she drew on her coat and picked up her purse.

Calm down, Jane. You can do this. You can blame your strange reaction on shock.

Garrett was waiting outside her door when she emerged. "Are you all right?"

She couldn't look at him right now. She certainly couldn't acknowledge the concern shadowing those intense blue eyes.

"I'm fine." She went to move by him, but he held her arm in a gentle grip.

"You don't have to go with him," he said in a low tone. "You don't owe him anything."

For a moment, she fought the temptation to lean into his strength. But this situation had nothing to do with him, and after what he'd said to the board, he wasn't the person she wanted to turn to for comfort. She would deal with this herself.

"I know, but this is my decision." She fumbled with the buttons on her coat, annoyed that her fingers didn't want to cooperate, as she headed down the hall to where Donald waited. "I'll be back shortly," she said to Melanie.

Then, on legs as wobbly as overcooked noodles, she allowed Donald to lead her out the door.

"There's a coffee shop on the next block," she said tightly. "Though I don't see what we could possibly have to talk about." If she wasn't so worried about her heel catching in the crack of the sidewalk, or her legs giving out on her, she'd attempt to walk faster. Anything to get this ridiculous meeting over with as soon as possible.

When they reached the diner, Donald held the door for her.

Jane chose a table nearest the door and sat down. She smoothed the hair off her forehead, making certain that despite her erratic heartbeat, she kept her features expressionless. "Why are you here? Are you on leave?"

As soon as the question left her mouth, she realized how absurd it was. Why would he waste a leave to come back to Canada? He had no real family left. His parents were dead, and his only brother was fighting in the war too. She was the only person left here that he would have any real connection to.

Donald took a seat, draping his coat on the bench beside him. His gray eyes were serious as he looked at her. "Not quite." His mouth thinned.

"Then why aren't you overseas?" Her patience was running out, as was her ability to control all the scathing accusations on her lips.

He paused to give a waitress their order. Then he folded his hands on the tabletop. "Not long ago, I was injured and taken to a hospital in France. Thankfully, I recovered."

"You're here to recuperate?" Jane still couldn't understand it. Even if he'd been discharged from duty, wouldn't he return home to his new wife?

"No, I'm not." The lines deepened around his mouth. "I was about to rejoin my unit when I received some terrible news."

It was then Jane looked past her own shock and anger and noticed the sadness in his eyes. A dullness she'd attributed to weariness from the war or from his recent travels.

She drew in a breath. "Your brother?" That would explain why he was back in Canada. To bury his only sibling and settle his estate.

He shook his head, his gaze falling to his hands. When he looked up, tears rimmed his lower lashes. "My wife, Moira, passed away."

Jane's mouth fell open, and she quickly snapped it shut. "Oh. I'm sorry." How surreal was it that she was offering her condolences for the woman who'd replaced her?

The waitress appeared and set two cups down in front of them. Donald discreetly wiped his eyes. Jane couldn't remember ever seeing him cry. Except when they lost their son.

Jane stared down into her mug. Nothing about this visit made sense. Why on earth would he come all this way to share this news with Jane? She was the last person who'd be likely to commiserate with his grief. "I don't mean to sound insensitive, Donald, but what does any of that have to do with me? Because as far as I'm concerned, you and I are nothing to each other anymore."

He winced and turned his head to stare out the window at the people walking by. After several seconds, he finally faced her. "The thing is . . ." He hesitated, raising his eyes to hers. "I have a child. A son."

Searing pain shot through Jane's chest as though someone had reached into her chest and twisted her lungs into a knot. Immediate tears burned the backs of her eyes, and she covered her mouth with her hand.

Really, Lord? How much more agony am I expected to bear?

"He's seven months old. And he needs a mother."

Jane bit her lip, struggling against a wave of dizziness.

"I realize it was unforgivable the way I left you," he went on. "And I know it's not much of an excuse, but I fell apart when we lost—"

She sucked in a sharp breath. "Don't," she hissed. If he uttered the words *our son* she would lose it right here in the middle of this diner.

He closed his eyes, seeming to try to pull himself together. Then he opened them again. "Joining the army seemed the perfect escape, since at that point, I truly didn't care if I lived or died. Being in constant peril has a way of taking your mind off anything else." He lifted a wry brow. "Then, one night on leave, I met Moira at a pub and—"

"I don't need to listen to this." Jane shoved back her chair and got to her feet.

"Wait. I'm sorry." He reached out a hand as though willing her to stay. "Please, if you'll just hear me out . . ."

His pleading tone, along with a look of sheer desperation, elicited a trickle of unwanted sympathy within her. She hesitated, then sat down again.

"Thank you." The tension in his brow eased. He took a sip of his coffee, then raised his head, his gaze boring into her. "After Moira died, I realized the only true obstacle you and I faced in our marriage was our inability to have children. Now I find myself alone with an infant to raise. An infant I have no idea how to look after. And it occurred to me that . . . maybe we could help each other." He reached over to cover her hand with his, an earnest expression lighting his face. "I can give you the baby you've always wanted, Jane. We could be a real family, just like we used to dream about, if only you can find it in your heart to forgive me."

Cold chills raced down Jane's arms. She stared at him in disbelief. "Do you expect me to simply forget that you divorced me and married someone else? Forget all the hurt and agony you caused?"

Amazingly, more tears appeared in Donald's eyes. "I'm so sorry, Jane. You'll never know how terrible I feel about the way I abandoned you when you were in so much pain. As I said, there's no excuse for my behavior except that I was out of my mind with grief myself. Not only at the death of our son, but at learning I'd never be a father." He scrubbed a hand over his jaw, then fixed her with an agonized stare. "What do you think, Jane? Can we put all that behind us, so we can have the future we'd always dreamed of together?"

27

Garrett stared out the window that overlooked Isabella Street, as if by peering intently at the road, he could will Jane's return. It had been over an hour since she left. Not that he was watching the clock or anything.

"I can't believe he had the nerve to show up here." Melanie's disgust echoed over the now-empty stenographer's area. She was the one other person who knew about Jane's divorce. The one other person who was as flummoxed as he was by Donald's arrival.

"At least he had the good sense not to bring his new wife." She huffed out a loud breath. "What do you think he could possibly have to say to Jane?"

"I have no idea."

"Maybe he's here on leave to see his family and decided while he was here to apologize to her in person for what he did."

"Possibly." Garrett moved away from the window and dared to ask one of the questions plaguing him. "Do you think Jane could actually forgive him?"

The other question—did she still have feelings for the man?—would remain unasked. He didn't really want an answer anyway.

Melanie pursed her lips. "I don't know. *I* certainly wouldn't. But

Jane has a soft heart underneath her tough exterior. I wouldn't be surprised if she forgives him eventually."

Garrett crossed his arms over his chest. "I just hope his arrival doesn't bring back too much pain or cause Jane any new problems."

Melanie arched a brow. "Is there something going on between you two I should know about?"

"Of course not." He kept his voice firm. Melanie was the last person he would want to know about his feelings for Jane, given her inability to keep a secret.

"Are you sure you don't have a little crush on the boss?"

He jerked away from the wall where he'd been leaning. "Jane is not my boss." He gave Melanie his fiercest scowl. He could not afford to have her spreading such ideas around the office.

She had the grace to look chagrined, and Garrett hoped she'd let the matter drop.

Just then the telephone rang. Melanie rushed to answer it. "Toronto Children's Aid." Her eyes grew round. "Jane, are you all right?"

Instantly Garrett's shoulders tightened, and he moved over to the desk, straining to catch what was being said.

"I understand, but what did Donald—?" Melanie frowned and made notes on a pad, as if listening to instructions. "Yes, of course. Fine. I'll see you tomorrow, then. Call me if you want to talk." A variety of expressions flickered over her features as she hung up the phone.

Garrett hovered over her desk. "What did she say?"

"She said to tell you and the other staff that she's not coming back today. She wants me to cancel all her appointments for the rest of the afternoon."

"That's worrisome." He paced to the window and back, fighting the urge to rush out and find her. "How did she sound?"

Melanie shook her head, making her blond hair swing about her shoulders. "I've never heard her sound so shaken. But she wouldn't tell me what Donald wanted. She said she needed time alone to process everything." She shrugged. "I have no idea what that means."

Garrett pressed his mouth into a tight line. He didn't either, but it couldn't be anything good if it had upset Jane to such a degree.

However, there was nothing he could do at the moment. Jane said she needed time alone. He would give her the afternoon, but he fully intended to talk to her this evening and find out exactly what her ex-husband had said to cause her such distress.

——◆——

Jane had no idea how far she walked after calling Melanie from the diner. Hours later, she found herself standing by Lake Ontario, staring out at the strong waves pounding the rocks. She found a bench on a path overlooking the water and, despite the cool temperature, sat down.

After dropping his bombshell, Donald had seemed to be waiting for some sort of reaction from her. What did he expect? That she'd say she still loved him and that they could pick up where they'd left off?

Fat chance of that happening!

Once she'd managed to get her tongue to work, Jane had told him she needed time to think about the situation, and after a few more minutes of apologizing, Donald had scribbled down his telephone number and reluctantly left the restaurant.

Jane hadn't known what to do after he left. She couldn't go back to the office and face the questions everyone would have. Nor could she go home. Mama would want to know why she wasn't at work, and Jane knew exactly what her mother thought about Donald. Though she had felt it her Christian duty to forgive her ex-son-in-law, Jane had no illusions what Mama would say about the situation.

No, Jane needed to sort this out on her own.

The long walk did nothing to help clarify her feelings. They remained as tumultuous as the swirls of water on the rocks before her. She took a few deep breaths and paused to examine her emotions. First and foremost, she was still incredibly angry at Donald. The resentment she felt over his desertion and subsequent remarriage, as well as the damage to her self-esteem, ran far too deep to disappear with a simple apology.

And Jane's mistrust ran just as deep. How could she not see his abandonment of her as a rejection of the worst kind? And what guarantee did she have that he wouldn't do the same thing again if someone better came along, or if the circumstances of their life became too much to handle?

If you hold anything against anyone, forgive them, so that your Father in heaven may forgive your sins.

Her mother's often-quoted Bible verse sprang to mind, convicting her of the grudge she still bore against Donald.

But even if she did manage to forgive him, it didn't mean she could marry him again. And what would he expect of such a union? Would it be a marriage of convenience simply to provide a mother for his son, or would he want something more? Something that, at this time, she was in no way prepared to give him?

The questions raced through her mind with relentless fury, not allowing her time to even formulate a response.

And in the midst of her confusion, Garrett's face kept popping up. She'd begun to have strong feelings for this man—feelings that could be clouding her judgment concerning Donald. Yet Garrett himself had betrayed her trust. But compared to what Donald had done, Garrett's lack of faith in her professional abilities had been nothing more than a scratch that barely marked her skin. Donald's actions had cut her deeply, making her feel worthless and unlovable.

And really, what kind of future could she and Garrett have together? He clearly adored children, and Jane couldn't give him the offspring he deserved. At the same time, Garrett faced an uncertain future that could potentially paralyze him, or worse, kill him. Their connection was too new, too uncertain, to overcome such weighty obstacles.

But if Jane accepted Donald's proposal, she would have the security of a husband and, most tempting of all, she'd have a baby to raise as her own. She'd finally have the family she'd always longed for. And she'd be able to make sure Mama would be taken care of as well.

In theory, it all sounded wonderful. Yet her stubborn heart rebelled against the fact that she couldn't make her feelings align with what appeared to be the perfect solution to her circumstances.

A brisk wind blew up from the water, causing Jane to shiver. She rose and cinched the belt of her coat tighter. Clearly the answer wasn't going to jump out at her as she sat there. She'd better get home and start thinking about Mama's dinner. Then she'd spend the evening in prayer and hope that God would reveal what she needed to do. Only He could help her make sense of this unbelievable situation.

She found her mother in a severely agitated state when she arrived home.

"Jane? You need to come here."

She shrugged out of her overcoat, hung it on the rack, and followed the sound of Mama's voice into the kitchen.

Her mother's hair had come loose from her usual tidy bun and several pieces hung by her cheeks. She pointed to the far corner of the room. "There's a leak coming in from somewhere. I've put out a pot to catch the drips, but it's filling up faster than I expected."

Jane frowned, her spirits sinking even lower. "The rain stopped early this morning. Why is it leaking now?" She peered at the yellowing stain in the ceiling.

"Sometimes the water takes a roundabout route to its final destination." Mama went to lift the almost-full soup pot from its perch on a wooden plant stand.

"Here, Mama. Let me." Jane picked up the heavy aluminum

container, while Mama replaced it with another pot. Then she carried the full one to the sink and dumped out the water.

"I tried to call you at work, but you weren't there."

The accusation in Mama's voice stung Jane's conscience. Normally she tried to make sure Mama knew where she was at all times, usually by leaving word with Melanie should her mother call. But this time, she hadn't thought of her mother at all.

"I had an unexpected meeting off-site." Not entirely untrue.

Mama heaved a great sigh. "If only Brandon would come home. He'd be here to fix all the things going wrong in this house."

Jane sank onto a kitchen chair, reality seeping through her faster than the water dripping through the ceiling. Most likely, Brandon wasn't coming back, and even if he did, who knew what condition he'd be in. He would need time to heal and regain his health. It wouldn't be fair to place such high expectations on him.

No, she couldn't base her hopes for the future on Brandon. She would have to make her decision strictly with the facts she had on hand.

———— ❧ ————

After work that day, Garrett approached Jane's front door, not convinced he had any right to be there, especially given their recent falling-out over his report to the board members. All he knew was that the woman he'd grown to care for so deeply was hurting, and he couldn't sit by and do nothing. He had to at least offer his assistance—whether that meant lending an ear to listen or giving her a shoulder to cry on, he didn't know. He only prayed she didn't shut him out. No matter how much he deserved it, he wasn't sure he could handle that.

With a final vow to remain in control of his emotions, he checked the buttons on his jacket, adjusted his tie, then knocked on the door.

It took a minute for it to open, and then Jane stood there in front of him. The ravaged look on her face stripped away all his intentions of remaining unaffected. Clearly something devastating had happened.

But what?

"I hope you don't mind," he said, "but I had to see if you were all right."

Her chin quivered as she attempted to reply, yet no words emerged.

"May I come in?"

"I don't know if that's a good idea." She stared at him, her eyes awash with confusion.

Garrett stepped inside and closed the door with a soft click. "I'm simply here as a friend to offer support."

When she nodded, he held out his arms. She accepted his offering like a ship seeking a safe harbor, and her body trembled as she rested her head on his shoulder. "Mama doesn't know I've seen Donald," she whispered. "I didn't want to upset her."

"I understand. Do you want to talk in the kitchen?"

"Okay."

"Let me say a quick hello and I'll join you in a minute." He gave her hand a gentle squeeze, then walked into the living room, where Hildie sat in her favorite armchair, knitting needles clicking.

Her face brightened somewhat when she noticed him. "Why, Garrett. This is a nice surprise."

"Good to see you too, Hildie." He bent to kiss her thin cheek, noting she seemed a little off-kilter, her fingers trembling more than usual.

"I'm glad you're here," she said. "Maybe you can cheer Janey up. She hasn't been herself since she got home, and she won't say what's troubling her. I know it's more than the leaky ceiling."

"A leak? Whereabouts?"

"In the kitchen. But it seems to have stopped for now."

Garrett nodded. "I'll do my best to help. I promise."

With a prayer on his lips, he headed back to the kitchen.

Jane was seated at the table, twisting a saltshaker between her fingers. A large pot was situated on a wooden stand in the corner to catch the slow drips of water.

He stood inside the doorway for a second before walking over to take a closer look at the stained ceiling. "I can have a roofer come over tomorrow to find out where this leak is coming from, if you like."

He turned, prepared for her to refuse his offer, but instead, she nodded. "I'd appreciate that. Thank you."

His brows rose. She really must be upset to accept help so easily.

Garrett took a seat beside her, trying to decipher her expression. "It must have been a huge shock for you," he said carefully. "Donald showing up out of the blue like that."

She raised her eyes to his, misery rolling in their depths. "It was, but it was nothing compared to the news he came to tell me."

His gut gave a painful lurch. What could Donald possibly have said that would upset her to this degree?

She set down the saltshaker and laid her palms flat on the tablecloth. "At first, I thought he'd come in some misguided effort to alleviate his guilt." She sucked in a great breath that shuddered back out. "But he came to tell me that his wife is dead . . . and that he wants me back."

"W-what?" A bucket of cold water in the face couldn't have given Garrett more of a jolt. As he stared at Jane's bewildered expression, anger seeped through his veins. How dare the man even suggest such a thing after what he'd done to her? "I hope you told him exactly what you thought of that ridiculous idea."

Her lids fluttered closed, and a muscle ticked at her temple. "He has a baby," she whispered. "A little boy who needs a mother. He wants us to be a family."

Garrett leaned back heavily against the chair, his chest hollow. A thousand emotions churned through his system at once—outrage, resentment, then despair. Donald was offering Jane everything she'd always wanted. The one thing she thought she could never have. What could Garrett say to that?

He swallowed, forcing his own feelings aside for the moment. "How do you feel about the situation?"

"I don't know how to put it into words." Her lips quivered. "I'm tempted . . . so very tempted. This could be my one chance to be a mother, to give a baby all the love I have inside." She twisted her fingers together. "But at the same time, I'm so angry I could scream."

Even though her eyes remained dry, he handed her his handkerchief, searching for the right words to say. "You have every right to be angry, Jane, as well as confused. Who wouldn't be in this situation?" He paused, wanting to give her the wisdom she needed without adding his own bias. "But you don't have to make a hasty decision. Take all the time you need to consider the ramifications. Pray about it. Try to decipher what God wants for your life."

He could almost see her coming back to herself, the way she straightened her shoulders and nodded. "I'm going to do just that."

He had to force himself not to blurt out *What about me?* Their relationship was too new to even pose the question. Instead, another one rose in his mind. "What about your job? I assume Donald would expect you to give it up."

"I . . . I hadn't thought that far ahead." Her shoulders sagged. "But you're right. He needs a full-time mother for his son." She pushed away from the table and crossed to the counter. "Mr. Fenmore called this morning. He's narrowed down the candidates for the director's job, and I'm no longer in the running."

His heart squeezed with guilt. The chances were good that she wouldn't have gotten the position anyway, but his report had likely sealed her fate.

"Maybe this is a sign that God has another path in mind for me." She gave a humorless laugh. "All I have to do is forgive Donald."

He swallowed hard and rose to face her. Was she seriously considering going back to him? "Only you can decide if that's possible and whether you can trust him again." He balled his hands into fists. He couldn't stay here much longer and remain in control of his emotions. Not when all he wanted was to take her in his arms and claim her as his own. On unsteady feet, he headed to the door. "I'll be praying you make the decision that will make you happy."

"Wait." She moved toward him with jerky steps. "You haven't said how *you* feel about all this."

With effort, he met her gaze. "Obviously, I'm not happy about it."

For the first time, tears welled in her eyes. "That's what makes this so hard. If I didn't have feelings for you, my choice would be so much simpler."

Suddenly he'd become part of a tally sheet where his assets and liabilities would be compared to those of her ex-husband. And Donald had a big plus in the asset column: a ready-made family just waiting for Jane to claim. How could Garrett compete with that?

He resisted the urge to touch her, willing his emotions to steady. "You know I care about you, Jane. And you also know about my uncertain medical issues. I have no right to try to sway your choice. You need to make your decision without any undue influence from me or from anyone else. Trust yourself, and most of all, trust in God."

He leaned over and pressed a soft kiss to her forehead, letting his lips linger just a bit too long. Then he pulled away and headed blindly out of the house.

28

For the first time in her life, Jane called in sick to work when she wasn't actually ill—at least not in the physical sense. Mentally and emotionally, well, that was another story. But she simply couldn't face Melanie or her other co-workers. Nor could she face Garrett again until she'd made her decision. She knew Mama was worried about her, but she couldn't share her dilemma yet. Not until she'd made up her mind, one way or the other.

How did Garrett put it? She didn't need any "undue influence" on her decision. The only direction she needed was from God.

And to that end, she found herself walking into church in the middle of the day, hoping that within the sanctuary of those sacred walls, she'd be able to discern God's guidance and find a way to sort through all the variables. She also needed the Lord's help to truly forgive Donald, no matter what she decided to do. Because seeing him again had unleashed a storm of pain and resentment inside her. She'd fooled herself into thinking she'd overcome these debilitating emotions, when clearly she'd only pushed them beneath the surface, where they'd lain dormant all this time, ready to erupt when she least expected. For her own sake, she needed to make peace with the past.

In the largely empty church, Jane sat praying for what seemed like hours. She recalled the tears in Donald's eyes when he'd said how truly sorry he was for leaving her. It was the only way, he'd said, that he could get past his pain.

From the few sessions Jane had had with her minister after losing the baby, she'd learned that everyone dealt with grief in a different way. And that often men found it more difficult to process. At the time, she'd thought the minister was making excuses for Donald's behavior, but now, she found she could view the man's words in a more objective light.

Still, Donald had divorced her and married another woman. Could grief excuse him inflicting that type of pain on her? The answer to that remained as elusive as the concept of forgiveness itself.

After hours on the hard pew mulling over the last year of their marriage, as well as the past several months at work, one thing became glaringly obvious. Whether by intention or by chance, Jane had fallen into the role of victim. The victim of infertility, the victim of Donald's abandonment, and the victim of what she considered unfair treatment at work. She'd blamed God, blamed Donald, and even blamed Garrett for her misfortune. But if she wanted Donald to take ownership of his mistakes, then she could do no less.

From now on, she needed to reclaim her own sense of power and take charge of her life. Make the decision that was right for her and refuse to fall into the habit of blaming others for her unhappiness.

Whether she chose to accept Donald's proposal or not, she would do it with confidence, not with regret.

Thanking God for this small bit of clarity, she rose and made her way home.

When she arrived back at the house, Mama was resting in her room. Jane took the opportunity to call Melanie at the office.

"I'm feeling better, thank you," she replied to Melanie's concerned question. She was being less than truthful with her friend, but she wasn't ready to disclose all she was wrestling with just yet. "I'm just checking to see if there are any important messages."

"Not really. Mrs. Blackwood called to find out if you'd made a decision about Martin. When I told her you weren't in, she asked to speak to Mr. Wilder. I figured since he'd been with you at the interview, it would be all right."

"Yes, of course. But if anything else comes up, please let me know, and I'll return the calls from home. I'll be back tomorrow, so if the matter can wait until then, I'd prefer it."

"I understand. I'll see you tomorrow, then."

Jane hung up the receiver, her thoughts further muddled by guilt. In all the uproar over Miss Dupuis and Mr. Bolton, and then Donald's sudden arrival, Martin's placement had been pushed to the back burner. But a decision had to be made soon, preferably before the board named a new director and the boy's fate was taken out of her hands. As acting directress, she still had the power to decide his next move, but if someone else took over, they would make the final call.

This might be her last chance to fulfill her promise to Martin's mother, her last chance to—

A sudden idea slammed through her with the force of a tsunami. Her heart began to race as though she'd just sprinted a mile. She leapt up from the sofa and paced the worn carpet, her legs as shaky as a new lamb's.

If I married Donald, I could adopt Martin myself.

She and Donald could give him the family he'd longed for his whole life. He'd never have to go back into foster care again.

Tears bubbled up and brimmed over her lashes, baptizing her cheeks with joy. Not only would she have a baby to raise, but she could fulfill her long-held dream of finally giving Martin a real home.

A home with her. She could be Martin's mother for the rest of his life.

She sank back onto the sofa, dropped her face into her hands, and wept.

———— ❖ ————

"I was glad to get your phone call," Donald said as they strolled through St. James Park later that afternoon. He walked with his hands clasped behind him, staring straight ahead. Under a gray fedora, only a few strands of his blond hair were visible across his forehead. He'd lost weight, she noted, observing the way his suit jacket hung slackly on his now-thin frame.

"I figured we should talk again," she said. "Now that I've had time to recover from the shock and consider everything you told me."

"You always were the sensible one in our relationship. Much more so than me at times." He gave a rueful smile. "Which is why I have every confidence that you'll make the most practical decision for everyone concerned."

"I'm glad you have such faith in me."

"I always have." He glanced over at her. "May I ask if you've come to any conclusions?"

"Perhaps we should sit down for this." Jane gestured to a park bench tucked away out of the wind.

"Very well." He waited for her to sit, then followed suit. He seemed overly cautious, as if worried he would say or do the wrong thing. Or maybe he just didn't want to rush her.

"Where is your son now?" she asked, setting her purse on her lap. She'd been curious about that, not having had the presence of mind to ask yesterday.

"He's with the nanny. Mrs. Hedley is a friend of Moira's family, and she was good enough to come with me on the voyage over. I don't know how I would have managed alone. She said she'd stay long enough to help me get settled, but she'll be heading back to England soon. For now, I've rented an apartment until my plans firm up."

"I see. And will you be looking for work here?"

"That's my intention. Once I secure proper employment, I'll see about buying a house. Somewhere we can put down real roots."

"You plan to stay in Toronto, then? Not return to England?"

He glanced over at her. "Canada is my home, Jane."

"What about the boy's grandparents and other relatives?"

He shook his head. "Moira's parents weren't happy about my decision, and I did feel bad about taking Patrick from them, but in the end, I have to raise him as I see fit." He sighed. "I just couldn't see myself staying in England."

Jane straightened on the bench. She could understand his desire to return home, to the place he was most familiar with. She would have felt terribly homesick so far away.

A soft breeze blew up, ruffling Jane's skirt about her knees. Donald sat in silence.

On the expanse of grass in front of them, a mother rested with her young daughter on a blanket, while an older boy of about seven or eight rolled a ball to the little girl. A pang of longing pinched Jane's chest. That could be her family one day. Martin, the protective older brother, teaching Patrick how to kick a ball. The four of them, and maybe Mama, out on a picnic on a warm fall afternoon, laughing and enjoying the antics of the children.

If she accepted Donald's proposal, their future would be secure. With his tenacity, she had no doubt that he'd find work somewhere, doing whatever necessary to provide for them. The safety she'd been seeking for so long would be within her reach at last.

Finally, she drew in a breath. "I've tried to view the situation as objectively as possible, though I'll admit it was difficult to set aside my anger to do so. I concluded that I'm not ready to accept your proposal right now. It will take time to rebuild the trust you destroyed when you left."

A nerve pulsed in Donald's jaw, then he nodded. "You have

every right to be angry and distrust me. Unfortunately, I don't have a great deal of time. Mrs. Hedley has booked her return passage to England for two weeks from now. One way or another, I'll have to arrange for a new caregiver for Patrick by then."

She tilted her head. "Well, perhaps my idea will work."

"What's that?" Hope brightened his eyes.

"I propose that I work as Patrick's caregiver for a trial period. I'll accept the same wage you're paying Mrs. Hedley, and that way I can get to know Patrick. At the same time, you and I can spend time together to determine if we're still . . . compatible."

Her heart thudded in her chest. Would he read between the lines? Recognize her uncertainty that she'd be able to overcome her resentment toward him?

His brows rose slightly. "What about your job? I know how much it means to you."

Her breath caught on a wave of grief. She'd agonized over the pros and cons of giving it up. Yet, after the disappointment of losing the directress position—and even earlier than that, if she were honest—her heart just hadn't been in her work. Perhaps God had used that setback to make her more receptive to Donald's proposal. And since the agency was short of caseworkers right now, even more so after Miss Dupuis's departure, Jane was fairly confident she could get her old position back, if she had to.

"I'm prepared to give up my job, but I'll need a few days to wrap things up at the office. That should allow me some time with the nanny before her departure. In the meantime, I could come over in the evenings to spend time with the baby . . . and you."

He studied her, concern clouding his features. "What happens if you decide it won't work? Will the Children's Aid take you back?"

Jane forced her lungs to breathe. "I don't know for certain, but chances are favorable that they would." She was amazed at how calm she kept. After all, this felt more like a job interview than a potential marriage proposal.

He was silent for a few beats. "This is a big risk for you, and I understand your need to be certain." He gave a faint smile. "I won you over once. God willing, I can do it again."

"There are another few details I wish to iron out," she continued. She might as well get it all out in the open and gauge his reaction.

"And what would they be?" A glimmer of amusement shone in his gray eyes.

She twisted on the bench to face him more fully. "As I've mentioned, my mother is in frail health. I've been living with her since Brandon enlisted. If he returns from the war, we can reevaluate the situation, but until then—"

He held up a hand. "Of course Hildie is welcome to stay with us. Anything else?"

"Yes." She paused to level her emotions, unwilling to reveal just how much this next request meant to her. "There's a boy from the shelter I've become quite fond of—" she swallowed but kept her gaze even—"and if we decide to remarry, I would like us to adopt him."

The words hung in the air between them, laden with all the weight of their previous arguments on the subject. Was Donald remembering their heated discussions on the issue, or had his position possibly mellowed since then?

He remained silent, his hands clasped over his knees. "How old is this boy?" he asked at last.

"Eight, going on nine. I've been his caseworker since he was two, and we've developed a special bond over the years."

"Why hasn't he been adopted by now?"

She hesitated. "The agency hasn't found the right fit for him yet, mainly because of his epilepsy. Foster parents have a hard time coping with his seizures, but I've become adept at dealing with them." She pressed her lips together and willed herself to stay strong.

"I see." Donald got up and paced the ground in front of the

bench. She could almost see the wheels in his head turning. At last, he slowed and faced her. "It's hard to agree to something so important without having met the child. But if it means so much to you, then I'll consider it." He paused and rubbed his chin. "Perhaps while you're getting to know my son, I could do the same with this boy."

"That sounds fair." A measure of relief loosened the tightness in her chest. At least he was willing to consider adoption. "So, we'll have a trial period of two weeks, after which time we'll re-assess our respective positions."

"Agreed."

She rose, and as they shook hands, Jane prayed she wasn't making the biggest mistake of her life.

29

The next morning, Jane did her best to brace herself for the difficult day ahead, certain that nothing would really help. Tucked in the recesses of her satchel was her meticulously penned letter of resignation. Since she didn't know where to send it, the first order of business this morning would be to place a call to Mr. Fenmore and give him her verbal intention to resign. A bitter pill to swallow; however, it had to be done.

But the hardest part of all would be facing Garrett. Because no matter what, she couldn't deny she still had feelings for him. It no longer stung when she thought about his report to the board, and in all honesty, he'd been right. Though it'd been hard to admit, most times the logistics of the position did overwhelm her. Yet her main goal to overhaul the adoption criteria had been included in Garrett's report, so the new director would at least have her suggestions in writing. Not the perfect outcome, but better than no change at all.

And she had Garrett to thank for supporting her ideas. If she couldn't run the agency, then she hoped Garrett would. He had the integrity and vision to overhaul the organization and bring it into the future.

Now all she had to do was try to forget about him and move forward herself.

She found Garrett already at his desk, sleeves rolled up, his dark hair somewhat disheveled. Her treacherous heart constricted on a wave of longing, one she hoped would fade in time. His dark lashes cast shadows on his chiseled cheeks as he stared at the paperwork in front of him. His shoulders sagged, and deep grooves were etched into his brow. She couldn't help but remember how he'd brimmed with enthusiasm when he first came to the department and compare it to how defeated he looked now.

Had she done this to him?

He looked up. "Jane. Good morning." He stood and reached for his jacket on the chair behind him.

She entered the room, unable to force a cheery greeting in return. "I came to tell you that I've made my decision," she said without preamble, willing her spine to remain firm and her lips not to tremble.

His hand stilled as he let the jacket fall back on the chair. "From the look on your face, it doesn't appear to be good news."

"Probably not." She hiked the strap of her bag higher on her shoulder, staring at a point just below his chin. "I've decided to give Donald another chance. I'm going to be a caregiver for his son while we see if we can make our relationship work again."

Garrett's features solidified until his face appeared to be carved from granite. But his eyes came alive with anguish.

"You need to make your decision without any undue influence from me."

Why did he have to be so noble? Was it foolish to wish he would tell her he loved her and wanted to marry her, that they could adopt Martin together? If only he would, then she'd have another option to consider. One that could change everything.

She remained still, save for the frantic beating of her heart, awaiting his reaction.

"I see." He folded his arms in front of him, his shuttered expression now unreadable. "What does that mean for your job here?"

She blinked, and her mouth gaped open. Her job? That's what he was concerned about?

With considerable effort, she pulled herself together and once again donned her professional armor. "I will be tendering my resignation, effective at the end of the week."

His brow remained furrowed. "Are you sure about this, Jane? What if it doesn't work out? You'll become attached to a child who'll be taken away, and you won't even have your job to fall back on."

She pushed back the cold fissure of fear that opened in her chest. If she didn't take the risk, she'd always wonder if she could have had the life she'd longed for, being a mother not only to Martin but to a baby boy. One who would know no other mother but her.

"If that were to happen," she said, "I'm fairly certain I could get my caseworker position back. But if not, they're still hiring women in the factories." Her voice sounded as raspy as sandpaper. "I can always find another job, but the opportunity to have a family will only come along once. How can I not try?"

He shook his head sadly. "Then I pray it all works out the way you want, Jane. You deserve to be happy." He yanked his jacket off the chair. "Excuse me, but I have an appointment to get to."

Then he swept past her out the door.

———— ❖ ————

Blinded by his haze of pain, Garrett had no idea where he was heading as he strode down Isabella Street. But he couldn't stay in that building another second, not with a tidal wave of regret building in his chest. And not with Jane looking at him so expectantly, as though waiting for him to say something or do something. Like what? Propose to her himself?

Not that he wasn't tempted, but when it came right down to it, Jane was better off with Donald and the stable family her ex-husband could give her. All Garrett could offer was an uncertain medical diagnosis and a failing farm.

His gut gave a hard twist. The kindest thing he could do for her was take a giant step back, remain silent, and allow her to realize her dreams. No matter how difficult it would be for him. At least next week, she wouldn't be sitting down the hall from him any longer, and he could avoid the torment of seeing her every day.

After stopping at the boardinghouse to change clothes, then telephoning Melanie at the office to tell her he would be out for the rest of the day, Garrett got back in his car and headed home. The one place that always gave him solace.

The drive through the country seemed agonizingly slow until he turned at last onto the country lane that led to the farm. He parked the car and jogged up the steps into the house, expecting to find his mother hard at work in the kitchen as usual. But the room sat empty, and a strange pall hung in the air. Where were Mom and Cassie? Normally, they would be elbow-deep in some sort of baking at this point in the day.

He walked farther into the room and frowned. Two broken pieces of crockery lay on the kitchen table. He lifted one piece and ran his fingers over the jagged edge. It was his mother's favorite teapot, the one his grandmother had passed down from their English ancestors. Mom would be devastated over the loss. But what had happened to it?

He frowned. Last weekend, he'd sensed an underlying current of tension between his sister and his parents. He'd overheard bits of conversation alluding to fighting amongst the boys and escalating bad behavior on Kevin's part, but he hadn't had a chance to ask if Martin was a factor in this. Could this broken teapot have anything to do with that?

"Mom?" he called out. "Are you upstairs?"

Only silence answered him.

A chill of apprehension raced through his veins. Surely nothing had happened to her? Or to Dad? He strode to the back door, pushed it open, and stepped outside. Maybe she was feeding the chickens, or gathering the last of the vegetables from the garden before the first frost set in. He headed across the lawn until he saw a familiar figure standing at the clothesline, pinning the laundry in place. The wave of relief that crashed over him nearly buckled his knees.

Thank you, Lord. He must be feeling overly emotional after the episode with Jane.

"Hi, Mom," he called out, not wishing to scare her with his unexpected arrival.

She whipped around, a wooden peg falling from her fingers. "Garrett. What are you doing here in the middle of the day?"

He came to a stop as he noticed her swollen eyes. "What's the matter?" he asked. "Why have you been crying?"

She wiped a hand across her cheeks. "It's just been a bad morning, is all."

"For me too. That's why I came home." He frowned. "I saw the broken teapot. Is that what's upset you?"

She shrugged, then bent to pick up the wicker basket. "That's part of it. The boys were fighting at breakfast this morning, and Martin accidentally knocked the teapot off the counter."

"Fighting? As in physically?" It would take more than an argument to break crockery.

His mother nodded. "I've been trying to keep things under control, but Martin's behavior is getting worse instead of better. I'm afraid Cassie is at her wits' end with his bad influence on her boys. Kevin's become more belligerent, and Dale's vocabulary has taken a distinct turn for the worse." She released a sigh, her eyes clouding with regret. "I know we promised to keep Martin until you find him a new foster home, but I'm not sure it's fair to Cassie and the kids."

Garrett raked his fingers through his hair. Why hadn't his parents said anything about Martin before now? "We're about to make a decision regarding a foster family for him. Can you hang in for another few days?"

A cool breeze blew up, snapping the laundry out from the line.

"I'll try," she said. "As much as I hate to admit it, I don't think we have the stamina for him right now." She shook her head. "Especially after the news we got today."

"What news?"

Her mouth began to quiver. "Bad news about Jack."

His gut tightened as he sucked in a breath. *Dear God, no. Not Jack.* "He isn't . . . ?" He couldn't bring himself to say the word.

"No, at least we don't think so. The telegram said he's been injured in battle and taken to a hospital somewhere in Italy. But when Cassie called the war office, they couldn't give us any more details. Of course, your sister is imagining the worst." She gave a watery smile. "I guess that telegram brought back the horrible memories of the day we got the same news about you."

He reached over and pulled his mother's trembling frame into a hug. It struck him then that she seemed frailer than he'd always thought. "I ended up fine. Jack will too."

Another gust of wind blew Mom's dress about her knees, molding it to her frame. "Come on," he said. "Let's go inside and talk some more."

She sniffed. "Yes. I want to know what's brought you all the way out here in the middle of the week."

A few minutes later, Garrett had a pot of coffee brewing on the stove while Mom got out the cookie tin. Oatmeal raisin, his favorite. But today he had no appetite for them.

"Where's Dad?"

"In the orchard, clearing out the rest of the apples."

"I'll go help him after my coffee."

"He'll appreciate that."

Garrett poured the coffees and carried them to the table, carefully moving the broken teapot to the counter.

"So, what's going on?" Mom took her chair. "You didn't lose your job, did you?"

"No."

"Then what upset you enough to come home?"

He shrugged, avoiding her eyes. "Jane resigned this morning."

His mother gasped. "What? Why would she do that? She told me how much she loves her work."

Garrett tried to keep his tone light but knew full well his mom would see right through him. "Her ex-husband came back from overseas, and they've decided to attempt a reconciliation." The words scraped across his tongue like a rusty blade.

But it was his heart that bled.

"Oh no." Mom reached over to lay her hand on his arm. "I thought the two of you were . . . I mean, Jane seemed to really care about you. And you seemed to care a lot about her."

"I do." He stared at the brown liquid in his mug. "But Donald is a widower now, with a baby boy to consider."

"Oh, honey. I'm so sorry."

His throat seized up, and he swallowed hard. "I had to get out of the office. I'll schedule off-site meetings for the next few days until she's gone."

"Did you tell Jane how you feel about her?"

He shook his head. "It wouldn't have been fair. Not with my health situation. She's better off with Donald and his baby. Jane's wanted a child for a long time now. I have to try to be happy for her."

"Oh, Garrett. You deserve love and a family too." She sighed heavily as tears sprang to her eyes. "All the more reason you should push to get a specialist appointment. Maybe a new doctor could offer you fresh hope."

He shook his head again and rose. A specialist couldn't change the position of the shrapnel pieces. Or suddenly be able to operate when others had told him it was too dangerous. "I'd better go help Dad."

At least then he wouldn't have to see the pity in his mother's eyes.

30

"Jane, this is Mrs. Hedley, my son's nanny. Mrs. Hedley, this is Jane, my former wife."

Standing in the makeshift nursery in Donald's apartment, Jane smiled at the plump woman who she gauged to be in her early sixties. She wore a standard white apron over her dress, thick stockings, and sturdy shoes. "Nice to meet you, Mrs. Hedley."

"Likewise." She scrutinized Jane from head to toe. "I understand you're going to be Patrick's new nanny."

Jane hesitated, not sure exactly what Donald had told the woman. "That's right."

Donald moved closer to the crib. "Jane is eager to learn all she can from you before you head back home, Mrs. Hedley."

"I'm happy to help, sir. You know how much I adore little Patrick."

"I do indeed."

"If it weren't for my dear sister back home, I'd consider staying here with you." She shot Jane a wary look.

Jane couldn't blame the woman for her mistrust. After all, it was an incredibly unusual situation. "I promise I'll take the best care possible of Patrick."

The woman sniffed. "You will after I teach you all you need to know."

Donald seemed to sag with relief. "Could I have a few minutes alone with Jane and the baby, please?"

"Certainly, sir."

The woman left the room and right away there seemed to be more air circulating.

Donald shrugged. "She means well. She's just a little overprotective when it comes to Patrick."

"I understand." Jane peered over the rail, eager for a closer look at the precious baby. Her heart fairly melted as she gazed at him. The boy slept on his back with his hands flung out to the sides, a knitted blue blanket covering his body. Fair lashes matched the tufts of hair on his head. "He's adorable, Donald. He looks a lot like you."

Donald beamed. "Thank you." He reached into the crib and tenderly picked the boy up, laying him in the crook of his arm. "This little tyke has been through a lot in his short life. But I'm determined he won't suffer any more. That he'll have a mother who will love him as much as Moira did."

Almost as though the mention of his mother's name summoned him awake, little Patrick blinked and opened his eyes. Gray eyes just like Donald's stared back at Jane with such innocence that a sudden rise of emotion clogged her throat. This is what *their* son would have looked like. Jane swallowed and pushed her grief back where it belonged to focus on the child in front of her.

Staring at Jane, his little face crumpled, and he let out a whimper.

"Shh, it's all right," Donald crooned. "Daddy's here."

The boy instantly quieted, and his eyes drifted closed again.

Donald swayed with the boy in his arms. "He usually sleeps through the night, but right now his schedule is a little mixed up. I should have realized that when I invited you over."

"The poor thing. His whole world has turned upside down." Jane couldn't resist reaching out to smooth down a lock of wispy hair.

Donald eased the child back into the bed and repositioned the blanket. "He should sleep for several hours now. Would you like to come with me to the market before it closes? I have to pick up a few groceries."

Jane hesitated. She'd hoped to have longer with Patrick, but since that wasn't the case, the least she could do was spend time with the man she was considering remarrying. "That would be nice."

They left the door ajar and crossed a short hall to the living room, furnished with a rather worn brown couch and two armchairs. Mrs. Hedley came in from the kitchen with a cup in her hand.

"Jane and I are going to the market. Is there anything more you need, Mrs. Hedley?" Donald asked.

"I think everything is on the list I gave you. Do you have your food stamps?"

"I do. Thanks." He patted his jacket pocket. "We won't be too long."

The woman nodded. "Good night, Mrs. Linder."

For the first time, Jane's name jarred her. She still bore Donald's surname, which must seem odd to the woman.

By the front door, Donald helped Jane into her coat.

"Where does Mrs. Hedley sleep?" Jane asked as she tied a kerchief under her chin.

"On a cot in Patrick's room," he said. "I wasn't able to find a three-bedroom flat on such short notice. But it's only for a couple of weeks."

They descended the stairs to the street below. Though it was just after five o'clock, the sun had started its descent, casting a golden hue over the sidewalk. She'd left work a little early to come straight over to the apartment.

"I've been meaning to ask how Brandon is doing," Donald said as they made their way past several shops. "I assume from what you said that he enlisted?"

"He did. About a week after you." Jane swallowed back another rush of sadness. Right after her husband deserted her, the only other male in her life had abandoned her too. Deep down, she understood it wasn't personal and was proud of Brandon's desire to defend their country, but at the time, it had only compounded her depression. "Sadly, Brandon's been declared missing in action. We haven't heard anything in weeks."

"I'm so sorry, Jane. That's tough." Donald's mouth turned grim. "I'm lucky my injury was only minor. Enough to get me away from the front line for a while."

"Mama is convinced Brandon will come home to us. But I'm not so sure. Still, I have to let Mama stay optimistic until we hear anything definite." She pulled her coat tighter at her neck. "What about your brother? How is he doing?"

"Last I heard, Peter was fine, though it's been some time now since I've had a letter. Probably because he hasn't gotten word that I'm back in Canada."

Jane nodded. "I'll add him to my nightly prayers. If only this war would end. It's been dragging on far too long."

They entered the crowded grocery store, where Jane's senses were bombarded by the pungent aromas of garlic and onions and coffee beans.

Donald pulled a list from his pocket. As he picked out the items he needed, Jane couldn't shake the somber mood that had come over her with the talk of war. Sometimes it was better to avoid the newspapers and radio broadcasts and pretend that nothing was amiss in the world.

But then again, that was only avoiding reality.

When Donald had paid for his groceries and they'd retraced their steps back to his building, Jane hesitated at the entrance. The thought of going back up to the apartment had lost its appeal, knowing that the baby would be asleep. "I hope you don't mind, but I think I'll catch a bus home. Mama will be waiting for me."

Donald switched the brown bag to his left arm. "If you wait for me to put these things away, I can escort you."

She took a step back. "Thanks, but there's no need. I take the bus alone all the time."

"If you're sure."

"Positive." She forced a tight smile.

"Then I guess I'll bid you good night." He leaned toward her, and his lips grazed her cheek.

The familiar scent of his aftershave swirled around her, bringing with it a host of unbidden memories. As soon as she could politely do so, she stepped away from him. "Good night, Donald."

"Good night. I hope to see you soon. Perhaps I can meet Martin this weekend?" His fair brows rose over hopeful eyes.

She forced back the tide of uncertainty racing through her. Donald was making an effort. She needed to do the same. "I'd like that. I'll see if I can make the arrangements tomorrow."

———— ⚜ ————

Garrett paced the conference room where he awaited several of the board members. He'd been summoned to their location almost as soon as he reached the office and, being painfully aware of Jane's presence down the hall, had been only too glad to make his escape and avoid her.

Did that make him a coward? Probably. But he liked to think it was for her benefit as well, making her last days at work more comfortable.

Mr. Fenmore and Mr. Warren, along with seven other members, entered the room, followed by the woman who took the minutes. Mr. Fenmore shook Garrett's hand and indicated for him to take a seat.

Mr. Fenmore called the meeting to order. "All the members

couldn't make it today, but we have enough for a quorum. Let's get started, shall we? This shouldn't take long."

Garrett willed his heart rate to settle. Would they be ready to announce the new director already?

"Due to Mrs. Linder's recent resignation, the board has come to a decision. As a result of the good work we've seen from you so far, Mr. Wilder, we'd like to appoint you as interim director until such time that we make our final decision."

A bead of disappointment ran through him. But what did he expect? That they would forgo any other potential candidates and hand him the position on a silver platter? Hopefully, being the interim director would give him a longer opportunity to prove his merit.

Garrett cleared his throat. "Thank you very much. I graciously accept your offer."

"Excellent." Mr. Fenmore beamed. "Now, as to the matter of your salary." He swept his arm toward Mr. Warren, who nodded.

"We are prepared to increase your salary to the level of acting director." He named a figure that made Garrett's heart thump. "Is this acceptable?"

"It's more than generous. Thank you."

That amount would go a long way to help cover any loss the farm had sustained with the less-than-successful apple season.

Mr. Fenmore congratulated him with a hearty handshake, and Garrett forced a smile to accompany his enthusiastic acceptance. This was one big step closer to the goal he'd been working toward. So, why did a hole remain in the pit of his stomach?

Instead of taking the streetcar back to the office, he decided to walk. He had a few things to work out about the way he wanted to move forward in his new position. As interim director, he couldn't make many permanent changes, but he could act on the outstanding matters at hand. The first and most pressing one being to choose a foster family for Martin.

Garrett had spoken with Mrs. Blackwood the other day and

promised her an answer by the end of the week. That, on top of Cassie's reluctance to keep the boy at the farm, had sealed his decision. He pushed aside a twinge of guilt, knowing Jane wouldn't agree. But then Jane was no longer part of the process since today was her last day, and he had to make the decision he felt was best.

Still, he owed it to her to at least let her know what he'd decided.

As soon as he reached his office, he set down his briefcase and, steeling himself for the upcoming conversation, headed down the hall to Jane's office. He knocked on her closed door and waited, but there was no response. When he tried her door, he found it unlocked. However, when he peered inside, Jane wasn't there. Perhaps she'd gone over to the shelter to say her good-byes.

Somewhat relieved, he went back to his office and picked up the telephone. He placed the happy phone call first, making arrangements with the Blackwoods to deliver Martin to them on Monday morning. Then he called the Jeffersons to relay the news that they'd chosen a different family for Martin. He thanked them for their time and promised to keep them in mind for another child in need of placement.

Pleased with their easy acceptance of his decision, Garrett jotted a note on his pad to make a more thorough study of the children still at the shelter and determine why Jane hadn't placed one of them with the Jeffersons. If foster families were in such short supply, the least they could do was make use of the ones they did have available.

A knock at the door brought Garrett's attention back to his cluttered desk. "Come in."

The door opened and Jane stepped in, her presence drawing the very air from the room. "I hear congratulations are in order," she said. "Mr. Fenmore just called to relay the news."

"Thank you. It's only an interim post, but I'm hopeful it will lead to something permanent." He didn't know what else to say. How hard must it be for her to leave her job and hand it over to him? But maybe now she had a different goal to look forward to.

She hesitated, then came a few steps closer. "I have a favor to ask."

He laid down his pen. "What is it?"

"I'd like to bring Martin into the city this weekend to meet Donald. However, I'm not sure the best way to go about it."

Tingles of suspicion traveled up his spine. "Why would you want to do that?"

She twisted her hands in front of her, then squared her shoulders. "If Donald and I decide to remarry, I intend to adopt Martin. But Donald wants to get to know him first."

The floor seemed to drop out from beneath him. Whatever happened to Donald not wanting to adopt? Garrett dragged a hand across his jaw. "That might pose a bit of a problem."

"I know it's hard being so far out in the country. Donald doesn't own a car yet, so we can't go there to get him."

"That's not what I meant." He forced himself to remain professional. "I've just informed the Blackwoods that I'll be placing Martin with them as of Monday."

Her mouth fell open, and she grasped the back of the chair in front of her. "What?"

"I stopped by to let you know, but you weren't in your office. I figured there was no point in putting it off any longer." He glanced at her stricken face, his resolve slipping a notch. "Maybe I could bring Martin to your house on Sunday. He could stay with you overnight before I take him to the Blackwoods. It would give you and Donald the afternoon and evening with him."

She blinked several times. "I suppose that would work." But she crossed her arms, not appearing any happier. "So, you decided on the Blackwoods after all?"

"I did." They'd already been over the reasons he felt they were preferable to the Jeffersons, so he wouldn't justify his decision to her. But he could offer her a crumb of hope. "You still might be able to adopt Martin down the road if that's what you decide," he said. "I don't think the Blackwoods will adopt him straightaway. They seem adamant about only wanting an infant."

"But it would mean moving him again." Jane shook her head. "He was just getting used to the farm. I was hoping your parents could keep him a few more months. Would that be possible?"

A few months? His chest tightened. Was that how little time she intended to wait until she remarried Donald?

"I'm afraid things aren't going as well as we thought." He frowned, tapping his pen on the desktop. "I just found out that Martin has been creating problems. Cassie is worried about the influence he's having on Kevin and Dale. It's causing a considerable strain on the household." He dared to look at her then, a mistake on his part. His heart cinched at the agony in her eyes, twin pools shimmering with moisture.

"Cassie's even more on edge lately since she got word Jack has been injured. She can't really cope with the added stress." He deserved the guilt he felt now. After all, it had been his idea to bring Martin to the farm. He let out a slow breath. "I'm sorry things didn't work out the way we'd hoped."

"It's not your fault," she said at last. Then she stared at him, unspoken regret clouding the air between them. "We tried our best. I guess it wasn't meant to be."

His collar suddenly seemed too tight. "I'll call your mother's house on Sunday and let you know when to expect us."

"Thank you," she said. "And congratulations again. I know you'll make a great interim director."

With a final trembling smile, she walked out of his office.

Garrett's chest deflated with a long release of air. If only he could be as magnanimous toward Jane and her future endeavors. Maybe with enough time, prayer, and distance, he could master that particular skill.

31

On Sunday morning, after returning from church with Mama, Jane busied herself preparing a light lunch while attempting to ignore the nerves twisting her belly into knots. Today would prove to be momentous in more ways than one.

Today, Mama would see Donald again for the first time in years as well as meet his infant son. Jane held no illusions that it would be a happy reunion, since Mama had made her disapproval of Donald apparent every chance she got. Jane only hoped little Patrick would soften her heart enough to forgive Donald.

But it was Martin's arrival that was uppermost on Jane's mind. It was imperative that the boy make a good impression on Donald. Yet knowing the way Martin operated, he'd probably be reeling from the news that he was being placed with yet another foster family and would most likely act out. But Jane was running out of time. Once he went to the Blackwoods, she would have no way for Donald to meet him.

After she carried her mother's lunch into the living room and set it in front of her, Jane peered out the window to the quiet street beyond. At least the weather was cooperating with her idea for this afternoon. Wanting to do something active to keep Martin busy, she'd planned an outing to the harbor, where they could watch the boats come in. And afterward, perhaps Donald and Martin could bond by flying a kite in the nearby park.

So much was riding on this meeting today. It just had to go well. It was the only way her future made sense. The only way to justify walking away from her career.

Her fingers tightened on the window ledge as her thoughts drifted back to those last heart-wrenching moments in the Children's Aid office. On Friday afternoon, Jane had endured the heartfelt good-byes and good wishes of her co-workers, then waited until everyone had left for the weekend. In the hushed silence that remained, she took her final tour of the building that had meant so much to her, where she'd spent so much time over the last decade. The stenographers' pool where she'd first started as a clerk, the crowded rooms upstairs where she'd worked as a caseworker, the tiny staff room where she'd made numerous cups of cocoa and dried countless children's tears.

At Melanie's desk, Jane had let her fingers linger on the cool metal keys of the Underwood typewriter as she inhaled the familiar scent of paper, ink, and stale coffee—smells she would forever associate with the career she loved. After a final look around, she'd headed to the last room on her list. The most difficult room of all.

It was impossible to steel herself from the emotions swirling through her as she opened the door to Garrett's office and snapped on the light with a quiet click. Standing there, she absorbed the pure essence of him that permeated the room. The tidy desk, the lingering smell of his aftershave, the spare jacket that hung on the coatrack. All memories of the man who had come to mean so much to her. Reminders of the life she could have had if only the circumstances had been different.

Lord, have I done the right thing? I thought my place was here, helping children find a home. Yet my heart yearns so deeply for a child of my own. If marrying Donald and being a mother to his son is truly your will for me, help me to be brave and step boldly into my future with no regrets.

Jane had walked to the coatrack in the corner and removed the starched white handkerchief from the breast pocket of the jacket Garrett had left there. She held it to her nose, inhaling the memory of the man who invoked such strong feelings in her. Then, unable to relinquish this last reminder of him, she tucked the handkerchief into her skirt pocket. After a final lingering glance around, she'd turned off the light and closed the door firmly behind her, bringing an end to that chapter of her life in preparation to start another.

Jane pushed away those painful memories and let the parlor curtain fall back into place. Dwelling on the past wouldn't change anything. She needed to leave her memories firmly where they belonged and focus on the future.

"Jane, honey, there's someone here."

Mama's voice broke Jane from her dismal thoughts. Surprised she hadn't heard the bell, Jane whirled around and rushed to answer the door.

"Good afternoon, Donald." Her forced cheeriness sounded almost as false as her smile felt. Then her gaze fell to the baby and her insides melted. "Please come in."

She took Patrick from Donald's arms so he could remove his hat and overcoat. Under a knitted blue bonnet, little Patrick gazed up at her with unblinking eyes. Her throat cinched on a rush of emotion. This little one needed a mother. He needed *her*. This was the very reason she'd given up everything else. Surely it would be worth it in the end.

"I haven't been in here for years," Donald said, scanning the entryway. "The place hasn't changed at all."

"Come into the parlor and see Mama."

Donald walked in and hesitated in front of Mama's chair as though unsure how to greet her. "Hello, Hildie. It's good to see you."

Mama's cool stare held him in place. "Hello, Donald," she said. "I must say I'm surprised to see you again."

Donald nodded. "I know. I never expected to end up back here. A widower with a baby to raise."

"And Jane certainly never expected her husband would walk out on her." Her mother lifted her chin, totally unrepentant for her confrontational attitude.

"You have every right to be angry," Donald said with amazing candor. "I've apologized to Jane and told her how much I regret my actions. I promise to do my best to make it up to both of you."

Jane moved in to alleviate the awkwardness. "Mama, this is Donald's son, Patrick." She set the baby on her mother's lap. The little boy looked at her mother with a toothless grin, save for two tiny bottom teeth.

Mama's features softened like ice cream sitting on the counter too long. "Aren't you a precious thing?" she crooned as she jiggled the boy on her lap.

Jane turned to Donald. "Have a seat. I'll put on the kettle for tea."

She had just headed toward the kitchen when the doorbell rang again. Her feet froze, her heart beating a frantic rhythm that matched the nervous flutter in her belly.

Garrett was early. She hadn't expected him for another hour or so and had hoped to have time to speak with Donald about Martin and what to expect from the boy.

She took in a calming breath, smoothed her skirt, and opened the door. Nothing could have prepared her for the way her whole being jolted at the sight of Garrett standing there, so solemn and strong, his hand on Martin's shoulder.

"Hello, Jane." His voice sounded different, strangled somehow. He wore a simple blue shirt that made his eyes appear brighter than Mama's forget-me-nots in the spring.

"Hi." She couldn't seem to make her tongue formulate any other words, so she simply stared, memorizing every detail of his face. The finely shaped brows, the dark lashes, the cleft in his noble chin.

Garrett set a small suitcase on the floor. "Here are some of Martin's things. I'll keep the rest in the car until tomorrow."

"Thank you. Come on in, Martin."

The boy scowled, not seeming the least bit happy to see her.

Her stomach sank. If only she could reassure him that this stay was temporary, that she would be his mother one day soon. But it was too early for such promises.

"Well, who is this? You must be Martin." Donald came into the hallway, a wide smile on his face.

Jane cringed inside. This was not how she'd wanted to make the introduction. And certainly not in front of Garrett.

"Martin, this is my . . . friend, Donald."

"Hello, young man. Jane has told me all about you. We're going to take you out for a fun afternoon."

Martin stared up at Donald, a slight sneer curling his lip.

"Remember your manners, Martin," she warned.

"Hello, sir," he muttered. "I'm going to say hi to Mrs. Mitchell."

"We'll be right in." Jane attempted a light tone, but if her stomach twisted any tighter, she just might pass out.

"You're the guy from Jane's office, right?" Donald stepped forward and offered his hand.

"That's right." Garrett hesitated for a split second before he shook it. "Garrett Wilder."

Donald released Garrett's hand and draped an arm across Jane's shoulders. "Thanks for bringing the boy. I know it means a lot to Jane."

Garrett's steady gaze moved to her. "That's the only reason I'm here."

Her lungs seized, trapping the air inside as surely as the weight of Donald's arm trapped her in place. She wanted to shrug it off, to tell Donald this was all a horrible mistake, but then the baby let out a loud squawk from the parlor, and all her motivation for doing this came rushing to the forefront.

"That's my son." Donald laughed. "I'd better make sure he's all right. Nice meeting you, Garrett." Donald squeezed Jane's shoulder before he walked away.

She wrapped her arms around her middle, struggling for something to say, wanting Garrett to stay but needing him to go.

He studied her with an inscrutable regard. "I hope you understand why I didn't stay to say good-bye on Friday. I thought it would be better for the both of us if I wasn't there."

She nodded. "I needed to be alone, to leave in my own way." Her cheeks heated at the thought of his handkerchief tucked away in her drawer.

He stuffed his hands in his pockets. "I wish you nothing but happiness, Jane. I hope you find the family and the love you deserve." Though his words were even, a quiet despair filled his gaze. "I want you to know I'll do my best to carry on your hard work at the agency until the new director is named."

Unwanted tears burned her eyes. "I know you will." She swallowed. "And if you ever need advice, I'm available . . . for a small fee." She laughed a bit too loud.

When he joined her, the tension released inside her like air leaking from a balloon.

"I should go," he said. "I'll pick Martin up tomorrow morning around nine o'clock."

"Thanks again."

"You're welcome." He gave her a ghost of his regular smile, then headed toward his car without ever looking back.

32

"Here comes a good gust now!" Jane shielded her eyes, tilting her head to watch the shaky progress of Martin's kite as it weaved and bobbed across the sky.

The sun had already begun its slow descent. They'd spent a couple of hours walking by the water, enjoying the unseasonably mild November day, and watching all the different boats that moved in and out of the harbor, including the island ferry. When Jane had suggested the kite idea, Martin had shown the first real spark of interest.

"That's it. Let out some more line," Donald called, running alongside him. His always-immaculate hair blew across his forehead, his tie fluttering out behind him like his own kite tail.

Martin squinted upward as he jogged, holding his arms up as high as he could. When the wind suddenly dropped, the kite plummeted downward, just as Martin's foot hit a tree root. He sprawled to the ground, dragging the kite with him.

Donald skidded to a halt. His face grew taut, and his mouth compressed into a thin line.

Jane pushed the baby carriage over the grass to reach Martin. "You were doing great," she said. "Want to try again?"

Martin jumped to his feet and went to examine the kite. The wooden spine had cracked, poking a gaping hole through the fabric. The boy picked it up, his face contorting with a mixture of disappointment and rage. "Stupid kite."

"That's too bad." Donald rolled down his sleeves. "I guess that's the end for today."

"Flying kites is for babies anyway." Martin scowled and threw the kite on the ground.

But Jane could tell by the way his chin crumpled that he was about to cry, and she knew he wouldn't want anyone to see.

Sure enough, the boy darted across the lawn toward the street, his jacket flapping open as he ran.

"Take the carriage," she said to Donald. "I'm going after him."

Without waiting for a reply, she dashed across the uneven ground, scattering dead leaves as she ran. "Martin. Wait."

She had no real expectation he would obey, but to her surprise and relief, he came to a halt at the edge of the grass and sank down, bringing his chin to his knees.

If she hadn't been wearing a dress, Jane would have sat beside him. Instead, she leaned over her knees, trying to catch her breath.

"I'm sorry your kite broke," she said when she could talk again. "It wasn't your fault."

The boy dragged a hand across his face. "He thinks it is."

"No, he doesn't. He saw you trip. It was an accident." She pulled her cardigan tighter to combat the wind. "Come on. Let's go back to the house and have dinner."

Martin peered at her from under his unruly bangs. "Is *he* going to be there?"

"Well, yes. Donald's our guest tonight."

"Why?"

She hesitated for a moment, then decided to risk soiling her dress and sat on the ground beside him. As much as she wanted to give the boy some hope, some inkling of what might happen in the near future, she couldn't risk it all falling apart. But she could tell him a little about her circumstances.

"Donald used to be my husband before he went away to war. Now he's back, and he wants to be my husband again." Her stomach pinched at those words, but she ignored it and continued. "So, we're spending time together to see if that's what we both want."

Martin plucked a blade of grass. "Whose baby is that?"

Oh, she should have been prepared for that question. "It's Donald's. He had another wife for a while," she said. "But she died a few months ago."

Martin stared at her unhappily. "You're going to be the baby's mother?"

Jane nodded. "If we decide to get remarried, then yes, I'll be Patrick's mother." Emotion tightened her chest simply saying the words out loud. "Now, come on. Donald's waiting for us."

"I don't think he likes me."

She paused, not wanting to discount his feelings. "He just needs to get to know you better. We'll work on that at dinner. I'm making your favorite."

"Spaghetti and meatballs?"

"That's right." It was worth using some of her meat rations to make Martin's favorite dish. She rose and held out her hand to help him stand.

"Mrs. Linder? Why do I have to go to another home tomorrow? I know I shouldn't have fought with Kevin and Dale, but if I try harder, could I stay on the farm?" The sadness in his voice tore at Jane's heartstrings.

"Oh, honey, I'm sorry but no. It was too much for the Wilders with all the kids and the farm to run." She put a hand on his shoulder as they walked back to Donald and the baby. "But you had a good time there for a while, right?"

"Yeah. It was fun with all the animals. I'll miss Blackie a lot."

She wanted to promise him the moon and the stars, but she'd already said too much. "You keep saying your prayers every night, honey. I know God will find you the right home yet."

Jane only prayed it would be with her.

———— ❦ ————

Dinner was a rather strained affair with Martin trying so hard to be good that he basically said nothing at all. Mama wasn't herself either. Donald did most of the talking, recounting his adventures in England and a little of his experiences in the war. He seemed to hold back, as though sensing his talk of war might upset Mama, and of course, Martin didn't need to be exposed to such horrors. Little Patrick provided relief from the tension, playing with a wooden spoon and making funny noises, while watching every move Martin made, clearly fascinated with the older boy.

Before long, however, the baby grew tired, rubbing his chubby fists into his eyes and beginning to whine.

"I'd better get this young man home to bed." Donald rose, taking Patrick in his arms. "Thank you all for a lovely meal and visit."

Martin jumped up from his chair. "I'll help clear the table, Mrs. Linder."

"Thank you. That would be nice," Jane said. "You can stack the dishes on the kitchen counter."

She walked Donald to the front door and helped him put on Patrick's jacket.

"Thank you for trying so hard today, Donald. I think overall it went pretty well." She did her best to ignore her misgivings over the awkward dinner. After all, she never expected their first meeting to go perfectly.

He buttoned his overcoat. "I'm sure it will just take time for us to get used to each other. Will we see you tomorrow?"

Monday would be the first day Jane wouldn't be going to the office, and she would need a distraction to keep from mourning the loss of her career. "Yes, I plan to spend some time with Mrs. Hedley and become familiar with the baby's routine. How does nine o'clock sound?"

"Perfect. I have a job interview in the afternoon, so that will give us some time together. Perhaps we could even go somewhere for lunch?"

"An interview! How wonderful." She ignored the implied date-like invitation, not certain if she was ready for that. "What type of job is it?"

"A sales position." He shifted the baby to the crook of one arm, giving her a quiet smile that told her he was aware of her avoidance tactic. "Until tomorrow then, Jane."

He bent toward her, his lips claiming hers in a light kiss. She forced herself to relax as old memories fought to surface. Like the first time he'd kissed her on the front porch, how nervous she'd been that she didn't know what to do, and how sweet he'd been, never pressuring her for more.

Now, seeming to sense her hesitation, he kept the kiss brief. "Good night, Jane."

"Good night." She gave a self-conscious laugh and turned her attention to the baby, skimming a finger down his soft cheek. "Good night to you, sweet boy. I'll see you tomorrow."

After Donald left, Jane locked the door for the night and allowed a sigh to escape. It would take a while for affection to grow again. In the meantime, she needed to grant herself a little grace in that regard and take this new relationship one day at a time.

— ❖ —

On Monday morning, Garrett parked his car outside Jane's house, likely for the last time. After today, he'd have no reason to see her again. Maybe then he could stop picturing an entirely different future, or at least stop torturing himself by having to see her with another man.

Still, as he approached her house, an unwarranted flare of hope burned in his chest. Hope that she might have had a change of heart overnight.

But when Hildie answered the door, a wave of disappointment hit hard.

"Good morning, Garrett." She handed him Martin's small suitcase with a tentative smile. "Martin's all ready and waiting for you."

Sure enough, the boy moved into view from behind her. Garrett attempted to peer into the hallway, but Jane was nowhere to be found. Would she really let Martin go without a proper farewell?

"Jane's over at Donald's this morning." Hildie watched him with knowing eyes. "She's already bid Martin good-bye, and she said to thank you again for bringing him."

Garrett hated the searing defeat that seeped through his system at the thought that she'd obviously left early to avoid him. When would he accept that she'd chosen Donald and was now invested in her new life?

"Be a good lad for your foster parents." Hildie patted Martin on the back. "I hope we'll see you again soon."

Martin appeared unusually sullen as he said good-bye and followed Garrett to the car.

He supposed it was only natural for the boy to feel unsettled, being uprooted so many times over the past few weeks. All Garrett could do was try to reassure him that everything would work out in time.

"The Blackwoods are a nice couple," he said in his most convincing manner as he pulled away from the curb. "I interviewed them myself to make sure."

"Will they let me have Blackie?"

Garrett glanced at the scowling boy, then back at the road. "We discussed this before we left the farm, remember? Blackie is a big dog. He needs room to run around." He bit back the urge to promise he could visit one day, since he had no idea if that would ever happen.

Garrett drove for a while in silence. Finally, he couldn't resist asking about the previous day. "Did you have a nice time with Mrs. Linder and Donald?"

"I guess."

"What did you do?"

"We went to see some boats. Then we went to a park."

"That sounds like fun."

Martin shrugged, unsmiling. "It was all right. But I wish it was just Mrs. Linder and not him too."

Hmm. It seemed Donald hadn't made a great impression on the boy.

Martin turned to look at him. "Mrs. Linder said she's going to marry him."

His stomach sank. "She did?"

The boy nodded. "I think it's 'cause he has a baby."

Garrett came to a halt at a stop sign. He waited a beat, drumming his fingers on the wheel, and at last he couldn't resist asking, "Does Donald treat Mrs. Linder nicely?"

Martin shrugged again. "He kissed her good-bye when he left, so I guess he likes her."

Garrett's gut clenched hard. Served him right for prying. Yet he had a hard time believing Jane could move so quickly from resentment to kissing.

Not that it was any longer his business whom she kissed. He gripped the steering wheel harder and accelerated through the intersection.

A few minutes later, he pulled up in front of the Blackwood house. He shut off the engine and took a moment to focus on the present situation. "Martin, I know you're scared. But right now, I want you to do your best to get along with Mr. and Mrs. Blackwood."

Martin stared out of the window, his chin quivering slightly.

Garrett's insides felt hollow. He couldn't help but feel he'd let the boy down. Had he been wrong to suggest bringing Martin to stay at his parents'? Had he only subjected the boy to another disappointment? "I'm sorry you couldn't stay at the farm longer," Garrett said, regret pushing at his throat. "But I hope you'll always remember the fun you had there."

"I'm sorry I was bad, Mr. Wilder. I didn't mean to make them angry." A tear hung on the boy's lashes.

Garrett reached over and pulled the boy into a hug. "I know you didn't. But unfortunately, actions have consequences."

Martin buried his face into Garrett's jacket. "If I promise to be better, would they let me come back?"

How he wished he could say yes. Garrett swallowed hard in order to speak again. "Maybe you can come back for a visit one day. But for now, do your best here."

Martin stared at him for a second, and then his childish features hardened into an expression far too adult for an eight-year-old. He swiped his elbow across his face and pushed open the car door.

Garrett's heart ached for him, the way he seemed to expect nothing but disappointment from the adults in his life. And despite Garrett's good intentions, he'd been no better. He clenched his teeth together. For the first time, he truly understood Jane's obsession with finding Martin the perfect home and her feeling that she'd constantly let the boy down.

Lord, protect this child. Show him your love and find him the family that will give him the stability and affection he so rightly deserves.

Forcing his emotions back, Garrett took a deep breath and got out of the car. The Blackwoods would expect a professional representative of the Children's Aid Society to handle the transaction, not an emotional wreck.

The couple opened the door with a welcoming smile and gushed over Martin as they brought him into their home. Yet, as Garrett left the boy with virtual strangers, he couldn't rid himself of the sinking feeling that he was abandoning Martin to an unknown future.

Much like his own uncertain future.

One that continued to hold him hostage.

Garrett strode back to his car, anger twisting through every muscle. He got in and slammed the door. Suddenly, doing nothing about his health seemed more cowardly than pragmatic. Didn't he owe it to himself to live life to the fullest? If he could get a definitive answer from a specialist about whether surgery was even a possibility, shouldn't he at least try?

Maybe if he had a final diagnosis, good or bad, he could stop wishing for a life he wasn't meant to live.

33

Jane laid the sleeping baby in the crib, adjusted the blanket over him, and stood watching his tiny chest rise and fall. There was something about a sleeping child that wrapped a person's soul in wonder, their sheer innocence and beauty evidence of God's grace in the world. Very quietly, she backed out of the room and walked into the living room, where Mrs. Hedley was ironing the laundry.

It had been over a week since Jane had started coming to the apartment every day, and she and the nanny had developed a good rapport. Once Mrs. Hedley had gotten past her initial mistrust, she had eagerly shared all her expertise in caring for Patrick.

Donald had been offered the sales job and had started work the next day. Was Jane a terrible person to be less than thrilled that her husband-to-be was now a car salesman?

"Is the wee angel asleep?" Mrs. Hedley asked. Steam hissed from the iron as she slid it across the fabric.

"He is." Jane dropped into one of the chairs. "Who knew caring for one tiny being could be so exhausting?"

Mrs. Hedley chuckled. "And you get to go home at the end of the day. Imagine when it's all night too."

Jane grimaced.

The woman set the iron on its stand. "I will miss that boy when I leave, but I must admit, I'm glad to be going home."

"I'm sure you are."

Mrs. Hedley folded the blouse and set it aside, then gave her a funny stare. "What about you, Jane? Are you really ready to marry again? I'd imagine you'd be leery to trust Donald after what he put you through."

Jane straightened on her chair. What exactly did this woman know about her and Donald's past? It sounded like she was trying to warn her. "When it comes to Patrick, I have no qualms at all. But to be honest, I'm not certain about marrying Donald yet. Which is why I'm taking things slowly."

"You've given up your career," Mrs. Hedley said, her expression serious as she unplugged the iron. "I'd hate it to be for nothing if things don't work out."

Unease slid through Jane's system. "It's a risk I'm willing to take."

The woman's mouth turned down. "Overall, I do believe Donald is a good man. I just hope he isn't moving too fast." Mrs. Hedley reached over and patted Jane's hand. "Make sure you're marrying for the right reasons, luv. That's all I'm saying."

Then she rose and took the ironed clothes into the bedroom, leaving Jane with a sense of dread in the pit of her stomach.

———— ❖ ————

On the night before Mrs. Hedley's scheduled departure for England, Donald insisted on taking Jane out for a nice dinner.

"After all," he said, "we won't have a built-in babysitter once she's gone."

Jane wasn't sure she was ready to move to dating just yet, but at some point she'd have to put forth the effort if she intended to marry him again.

And so, she agreed to the dinner date.

Earlier, as she'd donned her best green dress, she'd smiled to herself, thinking of the little things Donald had been doing to please her over the past week. One night, he'd come home with a small bouquet of daisies. Another day, he'd brought her brownies from the local bakery she liked.

And now he was taking her to Chez Monique, a fancy restaurant in the heart of downtown known for its French cuisine.

As they entered the dimly lit dining room, with its flickering candlelight and soft music, a hard pang went through her. How she wished she were here with Garrett instead. To sit across the table from him in this romantic setting and stare into his vibrant blue eyes would be thrilling beyond measure.

But that kind of thinking wasn't fair to Donald. And as she smoothed her dress under her, she resolved to appreciate Donald for his own merits.

After an initial period of awkward silence, they passed the meal in pleasant-enough conversation. Donald recounted some amusing encounters at the car dealership. Jane did her best to listen politely and comment where it seemed appropriate.

"I don't intend for this to be my permanent career," he said quietly at the end of one story. Perhaps he'd sensed her less-than-enthusiastic response. "It will do for now, until I find a job I really want."

"What would that be? I remember when you worked for the hardware store after we were first married, you hoped to work in an office one day."

"True. I've always thought that banking would be a good fit for me. Wearing a suit and tie, having a nice office." He shrugged one shoulder. "A little easier than trying to sell cars."

She smiled. "That sounds like a good career choice." A banker's wife. Not something she ever pictured herself being, but it had the ring of respectability she liked.

Donald reached across the table and laid a hand over hers. "It would mean better hours. I could come home and eat dinner with my family every night and maybe take the kids to the park before bedtime."

Her heart stirred to a familiar dream. One they'd discussed so long ago, when they learned she was pregnant the first time. Before their dreams had been crushed by sorrow. "That sounds really nice."

And the fact that he'd said *kids* meant the world to her. It showed he was truly on board with adopting Martin. Maybe they'd even consider adopting another child down the road. Warmth that had nothing to do with her after-dinner coffee spread through her system.

"I wonder how Martin is faring at the foster home," she mused as she scraped the last of her chocolate mousse from the fancy dish. "I thought I might have heard something by now."

Donald set his coffee down, unease evident in the tension around his eyes. "Have you been in contact with Garrett?"

"No, I haven't. But he did say he'd let me know how Martin was doing, since he knows that I . . . we hope to adopt him."

"Will he be the one handling the adoption?" The soft question held a thread of disapproval.

She blinked. "I doubt it. I imagine he'll hand it off to one of the caseworkers."

"Good." He took in a deep breath. "I hope you don't think this is too forward, but I've sensed there's more between you two than just co-workers. And I couldn't help but notice some hostility toward me on his part as well." He stared at her intently enough to make her squirm. "Am I right?"

Jane swallowed her coffee. How did she answer that with anything less than the truth? "Garrett and I did grow close during our time together."

Donald frowned, grooves appearing between his brows, but he remained silent, waiting for her to continue.

"However, we both realized there were too many obstacles for us to ever have a future together." Her gaze fell to the pristine white tablecloth, hoping to mask the regret that must be evident on her face.

"I see," he said slowly. "Thank you for being honest with me. And since that's the case, I'd prefer if you didn't have any further contact with him now that you've made a commitment to me and Patrick. I hope you understand."

A bubble of irritation rose in her chest but quickly dissipated. She couldn't fault Donald for his request. And he hadn't spoken in anger. He'd simply stated a fact. To make a big issue out of it might make him believe there was more to her relationship with Garrett than there was.

"Don't worry. Once the issue of the adoption is settled, I'll have no need to contact him again." Her traitorous heart twisted at the words, and she glanced down once again to hide her conflicted emotions.

"I appreciate that. We already have enough obstacles of our own to overcome. We don't need any extra ones."

As Donald settled their bill, Jane sent up a desperate prayer. *Lord, help me to put Garrett in the past and focus my affections on what I have in front of me.*

Despite the crisp November air, they chose to walk the several blocks from the restaurant to her home rather than taking a cab, wanting a bit of exercise after the big meal they'd eaten. The streets were practically deserted at eight o'clock in the evening. Yet the glow from the streetlights and from the neon shop signs created the illusion of warmth as they walked.

In her haste this evening, Jane had forgotten her gloves, and even with her hands in her pockets, they were half frozen. At one point when they stopped to admire a window setting, Donald reached over and took one of her hands in his, his warmth curling around her fingers.

"Do you remember when we were first dating?" he asked softly. "How long it took me to work up the nerve to hold your hand?"

"I remember." She smiled, allowing the memory to drift over her. "I thought you'd never get around to it. But then that day after the football game, you walked me home and finally grabbed my fingers."

He laughed. "If memory serves, I got the nerve to do more than that once we got home."

Her cheeks heated. "Our first kiss."

"A rather awkward one, I'll admit. But I'd like to think I improved greatly after some practice."

She allowed her mind to travel back to those innocent days, before all the disappointments in life had worn them down. "You certainly did." She chuckled, recalling the many kisses they'd shared at the beginning of their romance. "One of the reasons we married so soon after graduation."

His arm came around her shoulders like a familiar hug. "I'm glad you still have some fond memories," he said. "That my actions didn't totally erase the good times we shared."

"No, they didn't." Her heart softened. "I guess it was just easier to focus on the bad times than remember the good."

"I promise I'm going to make it up to you, Jane. All I want is for us to be a family, and for you to be happy again." He brushed a soft kiss over her mouth, and this time Jane didn't shy away, allowing the warm feelings from the memories he'd brought back to carry forward into the lingering embrace.

Perhaps this relationship could work out after all.

They continued walking, holding hands, and when they reached her house, Jane hesitated. It was still early. Should she ask him in, or would that be inviting too much familiarity?

The choice was taken out of her hands when Mama opened the front door. "Jane, thank goodness you're back. Garrett called."

At once, the haze of new closeness between her and Donald vanished, and a cold burst of alarm spurted through her. "Why? Is something wrong?" Jane followed her mother into the house.

Mama twisted her hands together in front of her. "It's Martin. He's run away from the Blackwoods. Garrett thought perhaps he might have come here."

Jane's knees went weak, but she managed to rush into the parlor, where the telephone sat near Mama's chair. "Did Garrett say if he was at the agency?"

"Yes. But he was going to start looking for Martin."

"I'll try anyway, just in case." She began dialing the number, suddenly conscious of Donald standing before her.

The phone rang and rang. The start of a headache brewed at her temples as she slowly hung up the receiver. What could she do now? She didn't know the Blackwoods' number, and it wouldn't be appropriate for her to contact them anyway, since she was no longer employed by the Children's Aid.

But she ached for information. What had happened to drive Martin away? Where could he be now? Where would he go? The weather was turning colder by the minute, and if she remembered the forecast correctly, there was the possibility of snow tonight. Yet, until Garrett contacted her again, there was nothing she could do but wait.

She undid her coat and pulled it off, draping it over a chair.

"I'm sure he'll turn up soon," Donald said, a slight frown marring his brow. "Try not to worry."

"That's impossible." She paced to the fireplace and back.

Donald came up and laid a warm hand on her shoulder. "Maybe this is a sign."

"A sign of what?" Her gaze shot to his face.

Sympathy shone from his eyes, and one brow rose in a half-apology. "That perhaps the boy is too troubled for us to take on. After all, we have a young child to consider. I worry that Martin and his unpredictable moods may not be good for Patrick."

Jane stiffened, all the fear and worry balled up in her chest now aimed at Donald. "That's not true." Yet Garrett's words about Martin's influence on his nephews echoed through her brain. "I'm sure once Martin feels more secure, his behavior will change. I know it will." She pressed her lips together.

"Jane, I wanted to give it more time before I brought this up, but now seems to be the best time." Donald took her hand and led her to the sofa. "I keep thinking that there must be a reason no family will keep him."

"Of course there's a reason. No one has taken the time to show him unconditional love. Parents don't just give their child away when he doesn't behave exactly as they want, or when he has a medical condition that's inconvenient. A parent loves the child through everything, no matter what life throws at them."

The way you should have loved me.

Angry tears welled in her eyes, but she pushed them back and jumped up to pace the floor again. "Someone has to give Martin a chance and show him his true worth."

Donald stood, thrusting out his hands. "Why does that have to be you?"

She came to an abrupt halt to stare at him. "Why not me? I've loved him since I first met him as a bewildered two-year-old returned by his initial foster family. It was right after my first miscarriage, and I wanted us to take him then, but you said you didn't want to adopt. You wanted to try again for another baby."

"*He* was the child you wanted?" Donald's brows rose over incredulous eyes.

She nodded and bit down on her lip. "Not long after my second miscarriage, Martin came back to the shelter again. I brought up the subject of adoption a second time . . ." She trailed off, recalling how nervous she'd been to even ask Donald and the way he'd simply shut down afterward. The next day, he'd packed all his things and left their home.

"Since then, it's been one foster family after another. How much rejection can a child take before it breaks his spirit?" Her chin quivered and she turned away, unwilling to fall apart in front of him. Unwilling to let him see how much she still resented him for not allowing Martin to join their family back when they could have made a difference in his life.

Had Donald really changed since then, or was he only humoring her to obtain a mother for Patrick? Mrs. Hedley's warning came to mind about Donald acting too fast and about marrying for the wrong reasons. Perhaps Mrs. Hedley had feared the same thing.

A frantic knock at the door echoed through the house. Jane rushed into the hall to see Mama opening the door and Garrett standing on the porch.

"Garrett!" she cried. "Did you find him?"

"Not yet." His worried eyes told the story as he stepped inside. "I was hoping you'd be home by now and maybe have some idea where he might have gone."

She twisted her hands together. "I doubt he'd go back to the shelter, but you never know."

"I've already tried there. Mrs. Shaughnessy said she'd let us know if he turns up." He scanned her from head to toe, taking in her silky green dress and high heels. "I'm sorry. Did I interrupt your evening?"

"No, it's fine. We just got back from dinner." She paced the foyer as she searched her memory for any place Martin considered special. "He might come here."

"That's what I was hoping," Garrett said, "but he would have been here by now."

"How long has he been missing?"

"The Blackwoods aren't entirely sure. At least a couple of hours."

More than enough time to make it to their house. "Did anyone call the police?"

"Mr. Blackwood did, but they said to give it some time. That Martin would likely come home on his own like most runaway children." Garrett's eyes snapped with annoyance.

"Where could he have gone?" She stopped and raised her eyes to Garrett. "Do you think he'd head to the farm?"

"He might." His forehead crinkled. "Would he have any idea how to get there, though?"

"I don't know, but if the police won't look for him, we need to keep searching. It's too cold for him to be out all night." She raced back into the living room to grab her coat and search for her purse.

Donald followed her in. "You aren't going with him, are you?"

"Of course I am. I can't just sit here while Martin's out there all alone." She moved around him to snatch her purse from an armchair. "I'd ask you to come, but I know you want to get back to Patrick."

"I do." He stared at her, an expression close to hurt on his face. "Don't forget, Mrs. Hedley leaves tomorrow morning. I need you there to watch Patrick while I work."

"I haven't forgotten." She walked back into the hallway and grabbed her boots by the door. She'd change out of her heels once she was in the car. "Mama, you don't mind, do you? You'll be all right for a bit?"

"Land sakes, of course I don't mind. You go and find that boy. I'll be here praying for him all night if that's what it takes."

"Thank you." She kissed her mother's cheek, gratitude spilling through her. Then she turned to Donald. "I'll see you tomorrow."

Before he could utter another word, she followed Garrett out to his car.

34

Garrett closed Jane's car door and went around to take his place behind the wheel. The outside temperature had turned decidedly colder, and his breath hung in white puffs before him. Chances were good it would snow tonight.

All the more urgency for them to find Martin.

Jane rubbed her bare hands together and blew on them. "Did the Blackwoods say what made Martin run off like that?"

Garrett started the engine and turned on the heat as well as the car's headlamps. "Nothing they could pinpoint." He shrugged. "They did say Martin has been giving them a hard time. 'Testing their patience,' I believe is how they put it."

"But something must have triggered him to leave. What could it have been?" She started taking off her heels, exchanging them for the pair of winter boots. "You don't think they were mistreating him, do you?"

He did his best to ignore her familiar floral scent that drifted over to his side of the car. "I don't think so. They seemed genuinely distressed." He released a long breath. "However, anything's possible."

If he were honest, he'd tell Jane she could be right, that perhaps he'd made a mistake giving Martin to the inexperienced

Blackwoods. The couple had hinted as much when he went there tonight. Yet it didn't seem right to add to Jane's worries right now.

"Do you have any extra gloves in your car?" she asked.

"I wish I did." He glanced over at her. "I forgot mine too. But the heat should kick in soon." He increased the setting for the car's heater, then headed out of the city using Lakeshore Boulevard, praying Martin had come in this direction. "This is the route I took to the farm," he said to Jane. "It's more scenic by the water. I'm hoping Martin remembered that."

"Good thinking. Although I can't imagine him walking all this way."

"He might be riding a bike. The Blackwoods said there was one missing from their yard."

"I'm not sure if that's better or worse."

"I know. But on a bike, he'd have to stay on the roads rather than veer off onto the grass."

"Still, it's going to be like looking for a needle in a very dark haystack." She gave a loud sigh.

The car's headlamps illuminated the pavement ahead. Jane was right. It would be a miracle if they found the boy in the dark.

He shot her a sideways glance, his battered heart drinking in every detail of her. She sat staring out her window, her tweed coat pulled up tight at the neck, her hands clasped around her purse. He'd missed her more than he thought possible. Had it only been twelve days?

"I take it you and Donald were out on a date," he said in a voice that didn't sound like his.

"It was just dinner." She scanned the landscape from the side window, then peered at the road in front.

"Donald didn't seem overly concerned about Martin's disappearance," he said. "And he didn't seem happy about you coming with me."

She remained silent, her lips pressed together in a tight line.

"Can I ask if you're any closer to making a decision? About

marrying Donald and adopting Martin, I mean." The two-week trial period she'd mentioned was almost at an end. Judging by her fancy attire, things were moving in the direction he'd dreaded.

She whirled on him then. "Can we please just focus on trying to find Martin? Nothing else matters right now."

He gave a curt nod, regret pooling in his gut. He should be trying to comfort her, not adding to her distress.

Soon they came to the edge of the city where the streetlights ended, leaving nothing but an inky expanse of road with only the two beams from the car's lights to guide them.

Lord, please lead us to Martin. And please keep him safe until we find him.

Garrett tried to put himself in Martin's shoes. Where would he have gone if he'd run away? But he couldn't really compare his life to Martin's. Martin didn't have a safe place to run to. No friends or relatives. The one thing he loved was Blackie.

Who was at the farm.

Determination filled Garrett, more certain than ever they were on the right track. The problem was the great distance Martin would have to cover to get there.

"Keep your eyes open for anywhere he might have stopped to rest. A barn or farmhouse, maybe." He was suddenly grateful for the extra pair of eyes. It was hard enough to drive without trying to search the fields on either side of the road.

They continued in silence, Garrett's tension growing as rain began to fall, sliding down the windshield in sheets. He turned on the manual wipers but soon became aware that the precipitation contained more ice than rain, making visibility even worse. He purposely lowered his speed, not wanting to slide on the pavement that was growing slicker by the minute. He tightened his grip on the steering wheel until his fingers ached from the pressure.

"I can't imagine Martin being out in this weather," Jane said.

"He'd probably seek shelter of some sort. Keep looking for any place he might have stopped."

Several more painstaking miles went by with Garrett straining to keep the car on the road. He didn't want to alarm Jane, but the worsening weather had him concerned. Pretty soon he'd have no choice but to pull over or turn back.

The sleet had increased, now starting to coat the windshield and hindering his visibility even more. The car's heater couldn't combat the rapidly falling temperatures, causing Garrett's fingers to stiffen from the cold as much as from tension. There was no way around it. He had to stop. At least long enough to scrape the ice off the windshield.

He eased his foot onto the brake pedal.

The car didn't respond. In fact, their speed seemed to increase.

Adrenaline poured through his veins. He ground his teeth together and pumped the brakes harder, yet the car seemed determined to thwart his efforts. He turned the wheel to the right, struggling to pull over to the side of the road where the tires might find purchase on the gravel, but when he applied the brake again, it did little to halt their momentum. Instead, the car swerved out of control.

The metallic taste of fear coated his tongue. "Brace yourself!" he shouted.

Every muscle in his body stiffened as he threw all his strength into the wheel. But despite his efforts, the car skidded off the edge of the road. Jane's terrified scream tore through him as they shot over an embankment and crashed through some foliage. The left tires rode up over something, and the car tilted, hanging suspended in midair for several seconds before flipping onto its right side.

Jane screamed again as they both slid down the bench seat, Garrett's body thudding helplessly against hers. Pain shot through the side of his head, and the air slammed from his lungs. Stunned, he lay there until at last his chest muscles released enough to allow him to take in some air.

Jane!

In his awkward position, he struggled to lift his weight off her. "Jane, are you all right?"

She gave no response, lying much too still for his liking. Wings of panic beat in his throat. In the darkness, his shaking fingers found her face, and he felt for the artery under her jaw.

A fast but steady pulse beat there.

The breath he'd been holding leaked out. He fought to ignore his throbbing head and figure out what to do next. The car was sitting at an odd angle, making it difficult to move.

"I'm going to try to climb out," Garrett said aloud, even though Jane was most likely unconscious. The fleeting thought about what the jarring from the crash might have done to the shrapnel crossed his mind, but he shoved it aside. He couldn't worry about that now.

He squinted in the dark, his vision adjusting enough to make out vague shapes. Though the car headlamps were still on, the light was obscured by whatever they'd hit. He reached into the glove box and felt the cold metal of his flashlight.

"Please let the batteries work." He flicked the switch, and when a steady beam appeared, he let out a relieved sigh. Twisting, he aimed the light at Jane. Her eyes were closed, her hair disheveled, and a trickle of blood ran from her forehead. "Jane, can you hear me?"

She stirred a little and moaned.

Thank you, Lord!

Gradually she opened her eyes, but when she moved slightly, another moan escaped.

"Stay still. You've hit your head." He turned off the flashlight and shoved it in his pocket. Maybe if he was lucky, he could figure out a way to get the car back on the road. But first he'd have to climb out and assess the situation. Working mostly by feel, he grabbed the steering wheel and used it to haul himself upward. He braced one foot against the dashboard, the other against the back of the seat, and managed to roll the window open far enough to pull himself out into the storm's onslaught.

Hard pellets instantly stung his face, while icy wetness slid down his neck, making him shiver. He flicked on the flashlight and stood back to stare at the vehicle, his stomach plunging down to his wet shoes. The car was sitting at about a forty-five-degree angle in a deep gulley, its hood almost buried in a bush. There was no way Garrett would be able to right it, never mind get it back on the road.

And with the car in that severely tilted position, they couldn't really stay inside. The only other option was to find shelter somewhere until the storm lessened.

He squinted across the field. In the distance, he could make out a few dark shapes, one of which might be some type of structure. They'd head there first.

Carefully, he leaned his head through the open driver's window, making sure not to shine the flashlight in Jane's face. Thankfully, she seemed to be awake. "Are you able to move?"

She squinted up at him. "I-I think so."

"Good. I'm going to help you climb out."

She frowned, but the look she gave him was pure determination. "Okay. I'm ready."

He leaned in and stretched his arm toward her. "Grab my hand, and I'll pull you up."

She reached up to place her hand in his but let out a cry of pain.

"Wait. Are you hurt anywhere?" He should find out how bad her injuries might be before he attempted to haul her up.

"My head . . . and my shoulder."

Her breathing seemed shallow, and he worried she might be going into shock.

"All right. We'll move slowly, then. Use your good arm, and if it gets too much, just tell me to stop."

"I'm okay. I-I think it's only bruised." She sounded more cognizant now as she tightened her grip on his hand.

He drew her up as smoothly and steadily as he could, and after a minute she emerged from the window. Once she was safely out, he pulled her against his chest and held her until they both caught their breath. "Thank heaven you're all right," he whispered.

He never would have forgiven himself if she'd been badly injured. Or worse.

The freezing rain attacked them with renewed vengeance, covering the ground in more layers of ice. Jane pulled her scarf over her head and tied it under her chin.

He got the flashlight out again and turned it on. "Are you all right to walk?" He trained the beam at her forehead, relieved to see that the wound had stopped bleeding.

"I think so."

He squinted against the pellets to scan the landscape. "Let's head across that field. I think there's something out there, possibly a barn. But we'll have to walk slowly because of the ice." He shone the light in the direction they were going to head and held out an arm to her. "Ready?"

She nodded.

"All right. Let's go."

Jane shivered, her shoulders scrunched up to her ears, and with her hand firmly wrapped around his arm, they set out.

35

Jane pressed her face into the wool of Garrett's jacket, thankful for his arm around her. The stinging rain pelted her cheeks and eyes, blurring the landscape before her. Her forehead throbbed, as did her shoulder where she'd hit the passenger door, but she soldiered on. When her foot slipped suddenly on the uneven terrain, Garrett pulled her upright.

"Careful," he said. "It's like a skating rink out here."

She was eminently grateful she'd brought her boots. Otherwise, in the shoes she'd worn for her date, she'd have broken her ankle by now. She was also grateful for Garrett's steady arm keeping her vertical.

He pointed ahead. "Looks like there's a thicket of trees over there and possibly a structure."

The wind howled around them, whipping the edges of her scarf out to the side like a flag on a pole. Where could Martin be in this weather? She clamped her lips together to contain a cry of frustration. They were supposed to be rescuing him. Instead, they found themselves in a potentially worse predicament.

"It's a run-down barn," Garrett said, relief evident in his voice. "We should find some shelter there."

She squinted in front of them. Sure enough, a rough structure appeared out of the haze. It was indeed an old barn, though half its roof had caved in.

When they reached what appeared to be the main door, Garrett grasped the rusted handle and yanked hard. After two more tries, the coating of ice broke and the door creaked open. He aimed the beam of his flashlight into the interior.

"I'll go first to make sure it's safe," he said. "And that no animals are hiding inside."

She shivered but nodded. Huddling under a tree to wait, she stuffed her hands into her coat pockets, wishing again that she'd remembered her gloves.

Several moments later, he returned. "It's empty and a little drier at least."

She took his hand and together they went in. The wind whistled through the missing boards, but at the far end of the structure, a portion of the roof remained intact, providing them with a degree of shelter.

As they stood for a moment taking in their surroundings, she shook some of the moisture from her scarf and coat. The air was musty but breathable, although it wasn't ideal with the layers of dust coating everything. They moved farther down to a dry stall, where the flashlight's beam showed a thin layer of straw covering the wooden floor. Garrett looked around and gathered some burlap sacks from on top of a barrel, then arranged them on the floor.

"Sit here," he said. He helped ease her onto the ground, then crouched in front of her, setting the flashlight on the barrel, aimed toward her. "Let me take a look at your head."

His eyes were so intent on her—so close to her face—that her lungs seized. Maybe she'd hit her head harder than she thought. His chilled fingers brushed her forehead, tenderly probing the area around the wound. His gaze dropped to hers. "The cut isn't deep, but you'll probably have a large bruise."

His hands moved slowly down to feel her shoulder, and she winced.

"I don't think it's broken or dislocated, but you'll need to have a doctor examine it." He closed his eyes then and rested his forehead against hers. "I'm sorry. This is all my fault."

Ice beat against the roof, and farther down the enclosure, water dripped through various holes in the wood.

"I should have turned back as soon as the rain started," he said, thick self-loathing in his voice.

She reached up with her good hand to touch his cheek. "It's not your fault, Garrett. You can't control the weather."

"It's not just the weather." He moved away from her hand and slumped onto the ground beside her. "You were right about the Blackwoods. They're too inexperienced. I let my pride get in the way and ignored your advice." A loud sigh escaped. "If anything happens to him . . ." He broke off, squeezing his eyes shut.

"Martin is a survivor. He'll be okay. You'll see." She prayed she wasn't giving Garrett false hope, but she had to say something. She'd never seen him so defeated, so unsure of himself.

"Now I've involved you in a car accident and got you stuck in this horrible place. What is wrong with me?"

For a moment, she resisted the urge to say anything, not fully trusting herself. They were in a highly charged situation, heightening every emotion between them. Yet she couldn't deny the strong pull toward him. After almost two weeks of no contact, she now soaked in every detail about him. The familiar scent of his shaving lotion, the intensity of his eyes, the fierce way he cared about those around him. And most especially, the way he loved Martin as much as she did.

Gently, she touched his chin, forcing him to look at her. "Nothing's wrong with you, Garrett. Nothing at all." Then, before she could stop herself, she leaned over and kissed him.

His lips were cold, but it took only seconds for them to become warm. With a jerk, he sat up straighter, and his arm came around her, gently tugging her closer.

"Jane." He breathed her name like a prayer. "You have no idea how much I've missed you. Nothing has been the same without you."

His mouth claimed hers again, this time with more intensity, until her brain buzzed like a short-circuited wire, and warmth infused her very core. Even with the pain in her shoulder, she felt more alive in this moment than she ever had in the past two weeks.

Her mind flew to the few tentative kisses she'd shared with Donald, knowing his embrace couldn't begin to compare to Garrett's. And suddenly she realized why marrying Donald would never work. How could it when she was completely in love with Garrett?

Garrett held back a frustrated groan. Now he'd done it. One kiss was all it took to bring his feelings roaring back to life, larger and more intense than ever.

"I'm sorry," he said. "I shouldn't have kissed you that way. Not when you're with someone else now." He shook his head, the warmth beginning to fade from his system. "Can you forgive me?"

"I believe I was the one who kissed you." Her chin lowered until it rested on her coat. "You must think I'm a terrible person."

"Of course not. I could never think that."

When she raised her head to look at him, his stomach clenched at the sheen of tears in her eyes.

"Donald and I have come a long way these past two weeks, and his little boy is the most precious thing ever." She bit her lip. "But I think I've made a huge mistake."

"Why is that?" He held his breath, a fragile hope fluttering to life inside him.

She picked at the ice melting on the edges of her scarf. "I thought being a mother to Patrick and being able to adopt Martin would make it all worthwhile. That I could learn to love Donald again." Her lashes fluttered down. "But I don't think it's going to be possible—" she hesitated—"because of my feelings for you."

Her words made his heart soar, yet at the same time, the weight of an anvil sat on his chest. Had his selfishness sabotaged her last chance to have a family of her own? His own health situation remained the same, and even though he now had his name on a waiting list for the specialist, it likely wouldn't change anything. Still, he owed her the complete truth.

"I feel the same about you, Jane. If I could—if I had nothing impeding my future—I'd ask you to be my wife."

"Oh, Garrett." She covered her mouth with one hand.

"But the fact remains I have two pieces of shrapnel in my body waiting to destroy me. And it wouldn't be fair to subject you to that type of uncertainty. Nor would it be fair to Martin or any other child we might adopt. I could never be that selfish."

She tilted her head, her eyes huge in her pale face. "Only God knows the number of our days, Garrett. There's no guarantee that anyone will live to old age."

He quirked a wry brow. "No, but the likelihood seems far less certain for me."

"But I love you." The words erupted from her lips as tears shook loose to trail down over her face. "I love you, and I'm willing to take the chance."

His heart gave a leap at the unexpected beauty of her words, and he absorbed the pure joy of it for a heartbeat.

"I love you too, Jane." He expelled a long breath that hung in front of them in a wispy cloud. "But marriage is not a possibility. Especially since I won't be able to . . ." He clamped his lips shut. Frustration pulsed at his temples, through his veins.

"To what?"

"To love you the way a husband should. It would be too risky." He wanted to roar out loud at the unfairness of life. It would be pure agony to be married to her and not be able to share a physical union.

"I never thought about that." A blush bled into her cheeks.

Unable to bear her scrutiny, Garrett focused his gaze on the rotting wall beside him. "You should try to make it work with Donald. He can give you everything I can't." He closed his eyes, the mere thought of her sharing herself with someone else spearing his heart more than any piece of shrapnel ever could.

She took his hand in her cold one. "If you're worried about me, don't be. I love you, shrapnel or no shrapnel. We can make it work. I know we can."

Reluctantly, he turned back to face her. "That's noble of you." He gave her a wistful smile. "But I honestly don't know if I can say the same. To share my life with you, my bed with you, and not be able to love you, would be sheer torture."

Silence filled the barn, broken only by the fury of the storm outside.

"I suppose you're right," she said finally, staring at him with large, sad eyes. "Will you do something for me?"

"Anything."

"Will you see another doctor to find out if anything more can be done?"

His mouth twisted with the irony of it all. "As a matter of fact, I called the specialist last week. I'm on a waiting list to see him, but I'm not getting my hopes up. And you shouldn't either."

A smile hovered on her lips, but her expression remained sad. "I won't. But I will pray. Extra hard."

"Jane. I wish . . ." Frustration tore through him. He should have left her alone. Left her to make a life with Donald. Now he'd given her false hope for the future. *Why Lord? Why did you make me love her when I can never have her?*

"Let's leave it in God's hands," she said firmly. "I trust He has our best interests at heart. Until we know anything for certain, let's just be happy with the time we have right now."

He stared at her. She was so brave, so beautiful. How could he ever let her go? "I can do that," he said, only because there was no other option at the moment.

Breathing out a reluctant sigh, he laid his head against hers. He could already feel his limbs stiffening from the cold, and he forced his brain to focus back on their current situation. "Are you warm enough?"

"Not really. Could we try to make a fire?"

"I don't think so. We have no matches or any way to start one."

"Then I guess we'll have to keep each other warm until the sleet stops." She smiled at him through the tears still sitting on her lashes.

Resisting the longing to kiss her again, he reached over to snap off the flashlight. Then he put his arms around her, drawing her against his chest, and prayed the night would pass quickly.

36

Despite the cold, Jane fell into a fitful sleep, cocooned in Garrett's arms. Even amid their dire circumstances, she'd never felt safer. How long she slept she couldn't tell, but when she finally roused, Garrett was staring down at her.

"I think the weather has let up," he said. "I should leave and go for help."

She moved away from him, attempting to shake off her sleep and become more alert. "I'm coming with you."

He frowned. "You'd be safer here. A fall on the ice might damage your shoulder more."

"With you helping me, I won't fall. Besides, I don't do well sitting and waiting."

"All right," he sighed. "I know better than to argue with you." He pulled himself slowly to a standing position. "Between the cold and stiffness from sitting on the ground, I feel like an old man." He stretched his neck and shoulders, then held out a hand to help Jane to her feet.

Even without gloves, his hands were still slightly warm around her cold ones.

Her knees creaked as she rose, pain shooting through her

shoulder. All her joints felt fused, in need of oiling, like the Tin Man from *The Wizard of Oz*.

Garrett kept her hand in his as they made their way outside. From the lightness of the sky, Jane gauged it to be somewhere around six thirty or seven in the morning. Her empty stomach cramped. Mama would be so worried.

Lord, please comfort my mother and let her know I'm coming home soon.

The still-frozen ground forced them to pick their way slowly across the uneven terrain. She was surprised to be able to see Garrett's car in the distance, still sitting at a strange angle. Last night, it seemed they'd walked in the sleet for ages before coming upon the deserted barn.

As they got closer to the road, another car pulled up near Garrett's.

"Hey, we may be luckier than I thought," he said. "I think that's a police car."

They quickened their pace as much as they could. Up ahead, a man emerged from the other vehicle and stood, staring down at Garrett's car. From the man's uniform, it appeared Garrett was right.

"It is a policeman," he said. "Maybe he can drive us to a garage."

He waved his arms as they walked, trying to catch the man's attention.

At last, they reached the ditch and the car. "Hello," Garrett called. "Thank goodness you're here."

"Is this your vehicle?" the officer asked.

"Yes, sir. We slid into the ditch last night."

"Why were you out in such bad weather?"

"We were looking for a boy who'd run away from his foster home. The ice storm came on all of a sudden. I was trying to pull over, but the car had other ideas." He helped Jane navigate the trench and come up onto the roadside. "I'm Garrett Wilder,

307

interim director of the Children's Aid Society, and this is Jane Linder, the boy's caseworker."

"I'm Officer Samuels."

"Can you tell me if anyone reported a boy named Martin Smith missing?" Garrett asked. "Or better yet, if he's been found?"

"Sorry. I haven't heard anything. The call could have come in to a different division, though." He gestured to the car. "That's quite an angle. Must have been fun getting out. No one injured, I hope?" The officer peered at Jane's forehead.

"Jane got the worst of it. A bump on the head and a bruised shoulder."

"You should probably get checked out by a doctor, ma'am." The man scanned the landscape. "Where have you been all this time?"

"We found shelter in an old barn." Garrett pointed across the field. "It wasn't much, but it kept us dry at least."

The policeman raised his brows. "Lucky it was there. Would have been an even more miserable night without it."

"We could use a lift into town, if possible," Jane said. "My elderly mother will be worried sick about me." She shivered. "Are the roads drivable now?"

"They're still a little slippery but much better than last night."

Garrett pulled the collar of his jacket up around his ears. "If you wouldn't mind radioing for a tow service, I'll wait here."

"It's still pretty raw out," the officer observed. "Why don't I drop you at the nearest garage and you can wait in the warmth for the next available truck?"

"That sounds like a better idea." The lines in Garrett's forehead eased, and he gave Jane's fingers a silent squeeze.

A surge of relief spilled through her that she wouldn't have to be separated from him just yet.

The three of them climbed into the patrol car, with Jane in the middle between the two men. The heat blasting from the vents felt wonderful. She stretched her fingers out toward it.

Officer Samuels put the car into gear and pulled slowly away from the roadside. Gravel spun out from the tires.

Jane glanced over at Garrett. "What should we do next to find Martin?"

"I'll call the Blackwoods to see if there's been any news. If I can get my car back on the road, I'll continue from where we left off." Garrett peered around her to stare at the officer. "We'd appreciate any help you can give us with our search, sir."

The man stared straight ahead. "How old did you say the boy is?"

"Eight going on nine."

"I've got a son the same age. I can't imagine what I'd do if he'd been out alone in this weather all night." He shot a worried glance at Garrett. "When I get back to the station, I'll see if anyone's on the case and round up as many men as I can. Don't worry. We'll find him."

"You can let me off at the corner up ahead, Officer Samuels," Jane said as they turned onto her street. "My mother has a weak heart, and if she sees a police car pull up, it might be too much for her."

After the officer had let Garrett off at the mechanic's, he'd insisted on driving Jane home before heading into the station, an offer she didn't refuse.

For the first time, the man's lips twisted into a half-smile. "I understand." He glanced at her forehead, where she was certain an ugly bruise had bloomed. "Are you sure you don't want me to take you to the hospital?"

"That's not necessary. It's only a small cut. And my shoulder is only bruised." At least she hoped that's all it was. It still ached when she lifted her arm, but she was fairly certain it wasn't serious.

The car slowed to a stop by the curb a few houses away from

hers. "Thanks again for your help. We appreciate anything you're able to do to find Martin."

"My pleasure, ma'am. And try to refrain from sliding off any icy roads in the future." He gave her a wink, then handed her a business card. "I'll try to keep you and Mr. Wilder informed about the search for the boy. But here's my number in case you need to contact me."

"Thank you." She pocketed the card, then got out and closed the door with a wave.

The sidewalk was almost bare, the ice having already melted away. In the city's core, the temperature was always warmer. Perhaps they hadn't even had the same sleet as in the open countryside.

On a deep inhale, Jane opened the front door and went inside. *Please let Mama be all right.*

She removed her coat and boots and walked into the living room. Mama sat asleep in her chair, an afghan pulled over her. She'd likely stayed awake all night worrying about her.

Jane glanced at the clock on the mantel. Eight thirty. The whole trip back, including the stop at the garage, took a lot longer than she realized. She should have been at Donald's apartment by now so he could catch the bus and be to work at nine. But first things first.

"Mama." Jane gently touched her mother's shoulder. "I'm home."

Her eyes flew open. "Oh, Janey. I was so worried."

"I would have called if I could. We had a bit of trouble with the car and—"

"Your head!" Horror filled Mama's eyes.

"It's just a bump. Nothing to worry about." Jane smiled to reassure her. "How are *you* doing?"

Mama pressed a hand to her throat. "I had a bad night. Barely slept at all. But I'm fine now that I know you're home."

"I'm so sorry I worried you." Jane reached over to hug her.

"It was a long night, and we still haven't found Martin. A police officer drove us home. He's going to send out some men to search for him. I only hope Martin found somewhere to wait out the storm."

"I'm sure the good Lord is looking out for him." Mama gave a tired smile.

A rush of guilt filled Jane's chest. She'd been neglecting her mother lately. All the time spent with little Patrick had taken most of her focus and energy. By the time Donald got back in the evenings and Jane caught the bus home, it was too late to start making dinner, so Mama had even started to cook for them during the week.

"I'm sorry I've neglected you lately, Mama. Would you like me to get you something before I leave for Donald's? Or would you like to lie down?"

Mama just smiled and laid her hand against Jane's cheek. "You worry too much, Janey. I'm stronger than you think. It's been a nice change these last couple of weeks to help care for you. It gives me something to focus on besides being ill."

"Really?" Jane couldn't imagine that being the case. But other than looking tired, Mama did seem more like herself than she had in a long time.

"I know you think you have to do everything for me, but maybe it's not the best thing," Mama said gently. "Maybe it's time I started being a little more independent. Help you around here for a change so I won't be such a burden."

Jane grasped her mother's hand. "Oh, Mama. You've never been a burden. I just want you around for as long as possible."

"There's no need to worry about that." She gave a serene smile. "God's already got it all worked out."

The telephone rang, and Jane jumped. "That's probably Donald." She swallowed and picked up the receiver.

"Jane! Where are you? You were supposed to be here fifteen minutes ago. Mrs. Hedley has already left for the train station so there's no one to stay with Patrick." Donald's strident tone jarred her already-frayed nerves.

"I was about to call you. I'll be there as soon as I can. Garrett and I were in a small accident last night, and I—"

"An accident? Are you all right?"

"I'm fine. I'll tell you the story later. Right now, I need to call a cab."

She hung up before he could even say good-bye.

37

Garrett waved to the tow truck driver to indicate that the car was working fine. Other than a dent in the passenger door and another in the right front fender, the rest of the vehicle appeared intact. After checking the fender, the tow truck driver had said it wouldn't scrape against the tire, and with the engine starting on the first try, Garrett was ready to continue the search.

He'd used the telephone at the mechanic's to contact the Blackwoods, who hadn't learned anything new about Martin's whereabouts. They'd sounded upset that the police hadn't taken it more seriously. It wasn't until just after midnight that the department had finally sent out a patrol car. Garrett assured the couple that he'd keep looking for Martin and would let them know the minute he had any news.

Now, despite his eyes being heavy from lack of sleep, Garrett set off on the route he and Jane had been following. He only prayed Martin had found shelter somewhere and hadn't been out all night in the elements.

Half an hour later, he arrived at his parents' house, having seen no sign of the boy or a bike along the way. His last-ditch hope was that Martin had somehow made it all the way to the farm.

The front door opened before Garrett had even shut off the engine. His mother came out onto the porch, her brow pinched. "Garrett? What on earth are you doing here? Is something wrong?"

His spirits plummeted as he trudged up the stairs to kiss her cheek. "I'm looking for Martin. He ran away from his foster home yesterday, and I thought he might have headed here to see Blackie."

Her mouth tightened. "I'm sorry. I haven't seen him. And Blackie's been inside all night." She peered across the still-frosty grass to the barn. "Do you think he could be hiding somewhere on the property?"

"It's possible, though I think it would be a miracle if he made it this far in that sleet. I'll go check the barn and the other outbuildings. Then I wouldn't mind a cup of your coffee." He managed a faint smile. "It's been a rough night."

"I'll make a fresh pot." She pulled her cardigan more firmly around her and disappeared back inside.

Garrett made a thorough search of the barn, the sheds, even under the porch, anywhere he thought a child might fit. But, as he suspected, there was no sign of the boy.

Discouraged, irritable, and dirty, he strode back to the house, looking forward to a cup of coffee and something to eat.

His mom poured him a mug and set it on the table. "No luck, I take it."

He shook his head. "After I eat and shower, I'll head back to the city. Figure out what to do next."

Jett got up from his place on the mat beside Blackie and ambled over, his nails clicking on the wood floor. He laid his head on Garrett's knee, and Garrett rubbed the dog's ears. "You always know when I'm upset, don't you, boy?"

His mother set a plate of toast and scrambled eggs down, then stood, staring at him. "I feel like this whole thing is our fault. If we hadn't made Martin leave . . ." Her voice broke and she turned back to the sink.

"Mom, no. If this is anyone's fault it's mine. Jane tried to warn me the Blackwoods might not be a good fit for Martin. That another family was better suited." He speared his fork into the eggs. "I should have trusted her expertise instead of forcing my opinion on everyone." He chewed a large bite of toast and some egg, then took a long drink of the black coffee. "If anything's happened to him, I'll never forgive myself. Never be able to face Jane again." He set down his mug with a thunk. "She's considering remarrying her ex-husband just so she can adopt him. That's how much she loves Martin." His appetite waning, he got up and paced to the window, where he leaned his forehead against the glass, hoping the coolness would ease the headache brewing there.

Silence pulsed in the room for several beats, until at last, he exhaled, his breath fogging the window. A warm hand rubbed his back.

"I know how much you care for Jane, Garrett. This must be killing you."

Tension rippled through his muscles. "Yeah, it is. But I can't be selfish, Mom. I can't make her any promises when I don't know what my future holds."

"No one does, honey. Only God knows the number of our days."

Slowly, he turned to face her. "That's so strange. Jane said almost the exact same thing to me yesterday."

His mother's blue eyes twinkled. "I knew I liked that girl."

A strangled laugh escaped him, and then he quickly sobered. "You should know I finally called the specialist and put my name on the waiting list for an appointment."

She raised a hand to her mouth. "Oh, Garrett. That's wonderful."

He pointed a finger at her. "I don't want you getting your hopes up. Chances are nothing can be done. But you're right. I need to know. One way or the other."

The telephone on the kitchen wall rang.

"I'll get it." His mother whirled around, dabbing at her eyes. "Hello?" A small frown appeared between her brows. "Yes, he's here. One moment, please." She held out the receiver to him.

He walked over to take it. "Garrett Wilder."

"Mr. Wilder, this is Officer Samuels. I hope it's all right that I tracked you down."

"It's fine. What's going on? Have you found Martin?"

"We think so. We just received a call from a farmer not far from where I found you this morning. He reported a break-in to a shed on his property. He also found an abandoned bicycle nearby. We're on our way there now."

"Give me the address and I'll meet you there." Garrett reached for a pencil and paper on the counter.

After the officer rattled off the rural address, Garrett thanked him and hung up.

"Is there news?" His mother hovered near his elbow.

"They might have a lead. I have to go." He bent to kiss her cheek.

"I'll be praying you find him and that he's all right. Be careful."

"Thanks. I'll be in touch."

As Garrett sped along the road back toward Toronto, he did his best to keep from accelerating too much. The rising warmth of the day had melted most of the ice on the pavement, so at least he didn't have to worry about sliding off the road again, but he should be mindful.

He'd thought about having his mother contact Jane, but until Garrett was sure Martin was safe, he didn't want to get her hopes up. As soon as he had anything tangible to report, he'd call her himself. That way, he could hopefully tell her Martin was all right and be able to make sure she wasn't any the worse for wear after the accident and their night in the cold barn.

Twenty minutes later, as he slowed onto the country road, two police cars came into view, parked near a lane leading to a farmhouse.

Please, Lord, let Martin be safe. And give me the words to reassure him that everything will be all right.

Garrett parked behind the second police car and jumped out. The faint sound of voices met his ears, and he followed the noise to the rear of the house. Not far from a wooden shed, a small group of people, likely neighbors, stood huddled at the base of a tree, staring up at the brownish leaves still clinging stubbornly to the branches.

A German shepherd stood with its front paws on the gnarled trunk. They must have used the dog to track Martin's scent. Garrett strode over to where Officer Samuels watched from the edge of the group.

"What's going on?" he asked.

"Mr. Wilder. Glad you're here. They flushed the boy out of the shed, but he climbed the tree and won't come down. The owner of the property has gone for a ladder."

Garrett craned his neck to peer up into the leaves, and his gut clenched. The tree had to be more than thirty feet high.

"Come on down from there, son," another officer called. "Do as we say, and you won't get in any more trouble."

Garrett rolled his eyes. That wasn't going to entice the boy to cooperate.

"Martin?" he yelled up. "It's Mr. Wilder. Are you all right?"

The tree rustled, but there was no other response.

"You must be hungry," Garrett continued. "Come on down, and I'll get you something to eat. I promise you're not in any trouble."

He waited a few seconds, but there was still no response.

Garrett turned to Samuels. "Is it really necessary to have so many people here? I think I'd have better luck talking to him alone."

The officer shot him a disgruntled look, then nodded. "All right. I need to radio in to headquarters anyway."

"Thank you."

"Call off the dog," Officer Samuels ordered. "And everyone move back."

One of the men whistled, and the shepherd instantly backed down. The man led the animal away while the rest of the group reluctantly retreated.

Garrett offered a silent prayer as he approached the base of the tree, lamenting once again the pieces of shrapnel that prevented him from climbing up to rescue the boy himself.

"Martin," he called. "It's just you and me now. Can you show me where you are? Move some leaves or something?"

He held his breath and waited, peering up.

Finally, a faint rustling shook some of the decaying foliage. Garrett swallowed hard. Martin was incredibly close to the top of the tree. What possessed him to go so high? He scanned the distance from the bare trunk to the leaves. The boy would still have to come a fair way on his own. The ladder would only reach so far. "The farmer's getting a ladder. Can you start moving down? Very slowly?"

"I-I'll try." Martin's voice quavered as much as the leaves.

He sounded in rough shape. Likely cold, hungry, and possibly dehydrated. *Please, Lord, don't let him have a seizure now.* That would be disastrous.

Garrett rubbed a hand against his chest, but it did nothing to ease the pressure building there. "Take your time. Make sure the branch is sturdy before you put your weight on it."

"Okay."

The leaves swished and swayed, but Garrett couldn't see much except the odd flash of color. Seconds ticked by like hours as he waited, clenching and unclenching his fists in helpless frustration. He tried not to think about the fact that the storm might have weakened some of the limbs.

Suddenly, all movement stopped.

"The branches are too wet." Martin's tremulous voice drifted down. "I'm afraid I'll slip."

"It's all right. Take your time." By Garrett's calculations, the boy was more than halfway down.

The farmer appeared then, carrying a long wooden ladder under one arm, the rear being held by another man. The two leaned the ladder against the trunk, checking that the feet were secure. The farmer tipped his cap at Garrett. "Let me know if you need anything else."

"I will. Thank you." Garrett focused back on the tree. "All right, Martin. The ladder's here. You don't have much farther to go until you reach it."

The boy didn't respond, though Garrett thought he heard sniffling.

"Mr. Wilder, can you come up and help me?"

Garrett's insides twisted at the plaintive question. The poor kid was terrified. How could he possibly refuse to help? "I'll start climbing up while you come down a few more branches. I'll be waiting for you when you reach the ladder." Garrett glanced back at the farmer, who stood not far away. "Would you mind holding this for me?"

The man nodded, and then once he was in place, Garrett swallowed his trepidation and started up. Despite the frigid air, his back and palms slicked with sweat. The leaves above him rustled again as Martin began to move slowly downward. Finally, Garrett could see him through the thinning foliage. Martin's shoes were splattered with mud and his pants had a huge tear in one knee. "Almost there, buddy. You're doing great."

Garrett stretched one hand up toward him, anticipating the moment when he could wrap his arm around him and know he was safe. Just then, a loud splintering sound ripped through the air. The limb Martin was standing on cracked beneath him. The boy cried out, his arms flailing.

Garrett made a desperate grab to catch hold of the boy's jacket, just making contact when the ladder swayed beneath him. Panic clawed up his throat. The farmer's shouts from below barely registered as Garrett plummeted downward faster than a plunging roller coaster.

A thousand disjointed thoughts raced through his mind. *Please, Lord, don't let Martin be harmed. Please bless Jane and comfort her. Please forgive me . . .*

He landed on the rigid ground with a sickening thud that knocked the air from his lungs. Almost immediately, Martin's weight crashed down on his chest, sending a fiery pain shooting through his spine.

Garrett's eyes flew open. He struggled for air, willing his lungs to function as he stared helplessly at the angry gray sky above him.

Then blackness overtook him.

38

Jane rocked little Patrick in the living room of Donald's apartment, fighting to keep her own eyes open. Finally, after a valiant struggle, the little boy drifted off. She rose, crossed the hallway to the boy's bedroom, and laid him gently in the crib. When satisfied he wouldn't awaken, she inched her way out of the room and softly closed the door.

At last, she could indulge in a cup of tea and relax for a few minutes. In the tiny kitchen, she put the kettle on the stove, her worried thoughts instantly turning to Martin. Had anyone found him yet? Why hadn't she heard anything? She glanced at the clock on the wall. Though it was only three o'clock, the day seemed interminable. After very little sleep in the barn last night, then arriving late to face Donald's silent rebuke, her nerves were chafing her very skin. She could use some good news right about now.

A few minutes later, she carried her cup to the living room and set it on the table. The shrill ring of the telephone broke the silence. Jane dove to grab the receiver before the noise woke the baby. "Linder residence."

"Jane? It's Mama."

Adrenaline flooded her body. "Mama. Is everything all right?"

"Sarah Wilder just called. There's news."

321

Why did Mama sound so nervous? And why was Sarah calling instead of Garrett?

"What is it?" Jane's voice cracked.

"They've found Martin."

Her heart thudded heavily. "Is he okay?"

"He is, yes. But . . ."

"But what?" A chill slid down her neck, and her legs began to shake.

"Garrett was hurt. He's been taken to the hospital."

Jane gripped the phone, a loud roar filling her ears. "W-what happened?"

"He was trying to help Martin down from a tree, and somehow they both fell."

Jane's knees buckled, and she sank into a boneless heap on the sofa. *Dear Lord, no.* A jolt like that could cause the shrapnel to shift into his spine. Or, worse yet, into his heart.

"Jane?"

"I-I'm here."

"What are you going to do?"

She inhaled and forced herself to think rationally. "I have to stay here until Donald returns. But I'll make some phone calls and see what I can find out." Jane wavered as the familiar guilt churned inside her. "Will you be all right if I go up to the hospital right from here?"

"I'm fine. Don't worry about me. Just let me know if you hear anything more."

"I will. I'll call you when I can."

As soon as her mother hung up, Jane went to rummage in her coat pocket for the card Officer Samuels have given her when he'd dropped her off that morning. *"Feel free to call anytime,"* he'd said.

She planned to take him up on that offer right now. It took several rings for someone at the precinct to answer. When she asked for the officer, she was told to hold for a minute.

Her palms grew damp as she waited, and finally Officer Samuels answered.

"I'm glad I caught you," she said.

"I just finished my shift and came back to the station to write up the paperwork. I presume you heard we found the boy."

"Yes, that's why I'm calling. Can you tell me what happened and where he is?" She held her breath and prayed the man would be willing to answer her.

"I was there when it happened. The boy had climbed high up a tree and wouldn't come down. Mr. Wilder went up a ladder to help him." A sigh sounded over the line. "I'm not sure what happened exactly, but the next thing I knew, they were both on the ground."

Her stomach lurched. "Were they badly hurt?"

Silence ticked by for several seconds. "The boy seemed all right, but he started having a seizure right before they took him to the children's hospital."

Oh, poor Martin. He must be so scared. Tears blurred Jane's vision.

"Mr. Wilder took the brunt of the fall and was unconscious when they took him off in the ambulance."

A deep ache cut into Jane's heart. Of course Garrett took the brunt of the fall. He'd probably protected Martin with no regard to his own health. "Have you . . . do you know where they took him?" she choked out.

"Toronto General." The grim tone of his voice did nothing to calm Jane's fears. There was a distinct possibility he knew more but couldn't tell her.

Lord, please be with Garrett. Surround him with your healing grace.

"Thank you for your time, Officer. And for your help in finding Martin."

Jane fell to her knees and through her tears sent desperate prayers upward for Garrett, trying not to imagine how bad his injuries might be. When she recovered enough to speak again, she called the farm. Maybe someone would be able to give her more information.

Cassie answered, obviously in a state of tearful anxiety herself. She told Jane she didn't know the extent of Garrett's injuries, but that her parents were with him, and she gave Jane the number of the nurses' station at the hospital.

Jane called there next. All they could tell her was that Garrett was still undergoing X-rays. When Jane hung up, she wiped her eyes, unable to stem the flow of tears. She tried to focus on the fact that at least Garrett was alive. That was the most important thing.

Yet she was torn between wanting to see Martin and needing to know how Garrett was doing. Thankfully, the hospitals were located across the street from each other. She'd pay a quick visit to Martin first, then head over to see Garrett.

The moment Donald walked through the door, Jane jumped up and went to greet him.

"They found Martin," she blurted out. "He's in the hospital." She held back adding anything about Garrett, since it didn't feel appropriate.

Donald let out a sigh, a look of resignation coming over his face. "You want to go and make sure he's all right."

"Yes."

He stared at her and nodded. "I understand. Thank you for staying with Patrick. I know it must have been hard with you so worried about Martin."

But it wasn't Martin she was most concerned about.

"You're welcome." She walked to the door as she spoke and grabbed her coat. "I should get going to make the next bus."

"Call me later and let me know how he is."

"All right. I'll be in touch. Good night, Donald."

Jane practically ran to the bus stop, relieved when the bus showed up moments later. After one transfer, she got off near the children's hospital. Would Martin still be here? She prayed he would be, because if he'd been returned to his foster parents, she didn't know when she'd get the chance to see him. It wouldn't be appropriate for her to check in on him at the Blackwoods' home since she no longer worked for the Children's Aid.

She inquired about Martin at the main desk, and they told her that he was still there. An attendant directed her to the proper floor. She found Martin in a long, narrow ward filled with beds. Perspiration dampened her blouse as she approached him. He lay curled in a fetal position under the white sheet, his disheveled hair in a tangle.

"Martin, honey? Are you awake?" she asked softly as she perched on the edge of the bed.

His eyes flew open, and he gave a strangled cry, then flew into her arms, his sobs coming in great gasps.

"Shh. Everything is all right now." She rubbed a soothing hand over his back and tried valiantly to keep her own tears at bay. This poor child had been through more in his young life than any adult should have to endure. "Are you hurt anywhere?" She suddenly worried that in addition to the seizure, he could have other unknown injuries.

"N-no." He sniffed and moved away from her shoulder. "But Mr. Wilder is hurt bad. Do you think he's . . . dead?"

An icy fist gripped her heart.

"He's not dead," she said firmly. "But he was hurt, and they took him to another hospital." She gently pushed the bangs off his forehead. A raw-looking scrape ran across his forehead, likely from the tree branches. "I'm going over now to see how he's doing."

He sat back, and she propped a pillow behind him.

"Martin, I want to ask you a question, and I want you to tell me the truth."

He eyed her warily but nodded.

"Did Mr. or Mrs. Blackwood mistreat you?"

He shrugged one shoulder. "Mr. Blackwood yelled sometimes. But Mrs. Blackwood was nice."

"So, why did you run away?" She reached for one of his hands, still stained with dirt under the nails.

"It didn't feel like home." Tears welled again in his eyes. "Not like the farm. Or like your house. And I missed Blackie. I couldn't sleep without him."

Jane's throat thickened as she scanned the room. "Have the Blackwoods come to see you yet?"

He nodded again. "But I think they're mad at me for running away."

"Well, they were worried. You gave them a real scare."

"Yes, you did." Debra Blackwood came into the room. Dark circles hugged her eyes and lines bracketed her mouth. "Hello, Mrs. Linder. I understand you were out looking for Martin last night too."

"I was. But with the weather, we didn't have much luck." She attempted a smile. "Thank goodness he's safe. Did the doctor speak with you and your husband?"

"Yes. Except for a few scrapes and bruises, Martin's going to be fine. But they're keeping him overnight to be safe."

The woman remained standing at the foot of the bed, not showing Martin any affection or even attempting to comfort him. The somber expression on her face sent off tiny alarm bells in Jane. "I have to go and find out how Mr. Wilder is. Are you going to stay with Martin?"

"Yes. My husband and I will take turns sitting with him. Please give Mr. Wilder our best."

"I will." Jane bent to give Martin a quick hug. "I'll come back and see you tomorrow, honey. Get some rest now."

With effort, she dragged herself away from his stricken face. As much as she wanted to stay with him, her heart was urging her to get to Garrett. Not until she saw him for herself would the terrible fear inside her ease.

Mrs. Blackwood followed her out into the hall. "Mrs. Linder? Before you go, I'd like to talk to you about Martin."

From the woman's demeanor, Jane could already surmise what she wanted to say. A ball of raw anger swirled in her chest. She wanted to rail at all the people who'd let this boy down, but for Martin's sake, she forced back her outrage. "You likely haven't heard," she said coolly, "but I'm no longer with the Children's Aid Society. You'll have to speak with his new caseworker. Good night, Mrs. Blackwood."

She gripped her purse and walked briskly down the hall, a fierce determination rising up inside her. Once she made sure Garrett was all right, Jane intended to do whatever was necessary to become Martin's guardian. Now more than ever, she believed that God meant for her to be this boy's forever family. Since she was no longer the directress, there would be no conflict of interest. She had to believe that the Lord would make it possible for them to be together.

But first, she had to get to Garrett.

39

With her heart racing, Jane rushed into the emergency department of the Toronto General Hospital, dismayed to find the waiting room overflowing with all manner of patients. Across the room, a baby wailed. An old woman slumped in a wheelchair, rocking back and forth and moaning. Another man held a blood-soaked bandage around his hand.

Jane dashed by all of them to the nurses' station.

"Excuse me," she called over the chaos. "Excuse me, I—"

A nurse looked up and shook her head. "You're going to have to wait your turn, dear. We're swamped right now, as you can see."

Jane bit back an argument, realizing it wouldn't get her anywhere. Maybe in all the confusion, she could slip down the corridor and search for Garrett herself. She was gathering the courage to do so, when she noticed Dr. Henshaw emerging from one of the curtained areas.

"Dr. Henshaw!" She darted toward him before anyone could challenge her.

He turned and blinked. "Mrs. Linder. You're not here because of your mother, I hope."

"No. Mama's fine right now." She paused to catch her breath.

"A friend of mine, Garrett Wilder, was brought in earlier today after falling from a tree. I need to find out how he is."

The doctor's brow rose. "I was here when they brought him in."

"Were his injuries bad?" She clasped her hands on her purse strap to keep them from shaking.

His kind eyes radiated sympathy. "I don't know for certain since I didn't treat him." He made a discreet scan of the area and lowered his voice. "I can tell you that you'd likely find his family in the waiting room on the surgical floor. Level five."

"Thank you, Doctor. I appreciate it." She squeezed his hand, then took off at a brisk walk toward the elevators, thankful her frequent visits here with Mama had given her a good working knowledge of the hospital's layout.

On the way up in the elevator, she prayed silently for Garrett's well-being. The fact that he was on a surgical floor made Jane's legs go weak.

When the doors opened, she followed the signs toward the waiting area, her anxiety mounting with each step. She peeked inside and right away spotted Ben and Sarah sitting across the room.

Sarah immediately jumped up. "Jane! I'm so glad you're here." She came over and wrapped her in a hug.

Jane clung to her for a moment, then pulled back. "How is he?"

"He's in surgery." Moisture rimmed Sarah's eyes. "He injured his back in the fall. The X-rays showed the shrapnel had moved to a dangerous location, and they had no choice but to try and remove it."

"Is he going to be able to . . . ?" She couldn't even finish the sentence.

"They don't know." Sarah clasped her arms around her middle. "Only time will tell."

"You mean they won't know right away?"

Sarah shook her head. "It will depend on how well the spine heals after surgery." She gave a weak smile. "The good news is that the piece of shrapnel in his chest also got jarred in the fall.

It moved far enough away from his heart that the doctors believe it won't be a threat anymore."

The air leaked from Jane's lungs. Garrett's life was no longer in danger. Only his ability to walk. "That's some consolation, at least."

"It is indeed." Sarah sniffed into her handkerchief.

This time it was Jane who hugged Sarah, a mother in need of comfort. "May I wait with you and Ben?"

"It could take hours more." Sarah glanced at the industrial clock on the wall. "It's already been a long time."

"It doesn't matter. I'll wait as long as it takes."

Sarah gripped her arm. "Thank you. I know it will mean the world to Garrett. Why don't we sit down and you can pray with us?"

"I'd like that very much."

❖

Garrett came slowly to consciousness, as though winding his way through a thick fog. He blinked and opened his eyes, but only darkness met his stare. Where was he? He attempted to shift his position, but a bolt of pain shot down his back and through his left hip. He let out a groan. What was wrong?

"There you are. Back from the land of ether." A woman chuckled. "Don't try to move, hon. You've had back surgery."

The face of a woman in a white cap came into focus. Garrett tried to speak but his tongue felt two sizes too big for his mouth.

He grunted instead.

"Ah, your mouth is probably drier than dirt. Let me get you some water."

A few seconds later, she pushed a straw between his lips, and he drank thirstily.

"Not too much, now. You can have more in a few minutes when we see if you keep this down." She set the cup on the side table. "How is your pain?"

"Tolerable," he managed to rasp.

"That's good. You let me know if it gets any worse and I'll see about another shot for you." She patted his arm. "I'm going to let the doctor know you're awake. He'll want to discuss the results of the surgery with you. Back in a jiffy."

Garrett laid his head on the pillow, allowing pieces of memories to sift through the haze in his brain. He remembered climbing the ladder to get Martin, and he remembered the fall. But not much afterward.

Garrett squeezed his eyes shut. *Lord, help me get through this and to accept whatever fate you have in store for me.*

His thoughts turned then to Jane. Did she know they'd found Martin? Did she know about his fall? A sinking wave of depression washed over him. So much for meeting with the specialist to determine if there was anything that could be done. The matter had been taken out of his hands in a most disastrous manner.

Footsteps echoed in the room, and his parents appeared with a doctor right behind them.

Mom rushed to the side of his bed. "Garrett, honey. You're awake. How do you feel?"

"Sore."

"That's to be expected," the doctor chimed in. "I'm Dr. Littlejohn, your surgeon. I'd like to tell you how the procedure went and how we move forward from here."

Garrett gave a curt nod. "Go ahead."

"First, I noted from your chart that the piece of shrapnel in your chest has moved to a more benign location and will not require further intervention, which is indeed good news."

"Very good," Mom said with too bright a smile.

Garrett simply stared. He was more concerned with his back and why the doctor seemed to be stalling.

Dr. Littlejohn looked up from the clipboard. "Overall, I'd consider the surgery a success. We were able to remove the piece of metal and repair the damaged vertebrae as best we could."

"That's wonderful. Isn't it, Ben?" Mom turned her watery gaze on his father, as though to gather strength from him.

"It does sound favorable," Dad agreed. "Is there more, Doctor?"

"Yes." He cleared his throat. "We have no way of knowing if the nerve damage caused by the shrapnel invading the spinal column will be permanent."

Garrett stopped breathing.

"That will become apparent," the surgeon continued, "once the site has fully healed."

"And how long will that take?" Dad asked.

"That's difficult to determine. It could be as soon as a couple of weeks. Or it could take months."

Months! Garrett's stomach threatened to heave. He pressed his eyes closed and tried to breathe. His thoughts immediately turned to Jane and the words of love they'd both uttered. But was it fair to keep her hanging on, waiting to see if he'd ever walk again? Who knew how long that could take? And in the meantime, she'd lose her chance to marry Donald and be a mother to his son.

His throat ached. No, Garrett couldn't be that selfish.

He had to set her free to live the life she was meant to.

"Will he have to stay in bed all that time?" his mother inquired.

"Maybe just for the first week." He turned to address Garrett directly. "Then we'll start working with you to exercise the limbs and slowly help you gain strength to the point where we see if you can stand. In the meantime, we'll provide you with a wheelchair for use in the hospital and at home."

Garrett clamped his lips together to hold back the scream building in his chest. *A wheelchair.* His greatest fear was coming true, and there was absolutely nothing he could do about it.

After the doctor left, his mother came over and kissed his cheek. "It's all going to be fine, honey. You'll see."

"You don't know that, Mom. No one does." He shut his eyes

again. Maybe he could block everything out if he kept them closed.

"We have to count our blessings, son," Dad said in a low voice. "At least the other piece is no longer a threat to your life. That's cause for celebration in my book."

Garrett shook his head, his insides knotting. He knew he should be grateful. Yet right now, the possibility of paralysis outweighed everything else. Even though his family wouldn't see it that way, he dreaded the thought of being a burden to them. All he'd ever wanted to do was ease their load, not add to it.

Mom laid a hand on his arm. "Jane has been here with us all night. She's in the waiting room. Can I send her in?"

His heart threatened to shatter and become as useless as his legs.

"No," he said curtly. "I don't want to see anyone."

"But, Garrett, she—"

"I said no."

A strained silence settled over the room. Garrett wished he could take back his rudeness, but he couldn't even bring himself to say he was sorry.

"Come on, Sarah." Dad's voice was gruff. "Let the boy rest. This is a lot to take in."

"All right. But just so you know, Martin is fine."

Garrett swallowed hard and nodded. "That's good. Now, if you don't mind, I'm very tired."

He looked away from the hurt in his mother's eyes.

"We'll come by again later." She patted his arm. "And we'll be praying for you, dear."

Praying for him. The words ran through his mind, pounding harder and harder inside his brain. He laid there, not moving a muscle until he was sure his parents were gone, then he snatched the glass from his nightstand and hurled it across the room. It hit the wall and shattered into tiny pieces.

A nurse appeared several seconds later. He ground his molars together, not looking at her, his lungs heaving with the force of his labored breathing.

"I'll send someone to clean this up," she said and disappeared into the corridor.

Garrett gripped the metal rails of his bed until his fingers ached. Then he squeezed his eyes shut. Silent, useless tears spilled from under his lids, leaking onto the pillow until it was a soggy mess.

His mother could pray all she wanted. But he knew the truth.

It was far too late for that now.

40

In the early morning hours, Jane walked through the hushed hallways of the hospital, trying her best to tamp down her anxiety. She'd spent the entire night in the waiting room with the Wilders, alternating between praying and dozing off on the hard plastic chairs. They'd received word when Garrett was out of surgery and again when he was back in his room but were told that he would remain unconscious for some time. Visitors would not be allowed until he woke up.

When the nurse arrived a few minutes ago with the welcome news that Garrett was awake and that the surgeon wished to speak to the Wilders, Jane's emotions had become almost too raw too handle. Sarah and Ben left, promising to return with an update. Rather than wait alone in the empty room, Jane took the opportunity to go in search of a phone booth to call Donald.

Though it was still quite early, she presumed Donald would be up tending to Patrick already. As hard as this call would be, she needed to let him know that she wouldn't be coming back to babysit.

Not today. Not ever again.

Last night, it had become clear to her as she awaited word on Garrett's condition that her future lay in a different direction. She'd finally forgiven Donald, that much was true. But no matter

335

how she tried, she couldn't picture herself married to him again. Not when her heart was so firmly engaged elsewhere.

Perhaps she was taking the cowardly way out telling him the news over the telephone, but she couldn't afford the time to soften the blow in person.

As she walked, Jane tried to blink the grit from her eyes while attempting to ignore that every muscle in her body ached. Two nights in a row without a proper sleep was taking its toll. Finally, in a corner near the cafeteria, she found a phone booth. She slid inside and dialed the operator, who put her through to Donald's number.

"Jane," he said when he heard her voice. "Is everything all right? How is Martin?"

"He's fine, thank goodness." She paused. "But Garrett wasn't so lucky. I'm at the hospital now, waiting to hear the results of his surgery."

"The hospital? But what about Patrick?"

She took a deep breath. "Unfortunately, there's no easy way to say this. I'm afraid I can't continue as Patrick's caregiver." She bit her lip, awaiting the tongue-lashing she deserved. Technically, she hadn't gone back on her word. They'd agreed to a two-week trial period, which had just ended. She was within her rights to change her mind. Yet a bubble of guilt still pressed against her chest.

Instead of Donald's anger, complete silence met her ears.

"I-I don't understand," he finally said. "I thought things were going so well between us." He sounded more hurt than angry.

She swallowed. "I'm so sorry, Donald. I thought I could do it, I really did. But I've changed too much to go back to a life that doesn't fit anymore."

"I don't know what to say." The dejection in his voice filled her with another rush of guilt.

"I'm so sorry," she said again. "If you call the employment agency right away, they'll probably get you someone for Patrick by tomorrow."

"I thought you wanted a baby more than anything." He sounded dazed.

"I thought so too." She paused, but there was nothing else that could really explain her actions, except that she was in love with someone else. "I wish you and Patrick all the best."

When the call ended, she replaced the receiver with slightly shaky fingers and sat for a minute to allow her system to recover from the roil of conflicting emotions within her.

And prayed she wasn't making yet another terrible mistake.

———◆———

Jane headed back to the waiting room, hoping the surgeon had given Ben and Sarah good news about the operation and that she'd be able to see Garrett at last.

Sarah met her in the corridor, her lips trembling in a somewhat nervous smile. Not the one of unbridled joy Jane had hoped for.

"How did it go?"

An orderly moved down the hall, pushing a mop and bucket. Sarah moved out of the way, closer to the wall. Something about the way she was hesitating sent a chill of trepidation down Jane's back.

Sarah wrapped her arms around her middle. "The doctor said it went well, but they won't know the extent of the nerve damage until the spine fully heals."

Jane swallowed. "So, they don't know if he'll walk again?"

"They're hopeful. That's all they'll say."

Jane inhaled, reaching deep for her optimism. "Well, Garrett's strong. He'll do everything the doctor says, and he won't give up. I know he'll be all right." She managed a small smile. "Can I see him now?"

Sarah's features crumpled. "I'm so sorry, Jane. I don't know how to tell you this, but Garrett doesn't want to see anyone." She shook her head. "It's not personal. It's just . . . he's taking this all very hard. The doctor mentioned a wheelchair, and he shut down. He needs some time to adjust, that's all."

Jane pressed a hand to her mouth and leaned against the wall. Poor Garrett. His whole future must seem to be hanging in the balance right now. But he needed to know that she would stand by him no matter what.

She straightened and turned to face his mother. "I have to talk to him, Sarah. He needs to know that his life isn't over and that I'm here for him."

Indecision played over the woman's features.

"Please, Sarah. If he tells me he doesn't want me there, I'll leave. I just . . ." Tears brimmed in her eyes. "I have to at least see him for myself."

Sarah gave a huge sigh. "Far be it from me to stop you. Who knows? Maybe you can get through to him better than we could."

"Thank you." Jane wiped her eyes, relief flooding her muscles. "He's in room 522. But please try not to upset him."

"I'll do my best."

Jane's legs shook as she walked along the corridor, searching the room numbers. Would Garrett be furious with her for ignoring his wishes, or would he be relieved to see her? Either way, she'd have to respect his decision.

She paused outside his room to pray. *Lord, please use me as an instrument of your peace. Let me bring Garrett comfort and assurance and help me prove my love for him. Amen.*

Inside the door, Jane scanned the area. The bed on the right side of the double room was empty. A white curtain was pulled around the other bed, where Garrett must be. She steeled herself for his reaction as she quietly pushed the curtain aside.

He lay on his side facing the wall, his eyes closed. Tubes ran into his nose and arm, attached to machines that hummed. Her heart ached to see him lying there so helpless. He'd risked everything to save Martin, sacrificing his very health.

She came closer, loath to disturb him, but needing him to know she was there. She thought of the occasions he'd sustained her through trying times. Now she needed to be there to support him in the same way.

Jane brought a chair closer to the bed and sat down, her determination returning. She'd wait as long as it took to say her piece. Then at least he'd know where she stood. It may take him a while to accept whatever direction his life would take from here, but he wouldn't be doing it alone.

She sat there for several long minutes, until at last he opened his eyes. Her pulse jumped as his blue gaze met hers, but far from the welcome she'd hoped for, his features remained blank. Likely he hadn't been asleep at all but pretending so she'd leave.

Remember what he's facing, Jane. Of course, he's not himself.

"I know you don't want visitors," she said, "but I have a few things I need to say." She smoothed a hand over her blue flowered dress, trying not to be unnerved by his stony silence.

"First, I want to say how proud I am of you. And how sorry I am that you got hurt."

A flash of pain crossed his features, but still he said nothing.

"I understand your prognosis is uncertain, and it'll take time to know the outcome. But I'm confident you will walk again. You're persistent and determined, and I know you'll do whatever it takes to make that happen."

His jaw muscles twitched as his scowl grew deeper. What could he be thinking?

She leaned closer to make sure he heard her next words. "Even if the worst happens and you end up in a wheelchair, it doesn't mean you can't have a meaningful life. If Franklin Roosevelt can become the president of the United States in a chair, then you can certainly be an effective director of the Children's Aid and still make a difference in the lives of those children."

She reached for his hand, and when he went to pull away, she tightened her fingers around his. "I also want you to know that no matter what happens, I'll be here, waiting for you. And together we'll face whatever future God has in store for us."

When he started to shake his head, she rushed on, needing to finish what she started so he'd truly understand her position.

"Ever since my miscarriages, when my marriage fell apart, I've been struggling to find my place in this world. But now I know where I belong." She blinked, fighting the burn of tears. She needed to lay her heart on the line, no matter the consequences, so there was nothing left unsaid. Her breath hitched, her throat constricting on a surge of emotion. "My place is here with you, Garrett. Because I love you so very much." She kept her gaze fused to his, willing him to accept her offering.

"Jane." His voice was as tormented as the expression on his face. "I can't . . . I *won't* saddle you with a husband trapped in a chair."

"You'll only be *trapped* if you view it that way."

Garrett gave her another fierce scowl, but she ignored it, refusing to be put off.

"No one knows what challenges life will bring. All we can do is trust God to be with us through the hard times and help us find joy no matter what our circumstances." She placed her palm against the rough stubble on his cheek. "And you will find joy again, Garrett. This is only a setback. One I know you can overcome." She resisted the strong urge to kiss him. Now was not the time.

His features softened just a little. Yet she sensed his underlying reluctance. He needed time to process everything. Time to rest. And she had overstayed her welcome.

"I should go." She rose and took a last look at him, his tousled hair, his weary eyes, and her chest filled with warmth. "If you need anything, I'm only a phone call away."

"Wait." He frowned. "Have you seen Martin? Is he okay?"

She hesitated, then nodded. "He's going to be fine. They kept him overnight at the hospital just to make sure."

The lines etched in his forehead relaxed. "I'm glad. But what about the Blackwoods? Are they going to take him back?"

Jane bit her lip. She didn't think he needed to hear all this now. But if it were her, she'd want to know. "I saw Mrs. Blackwood in the hospital briefly. I got the impression she wants to return Martin again. I told her I didn't work there anymore and to contact the agency."

He shook his head, his eyes clouding over. "You were right about them. I was too stubborn to listen." He sighed. "What are we going to do now? Send him back to the shelter?"

"Actually, I had another idea." Nervously, she moved closer to the bed. "I'm going to apply for temporary guardianship of Martin myself, with the intent to adopt him." She gripped her purse tighter. "I was hoping that as interim director, you'd support me in this and approve the necessary paperwork." She held her breath. His answer could make or break her dearest wish for Martin.

A host of emotions flicked over his features. "I would, but I don't know when or if I'll be able to resume my position. The board might want to assign someone else in my place."

A flood of disappointment raced through her, but she nodded. "I understand." She gave him a tremulous smile. "Speaking of the board, has anyone informed them of your accident?"

"I don't think so."

"Would you like someone to call them? Or would you prefer to do it yourself?" She looked around the room. "I can have them find a way to bring a telephone to you."

His lips twitched at the corner before he let out a sigh. "Perhaps you could call Mr. Fenmore. Inform him of my surgery and request that he come by the hospital so we might iron out some of the details for my recovery."

A band of tension loosened around her shoulders. "I'd be happy to. Is there anything else you need?"

He studied her for a moment, the last traces of irritation fading from his features. "No." He reached out to brush his fingers over her hand. "I can't make any promises right now but knowing you're on my side will make all the difference."

Her heart started to pump faster. Clearly, he wasn't ready to commit to anything until he had a better idea of what was in store for him. Which was fine. She'd said she'd wait, and she meant it.

She bent over the metal rail to kiss his cheek. "I'm going to let you get some rest."

He gave her a warm look. "Thank you, Jane. You've given me the first real spark of hope since I woke up."

Her lips curved, gratitude spreading through her. "A spark is a good place to start. That and a great deal of prayer."

41

Lying in his hospital bed the next day, Garrett had entirely too much time to think. Time to imagine living his life confined to a wheelchair. It would be a huge adjustment to make, physically as well as emotionally. Yet Jane's words had given him the first glimmer of optimism for the future.

But what did that mean for the two of them? *"My place is here with you."* Jane seemed determined to stay by his side, but could Garrett allow her to sacrifice her life that way? He pondered the idea of how he would feel if their roles were reversed. If Jane had an accident and ended up in a wheelchair, would he love her any less?

No. He would still want her in his life.

Then how could he deny her the same choice?

And yet, a thousand worries plagued him. What if he grew weaker, not stronger? What if he couldn't even lift himself into the chair without her help?

He let out a soft sigh. Maybe he couldn't figure out his relationship with Jane right now, but at least she'd given him hope he could still have a meaningful career.

"Hello, Garrett." His father walked around the curtain. "How are you feeling, son?"

"Hi, Dad. I'm doing better."

"Good to hear." Dad pulled up a chair and sat down. "I sent your mother out for some fresh air. It will give us a chance to talk man-to-man."

Garrett's stomach swooped. That didn't bode well.

"How are you really doing, son?"

"Going a little crazy, if you must know. It's the uncertainty that's killing me, not knowing if I'll be able to walk again."

Dad nodded thoughtfully. "A difficult prospect to face."

"It is. But something Jane said gave me hope. She reminded me that President Roosevelt runs the United States from a wheelchair. I suppose if he can meet the demands of such a powerful position, I can make a worthwhile life for myself too."

"I agree." Dad pinned him with a stare. "But I know you, son. You'll use every last bit of strength to get back on your feet."

"I intend to give it my best shot."

"Just know that your mother and I are here to support you however we can."

"Thanks, Dad." Garrett swallowed hard. He'd hoped to be the answer to his parents' financial difficulties. Not add to them.

"Take this time to examine what's truly important, son. What you want out of life. And to ask God what He wants from you."

Garrett nodded. "I will, Dad. Thanks."

Footsteps sounded entering the room. "Excuse me, Mr. Wilder. Is this a bad time?"

Garrett looked up. "Mr. Fenmore. No, it's fine." He tried to move up higher against the pillows. "This is my father, Ben Wilder."

"Nice to meet you, sir." Mr. Fenmore shook Dad's hand.

"Well, I'll let you talk business." Dad edged toward the door. "See you later, son."

Garrett waited for his father to leave, then focused on Mr. Fenmore. "Thank you for coming to speak with me, sir."

Fenmore waved the comment aside. "Please accept my condolences on your accident. We were distressed to hear it happened while searching for one of the agency's wards. That's taking your commitment to your job a bit far, wouldn't you say?" His gray brows rose.

"Perhaps. But all I could think about was Martin's safety."

Mr. Fenmore nodded. "This certainly proves we made the right choice in appointing you as interim director." He gave a wry smile. "Though I never thought you'd take such a hands-on approach."

Garrett shook his head. "Thank you. I'm only sorry I'll be incapacitated for a while." The beeping of the equipment suddenly seemed louder, and he'd never felt so feeble in his life.

"Speaking of that, Mrs. Linder has offered to fill in until you're ready to come back to work. What would you think about that idea?"

"I'd welcome it. Jane will keep things running smoothly in my absence."

"Good. Then we'll make it official at our next meeting. In the meantime, I don't want you to worry about anything except your recovery. And to ease your mind, we're prepared to offer you the director position permanently."

Garrett's mouth fell open. "Really? But what about the other candidates?"

"We had a few promising applicants, but no one could match your proven commitment to the job."

"I don't know what to say. I'm honored, sir. Thank you very much."

Mr. Fenmore handed him a brown envelope. "Mrs. Linder asked me to bring you this. It's the Blackwood family's release papers. After this latest episode, they've decided they can't keep Martin any longer."

Garrett took the envelope, regret filling his chest. "I should have realized they wouldn't be a good fit."

"Mrs. Linder and I had a conversation about that. I understand you had another idea concerning Martin's placement. A more unconventional one?"

Garrett's heart picked up speed. Had Jane already pled her case? "Actually, it was Jane's idea, part of her recommendations concerning unconventional adoptions that I included in my report. Martin is the perfect example of a child who needs more one-on-one attention."

"I see." Mr. Fenmore stroked his chin. "I understand Mrs. Linder is divorced and lives with her widowed mother. Do you truly feel she would be a good fit to adopt the boy?"

"I do. Jane and Martin share a unique bond, and I believe he'd do well with her."

Mr. Fenmore gave a thoughtful nod. "Well, with so many fewer foster parents available, we need to come up with creative solutions to find the children a home."

"Thank you, sir. I look forward to getting back to work to implement those ideas."

"If there's anything we can do for you in the meantime, don't hesitate to call." Mr. Fenmore cleared his throat. "Should your recovery be delayed, we can always reconfigure the office to suit a wheelchair."

Garrett's brows rose. "You'd be willing to do that?"

He nodded. "To be honest, it's something we should have done years ago. Especially now that our injured veterans are returning home." He gave Garrett a pointed look. "You just concentrate on getting well enough to be released." He tipped his hat and left the room.

Garrett stared after him for a moment. Mr. Fenmore was being more than generous. And knowing they wouldn't rescind his job if he remained paralyzed was a freeing notion. He looked down at the envelope with Jane's neat script on the outside. He opened it and found the paperwork from the Blackwoods withdrawing their guardianship of Martin. Right underneath, he found the form granting Mrs. Jane Linder custody of Martin Smith with the intention of adopting the boy after the mandatory two-year waiting period. Jane had signed the form, and now all it needed was his approval.

He smiled as he read it over. He'd gladly sign this. At least, he'd have helped make one of Jane's dreams come true.

He only hoped that one day he could make the rest of her dreams come true as well.

42

Jane pulled the front door of the Children's Aid office firmly closed and locked it. It had been another long day, the middle of her third week filling in for Garrett. Next Monday, so Mr. Fenmore had told her, Garrett was due to return to his position, if the ramp out front could be installed in time.

She knew from her frequent conversations with Sarah that Garrett still wasn't walking, causing no end of frustration for Garrett and a great deal of worry for everyone else, Jane included.

As she made her way to the bus stop, she couldn't quite manage to shake her somber mood. She hadn't seen Garrett since he left the hospital and moved out to the farm to finish his recuperation. When she went to see him the day he left, he'd warned her that he would need time alone to concentrate on his recovery and asked for her understanding. What else could she do but agree?

Still, Jane called the house almost every day, and Sarah continued to keep her updated on her son's progress. The Wilders had set up a bed on the main floor for him, and the hospital had arranged for a physical therapist to come to the house three times a week to work on strengthening his leg muscles so that when the nerves had fully healed, he'd be strong enough to stand.

But whenever Jane asked to speak to Garrett, Sarah always had an excuse why he couldn't come to the phone. And if Jane suggested trying to visit, there was always a reason why it wasn't a good time for her to come out. Jane wasn't fooled by all the excuses. She knew Sarah was only abiding by Garrett's wishes, and it was obvious that he was distancing himself from her in case he never walked again.

If only she could she make him understand it didn't matter to her.

Jane pulled her collar higher against the sharp bite of wind, peering down the street to catch sight of the bus. Perhaps she was being impatient, expecting too much too soon. After all, this was a life-changing event for Garrett, and he deserved the chance to come to terms with it in whatever way he could.

Trust. The word kept popping into her mind at the oddest times, a subtle reminder that she needed to trust God's timing.

I'm trying, Lord. I really am.

She needed to remember that God was in control, and it was His will that would prevail. Because of that, she was doing her best to respect Garrett's wishes and give him the space he needed to come to terms with his circumstances.

The bus pulled up with a squeal of brakes, the doors whooshing open in front of her. As she climbed aboard, she made the conscious effort to push all negative thoughts away and concentrate on her blessings instead. Her spirits rose, knowing Martin would be waiting when she got home. He and Mama had fallen into a routine every afternoon. Mama would have a snack waiting for him when he got home from school, and then together they would prepare the vegetables for supper, so that by the time Jane arrived, much of the work would be done.

Martin had thrived in the short time since he'd come to live with them, which thrilled Jane to no end. Knowing he had a family who loved him, no matter what that family looked like, had made all the difference to him. He even enjoyed school and didn't balk at doing any of the assigned homework.

Mama too had benefited from Martin's presence. She seemed to have more energy and a new lightness to her being, enjoying her role as grandmother. When Jane discussed the apparent improvement with Dr. Henshaw, he told her that although Mama's heart condition remained the same, the change could be due to a lifting of her spirits.

Quite often, he told her, patients became despondent over their situation and that melancholy was almost as detrimental to them as their physical condition. He'd tried to assure Jane that she'd been taking wonderful care of her mother, but that perhaps having a child in the house had given her mother a new lease on life as well as a renewed interest in doing the little things she could, like knitting and some light cooking. Jane reflected on this and determined that Dr. Henshaw was right. Depression might have been as debilitating to Mama as her weakened heart. If Martin could help with that, then he was even more of a blessing in their lives than Jane had imagined.

As she got off at her stop, her steps felt lighter. God was good and faithful all the time, and in the end, that was all that truly mattered.

If one corner of her heart remained empty, she had no right to complain. She only hoped that Garrett would find happiness and fulfilment in his life, whatever the future held for him.

And if that life didn't include her, she prayed she could learn to accept it. Until then, she held tight to the hope that Garrett would eventually realize he wanted her in his life.

------- ❖ -------

Garrett rolled his chair down the hall and into his parents' kitchen. His therapy session had gone as well as most of his previous ones, yet today frustration screamed through every cell in his body. The tingles in his shins and feet told him that feeling was slowly returning. It had been over a week now since the sensations had started, but his doctor still wouldn't allow Garrett to attempt to stand.

"Give it a bit more time," Dr. Littlejohn had said during his last visit.

A bit more time? Next week he was due to start back to work. Still, the rational side of his brain understood that rushing his recovery could cause a setback, and he certainly didn't want that.

Yet, at the heart of it all, he ached for Jane. He'd promised himself he wouldn't see her again until he could walk up to her on his own two feet. And until he could come to grips with his new circumstances, he thought it best to give them both a little distance.

In the kitchen, Garrett maneuvered his chair past the counter to the long farmhouse table.

Mom was seated in her usual spot with a mug of tea in her hand. "Hi, honey. How did your treatment go today?"

She asked him the same question every time. And every time he answered in kind.

"Fine, as usual." He pulled his chair up to the table where a pitcher of water and a glass sat ready for him.

As he poured himself a drink, he glanced at his mother. Her brows were knit together, and she stared absently into her cup. Garrett held back a sigh. Things still hadn't improved much on the farm. Dad looked beaten down lately, which was likely the reason for his mother's worry.

And another reason Garrett needed to get out of this chair. Once he was fully recovered, he'd be able to help out more, now that he didn't have to worry about the pieces of shrapnel. He could put in his hours at the office, and if he had to, he'd drive out here each night to help his dad in whatever way he could.

Right now, with the start of December upon them and a new dusting of snow on the ground, the work had trailed off. Still, there were always fences to mend, repairs to be made in the barn, and feed to ready for the animals.

He took a long drink of water. "Is there anything I can do for you, Mom?"

She raised her head and mustered a brief smile. "You could peel some carrots for supper."

"Happy to." She always found some task to make him feel useful.

"Are you sure you're ready to go back to work on Monday?"

He gritted his teeth. This was the hardest part of recuperating at home. Not that he didn't appreciate her concern, but at times he felt like an eight-year-old kid instead of a thirty-one-year-old man. "Yes, Mom. I feel great. I just wish I could walk into the office on my own steam. And that I didn't have to bother Dad to drive me back and forth each week."

Thankfully, the boardinghouse where Garrett was staying already had a ramp up to the front door, and his landlady had kindly offered him a room on the first floor, so he'd be able to get in and out. He was also looking into city transportation options for people in wheelchairs.

She reached over and patted his arm. "Be patient a while longer."

"Unfortunately, patience isn't one of my finer qualities."

"You're right there." She chuckled as she rose and went to the sink. "Have you talked to Jane yet?"

A dark cloud instantly enveloped him. They'd had this same conversation over and over, and it was growing tiresome. He'd briefly spoken to Jane once or twice about work, but that wasn't what his mother meant. "No, Mom. And you know why."

"Honey, she calls every day to ask how you are. She cares for you, regardless of whether you can walk or not."

He scowled at the table. "It's not up for debate. When the time is right, I'll talk to her."

His mother only sighed and shook her head.

A loud knock sounded on the front door, followed by footsteps in the hall.

"I'll get it." Cassie's voice drifted back to the kitchen.

A few seconds later, she walked slowly into the room with little Mandy right behind her. Cassie stared at an envelope in her hand, her face ashen.

"What is it?" Mom dried her hands on a tea towel.

Cassie sank onto a chair, tears blooming in her eyes. "It's a telegram from the war office."

Garrett's gut gave a painful lurch. *Please, no more bad news.* He didn't think his family could take one more blow.

Cassie held out a shaky hand to their mother. "Could you open it, please?"

"Of course." Mom took the envelope and stared at it for a moment, as if weighing the gravity of its contents.

Mandy hopped up and down by the table, clutching one of her dolls. "Mommy, can I have a tea party?"

"Not now, sweetheart," Cassie said. "Maybe later." Her gaze remained glued to the envelope their mother was now opening.

Garrett's own heart thudded unevenly in his chest. He could only imagine the somersaults his sister's must be doing.

Mom pulled out the paper and scanned the contents, then a hand flew to her mouth.

"What does it say?" Tears had started to stream down Cassie's face.

Mom held it out to her. "Jack's coming home."

"What?" Cassie snatched the paper and read it. A smile broke through her tears. "It's true. They're sending him home. Thank you, Lord!" She cried harder, her shoulders heaving.

Relief and joy spread through Garrett's body. Finally, some good news. Jack would soon be home with his family, where he belonged.

A movement beside Garrett caught his eye.

"Mandy, no!" He sprang forward in time to prevent the hot teapot from crashing down on the girl. He shoved the pot back where it belonged and took Mandy's hand in his, checking to make sure she hadn't burned her fingers. "Are you all right?"

She nodded, her eyes huge.

Relief morphed into exasperation. "What did Grandma tell you about touching the teapot? You could have burned yourself very badly."

He glanced over at his mother and sister, expecting them to chime in, but they were both staring at him, their mouths open.

"You're standing." Cassie pointed to his legs.

Garrett slowly looked down, and goose bumps shot up his arms. He'd jumped up without even thinking to save Mandy from being scalded. Now his legs began to tremble, and he lowered himself back to his chair.

"Praise the Lord." Mom's eyes filled with tears.

He blinked, still dazed by what had happened. To test himself and make sure it wasn't some anomaly, he slowly pushed himself upright again, grasping the edge of the table for support. This time his legs seemed steadier. A grin twitched his lips as he attempted to take a step.

"Be careful." Mom rushed over to support him. "Take your time."

He took a few more halting steps until he reached the counter. Then he threw his head back and laughed out loud, his chest filling with elation. "I can't believe it. It's a day of miracles." He threw his arms around his mother. "I think this calls for a celebration!"

"I agree." Cassie came to hug him as well, fresh tears on her cheeks.

"Can we have a tea party, then?" Mandy peered up at them.

The three of them burst out laughing.

Cassie picked Mandy up and twirled her around the kitchen. "We can have a tea party and cookies and whatever else you want, sweet pea. Your daddy's coming home. And Uncle Garrett can walk again."

43

Jane closed the oven door. Another half an hour and the roast would be ready. She checked the pan of potatoes on the stove and replaced the lid with a smile. Sunday dinners were becoming her favorite time of the week. She always saved some of her weekly meat rations for the weekend as well as her sugar rations to make a nice dessert. Despite the war, Sunday dinner was a family tradition from her childhood that she wanted to pass on to her son.

Now that they had Martin, their lives seemed to have changed from black and white to Technicolor. Having a child to share their home, someone who appreciated family life, was a true gift. One that made her and Mama even more grateful for all they had.

Their lives would be even better if they could just hear some good news about Brandon. But after contacting the war office and learning they had nothing further to report—and likely wouldn't until the hostilities ended—Jane had tried her best to put the matter out of her mind. As Mama said, they would have to leave Brandon's fate up to the Lord.

The other matter weighing on Jane was the possibility she might need to find a new job. Once Garrett resumed his position as director, she wasn't sure she could go back to being a caseworker, not with the way he'd been avoiding her. It would probably be better for the both of them if she found work somewhere else. A prospect she did not look forward to.

Just then, Martin came barreling into the kitchen. "There's a truck in front of the house, Mom."

Jane's heart melted into a gooey mess every time he called her that. "Is there, honey?"

"Yup. It looks like Mr. Ben's truck from the farm."

Jane frowned and laid her potholders on the counter. What would Ben be doing here? She drew in a deep breath and forced her pulse to settle. He was probably bringing Blackie over for Martin. She'd mentioned to Sarah that Martin was pining for the dog, and Sarah had promised to talk to Garrett about it. Jane hadn't heard anything more and hated to bother them, knowing how preoccupied they were with Garrett's recovery. She figured that when the opportunity arose and Ben came into town again, he'd bring the dog.

But why would he have come into town on a Sunday afternoon?

She dried her hands on her apron, pulled on her bulky cable-knit sweater, and followed an excited Martin to the door.

Sure enough, Ben's red truck was parked in front. Blackie stood in the back of the vehicle, his tail wagging furiously. When he spied Martin, the dog jumped out onto the ground and dashed toward the boy.

"Blackie! You're here." Martin knelt and buried his face in the dog's fur. Blackie's whole body wriggled with joy as he licked the boy's face.

Ben came around the front of the vehicle, dressed in his usual plaid shirt and denim overalls, this time with a sheepskin coat over top. "Hello, Jane. Hope you don't mind us dropping by unannounced."

"Not at all, Ben." She smiled and stepped off the porch, pulling her sweater tighter. It was growing colder by the minute. They would probably get their first real snowfall of the season soon.

"Thank you for bringing Blackie. I hope you didn't come all this way just for that."

Ben's eyes twinkled. "Not just that. I have something else to deliver too."

It was then she noticed someone in the passenger seat. The door opened, and a pair of long legs swung out, followed by the end of a wooden cane.

Jane's heart froze in her chest. Her gaze traveled up from the legs to the man attempting to stand.

Garrett!

Her lungs stopped working as she drank in the sight of him, so handsome in a black corduroy jacket and tan-colored pants. His dark hair was longer than usual, but his vivid blue eyes were exactly as she remembered. She wanted to run across the lawn to help him, but her feet remained fixed to the walkway. Once he gained his balance with the aid of his cane, he stood smiling at her for a second before taking a halting step forward.

Jane's hand flew to her mouth. She looked at Ben. "He can walk?"

"Yes, ma'am. And after practicing for a day or so, the first thing he wanted to do was come here."

Tears burned her eyes. She blinked hard and moved toward him but came to a halt, unsure what to do next. She longed to throw her arms around him but worried they might topple to the ground.

Instead, she smiled through her tears. "When did this happen?"

"Friday afternoon. Around four twenty to be exact." Garrett's grin was a wonderful sight to behold. Joy radiated from his face, making his eyes even more vibrant.

He looked beyond her. "Hey, Martin. Will you take my dad inside to say hello to your grandmother?"

"Sure, Mr. Wilder. Thank you for letting me have Blackie."

"You're welcome. I'll bring the rest of his things inside in a minute. I need to talk to Jane first."

Despite the cold bite to the air, a wave of heat rose through Jane's neck and cheeks. "Do you want to sit on the porch?"

"If you don't mind, I'd prefer to stand for a bit. I've had enough sitting these last few weeks, and I'm still trying to strengthen my legs. Get them used to moving again."

Moisture dampened her cheeks. As much as she tried, she couldn't seem to stem the flow of her tears. "This is such wonderful news. I've been praying so hard for you."

He reached over to thumb away the moisture. "I know you have."

"I called every day."

"I know that too."

"But you wouldn't talk to me."

"I'm sorry." He lowered his chin, his expression contrite. "I couldn't let myself until I knew if I would ever walk again. It was prideful, I know. But I needed to come to terms with my situation before I made any major decisions about my life."

She searched his face, needing honesty. "And what if you never could walk again? Would you have come to see me? Or would you have just left me when things got bad, like Donald did?"

He winced, an expression of sorrow flashing over his face. "I never meant to hurt you, Jane. I was trying to protect you."

"I didn't need protecting," she said softly. "I told you it didn't matter to me. That I loved you no matter what."

He let out a contrite sigh. "I'm pretty sure I would have broken down and come to see you eventually. I don't think I'm strong enough to stay away from you. I never have been."

She lifted her chin. "And do you promise never to shut me out again?" She waited, her heart thudding hard, needing the reassurance that he could be the man she needed. The one who would walk beside her through all life's ups and downs.

His beautiful blue eyes grew damp. "I do. I promise to share everything with you—the good and bad. I can't believe I forgot what a good team we make."

One arm came around her as he drew her toward him. Then, slowly, he brought his lips down to meet hers. Her whole being sighed in response. *At last*, her soul seemed to say. At last, everything in the universe had come into perfect alignment. How she'd missed him. The feel of his arms, his warm lips on hers. He pulled away too soon for her liking, but she rested her head against his shoulder, inhaling the clean scent of him.

"I've waited so long to do that," he breathed into her hair. "At times, I thought I'd never be able to hold you like this again."

The urge to give in and weep almost overwhelmed her, but she wouldn't cry any more than she already had. He deserved a celebration, not tears. "I've missed you too. So very much."

He brushed another quick kiss against her lips, then smiled. "I have something for you. Wait here." With the aid of his cane, he walked carefully across the hard brown lawn to the truck, reached inside the open door, and came back with a glass container in one hand.

He handed her the Mason jar decorated with a red-checked cloth and tied with twine. "It's Mom's homemade applesauce. She wanted you to have the recipe—including her secret ingredient."

Jane stared at the slip of paper attached to the jar. Though she was flattered that Sarah would entrust her with a family secret, she couldn't quite hide her disappointment. She'd thought it was a gift from Garrett, something more personal. "Tell her thank you. We'll enjoy this with our dessert tonight."

Smiling, he pointed to the lid. "There's something else." A twinkle lit his eyes.

Sure enough, something gleamed from within the large twine bow. Nerves fluttered to life in her belly. "Is this . . . ?"

He leaned his cane against the porch, then reached over, untied the bow, and removed a ring. The diamond glinted in the light as he held it out to her with unsteady fingers. "I love you, Jane, more than I ever thought possible. I know now, with absolute certainty, that my place is with you, and I don't want to spend another day without you. Will you marry me? Will you and Martin be my family?"

More tears blurred her vision. She couldn't seem to find the words to speak. She pressed her fingers to her trembling lips.

"I would get down on one knee, but right now, I'm not sure I could get back up again." He searched her face, a hint of uncertainty mixed with the amusement in his eyes.

She bobbed her head. "Yes, Garrett. I'd be honored to marry you."

A smile broke free as he slipped the ring on her finger. "A perfect fit. Just like you."

Then he gathered her to him for another kiss. This time he seemed steadier, wrapping both his arms around her, as though he never intended to let her go.

Loud cheering from behind them broke through the haze of their embrace. Jane swiped the happy tears from her cheeks as her mother and Ben came toward them.

Mama beamed at her. "Congratulations, Janey. I'm so happy for you."

"Thank you, Mama."

Ben kissed her and shook Garrett's hand.

Martin stood a little behind, his hand on Blackie's back, unsmiling.

Jane's spirits deflated at his grim expression. Should she have asked Martin first before she accepted? "Martin, what do you think about having Mr. Wilder for a dad?"

When he didn't answer right away, her insides twisted harder. Had she made a mistake? She went to kneel in front of him. "What is it? You can tell me."

Martin looked at her with hurt-filled eyes. "If you and Mr. Wilder get married, you'll have babies and forget about me."

"Oh, honey, that's not true."

Garrett came to stand beside her and laid a hand on Martin's shoulder. "First of all, even if we did have more children,

360

we would never forget about you, son. That's a promise. And second—" Garrett glanced at Jane, his gaze seeking permission. She nodded. "The doctors have told Jane she can't have any babies, so that's not going to happen."

"Oh." Martin's brows rose.

"One day, though," Garrett continued, "we might want to adopt another boy or girl who needs a home, like you did. But we'd make sure that you're included, and we'd decide together as a family. Does that sound fair?"

"I guess so."

Jane opened her arms, and Martin came to her for a hug. She held on tight, relishing these rare moments, knowing the time might soon come where he wouldn't want a hug from his mother. She squeezed him and kissed his cheek. "You will always be very important to me, no matter what happens in our lives. I hope you believe that."

He smiled then, relief spreading over his features. "I do, Mom. You always keep your promises."

She hugged him again. "I try my best. Even if it takes a long time."

As she headed back toward the house, Jane reflected on the truth of that statement and how the same could be said of God. He always kept His promises, even if it seemed to take a long time.

On the porch, Garrett pulled her gently against him for another slow kiss, one that sealed his promise for a lifetime of happiness ahead. They'd already proven that they could weather any storm—even an ice storm—together. Jane was more than ready to see what else life had in store for them, knowing with complete certainty now that they'd face both the good and the bad together.

She smiled up into Garrett's eyes, amazed at how God had taken three broken and wounded people and knit them together to form the perfect family. One she would cherish for the rest of her days.

Epilogue

May 1945

Standing in the Wilders' farmhouse on a bright Saturday afternoon, Jane surveyed the scene before her with a grateful heart. Little Shannon, the newest addition to her and Garrett's family, sat at the kitchen table with Mandy, both girls engrossed in drawing pictures of the barn kittens they'd just been out to see. Drawing was far too sedate an activity for Kevin, Dale, and Martin, who opted to stay outside with Ben, which suited Jane just fine. Shannon was still adjusting to her new family and sometimes found the three boys overly rambunctious.

Jane walked over and laid a gentle hand on the girl's shoulder, eliciting the barest of smiles. Dr. Henshaw had brought the orphaned four-year-old into the shelter three weeks ago and, knowing that Jane and Garrett were hoping to adopt another child, had called them right away. It had taken Jane all of five minutes to fall in love with the tiny redhead, and once they'd gotten Martin's approval, they'd eagerly applied to be Shannon's foster parents.

Garrett came into the kitchen and winked at Jane, his eyes crinkling at the corners as he crossed the room toward her.

Her pulse sped up at the intimate expression that crept across his face. Today they were celebrating their first wedding anniversary. She wasn't sure what he had planned, but knowing her husband, it would surely be memorable.

"Are you ready to get out of here for a while?" he whispered in her ear.

"Why? Where are we going?"

"You'll see." His mischievous grin made her pulse soar.

Sarah poked her head out of the pantry. "Don't worry about the kids. Ben and I will keep them busy."

Sarah had been thrilled with the addition of Shannon to the family. "The more Wilders the better," she'd said. "And Mandy will love having another girl around." A statement that had proven true, as the girls had already become fast friends.

The banging back door announced Martin's arrival. He headed straight to the sink to wash his hands.

Jane went over to join him. "Dad and I are going out for a while. Will you help Grandma and Grandpa and watch out for Shannon while we're gone?"

"Sure." He wiped his hands dry on a towel. "I guess it's my job now if I'm going to be her big brother."

Jane's throat tightened, and she squeezed him in a warm hug. "You're amazing, Martin Wilder. I'm so proud of you."

He shrugged out of her embrace. At ten years old, he'd begun to tolerate her hugs less often. "That's not my name yet."

Garrett came up behind them. "Maybe not, but it won't be long now. Only a few more months until the adoption is final." He winked at him. "Then you're stuck with us for good."

Martin grinned. "Nope. *You're* stuck with *me*."

Jane blinked hard to stem the happy tears forming, still unable to believe how incredibly fortunate she was to have this amazing family.

———— ❖ ————

Garrett hummed to himself as he steered his dad's truck down the gravel lane toward the orchard. Although he loved spending time with his family, he couldn't deny the thrill of having his wife all to himself, even if only for a few hours.

And on this special day, he couldn't help but marvel at all the blessings in his life and at the changes that had occurred recently. Only days ago, the whole city had celebrated the surrender of Germany with a ticker tape parade and dancing in the streets. He and Jane had joined in the festivities, reveling in unbridled joy with their fellow Torontonians.

Their happiness, however, had been tempered with sorrow when Hildie had received official word of Brandon's death. Though his remains had never been found, eyewitness accounts of the last battle he'd been in seemed enough for the military to finally upgrade his status from Presumed Dead to Killed in Action. Jane and Hildie had taken the news with stoic realism, having come to terms with the inevitable outcome long ago.

The truck's tires hit a rut, lifting Jane and Garrett off the bench seat to come down with a hard thud. He grinned over at Jane.

"Watch it, Mr. Broncobuster." She shot him a mock glare. "Just because your back is healed doesn't mean you need to be reckless."

"Yes, ma'am." His grin widened until she burst out laughing and shook her head. She looked so pretty today that he was having a hard time keeping his attention on the road.

"I take it we're heading to the orchard?"

"That's right. Can't miss the apple blossoms. If we don't go now, they might be finished by the next time we're here."

"True. I bet Martin and Shannon would love to . . ." She trailed off and gave him an apologetic shrug. "Sorry. I said we wouldn't talk about the kids, but it's so hard not to."

"I was thinking the same thing." He gave her a warm look. "But I was also thinking about our wedding day one year ago. It was an even nicer day than this, with the leaves in full greenery, and, of course, the gorgeous blooms."

"I'm so glad we decided to have our reception here. I can't think of a more perfect place."

They'd been married in the Huttonville Community Church in an intimate ceremony. Afterward, a few friends and neighbors had joined them for the outdoor reception near the orchard.

It had been a magical afternoon. One he'd never forget.

He reached over to take Jane's hand. "Everything about that day was perfect. Especially the bride. You never looked more beautiful."

"Thank you." Her cheeks grew rosy. "My dress today is almost the same color as the one I wore then."

"Mm-hmm. And almost as breathtaking."

Jane hadn't wanted to wear white, since it was her second marriage. Garrett hadn't cared what she wore as long as she showed up at the church. And truly, with her hair wreathed in spring flowers and a bouquet to match, she'd looked lovelier than he could have imagined.

He stopped the truck near the orchard and went around to help her out, unable to resist pulling her into his arms for a lingering kiss. "Happy anniversary, Mrs. Wilder."

"Happy anniversary." She gazed at him with such love that his heart seemed to swell in his chest. She placed a palm against his jaw in a soft caress. "I never imagined my life could be this wonderful. And it's all because of you." Then she leaned in to kiss him again.

"I think the Lord might have had more to do with it than me, but I'll gladly take the credit." He laughed out loud, a sound so liberating it felt his soul could break free to fly above the treetops.

She laughed too, then sobered. "Do you think Shannon is doing all right?" She searched his face so earnestly that he had to kiss her again.

"She's still grieving the loss of her mother and adjusting to life with us. But overall, I'd say she's doing fine."

"Sometimes, when I go into her room at night, I find her sleeping on the floor. Why would she do that when she has a comfortable bed to sleep in?"

He drew her closer, needing to ease the worry from her brow. "Remember what Dr. Henshaw told us. Shannon and her mother had been living in the slums in a one-room hovel. She's probably used to sleeping on the floor." He tucked a stray piece of hair behind her ear. "It will take a little time until she adjusts completely. You're doing everything possible to show her she's safe and loved."

Jane sighed. "I guess you're right. It just hurts my heart to see her that way."

"Spoken like a true mother." He kissed her nose, then reached into the back of the truck for the picnic basket and a blanket. "How about we get this celebration started?"

When Garrett smiled down at her with such love, Jane's heart did a slow roll in her chest. What had she done to deserve such a wonderful man in her life? One who would do anything to please her, including adopting another child?

In addition, he had no qualms about her working as a caseworker at the Children's Aid office three days a week. She never dreamed she could have a career and a family too. But her husband understood how important it was for her to help troubled children find a permanent home, a place for them to belong and to be loved. Now that they had Shannon, Jane had taken a leave of absence until the little girl started school in the fall. Then Jane would happily resume her position again.

The late-afternoon sun was still high in the sky as they headed toward the trees, dappling the apple blossoms with filtered light. Garrett picked a grassy spot with a good view of the blooms, laid out the blanket, and set the basket down.

"I think we're in for a bumper crop of apples this year," he said as he waited for her to get comfortable beside him. "Just look at all those blossoms."

Indeed, it was more beautiful than a painting with the sea of pink and white flowers surrounding them. Jane was so thankful Garrett's brother-in-law Jack had decided to continue living with the Wilders to help Ben and Sarah with the farm. It relieved a huge burden from Garrett and allowed him to concentrate on his job and his own family without any guilt. Still, Jane knew how much the place meant to her husband, and they spent as much time with her in-laws as they could.

She glanced up at the endless blue sky above. Every now and then, a breeze shook a few petals loose to fall gently down on them, like nature's own confetti.

Garrett brushed a few stray petals from her hair, his hand lingering against her cheek. "You've made me happier than I ever dreamed possible, Jane. I thank God every day for bringing me to the Children's Aid doorstep—and to you."

Tears rose in her eyes. "I thank Him for the same thing. For you, for Martin, and now for Shannon. I can't help but think that if it weren't for Martin running away that night, I might have made the biggest mistake of my life."

His fingers caressed her cheek. "That's all behind us now."

She let out a soft sigh. "Once I followed my heart, everything happened as it was meant to. As God intended."

Garrett leaned over and kissed her tenderly once more. And there, among the apple blossoms, sheltered in her husband's arms, Jane knew she'd found her perfect place at last.

A Note from the Author

ear Friends,
   In researching the Toronto Children's Aid Society, the setting where most of this book took place, I had help from a wonderful resource, a book called *A Legacy of Caring: A History of the Children's Aid Society of Toronto* by John McCullagh. I read this book several times during the creation of *To Find Her Place*. Most of my renderings of the CAS were true to historical detail; however, I did take author's license in some cases to enhance my story. I would like to clarify some of these areas and ask any historians to forgive the liberties I took in telling Jane and Garrett's story.

   Mr. Robert Mills was indeed the Managing Director of the Toronto Children's Aid from 1923 to 1947. To my knowledge, the real Mr. Mills did not suffer from any heart condition, nor did he undergo heart surgery. I used this fiction to serve the purpose of my story. In reality, Mr. Mills resigned from his position in December 1947 and went on to enjoy a decade of retirement. One of Bob Mills's greatest contributions to the society was the stabilization of its finances and the guarantee of funding for its programs. He also worked in tandem with Vera Moberly to create the foster care system for both infants and older children. Mr.

Mills was described as "a child welfare pioneer, whose compassion, integrity and insight contributed to making Toronto a better place for children." Without consciously doing so, these are the exact qualities I gave Garrett Wilder.

While the Children's Aid Society did depend on volunteers in many areas, including the bookkeeping, there was never to my knowledge any instance of money skimming. This was strictly fictional, as was the instance of an unwed mother paying a caseworker to give her baby a better placement. In no way was it my intention to cast any aspersions on the sanctity of this institution.

Many of the recommendations Garrett made to the board members were actual practices that Mr. Mills instituted during his time at the Children's Aid. The space limitations I described during Garrett's tour of the offices were very real, as were the host of difficulties created by World War II. The real Children's Aid office on Isabella Street was a very plain, almost industrial-looking building. I am so grateful to the Bethany House team for making the Children's Aid building on the cover such a beautiful-looking structure.

The staffing of the Toronto CAS was far more extensive than portrayed in this book. I purposely kept it simple in order not to clutter the story with too many characters. This is how Mr. McCullagh describes the agency: "In 1939, the field staff consisted of a supervisor and 9 workers in child protection, a supervisor and 23 workers in child placement (adoption), a full-time physician and psychologist, and 2 workers in the clothing room to outfit the children. The clerical staff consisted of an office manager, 8 stenographers, a bookkeeper, and a switchboard operator." This was not including the volunteers. And the statistic Garrett quoted about the caseworkers seeing over two hundred families a day was indeed true!

It was difficult to find information on the exact adoption criteria the Toronto CAS held for determining who would be deemed worthy of adopting a child, be it an infant or an older child. From what I could tell, adoption by an unmarried person wasn't strictly forbidden; however, it seemed that this rarely, if ever, occurred. I took the liberty of putting my own spin on this subject.

The other tidbit I wanted to share with you was my inspiration for the Wilder farm. Huttonville is a real town near my home. As a child, we went there every fall to pick apples in the beautiful orchard. I remember with great fondness the tractor ride to the orchard, and the joy of picking the apples and eating the crisp fruit right off the tree. It was such fun to add the orchard scenes with Garrett and Jane and the children and to relive these treasured memories from my childhood. Sadly, the two main orchards in Huttonville have been sold to developers who plan to build houses there. This was my small way of immortalizing those farms, and I hope you enjoyed the time in the Wilder orchard as much as I did.

Best regards,
Susan

Acknowledgments

Jane and Garrett's story turned out to be a lot more difficult to write than I imagined! Perhaps it was because I was dealing with the history of such a renowned institution as the Children's Aid Society. But through prayer, perseverance, and some great editing, I managed to get it done.

Thank you once again to David Long and Jen Veilleux, my editors at Bethany House, whose advice helped to make this story shine. And thank you to the entire team at Bethany House, who work so hard on our behalf, especially during the trying times of the pandemic.

I'd like to thank my agent, Natasha Kern, for all her support and kindness, and for giving her all to her job despite any hardships in her personal life. I appreciate your dedication!

My gratitude goes to my dear friend and critique partner, Sally Bayless, who gives me such great advice and helps me meet my deadlines. And, as always, thank you to my family for their love and encouragement.

Lastly, thank you to my wonderful readers and influencers. I appreciate you all so much, especially those who take the time to leave reviews and who help promote my books. It means so much to have your support!

Blessings and best wishes,

Susan

To learn more about my books, please check out my website at www.susanannemason.net.

Susan Anne Mason describes her writing style as "romance sprinkled with faith." She loves incorporating inspirational messages of God's unconditional love and forgiveness into her stories. *Irish Meadows*, her first historical romance, won the Fiction from the Heartland contest sponsored by the Mid-American Romance Authors chapter of RWA. Susan lives outside Toronto, Ontario, with her husband and two adult children. She loves red wine and chocolate and is not partial to snow, even though she's Canadian. Learn more about Susan and her books at www.susanannemason.net.

Sign Up for Susan's Newsletter!

Keep up to date with Susan's news on book releases and events by signing up for her email list at susanannemason.net.

More from Susan Anne Mason

Haunted by painful memories, Olivia Rosetti is singularly focused on running her maternity home for troubled women. Darius Reed is determined to protect his daughter from the prejudice that killed his wife by marrying a society darling. But when he's suddenly drawn to Olivia, they will learn if love can prove stronger than the secrets and hurts of the past.

A Haven for Her Heart
REDEMPTION'S LIGHT #1

You May Also Like . . .

At Irish Meadows horse farm, two sisters struggle to reconcile their dreams with their father's demanding marriage expectations. Brianna longs to attend college, while Colleen is happy to marry, as long as the man meets *her* standards. Will they find the courage to follow their hearts?

Irish Meadows by Susan Anne Mason
COURAGE TO DREAM #1
susanannemason.net

In the aftermath of tragedy, Grace hopes to reclaim her nephew from the relatives who rejected her sister because of her social class. Under an alias, she becomes her nephew's nanny to observe the formidable family up close. Unexpectedly, she begins to fall for the boy's guardian, who is promised to another. Can Grace protect her nephew . . . and her heart?

The Best of Intentions by Susan Anne Mason
CANADIAN CROSSINGS #1
susanannemason.net

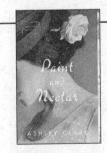

In 1929, a spark forms between Eliza, a talented watercolorist, and a young man whose family has a longstanding feud with hers over a missing treasure. Decades later, after inheriting Eliza's house and all its secrets from a mysterious patron, Lucy is determined to preserve the property, not only for history's sake, but also for her own.

Paint and Nectar by Ashley Clark
HEIRLOOM SECRETS
ashleyclarkbooks.com

BETHANYHOUSE

More from Bethany House

When his reputation is threatened, Aaron Whitworth makes the desperate decision to hire a circus horse trainer as a jockey for his racehorses. Most men don't take Sophia Fitzroy seriously because she's a woman, but as she fights for the right to do the work she was hired for, she finds the fight for Aaron's guarded heart might be a more worthwhile challenge.

Winning the Gentleman by Kristi Ann Hunter
HEARTS ON THE HEATH
kristiannhunter.com

Mireilles finds her world rocked when the Great War comes crashing into the idyllic home she has always known, taking much from her. When Platoon Sergeant Matthew Petticrew discovers her in the Forest of Argonne, three things are clear: she is alone in the world, she cannot stay, and he and his two companions might be the only ones who can get her to safety.

Yours Is the Night by Amanda Dykes
amandadykes.com

When Sylvie Townsend's Polish ward, Rose, goes missing at the World's Fair, her life unravels. Brushed off by the authorities, Sylvie turns to her boarder and Rose's violin instructor, Kristof Bartok, for help searching the immigrant communities. When the unexpected happens, will Sylvie be able to accept the change that comes her way?

Shadows of the White City by Jocelyn Green
THE WINDY CITY SAGA #2
jocelyngreen.com

✦BETHANYHOUSE